WRATH

WITCH WARS

BOOK ONE

HM HODGSON

Ebook ISBN: 978-0-6454516-9-6

Amazon paperback ISBN: 9798280811652

IngramSpark paperback ISBN: 978-0-6455598-0-4

Edited by Sarah Proulx Calfee, Three Little Words Editing https://threelittlewordsediting.com

Proofread by Jo Speirs, Nurturing Words

https://www.nurturingwords.com.au

Cover by Laura Hidalgo, Spellbinding Designs https://www.spellbindingdesign.com/

Internal character art by Ashley Nobes, Ashley Nobes Art https://www.ashleynobesart.com/

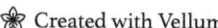 Created with Vellum

CONTENTS

To the readers:

May nothing stand in
your way of finding joy
between the pages.

Magic has a will and a way
that no battle line,
visible or not, can contain.

Vella slid into Councilor Matthias Medea's bedroom suite and, with delectable hints of sandalwood and spice warming the air, hit the timer on her watch.

Eighteen minutes and thirteen seconds to locate the runes and get out. Frigging goddess, how many more would Vella need to steal?

If only she could sneak out of this obnoxious mansion and the kiss-ass party and run back home to a good book, a splash of Fireball Whisky, and a chat with Sara about their latest antique acquisition—but tonight *was* about Sara, and Sara was all that mattered.

Holding her breath, she paused. Listened.

The party caroused on full steam below. Music and voices echoed up from the Magicae's fancy-ass mansion's ground floor. But otherwise ... perfect silence in the bedroom suite.

Exactly as her Div foreseers had predicted. As always.

Well, the delicious scents hadn't been part of the vision. Pity their foreseers didn't have Smell-O-Vision.

Time to work. The sooner she found the runes, the sooner she could get back to Sara.

She toed off her ridiculous heels, adjusted the neckline of her strapless ballgown and shone her cell flashlight on the extravagant room. She passed the bathroom, dressing room, sitting area and the biggest monster of a bed she'd ever seen.

Rumor was Councilor Medea brought his guests back here to bang after his clubs closed at dawn. Given the other rumors of his sexual prowess and his *many* fans, he probably needed a bed this big to fit them all in.

Typical—Magicae were infamous for using their spell-casting magic on hedonistic pursuits, unlike the Divinators who worked tirelessly to make the witch world a better, safer place.

Vella had been doing her bit for years, keeping witchkind secure by removing powerful arcana out of the hands of the lesser covens, since those who didn't have enough power to control them could harm themselves or others. And there was Sara. The doctors still couldn't figure out what was wrong, and Aunt Ellaine was using every single powerful arcana Vella could retrieve to scry for a cure.

Vella pushed down the old familiar sorrow and focused on her task: find the runes. Aunt Ellaine had hinted this set might be powerful enough to be successful.

Her flashlight hit a set of gleaming antique mahogany timber drawers in the far corner. George the Third, judging by the satinwood inlaid marquetry and the elegant, simple lines. Beautiful. And located exactly where their foreseers had said it would be.

Vella took a deep breath. The timber was smooth, warm, even on this icy early winter night, and solid. Somehow, she'd expected the piece-of-shit spellcaster to surround himself with more flashy furniture. Not that his timber choice mattered.

She eased the top drawer out and found a rectangular, padded leather box. The lid lifted off without a sound, but damn—just a bone-handled knife on one side and an intricately carved sheath, clearly a matching set, on the other—

Oh *shit*. The knife had a *bone* handle.

Vella bolted. Screw stealing and screw the runes and screw … shit. She couldn't run away. Five feet from the door, she pulled up and forced herself to resist the urge to bolt out of the room.

Sara. Sara mattered. The bone-handled knife did not. And Vella would be fine. She'd just put the lid back on the padded leather box and move to the next drawer.

But two feet away, she froze.

As long as her hand, with Celtic designs carved into every inch of the yellowed, worn bone, the entire knife radiated age and history. With any other object, her love of antiquities would have her oohing and aahing.

But not this.

Never this.

And Vella would bet her favorite 1908 Royal Doulton Witches teapot that the knife was magical. Goddess, it *felt* magical. Even Vella, with her weak talent, could sense it. An itch was prickling at the base of her neck, and she rubbed the skin before she could stop herself.

With blood rushing through her ears, Vella forced herself to take a step closer.

"Come on, Vel," she whispered. "You can do this. You don't have to touch the bone for frig's sake."

"Hello? Finally," a woman's voice, lilting with an unfamiliar accent, snapped into the room. "A daughter, after all these years. Thank the gods."

"What—" Vella whirled around, but the room was empty. *Empty.*

An entirely new shiver chased up her spine.

"What is your name? Who's there?" the voice said again. "Hello? Why are you going silent? No, I will not have it. Make contact so I can see you."

Her blood turned to ice. Oh shit, oh shit, oh shit. The bone was *speaking* to her? A hallucination, that's all. No one was talking to her—she'd tripped, hit her head or something. Because that couldn't happen. It wasn't *allowed* to happen.

"Oh no. No, no, no."

"Oh yes. Yes, yes, yes," the voice responded.

"What—"

"No, not what. *Who*? Who are you, Daughter?"

"Oh my gods!" Vella's heart triple timed. She gaped at the bone-handled knife. Frigging Mors frigging Dicen. What the fuck? What was she going to do?

"I demand you make contact," the knife said. "It's been far too long."

"Quiet," Vella hissed. She could do this—for Sara. "Not listening, not listening," Vella muttered under her breath as she reached out with shaking fingers.

"You are listening. Clearly, you can hear me perfectly well. Although why you are pretending not to, I have—"

Vella slammed the lid on the box and shoved the drawer closed.

Silence. Blessed silence.

And she was still alive! Her heart was still racing, her mouth dry. That had been close, though. *Fuck!* And if Aunt Ellaine ever found out—

Oh dear sweet goddess. Vella had practiced Mors Dicen magic somehow. The knife ... *it* had been a Mors

Dicen weapon. Panic rose, and Vella could feel herself beginning to hyperventilate.

Get it together, Vel.

She clamped down on the panic and forced herself to breathe and focus on Sara—Sara was depending on her. Nobody had seen. Vella would never tell a soul. It would be fine. It had to be.

Vella rechecked the timer ... thirteen minutes and forty-eight seconds before someone else entered the room.

She yanked out the next drawer. Candles, a sectioned box filled with crystals and herbs, strong in fragrance and clarity, and another box that held a piece of folded paper. A quick flick and the sheet straightened out, revealing eight ornately drawn runic symbols across the top.

These weren't exactly the divination runes that Aunt Ellaine wanted, but maybe it would suffice. That funny, itchy feeling gathered at the back of her neck again. She tucked the paper back away and—

"Well, well, well," an unfamiliar masculine voice purred from behind her. Two large hands grabbed her arms.

Adrenaline spiked. Vella dropped the box on the floor, and jabbed hard with her elbow—hit a wall of solid muscle. *Ouch.*

"Oof." The male tensed. "Well, hell, aren't you ferocious? Normally an attribute I admire. Now, who are—"

"Then admire this, asshole." She kicked backward, part of her rejoicing in the physical violence, but her floor-length skirt got in the way.

"Uh-uh." He yanked her back to his hard torso. "I said stop. I don't want to"—he dodged her next elbow, damn it —"hurt you."

"Well, bad luck, I want to hurt you." And she did. Fury,

oh so much better than the fear, coursed through her. No one manhandled her. She butted her head back, aiming for whatever part of his body was behind her.

The man whispered barely intelligible words, and something invisible locked around her legs and arms in a vice-like grip.

Vella's blood ran cold. Spellcaster magic.

"Good. You've stopped fighting—nice to see you can obey an instruction."

"Let me go, or you're dead. You don't know who you're dealing with."

"The audacity." A bitter laugh echoed in her ears. "*You've* entered my bedroom without my permission, and now you're threatening me. Now, let's take a good look at you."

His room? Oh no. Shit, shit, shit, no. It couldn't be. She took a breath—the sandalwood and spice she'd scented earlier filled her lungs.

The man stepped back, and moonlight haloed his tall silhouette, clung to his hair, hugged the width of his shoulders as he crossed the window then flicked on the lights.

Before her stood tall, imperious, masculine perfection with black jacketed shoulders. A hard jaw and a long, straight nose. Full lips, and slashes of brows as dark as his midnight hair, shaved at each side, with the top tied back, the ends down to his shoulder blades. Eyes like moonlight through cut crystal.

Tattooed snakes with red eyes, the sign of the Magicae coven, wound up each side of his long neck, their fangs poised, ready to strike. Ruby studs tracking up his right ear and more rubies on the rings on his long fingers.

Ridiculously, outrageously hot.

Magicae Councilor Matthias Medea.

Her mouth went dry. WTF, frigging foreseers? Had they been drunk during their vision seeking? Nobody was supposed to be here.

"I'll say it again. Well, well, well." A strange smirk curved his beautiful, sculpted lips. "You are the Divinator Councilor's niece." He whispered a few words, and the binding released her. "Interesting. I've always wondered, why is it that you don't have any Div tats?"

"I'm allergic to ink." She fumbled for the necklace around her neck and held up the pendant. "You want to see my all-seeing eye? And I'm here ... to find out what the fuss is about Magicae in bed. I'd love to party ... with you."

"It's Velvet, correct? Velvet Knight."

He teased her full name out, like he was savoring it with his British accent, and her lady parts cheered. *Oh, ew. No way, lady parts!*

"Just Vella," she ground out, attempting a smile.

"So that's your excuse for why you're here?" One brow rose. "A private party?"

The Magicae undid the top button of his white shirt, revealing a vee of deeply tanned skin. And while her heart still raced, a new heat pooled in her belly. Goddess but he was hot. Like off the charts smoking. How could she be *this* turned on when absolutely everything was falling apart?

Was it spellcaster magic? Had he enhanced his sex appeal? Made it so her nipples tightened and her body suddenly clenched like it was aching for something she'd had no idea she wanted until this very second? She wouldn't put anything beyond a spellcaster.

The little box on the floor caught her attention. *Pull yourself together, Vel.* Completing the mission and getting that box with the weird symbols on the paper was the goal

—if that meant faking an interest in the spellcaster, so be it.

She stepped closer. "Downstairs is so packed, I thought I'd see if you were free for some ... one-on-one time. After all, you're known for your parties. That's your business, right? Exotic clubs and all that."

"And do I get a choice in this private party?"

Vella recoiled. "As if I'd force you."

"And yet, here you are. Brazenly walking into my bedroom and demanding a private party. Typical Divinator entitlement if I ever saw it."

"Councilor Matthias, I would never order you to do anything."

"So you're not one of *those* Divinators."

Vella's skin crawled with the ick. She knew what Medea meant. Aunt Ellaine, her cousin Derrick, and the others from Div Tower *would* most likely demand, believing it their right to order a Magicae to obey their wishes—but no. That attitude was part of the reason Sara had wanted out in the first place. At least she and Sara had their own place now, away from the oppressive Div Tower.

"I would never force anyone." Vella stilled and kept her gaze directly on Medea.

Medea returned her stare before inclining his head. "Very well."

Vella let out a surreptitious breath. Shit ... so now what? She just needed to stay long enough in the room to distract Medea, grab the box and run. There was little he could do once she had his property and left his bedroom.

Surely, he'd never dare accuse Velvet Knight, niece to the Divinator Councilor, of being a thief. And even if he did, it would be Vella's word and against his, and they both knew who Aunt Ellaine would choose to believe.

"You know ..." Medea's sinful voice rolled over her.

"What?" She forced her focus back to Medea. *Think, Vel.* How far did she have to take things to distract him?

"You've captured my interest, Velvet Knight. And since you're here, I'm all for us enjoying a private party. But if you really want to fuck a spellcaster, it has to be on at least one foundation of truth."

"An honest Magicae?" This time, she couldn't restrain a snort. Of all the tales told to Vella growing up, not one had included a truthful witch from the Magicae coven.

"I know, scruples shouldn't stand in the way of a good time, right?" His lips twisted. "But alas, I must insist."

"So what? You want my favorite color? Easy. Black. Favorite music? Anything from Imagine Dragons to Linkin Park. Throw in some Foo Fighters too."

"As interesting as your music choices are ... no, I'm thinking more along the lines of why you're in my room?"

Time for another lie ... but Medea had given her an excuse to stay in his room, and she was running with it.

Sure, tell yourself that, Vella.

Shut up, inner voice.

She rose on her toes and whispered into his ear, "I am all about fucking you right now." Not an outright lie. Just missing a few key words. She was going to fuck him over.

2

Holy fuck! Matt had set out his lures, a few mildly powerful divination arcana around his bedroom, plus the Mors Dicen knife—and he'd not only caught the Div thief red-handed, but she was Velvet Knight, the Div Councilor's fucking niece.

Who had also just practiced Mors Dicen magic.

Mors fucking Dicen. This changed *everything*. The most immediate, he could no longer spell the thief, question her and disappear her.

He had to get some answers, though, *and* figure out a way to keep his secrets and leave the Div breathing. Shit. Fuck.

The Div's gaze met his—and damn, but her eyes were exquisite, a rich, glowing amber brown. Lioness eyes. And right now, burning brighter than a flame as she watched him like some hunting cat surveying its next meal. And fucking hell—he was turned on.

By a Div. By his *enemy*.

"Sex. Right. Want to see if the rumors are true, do

you?" He held back the urge to sneer. For fuck's sake, of course she did. They all did.

The Div scowled at him. Except, what did she have to be upset about? Well, apart from being busted mid-banned magic, and mid-thievery.

Just as soon as it had appeared, her expression cleared, and she took a breath; the swell of her breasts rose higher above the neckline of her fitted bodice, making the crimson silk, covered with jet and red beads, gleam in the lamplight.

Spectacular.

Then she stepped forward and kissed him.

Firm and delicious, rich and intoxicating, her lips caressed his for one second before her tongue swept and then plundered.

Primal magic clawed in Matt's chest, tore through his veins. Demanded to be let out. But he restrained it with total determination. What the hell was going on? He hadn't lost control since he'd been a randy teenager.

"I need to touch you," she whispered into his mouth.

Fuck, yes. "Then touch away."

Matt kicked away the box with the symbols that he and Sylvie had discovered in the lining of the Mors Dicen knife container. He drew the Div toward the bed. She ran her hands along his shirt and traced the tattoos on his neck, then she pressed her lips against them, followed the snake winding to his jaw—

Hot shivers gathered at the base of his spine, raced up his back. Maybe seduction *was* the way forward?

"Do I get to touch too?" He growled.

"Goddess, yes."

He spun her around. Kissed his way to her ear and inhaled the perfume of her skin, musky and scented with something buttery and earthy.

Mouthwatering.

He slipped a hand into the neckline of her dress and cupped her warm, silky flesh. The velvety tip of her breast tightened against his palm; she arched into his touch, and every bit of blood left his head and shot to his cock.

Gods, but she was hotter than fire in his arms.

Fuck. *Head in the game, Matt.*

"What are you really after?" He nuzzled into her ear. Grazed his teeth over the delicate pad of her lobe.

"What?" She pressed against him harder. "And lower. Touch me lower."

He ran his hand down to her skirts, gathered the material up until he found her thigh. "Tell me the truth, Divinator." Shifting his caress, he swept up to her core, groaning at her dampness.

Focus, Matt. Focus, focus, focus.

"What is your true purpose for entering my private bedroom?" He dropped to his knees. Her legs drifted apart. Fuck, had to kiss her silky skin—

Then she stiffened and pushed him away. "Why are you still talking?"

"I'm not allowed to talk and fuck?" He let her skirt drop with more regret than he bloody well should and rose to his feet.

"No." She crossed her arms. "You're the one with the rep around here, Councilor. What's so hard to believe about someone wanting to experience the wild side?"

"Hmm. I almost believe that."

"You're the spellcaster." She flicked her fingers. "Why don't you do a spell to see if I'm telling the truth?" She said the words casually, but her arms tightened around her torso.

"I'd been planning on it," Matt murmured. "The problem is you're going to run and tattle to your auntie about the big bad Magicae questioning her precious little thief. You're working for her, aren't you?"

Vella flushed bright red, and Matt had his confirmation, but—

Hell, he needed time to think. He shifted back, and Vella sidestepped away from the bed, her gaze roving the floor.

"Why do I get the sense you're still looking for something?" he asked.

"Just admiring your room. That chest of drawers—nineteenth century, George the Third, right?"

"It is indeed." Matt bent down and picked up the little box. "Any chance this is what you're searching for?"

The bedroom door clicked open, and Vella's gaze shot over Matt's shoulder.

"Matthias, did you capture the—" Matt took his time turning around to face Ronin, who was standing in the doorway. His green eyes flicked between Matt and the Div. Narrowed. "Holy fucking shit. Her *niece?* We can't—"

"No, we cannot. Unfortunately." Matt forced his laziest smile. "Velvet Knight, meet Ronin Daniels, our coven's Second."

Ronin's lips curled back in what could no way be called a smile.

And Vella clearly read Ronin's reaction correctly because her eyes narrowed, and she lifted her chin. "Clearly, you two have business to attend to. I think it's time I left."

Fuck. Vella now presented a real and present threat.

Matt shifted to let her leave, but as she passed, whispered in her ear, "I *saw* you do Mors Dicen magic, Div. Be very careful what you say to your auntie or there will be consequences."

CRAP, crap, crap. Vella's heart ran in her chest like she'd just finished a mile-long sprint. Mors fucking Dicen fucking magic that Councilor Medea saw. Her heart raced still as they descended the grand staircase—ostentatious marble balustrade and gold plaster scrollwork—with the Magicae Councilor and his Second crowding so close at her back that their breath made her skin crawl.

And frigging goddess, she'd failed to get the runes. What if those runes were the divination tool that helped their coven find a cure for Sara?

Her fists clenched, and she forced back the urge to spin around and run back upstairs. Who knew when they'd be able to engineer another opportunity to get them?

Her stomach knotted, but before she could do anything rash, the stairs turned and opened to the foyer and into the mingled voices of witches laughing and talking like they weren't all hyper on edge, their magics no doubt ready to cleave a path out of there the moment the shit hit the fan. Which could be any minute, judging by the heightened sense of awareness—understandable after yet another Darkling report only that morning—fizzing in the air.

A shiver raced up her spine.

Or that could be the fact she'd been caught making outlawed magic. Or that she'd failed in her mission.

Frig, frig, *frig*.

The knots in her stomach tightened. What was going to be worse—telling Aunt Ellaine she'd failed or Councilor Medea exposing her? And that kiss, holy shit.

At the last moment, Matthias took her hand, forcing

her to pause, and strolled around her, bringing her knuckles to his lips.

His lips were *so* warm, and her core clenched without her permission.

"What are you doing?" Vella gritted out. Around them, witches stopped and stared.

With his back to the room, no one else could see the mocking light in his crystalline silver eyes, but goddess, she wanted to wipe that expression off his face. Thank fuck he released her before she did something stupid—like smashing her fist into his nose.

"We need to talk. When can I meet you again?"

"Never." Conscious of the attention they were drawing, she forced a cool expression and gritted out, "This will be the end of our acquaintance."

"Oh, I think not."

"Councilor Matthias," a cool voice called out. Over the spellcaster's shoulder, Vella met her aunt's gaze, and her tension eased. "I see you've met my niece."

At sixty-five years of age, shorter than Vella even in heels, and with icy blond hair cut in a perfect bob, Aunt Ellaine might seem harmless, but only a fool would treat the head of the Divinator coven with anything less than total respect.

"Ah, Councilor Priestly." Councilor Medea bowed. "You are as lovely as ever. I cannot express my delight that you are attending our winter ball. You honor the Magicae with your presence. And you even brought your niece. We just had the pleasure of getting"—he lifted one eyebrow, and his mouth twisted into a partial smile that didn't quite reach his eyes—"*acquainted.* May I get you anything?" He leaned toward Vella. "*Do* anything for you?"

Beside him, his Second stood at ease, gazing at Vella in

a manner she didn't appreciate. Their eyes met, and he flashed her a bizarre grin that was all teeth.

Why were they acting so ... weird?

"That will be all, Matt," Aunt Ellaine snapped. "You're dismissed."

"Of course, Councilor." He made a flourish with his arm. "Please enjoy *all* the hospitality my house has to offer."

Medea's gaze touched on Vella one last time before he swept away, Ronin at his side.

Another shiver—this time, cold and brittle—flew up Vella's spine. His constant one-eighties, from seducer to flirty to threatening to obedient, made her head spin. Nothing added up here. Something deeper ... darker ... was brewing.

She should warn Aunt Ellaine—but no. Medea had *seen* her practice Mors Dicen magic. If he followed through on his threat and told anyone ... The knots in her stomach sank like a heavy chain to the bottom of her belly.

3

———

"You met him," Aunt Ellaine murmured as they wound through the ballroom. "How?"

Vella took a deliberate sip of champagne—*ugh*, she'd prefer a good whiskey any day—and gave herself one more moment of reprieve before she confessed to failing. She hoped Aunt Ellaine's retribution wouldn't be too harsh. "He entered his bedroom before I located the runes."

Her aunt's lips pinched for one moment, and she spoke calmly. Quietly. "Are you certain of your timing?"

This was Aunt Ellaine at her most frightening. Vella's mouth went dry, and she took another drink just to get the words out. "Absolutely. Everything else worked like clockwork."

"I take it you found a satisfactory way to explain yourself for being in his rooms?"

Almost. And if he'd finished kissing his way to your—

Shush, inner voice.

"You could say that, too." Vella's stomach tightened.

"Did you fail entirely, Velvet? Did you find *nothing* that

might help Sara with her illness? Was there anything else? Not even a Mors Dicen relic of some kind?"

Vella winced, and her heart went back up to triple time. Sweet frigging goddess, did Aunt Ellaine already know? Had the foreseers told her what Vella had done?

"Calm yourself, Vella," said Aunt Ellaine. "Your cowardice around anything to do with Mors Dicen is showing."

Cowardice? Vella's spine stiffened. How could she not be afraid of Mors Dicen bones after what had happened to her parents? An atrocity Vella had witnessed with her own eyes.

"You must overcome this fear, Vella. This is exactly why I didn't mention the potential provenance of the runes."

"The ... runes are Mors Dicen?" But the knife—

"Possibly. Besides, we weren't quite sure if ... well, let's just say their arcana is famously difficult for us to see. But our foreseers sensed something old, something powerful."

It was that knife! Vella breathed deep through her nose. But ... she just *couldn't*.

"Well? Did you see anything useful at all?"

"There was a bit of paper," she blurted. "With runic symbols on it."

Aunt Ellaine went still. Two spots of color brightened her pale cheeks. "Describe the symbols. Every detail."

As soon as Vella finished, Aunt Ellaine leaned closer. "Hmm. It could be something. You're certain about the scrollwork around the markings?"

"As much as I can be, yes."

"Matt must have a lead of some kind." Aunt Ellaine's eyes lit up. "What else was on this paper?"

"Nothing else."

"If only you had done your job, Velvet." She let out a

deep, annoyed sigh. "It's like you don't care whether your sister is cured or not."

Vella jolted, and her hands balled into fists as if Aunt Ellaine's words had been a physical slap.

Control, Vel. Don't show anger; don't show anger.

Finally, the rush of fury subsided, and she faced Aunt Ellaine with the traditional Div calm.

"I had to get away ... we sort of kissed—I needed a reason for being there—and he maneuvered me out of the room."

"You will get me that paper. Do you understand me? It could lead us to runes so powerful they could find a permanent cure for poor Sara."

A *total* cure? Hope bloomed in Vella's chest. "But surely Councilor Medea would honor a formal request from you?"

"Matthias is an unscrupulous flirt and, like all Magicae, practices his craft with just as much dishonesty."

"Dishon ... is he dangerous?" A chill scrabbled down Vella's spine. If Medea had been using magic to make her body respond physically back in his bedroom—

"Bah. Magicae spells these days have nowhere near the power to be a threat. No, Matthias' most powerful spell is making himself look better than he is. However, if he knows I want something badly, he's likely to turn it around and sell it to the highest bidder. No, your covert acquiring is best."

"I could try again now. He's down here, so his room is empty—"

"Patience, Vella."

Patience? Vella restrained the urge to grind her teeth at the internal chafe of that word. How to be patient when something might exist that would improve Sara's quality of life? It would also be nice to win just a little bit of Aunt

Ellaine's approval. Medea was busy right now—head bent with Ronin, standing as close as lovers. Vella squashed her sudden flash of envy.

"We never act without our foreseers," Aunt Ellaine continued. "There is a reason Divinators are so successful —and that is because we do not act without knowing all the outcomes. Who knows what might happen in five minutes' time? And if Matt finds you in his rooms again, we will have much more difficulty concealing your purpose for being there. Right now, I need you to circulate and pretend you're here to represent our family at this waste of a party."

But hadn't her aunt just said foreseers couldn't accurately divine Mors Dicen arcana? Vella shook her head. She had learned early on it was *never* worth arguing with her aunt about it. "Yes, of course. And I'm *so* sorry I let Sara—us all—down."

"As you should be. I'm very displeased with you. Keep that in mind for your next project tonight."

A crystal ball held by a family of Crystallos in the Bronx. No fancy tech from Sara required—they weren't swimming in security like the Magicae.

"I know you dislike these events, but we must maintain our cover." Aunt Ellaine glanced over Vella's shoulder, and her social smile rose perfectly into place. "Ah, Derrick, there you are. Take your cousin and make it clear she's our guest—I want no suspicion of why she's here. I need to chat with Charles."

Aunt Ellaine swept away toward the Elixir Councilor, people automatically parting before her.

"How's Sara been lately?" Derrick took her by the arm as they strolled across the parquetry timber floor, maneuvering between high-ranking witches from the remaining great covens. "Grandmother said you had an appointment with the new specialist?"

"They ran more tests yesterday."

"And ..."

"Same as always. Autoimmune disease, but they can't pin down why." Frustration and guilt and fatigue churned around and around in her belly, and Vella had to swallow the bile that rose fast.

"Hey, you okay?" Derrick squeezed her arm.

"Yeah. Just—" She sighed and dropped into the nearest seat.

"I get it. I can see you're worried." Derrick sat opposite her, his expression grave.

"I'm trying to hide that."

"Save it for everyone else. You don't need to with me. Of course you're worried; we all are."

"There's more. Tonight wasn't ... successful, *and* Aunt Ellaine isn't particularly happy about it."

Vella bit back the urge to blurt out everything. Six years older than her and their only cousin, Derrick had been the one person she'd turned to on the rare occasions she couldn't contain the urge to vent or cry or even celebrate as she'd been growing up. But if she told him everything, *he'd* be in the same challenging position as Vella.

"Why don't you come home and stay this weekend at Div Tower?" Derrick gestured with his drink. "You can relax; the staff will be there. You won't have to lift a finger."

Relax? Vella mentally shook her head. How Derrick could contemplate unwinding in the Divinator's Tower of Power with all that glass and marble and priceless works of art that must only be looked at and never touched—let alone living in a penthouse atop the forty-story office tower that was the Divinator coven headquarters, along with the Witches Council chamber and the jails in the basement—Vella had zero clue.

"No," Vella murmured. "Sara's most comfortable in her own bed." At least that was the truth. "Plus, aren't you and Aunt Ellaine up in Boston?"

"We are. Just Council business. But we're only a phone call away."

Derrick's kindness made Vella squirm with guilt for not being completely honest. She *wanted* to talk to her aunt about the knife, but she was terrified of the Mors Dicen. How could she not be? She knew barely anything about the Mors Dicen except for—well, what they'd done to her parents. Growing up, Aunt Ellaine had kept her and Sara's education totally streamlined, something Sara had always raged about. So perhaps Vella's fears were overblown? Maybe she *could* talk to Aunt Ellaine about how she'd accidentally practiced illegal, banned magic?

"So ... this may sound strange," Vella said, "but, uh, what do you know about the ..." Vella lowered her voice. "Mors Dicen?"

Derrick stared. Crossed his arms. Whispered, "Apart from the fact they started the rebellion against the Council that led to a two-year conflict and the deaths of both our parents?"

Oh goddess. This was not going well. "I mean, what do we know about their magic?"

"They were barbaric—and almost as bad as the Druids. The Mors Dicen sacrificed witches for their bones and practiced unnatural rituals on their bodies. And most of the time, their magic was deadly to both practitioners and others. Why do you think that magic was banned after the rebellion?"

"But ... have you ever heard of Mors Dicen magic happening without intention? Like, accidentally?"

Because surely that's what had happened when she'd touched the knife. Some fluke of magic.

"Accidentally talking to the dead through a bone? Not that I know of." Derrick frowned. "Technically, it might be possible if you found an uncursed Mors Dicen bone and somehow said or accessed a ritual without realizing what you were doing. Why? Has something happened? Have you seen someone practicing—"

"No! No, I'm just curious how it works. How they worked."

"Their power was a terrible thing, Vella. Our world is safer without them. Those bastards *partnered* with Magicae to curse their bones so they'd instantly calcify innocent Divs and Elixirs trying to purify this world of their evil."

Vella couldn't hold back a shiver. That's how her parents had died, after all. "I could never forget that," she whispered.

"Ah, hell. I know, and I'm sorry—I wasn't thinking." He rubbed her arm, but nothing could erase the chilling memory of her parents' deaths. "Listen, I know you're upset about tonight, but we'll get another chance. Matt's not someone you need to worry about."

Matt? "Hold on. You call the Magicae Councilor Matt?"

"Please. Like he's any threat." Derrick snorted. "Most of his blood is circulating downstairs, if you get my drift." Derrick patted her hand, much like Aunt Ellaine had. "And, come, it's time to put on a show. I'll take the lead."

His usual million-watt smile shot into place—dimples, golden hair and sparkling brown eyes all manufactured to make him appear harmless—as a Divinator couple approached them, their coven symbols painted up each arm.

Vella made sure her all-seeing eye was turned around

correctly—the insignia might be small, but she rarely joined official witching events, so every indicator of her coven helped.

But as she forced herself to make small talk, the hairs on the back of her neck prickled, and she gave into one last urge to check behind her ... Nothing. But in the far corner, Charles and Aunt Ellaine were having an animated conversation.

"Is everything okay with your grandmother and Charles?" she whispered to Derrick once they were alone. "They seem ... tense."

"And you're perceptive." Derrick took another sip of champagne.

"Out with it, Derrick. I know you're up on more gossip than anyone else here."

"I gather important information." He rolled his eyes. "That is my job with the SI team, after all."

"So? Clearly, this is something you know about. Spill."

"Charles is pissed about the turnout tonight. Matt's winter ball is packed, and he's just a *Magicae*, but the Elixir autumn festival only had half the witches here. He's pushing to remove Matt from the Council entirely, but Grandmother finds him useful. Personally, I think Charles is jealous."

"Of a Magicae?"

"Of Matt's growing wealth. And his magic dick."

4

At the far end of the ballroom, Matt and Ronin looked out the expansive bay window to the Bronx skyline beyond. As Matt tried to pull his racing thoughts together, two Div women approached.

They grinned at him, the closest licking her lips and her friend winking. Lip-licker said, "Do you ever do any private PDS shows outside of your clubs?"

Matt tilted his head to one side, gave a confident half smile. "For you? Absolutely. Here's my card."

Their fingers brushed as Matt passed it over. The Divs strolled away, their heads bent together, and Matt could swear he heard the words *magic dick*.

Fools. But they'd left him and Ronin alone, which was all he wanted.

"I hate it when you have to do that," Ronin muttered, his voice inaudible to normal witch ears.

"Same," he gritted out through the fucking smile he fucking forced in place.

"Then why the hells did we not follow through with the plan? Who cares if the thief is E's niece? We should've at least questioned her. Especially now we've confirmed E *must* be stockpiling all that arcana."

"Ronin, she—" Matt's whole body tingled, remembering Mors Dicen magic performed before his eyes. The last time he'd seen it practiced was at Madgewick in his childhood. It had been rare enough even in those days. He got closer to Ronin, putting his arm around his shoulders, and whispered, "She can *talk* to the knife."

Ronin recoiled, his face white, his eyes staring. "This means—"

Matt played with the lapel of Ronin's suit. "Fucking chill. You're drawing attention. We'll discuss *that* later ... but we need a lot more intel before making another move. What do you have on her?"

Ronin flashed a grimace, but then his mouth firmed. "Not much. She has a younger sister who's in and out of hospital. One year ago, she opened a shop called Arcane Antiquities in the West Village."

"Hmm. That's rather far from their tower."

"Especially since most Divs prefer to live close to their home base in each city."

"So why not *this* Div? Think I'll pay our would-be thief a visit first thing tomorrow morning."

Ronin pulled out his phone and scrolled. "Her background is ... odd. We don't have much on Miss Knight because Ellaine has had her and her sister pretty much sequestered at Div Tower. We know she didn't physically attend any public or private school or university. She must have been educated at home or online. She has zero social media presence outside of the shop, and look, she's barely speaking to any of her coven. She's either hanging out with her creepy cousin or on her own."

In the center of the room, Vella stood with Derrick, the Div Second, but as much as she appeared to be listening to Derrick talk, she also seemed ... alone ... and as if an invisible barrier wrapped around her, witches kept a space between them. But that meant Matt had plenty of room to consider the Div.

The black-shot red silk of her dress followed the curves of her strong, lithe body—stronger than most Divs for sure—the jet and garnet beads gleaming under the ballroom lights, but even so, the true glow seemed to come from her. Did everyone else see that?

His magic coiled and surged low in his belly—damn it. He locked it down and distracted himself by pulling up the Arcane Antiques website. "She's only—twenty-three, twenty-four at most—and according to her website, she already has degrees in art history and archaeology, specializing in ancient arcane ceramics?" He flicked through the business website on his cell. "Interesting. Her bio also says she works as a consultant for buyers 'wishing to add to their ceramic collections.' Hmm."

"How much of it is legit, do you reckon? It's so weird—so young, all that education, and she's like a freaking Rapunzel hidden by the evil sorceress. *And* she's been stealing for said evil sorceress on the down low for who knows how many years. What does it all mean?"

"We need to dig hard. I want every detail you can find about her, her sister, their business. Also, starting now, we surveil them twenty-four hours. Let's shake some trees, too. I want to see what happens when we use jammers around Arcane Antiquities. I bet you anything the evil sorceress is keeping a close eye on her Rapunzel."

"Ugh. Why is this happening now, right before Dave and Clay's wedding anniversary? I was looking forward to that." Ronin turned and glared out into the night. "The Divs ruin everything. Like always."

Matt shifted to brush Ronin's shoulder with his. Pack

needed physical solidarity as much as emotional, something Matt could hardly show here, but he did as much as was possible. "I know. We'll figure it out. But, Ronin, this could be huge. This might be the beginning."

"If it is ..." Ronin stood straighter, his jaw tightened, and he stilled in that preternatural way of his that Matt knew signaled the second-most dangerous person in the room was ready to fight.

A blond-haired server approached, holding a silver tray with two crystal tumblers. The server held the tray up as he reached them and nodded at Matt. "Sir, your whiskey."

"Thanks," Matt murmured as he handed one tumbler to Ronin and kept the other for himself. The server melted back into the crowd.

"We're celebrating *not* killing the thief?" Ronin asked as he sniffed his drink.

"Stop!" Matt grabbed Ronin's wrist. "You didn't order these?"

"No, I assumed you did. Fuck." Ronin's eyes began to glow.

"Keep it together," Matt growled. "Not here."

Ronin's jaw clenched, but after a moment, his eyes returned to their standard green. "I'm good. Let's go."

"Be careful with the whiskey—don't give it to anyone else, don't even let it touch your skin. It might be lethal on contact, not just ingestion."

They wove through the crowd, Matt going left, Ronin to the right. The server turned around and looked over his shoulder, back to where Ronin and Matt had been. He was maybe mid-twenties, medium height, medium build. The would-be assassin's eyes narrowed, and he picked up pace toward the foyer.

Matt sped up, too, and with a last large stride, collided

with the server from the side, exactly as Ronin bumped him from the other direction.

"Oops, how clumsy of me," Matt drawled even as he took the server's arm. "Here, let me steady you."

"I'll help, too," Ronin murmured.

"Let me go." The server pulled at Matt's and Ronin's grips.

"No need to be so hasty. I am your employer, after all. And I must say, you delivered these drinks so nicely."

The server's hazel eyes widened. "Get them away—"

"Away where? As in, back on your tray?" Matt kept his host smile in place but pitched his voice low. "We need to talk."

"What? Why? Let me go!"

"Uh-uh. No shouting." Around them, guests were reacting to the conversation, but no one made a move—they wouldn't, not with Matt being a Councilor. "We simply want to know what we're drinking. Why don't you take a sip and tell us?"

He held his glass up to the server, and Ronin did the same.

"Don't—"

"Don't hold them too close? Hmm, we thought so." Matt let a hint of his true nature slip through his grin. "Which means you know what's going to happen next since your attempt was unsuccessful. I suggest you come with us quietly; otherwise, this party isn't going to have the ending you were hoping for—in all ways."

"Get the fuck off me." The server pulled away harder.

"Careful," Ronin said with his wolfish grin. "You don't want us to accidentally ... spill these on you."

"Matt, what is going on here?" Ellaine's imperious voice rang out above the crowd.

Fuck. He'd hoped to do this away from his fellow Councilors' view.

Holding fast to the server, he faced Ellaine, and very much against his will, his eyes traveled over to Vella. She stood shoulder to shoulder with her aunt, her golden eyes narrowed. Heat and magic licked through him. *Seriously?* He was turned on *now*?

"A small staff matter." He forced his easy smile. "I do apologize."

"Typical Magicae carelessness." Ellaine sniffed. "Conclude this matter *away* from the ballroom."

"Of course." Matt's voice remained calm and pleasant. "We'll take care of this back of house."

"Fuck off, you will." The server flipped forward, breaking Matt's and Ronin's hold. Just as fast, he knocked the glasses Matt and Ronin held high into the air.

"Move," Matt yelled.

Together, he and Ronin pushed everyone back.

The glasses hit the parquetry floor.

Purple bubbles hissed, frothed. A lilac vapor oozed through the air.

"Get off me," Ellaine snapped. "We're safe enough here."

Fuck! He'd fucking saved Ellaine's life. Goddess damn it. He retreated and met Vella's wide gaze for one moment and realized he'd saved her too. Something deep, something primal, was satisfied at that knowledge. What the hell was wrong with him?

Ronin had the assassin—no doubt, now—trapped by one arm, but he shook a blue vial loose from his sleeve and hurled it at Matt.

Matt took two fast breaths and held the second. "Wind run hard and fast to me, as I say, so it will be." On his exhale, his spell flew free. But no simple witchwind would be enough, so he heaved on every air molecule within reach and bolstered his magic.

The ballroom windows shattered. People shouted. Glassware smashed.

Wind blasted through the room, picked up the vial flying at Matt and spun it back to where it came from.

The vial broke against the assassin's chest. Purple froth spread over his shirt—up his torso, down to his legs—until he was covered, and his cries were drowned beneath the fizz and pop of the bubbles as they encapsulated him, head to toe. Good, the asshole deserved it. He'd hurled that vial without a care about anyone who'd stood near him, who might be killed too.

Fuck.

Ellaine.

Matt cut the spell, dropped the air.

"Councilor Matthias Medea," Ellaine said, her voice cold as ice. "*What* magic spell was that?"

Focus, Matt. More than anything in your life, fucking focus. He breathed deeply and slowly. For all the people he loved, for everyone he was responsible for, he *had* to get this right.

"I merely stopped the vial from hitting anyone." He smoothed his hair back. "That was Elixir-made, wasn't it? Same as the whiskey this fake server tried to give me and my Second."

Ellaine's glare didn't waver. "I repeat. What was that spell you called?"

Matt made his face go soft. "Aren't you the least bit concerned about my assassination attempt?"

"He is dead and you are not, so problem solved. *You*, however, called a magic spell that has yet to be approved by the Council."

"I apologize, Councilor Priestly. It's just new," he lied.

"I expect you to submit it immediately, Matt, and if it is not, you are forbidden to ever cast it again. You may only *ever* use spells from the pages of the Council-approved Magicae spellcraft books at the Central Library at Div Tower. Do you understand me?"

"Yes, Councilor. It was an oversight, I assure you. Charles, as our potions expert, what do you make of the poison? Did you make it, perhaps? Do you happen to know the server?"

"Of course not!" Charles said. "I've never seen this man in my life, and I have no knowledge of lethal agents. This is outrageous. Are you insinuating this potion was created inside my research labs?"

"Matt," Ellaine snapped, "you know perfectly well Elixirs work solely on medicines and potions to help witchkind, not kill them. I suggest you tread carefully when you question the important work the Elixirs perform."

Matt dug his nails into his palms. He bowed. "Forgive me, I'm a little upset. Does anyone recognize my would-be killer?"

"This is a job for the Special Investigators." Ellaine nodded at Derrick. "Find out who this person is and make sure there are no others."

"And given the poison on my floor is probably still lethal"—Matt found his eyes locking to Vella's, the urge to keep her safe frankly irritating—"I suggest everyone leaves the ballroom."

Matt managed to maintain his bland expression as guests filed out, most craning their necks to look at the mutilated corpse, but when Vella strode past, he felt drawn to her, like the air around her was warm, fizzing ...

Screams erupted from the foyer where the crowd of departing guests was the densest.

"What now?" Ellaine looked annoyed.

"Darklings!" someone cried out. "Darklings at the gates."

Fucking hell. "Ronin, the lights. Everything on full. Now."

In brief seconds, the floodlights he'd fitted outside blazed over the grounds and blasted everyone with an almost-blinding light.

Matt, followed by Ellaine, Vella, Charles and Derrick, went outside to assess the damage. Several witches moaned in pain with bloody slashes along their arms and hands, but nobody else was dead.

There was also no sign of Darklings; the floodlights had done their job.

"Matt," Ellaine said, "this winter ball has been ... disappointing."

5

Snow-covered cars, lampposts and stoops were icy companions on Vella's early morning run, and after the events of the night before, she forced herself to push hard—set her breathing in cadence with her stride and shoved the memory of bone-handled knives, that *kiss*—and what had followed, out of her mind.

But even so, her lips tingled, as did other body parts.

"Frigging hell," she muttered. "Why him?"

She pushed hard for the next two blocks, slowing only when she reached Crystal Brew, the laneway coffee place one block from her shop.

"Vella, you are mad, girl." Jacqui Ashlin, Crystallo witch, good friend, and the coffee shop owner, shook her head. "What are you doing out this early?"

"Running," Vella deadpanned and stretched her legs under the heaters.

"Well, I hope you're running to something warm and toasty. Maybe a nice hunk of—"

Matthias' face flew into Vella's mind. How delicious he'd been on his knees kissing her thigh— "Ugh, no!"

"What, you don't want your regular?" Jacqui's nose scrunched.

"No, I meant—sorry, I didn't hear you ask for the coffee. I was thinking about someone, some*thing* else. Absolutely yes to the coffee. That's the toasty warmth I'm after."

"Well, coffee, I can do. Now, tell me all about the party last night. How did it go? What did you wear? Did you see the Magicae Councilor? Are his eyes really silver?"

"Who saw the Magicae Councilor?" Tanya, another early-morning customer paused with her coffee midway to her mouth.

"Vella." Jacqui waggled her eyebrows.

"And how do you even know I was at a party last night? They're not my normal gig."

"I run a coffee shop, hon. I know everything."

"Wait, you were at a party with the Magicae Councilor?" Tanya's eyes widened, and then she turned to Jacqui. "Isn't he a knight or something? That accent is divine. And have you heard the rumors about having sex with a spellcaster?" She fanned herself. "Makes me wish I was a witch myself."

"Oh yeah, I know *those* rumors." Jacqui smirked as she finished pouring the coffee. "So, how *was* the party? C'mon, give us something."

Hmm … failed arcana retrieval, attempted murder, a dead assassin, a hot-as-hell asshole spellcaster, oh, and a Darkling attack to cap off the night. Frigging brilliant.

"It was a party, people partied," was all she said. "One thing you should know—there was an attack on the grounds."

"Darklings?" Tanya shuddered.

"The Council think so. And they don't like bright

light." Vella looked around the shop. "But you're out here before sunup, so you need to be careful."

"Same to you, hon. At least I'm good in here. You're running about the streets—and the park—in the dark."

"I can run fast," Vella murmured. Plus, how could she explain that the dark felt safe, way safer than some places in the light, anyway? "Thanks for this. See you next time."

"Blessings to you, Vella."

"Back atcha. And you too, Tanya." She raised her travel mug and nodded before taking off for her shop and, within two minutes, rounded the corner of her building.

A contented sigh eased from her as she entered her beloved townhouse, *their* townhouse, a place just for herself and Sara away from Div Tower.

It was built over four floors, with the cellar used as storage, the street level cut in two with the shop at the front and office space at the rear, the first floor with their kitchen and main living area, and their bedrooms at the top.

Cradling the two coffees, Vella found Sara in their office.

"Surprise, surprise." She forced all tension from her voice. "You're up early."

"Vel, you're back!" At least Sara looked as well as she normally did. Then her eyes widened at the coffee, and she reached out. "Goddess, yes."

"How are you feeling?"

"Feeling?" Sara's nose scrunched. "Like every other time you've asked, I'm fine."

"You don't have to put on a show with me," Vella murmured.

"I know, and I'm not." Sara took a sip. "PS, girl, you should be worrying about your own bonkers self. You had that party and after you"—she did air quotes with her fingers—"*liberated* the sphalerite crystal ball, locked it up at Div Tower, you still went on your morning run. You're not looking your best. And I resent Auntie E for still making you go out last night after a ball *and* Darkling attack."

"Don't call her that; you know she hates it. And we owe her our loyalty and obedience. She's done everything for us. She raised us after Mom and Dad died, *you* from a baby, she's paid all your medical bills, she's paying the Elixirs to keep you"—*alive,* she didn't say—"on your special meds, she paid for both my degrees, she loaned me the money to start Arcane Antiquities."

Sara fiddled with her phone and put on some indie-rock girl music. "I don't care. She doesn't treat you well, Vel, she never has. *And* I don't think it's right to take arcana from fellow witches. I only hack your way through high security to keep *you* safe, not for Auntie E. And look at the poor Winchesters. That crystal was foundational to their whole business. They might lose everything now."

"It's for the—"

"Good of witchkind, blah, blah, blah. Is it, though? Really?"

A loud knock banged on the front door. Sara tapped on her mouse and up popped a visual of outside on the screen.

A dark, sleek, fancy car was parked out front, and standing on her doorstep, punching something into his cell, stood the asshole of the moment. Matthias fucking Medea.

Perfectly cut charcoal coat hugging that impressive frame, dark hair pulled back again, revealing the intriguing planes of his face, piercing silver eyes—

"Who the hell is *that*?" Sara murmured while taking

screenshots. "Ooh, I'm using him as inspo for my next romance hero. D*aaaa*mn."

"No, you are not," Vella snapped and stomped through the front room and yanked open the door. "What are you doing here?"

"You've been running?" His eyes narrowed on her leggings and then lifted to her face. "In the dark? Alone? That was foolish, Velvet—"

"It's Vella. Or how about *nothing* since I don't want you here on my doorstep?"

"Actually, I rather think you should listen to what I have to say."

"At seven a.m. on a Saturday?"

"Which you should be thanking me for. After all, I have a business proposal for you, and to avoid interrupting your shop hours, I came early. And I'm here in person because you would've ignored any message that I sent you otherwise."

She didn't bother hiding her eye roll. Hell, yes, she would've ignored him. "I need to shower, change and prep my shop. So no, I don't want to chat about anything, thank you."

"That wasn't the tune you sang last night."

"Is that why you're here? I'd have thought you'd never want to show your face in public ever again. Aunt Ellaine said she was *disappointed*."

Matt leaned forward and whispered, "I don't give a flying fuck if Ellaine is disappointed. But I confess, I didn't hate our make-out session, even if, on reflection, it wasn't my finest moment."

"We didn't—" She glanced around. Crap, this wasn't a conversation for her shop doorstep. She ground her teeth. "I was talking about you killing a person—"

"Who was trying to kill me." He shrugged like he'd

done nothing more than empty a bin of used sage smudges. "And others. In fact, if I hadn't killed him, he'd still be dead, just in a much nastier method after the SI got through with him."

"Sure, tell yourself that. Goodbye, Mr. Medea." She slammed the door shut … and it bounced open on his foot. Goddess damn it.

"Matthias. Surely, we're on a first-name basis?"

"No, *Mr. Medea*, we're not."

"I'm here to talk to you, *Miss Knight*. And this is something you might not want discussed on your doorstep. Or, maybe you do, after all, you were quite keen to experience my services last night, I suppose—"

"Frigging hell. Get inside."

She slammed the door shut after him. The bells jangled violently, and even the lavender and sage above didn't help her relax.

Medea stopped in the middle of her business and looked around, but whatever he thought of the shelves filled with witchy wares from years past, the wingback chair beside a traditional potbelly stove, or the indigo ceiling Sara had hand painted with gold leaf to reproduce the twelve zodiac constellations, Vella had no clue because the spellcaster's expression gave away nothing.

"Interesting," he finally murmured. "Is everything antique?"

"They're all real." She stiffened. "I don't deal in fakes."

"You must have some amazing contacts, but then, as a Divinator, who'd say no to you?"

"People do business with me because I've got integrity and pay a fair price," she ground out. "Not because of my family."

"You do, however, have a talent for securing harder to … obtain items for your auntie? I've heard that, as recently as last night, the Winchesters lost their crystal ball. And now, their entire world is going to come crashing down, along with everyone and everything they love, isn't it?"

Guilt twisted in her heart—but she hadn't done it for her benefit.

"Aunt Ellaine is a respected leader, not an evil monster. What? What is that look for?"

"Nothing." Medea's features smoothed out like he hadn't, for a moment, looked ready to kill. "So, to business."

"I'm not doing business with you."

"Oh, but I think you will." His expression remained bland. Too bland. Her stomach dropped. "I wouldn't want to repeat to anyone about how Councilor Priestley's niece—"

"I DON'T KNOW what you're talking about." Color flooded the Div's cheeks and the glow in her lioness eyes changed to outright destruction.

Matt's magic rose again to the surface. He *wanted* her to destroy him. *Deep breaths, Matt.*

"Oh yes, you do." His voice was gruff but at least steady. "My bedroom, last night, you talked to an ancient Mors Dicen knife. By the way, your thiefness, I'm fairly certain your *auntie* would literally kill to get her hands on it. And because I couldn't quite believe my ears ... and eyes"—no lie there—"I also recorded it." Now, that part was a lie, but he wasn't averse to a strong bluff.

"If that's true, why don't you report me?"

"Well, I could, of course. But I think there's a better option. I want you to kit out all my clubs—New York and

London to begin with. Maybe Edinburgh. Give them a witchy vibe."

He strolled to the comfortable-looking reading chair by the fireplace and ran a hand over the fabric. Not new, but quality. The latter he expected, the former made him pause. Exactly who was Vella Knight? He turned back to her.

"I'm not asking for much. I'll pay you handsomely, of course. I just want to spend some time with you. We'll do a bit of traveling. Get to know each other. Figure out why you can practice Mors Dicen magic ... talk about some of the ... lesser-known practices of the Divinator coven ... so, do we have a deal?"

"You want me *to spy*?"

"No, no, don't be so crass. Just a little chitchat."

"Fuck you and your crass. No way under the goddess's moon or sun am I spying for you."

"Such language. Rare for a Div, no? And while Ellaine is your aunt, she is the Council, and believe me, *she* is the one with a vendetta against all Mors Dicen ... and any coven or magical creature she sees as a rival or distasteful to her. Have you ever visited the jails beneath your auntie's tower? The ones filled with witches not outrightly killed for practicing any magic not expressly 'approved' of by Ell—I mean, the Council."

"You are batshit!" Vella's hands clenched at her side. "No one is killing witches—"

"You're the loco one if you think that's the case." He forced a casual shrug. "I simply caution you to do your due diligence for your sister's sake. It's Sara, right?"

"Don't you dare say her name."

"Me saying her name is the least of your concerns right now."

"Vella? You okay?" A young witch wearing leggings

and an oversize sweater, which only made her fragility more apparent, entered the shop from the back door. Apart from the tawny hair tumbling over her shoulders, her features were so like the Div's, down to the uniquely colored eyes and pointy chin; this had to be Sara.

But a pallor to her skin made his stomach clench. The sister was clearly unwell, and Vella's protectiveness for her resonated with him. Bloody hell. No, no sympathizing of any kind with the Div.

"Sara." The Div shot him a filthy look before turning back to her sister. "Sorry we were a bit loud. Can you give us a minute? Mr. Medea will be leaving soon."

Sara's eyes narrowed. "Well, I'm right here if you need anything."

Clearly, the protectiveness went both ways. Ugh. Why did they have to make themselves human to him? Empathy for Ellaine Priestley's nieces, witches from the coven he despised more than any other? Not bloody likely.

"Winter blessings to you," Matt said before he could stop himself.

"And to you." Sara winked at him. Winked! Then disappeared back through the interconnecting door.

"You are never to talk to her again." The Div stalked toward him, her lioness eyes screaming that if she had a weapon in her hands, she'd use it. On him.

He mentally cheered. Please take me. I'm yours.

For fuck's sake, Matt. Focus.

"You want me to never talk to her again?" Matt crossed his arms. Whether to stop himself from doing something stupid like grabbing her, begging to worship her body, or to act as a barrier from the impact this lioness of a witch was having on him—who knew? And hells, right now, it was likely both. "Fine. You have the power to make that happen, Div."

"Oh really, *spellcaster*?"

"Yes. Meet me at my club. Nocturnal. Tonight. Nine p.m."

"You're loco—"

"And you broke the law on banned magic—"

"Fine," she ground out. "But shut up about the Mor—about you know what."

He forced back the urge to shout his triumph, to let out the ferocity rushing through his veins, because yes, he had her now. He leaned forward and whispered in the shell of her ear. "Also, let me know if at any point you get a phone call about your computers or surveillance being down? Kay?"

And he strolled out just as her gorgeous mouth popped open—no doubt to demand what the hell he was talking about.

"Now, are you sure you're good for me to go out?" Vella asked, resting a hip on Sara's desk, checking out the artwork on her monitor. She almost choked. "Sara!"

"I know, right? It's based on an NSFW scene—that's Not Safe For Work, in case you're wondering. Isn't he *perfect*?"

It was basically Matthias Medea as an orc with an extremely large ... organ. Vella cleared her throat. Tried to speak. Cleared it again. "First of all, I know what NSFW is. I'm not that uncool—"

"Yeah, tell yourself that."

"—and, like artistically, it's quite lovely. Umm, his appendage is so green, though."

"Yep. It's great, isn't it?! I'm hoping to complete this for my author by solstice, so I'm pushing hard. Get it? *Pushing hard*?"

"Good gods, Sara. And please, try to go to sleep at a decent hour. You need your rest. And stop rolling your eyes. And pretending to gag to death."

"I'm fine, *Mom*. And yes, I'm good for you to go out tonight. Now go, do your clubbing thing." Sara's eyes narrowed. "Wait. Are you going out in that?"

"Clearly." Vella scowled. "Why?"

"Your meeting is with this very hot orc, um, spell-caster, I mean, and you've got this awesome opportunity to go to England and Scotland if you land the contract. Pfft, how is that so hard? What I wouldn't give to travel."

"Sar—" Vella's heart twisted.

"And it's Nocturnal," Sara continued, thankfully oblivious to Vella's heart. "Right now, you look like you're staying in for the night with me, not going to *the* club of the year. Every witch who is any witch, plus humans and nons, go there. Don't you want to make a good impression?"

"Not really," Vella muttered under her breath. But Sara was on her feet and grabbing her hand. "Come on, do you know how much I would love to go to Nocturnal? Please, for me—even if you don't want to dress up, let me live a little through you, okay?"

"You're serious, aren't you?"

"Totally. No, not your room, uncool person who only ever wears Auntie E's approved beige *or* eye-watering neon athleisure. My room. We're the same height."

"Just two sizes different. I've got the dress I wore the other night—"

"That's a big no—he already saw you in that. You need something different to impress."

"I'm not trying to impress him, Sara." The opposite, in fact. She had a plan for tonight, and Medea wasn't going to like it.

"Why not? I did a little light cyberstalking and dude is single. Very single. I mean, single in the way where he bangs everyone. You could use a little, uh, banging in your life. And have you heard the rumors about sex with a spellcaster?"

"Why is everyone obsessed with his dick? And you've been staring at your spicy art for too long if you think I'm ever going there."

"What? Why? Banging one is like a once-in-a-lifetime experience—as in you see the stars or something."

"Ew. No, no, no." Except, fine, seeing stars with someone other than her vibrator did sound good. Just not with the asshole trying to make her *spy* on her coven. And talk about ... that other stuff. Nope, she had her plan, and *she* was going to win.

"I'm just saying if you get the chance, do it for me." Sara smirked.

"Banging for my sister's sake. I'll keep that in mind."

"Good. Because you never know when the opportunity might come. Come—get it?" Sara's wicked little smile lit up. "Now, don't worry, I've got something short and roomy." She flicked the hangers across. "Here, this one." She pulled a red piece of slinky material out of her closet. "Perfect!"

"I swear you just want me to show off my legs."

"Hell, yes! I would if I had your legs. Come on, you're not breaking and entering tonight. This is an actual *client* who could pay us loads. Vel, imagine it. If we could just run this shop like normal people and not worry about all Aunt Ellaine's bullshit. And this dress is perfect for the club you're going to. *Please.*"

"Oh goddess, put away the doe eyes. Fine."

"Yes!" Sara did a victory dance, but she tired fast and flopped onto her bed.

"Hey, you okay?" Vella clutched the dress tighter. "I can stay—"

"No freaking way! Go. I'm fine, just tired—as always."

"If you're sure? Wow, a second eye roll? Okay, okay ... I'm going. I'll set the alarm on the front door and see you sometime ... later. Before midnight, though. And if you can't get me, here's the number of my contact; you can reach him in an emerge—"

"Oh, sweet goddess, just go." Sara flapped her arm about, not lifting her head. "I've got your cell. I've got the backup for Nocturnal. I've got Jac's from the coffee shop. I've got the coven emergency number. Bye!"

7

Nocturnal NY took up an entire three-story red brick building. Sara had been right, too, that the club was one of the city's fanciest nightspots. Despite the cold and relatively early hour, a queue already extended along the sidewalk from a set of red glass doors, with floodlights set up to keep the entire area brightly lit.

Was Medea really that thoughtful to keep everybody safe from Darkling attacks? Or, more likely, Medea realized without the lights, no one would line up to drop their cash in his sexy pockets. Yeah, that fit far more with the Medea she knew.

Medea had sent a message telling her to give her name to the door person, and a moment later, she was ushered from the falsely bright, cold sidewalk into an opulent kaleidoscope of velvet and leather, richly hued lights, heavy beats and a sea of bodies moving to the rhythm of the music.

And a diverse crowd—humans, witches from all the

covens, Crystallo, Magicae, Elixirs, and even some Divs—well, non-tower Divs, anyway, from their tats.

Was that a shifter? And holy hell, a *vamp*?

A vaulted ceiling soared three stories above the main dance floor. Bar to her right, stage straight ahead, and on the left, a first-floor balcony overlooking the dance floor and a second-floor wall of more of that smoky red glass. Stairs leading up to the higher floors were tucked into the corner.

She was impressed—no, no she was *not*.

And speaking of ... beneath the strobing lights, Medea appeared on the first-floor balcony in black pants and a white shirt with the sleeves rolled up—showcasing yet more snakes winding up his arms—with his hair tied back in a knot, the snake tattoos at his neck visible as well.

A walking smorgasbord of delicious, mysterious, bad boy—fuckboy—energy. And the object of almost everyone's gazes.

Was he aware of the attention?

Pfft. Of course he was.

Then he looked over at Vella, and a million watts of his energy locked on her like she was the only being in the entire club. And her traitorous body turned to fire all over again, like it had each time she'd been near him.

Crap.

Asshole. Prick. Motherfucking blackmailer. But Vella had a plan of her own now, and it didn't involve ogling snake tats.

She held her ground as he made his way down the staircase, stopped by numerous patrons and staff who he spoke with amiably, as if he had nowhere else to be.

"Vella, welcome to Nocturnal." He picked up her hand and brought it to his mouth, and his lips were *so* warm and she imagined them down—*no*, Vella.

She yanked it away. "Ew."

"I have to say, your dress is spectacular. Tell me you wore that color for me."

"Listen, you brought me here, now where can we talk? The faster we get this over with, the better."

"At least let me get you a drink."

"No. Where can we talk without yelling?"

"Well, why don't we go to my office?" Medea gestured for her to precede him. "It's on the second floor, and we can go over our agreement in quiet."

"Suits me. Do we take the stairs?"

"We could, or we can take the staff elevator." He grinned suddenly. "I've been looking forward to being alone with you again."

As he took off across the club floor, that surge of unwelcome—irrational—heat zapped to her core.

Get a grip, lady parts. You so do not need this right now.

"Matthias!" Three women, humans based on the lack of any coven marks, wearing about as little clothing as could be called dressed, swarmed the Magicae Councilor, cutting Vella off.

"Welcome back," Medea's voice rolled out like decadent silk. "This humble club doesn't do justice to your beauty."

Seriously? This a-hole was wasting her time by flirting?

"We've booked a salon tonight," the closest purred. "Coming to join us?"

"As tempting as that offer is, unfortunately, business demands me this evening. But I am sure you'll enjoy yourselves nonetheless."

"Not nearly as much as with you." They pouted and laughed and kissed his cheeks until he extricated himself and gestured for Vella to go before him. "The lift is this way, Ms. Knight."

Vella glanced back over her shoulder to find all three glowering at her as if she'd personally ruined their evening. Yeah, right. Like she was ever going to fight someone for Matthias Medea.

They got off the lift and stepped into the office area. Two lovely young women dressed in the club service uniform—very chic and sexy—were taking a break in what had to be the fanciest staff lounge ever. Medea waved at them as he passed by, and the blond one hurried over saying, "Winter blessings, Mr. Medea."

"And to you too, Susan. And just Matt, please."

"Sorry if I'm interrupting anything, but I just had to say thank you. My little girl was so sick, and she wasn't getting any better, and I couldn't afford Elixir prices—"

"Please, don't mention it; it was my pleasure. How is she now?"

"She's back at school and playing with her friends." Susan's eyes began to well up. "You can't imagine what it's meant to us."

Medea nodded and shifted his warm, genuine smile to the redhead. "And how are you, Lilly? Hope the car situation is all sorted now?"

"Yes, we got it fixed last week. Thanks again for the advance."

They said their goodbyes, and Vella found herself staring at Medea. He'd never looked at Vella like that, his face all soft and kind. She hadn't even known it existed in his facial expression repertoire. There was fake Medea when he was all apologies and agreeable to Aunt Ellaine, and Vella had been the frequent recipient of 'fucking angry and/or resentful' and 'weirdly sexy.' Although those had been pretty damn genuine too.

But what would it be like to work for someone who

actually had your back ... rather than counted every favor as a transactional?

"Your stare is almost a weapon," Medea said.

Then something began to glow in his eyes—dark and sparkling, like he was hiding a galaxy behind them—yep, he was *doing* it again.

"Listen, spellcaster, I'm here instead of looking after my sister because you're blackmailing me. I'd like to get this over with and get home."

"Like I said, I just want a little friendly chat. And to make a deal that will very much benefit Arcane Antiques financially. I think you're pissy because you're jealous." That teasing smile—and those dimples—came out to make him seem boyish almost, something he was absolutely not. "But you don't need to worry; you have my undivided attention." He gestured for her to follow and strolled off without looking back.

"You think I'm jealous? No way."

Liar.

Shut up, inner voice.

8

"Wow, some offices." Vella made her way to the window on the far end. "One-way glass, I take it. I can see the club through this section, but why is the other half dark?"

"Those rooms are our salons. We mainly book them for PDS—public displays of sex."

"Do you participate often?" Vella asked, her voice carefully controlled, but Matt could swear he smelled her arousal.

And his elemental power surged in answer, clawing under his skin, a-*fucking*-gain. He was not a randy teenager anymore, dammit. It was as if his fuse constantly short-circuited around this particular Div. Matt ground his teeth. Mr. and Mrs. B, the people of Madgewick, his coven ... all those people were counting on *him*, and no fucking way was he letting them down. He hauled in a deep breath, held his energy in a tight grip until it settled.

He'd managed to successfully lure Miss Knight to the exact location he wanted her, and he could not, *must* not, fuck it up. *Stay cool, calm, collected.* And keep the Div on the back foot.

He relaxed his shoulders and grinned. Leaned toward her. "Is that a request?"

"Eyes up here, spellcaster."

Matt tore his gaze away from those long, toned legs. "Of course, apologies for admiring the view."

Vella glowered and crossed her arms. "You're up to something, and I've got zero time for this bullshit. Here's the deal. I'm turning your blackmail back on you. If you tell the Council about me accidentally practicing Mors Dicen, I *might* get in trouble. But if I tell Aunt Ellaine about your attempts to get me to commit treason on my own coven, you'll absolutely suffer her full wrath. So, instead, I demand you hand over that bit of paper I tried to liberate—"

"Steal has a much truer ring, don't you think?"

"—from you and we never speak again. In fact, you forget I even exist."

"Actually, no, that doesn't work for me." He rocked back on his heels. Damn, but he enjoyed baiting this Div.

"What—" The Div's mouth dropped open, though just as fast, she snapped it shut, and true fury glowed in her glorious eyes.

"I'm engaging your services to provide décor for my house upstate and my clubs, so we have a solid excuse to spend time together." Matt opened the door to the salon. "Come, I've drawn up a legitimate contract, and I'll pay you well."

Matt strode inside, leaving the room dark. Vella followed him, outraged and hissing about selfish, untrustworthy spellcasters.

Shannah slammed the door shut, and Ronin flicked

on the lights. The two flanked the Div, grabbing her arms. Sylvie and her brothers, Tannis and Alexander, sat in the middle of the scallop-shaped booth against the back wall. On the teak coffee table before them was the Mors Dicen bone-handled knife in its box, the lid open.

Vella froze, staring—her face deathly white.

Matt *almost* felt bad.

But tonight, he was getting answers. Answers that might just be a stepping-stone to a world where all magical creatures could once again exist in peace without threat or fear.

Staying away from the Div's direct line of vision, he released all his other incantations, took the three breaths needed for the most complex spellcraft and, holding the last, whispered as quietly as he could, "Bind all senses to my spell, from those whose vision I wish to quell. From night or light, hide from their sight. As I say, make it be."

He sent his power in a wall of energy through the room, the hairs raising along the backs of his arms as the spell formed.

"We're clear," he said.

It started as an itch nibbling at the back of Vella's neck, then coalesced into an outright scratching. Magic. Here and now. And she saw, once again, her parents touching a cursed Mors Dicen skull, their living flesh calcifying to bone. "Let me go, you fucking assholes!"

"Daughter, I can hear you!" the woman's voice from the knife shot through the room. "Make contact and I can help you."

Not again! No, no, no.

Vella wrenched her gaze from the knife to Medea, who was now lounging on the edge of the scalloped booth next to the three strangers who were ... *vamps*? Good Goddess. Two males, one female, all lethal. She fought against Ronin and a woman with green-tipped midnight hair gripping her arms, but they were too powerful.

"Is this your plan, Medea?" Vella snarled. "Ambush and poison me with your Magicae spellcasting? Turn *me* into bone, too?"

The knife demanded, "Well, Daughter? Make contact! Please, it has been so very long."

"Stop," Vella shouted.

"I am Brianna. My purpose is to teach and protect. Now answer me. Please."

Vella began to shake; her heart was racing; she felt hot, nauseated, like the world was closing in on her. Without realizing what she was even doing, she managed to free one arm and slam down the lid of the box.

Silence. Blessed silence.

"Shannah," Medea said to the woman with the green-tipped hair, "secure her. Vella, don't try to deny it." Something flared in his eyes. "The knife is talking to you, isn't it?"

The three vamps rose and came forward. The female purred, "Vella, hello. Aren't you delicious?" She smiled, revealing her fangs. "Tell me, what is the name of the blade? And I suggest you answer truthfully if you wish to remain ... let's say ... *not* exsanguinated."

Vella's mouth went dry. She swallowed hard. "She called herself Brianna."

Was she practicing Mors Dicen magic?

The two males dropped to their knees, and the female raised an eyebrow before slowly nodding. "How interesting."

What the frig was going on now?

"Sylvie," Medea snapped. "Stop messing around. What's your opinion?"

"Well, she can speak to Brianna without the aid of arcana or ritual. That means she is not only Mors Dicen, but possibly a Bone Wielder, and most likely directly related to Brianna's family, who were very powerful witches indeed."

"Will you help us now, Sylvie?" Medea asked.

"My pledge is to honor the Mors Dicen, but since your ... guest is Councilor Priestley's niece and actively working for her ... hmm. This is a most unusual situation. Under the circumstances, yes, I believe we can be flexible in our interpretation of how to execute our pledge."

"Very good." Matt's face went as remote and cold as she'd ever seen it. "Please proceed."

The tiny vampire grabbed Vella's forearm.

"What the fuck are you doing?" Vella struggled harder, but the vamp was like a machine, with zero give in her grasp.

Sylvie brought Vella's wrist up to her mouth and gently pierced her skin with one sharp fang. A bead of blood welled up, and Sylvie delicately licked it. "I'm ready."

"First thing you need to understand, Rapunzel," Medea growled, "is Sylvie here can confirm or deny whether you're answering truthfully now that she's tasted your blood. And I have questions you need to answer."

"You've got zero right to interrogate me." Anger and fear churned in her belly, but she refused to let either take control. "And my name is *Vella*, asshole."

"Given your aunt locked you away in Div Tower and kept you purposefully removed from all other covens and Divinators ... at least until about a year ago ... I'd say I have every right to understand who the fuck you are. And moreover, we have people outside your home, where your sister is sleeping. So, I recommend you share information enthusiastically and truthfully."

Vella froze. He was threatening Sara.

"Motherfucker." She yanked harder than ever on the hands holding her. "If you hurt her—"

"Simply tell me what I want to know, and your precious sister will be fine."

"I don't know anything."

"Now there you're wrong. You've been stealing for your aunt, and we have questions. The big one first: does your auntie know you are a Mors Dicen?"

"I'm not a fucking Mors Dicen!"

"That's what she believes," Sylvie said.

"Why is Ellaine stockpiling powerful arcana? What is her purpose?"

"To protect witchkind from—"

"Bullshit," Sylvie murmured, examining her very long, very red fingernails. "One more chance."

"We're doing it for Sara. She's sick and the doctors have no answers. Aunt Ellaine is giving the arcana to the foreseers to try and find a cure."

"She also believes this to be true."

"What has Ellaine informed you about escalating her Divinator regime? Particularly regarding England and Scotland?"

"This is ridiculous! Let me go!"

"Shannah," Medea said, "please show Rapunzel where our surveillance teams are right now."

Shannah pulled out her cell phone so Vella could see several blue dots surrounding Arcane Antiquities on the glowing map. Rage and terror burned bright. She was going to kill every single last one of them. Starting with Medea. "Nothing," Vella replied. "She tells me nothing!"

"True."

"What do you think would happen if your auntie knew about your connection to the Mors Dicen?"

"I don't know."

"Half-truth."

Medea closed the space between himself and Vella, crowding her, towering over her, with black stars burning in his silver eyes. "What do you *fear* will happen?"

Oh Goddess, what Vella feared? So many fucking things.

"That ... that she will punish me." The words were out before she could stop them.

"Half-truth."

"Try again," Medea snapped.

"*Fine*." Bitter tears burned at her eyes and no matter how hard she tried she couldn't stop them falling. "Make me disappear."

"True. And disappear can have many interpretations." Sylvie nodded to the male vamps who'd remained kneeling, still as statutes. "Alexander, Tannis, come. We're out of here. Matt, we're done with this. Bring the Mors Dicen back to me *when* she is ready to accept her heritage, and only then will I offer more information. See you at the party."

The three vampires exited.

Medea drew out a linen handkerchief from his pocket and gently wiped Vella's face, but she jerked away.

"Getting your fucking hands away from me, you monster."

"Velvet, Velvet, Velvet." Medea tsked like she'd disappointed him. "I can see that your moral compass is set to your sister, and I can appreciate that, even admire it. So I want you to take into consideration that if *you* are a Mors Dicen, Sara most likely is too. If your auntie were to become aware of this information, any consequences would land on her head as well."

Vella bit hard on the inside of her mouth, using the pain to refocus her screaming, panicking heart into her deep rage and hatred of this man.

"So here's what's going to happen next." Medea shoved a computer pad before Vella, the screen glowing with a contract. "I'll pay you thirty thousand dollars, and you will travel with me to my clubs, decorate them as you see fit, and answer all the questions I have.

"You'll also take possession of Brianna, like the good Mors Dicen you are, and learn how to wield her. We have projects to accomplish together, you and I. Last but definitely not least, keep those pretty lips sealed. If you do one. Single. Thing. That endangers my coven, I will remove the threat you and your sister pose without hesitation. Am I clear?"

Vella nodded once, and Ronin and Shannah finally released her.

Medea handed Vella a plastic pen and pointed to the screen. "Now sign this."

She accepted it, and while Medea was bending toward her, she smashed her forehead hard into his face. His nose made a very satisfying crunch.

"Fuck you!" She lunged for the doorway.

Medea stumbled backward, swearing, and Shannah and Ronin leaped at her, but Vella was already sprinting out the door.

As she bolted down the corridor, an alarm suddenly wailed, blinding white lights blazed on, and she heard over the speaker system on repeat: "Alert, Darkling activity reported near and around Nocturnal. Seek shelter in all brightly lit locations; Alert, Darkling activity reported near and around Nocturnal. Seek shelter in all brightly lit locations."

Vella slammed through the first staff stairwell she saw with an exit sign, heading for Sara and home.

She didn't give a gnat's ass about Darklings; *they*'d better watch out for *her*.

9

Vella lay in her bed, mind racing. Sara was safe, thank the goddess, fitfully asleep in her room.

After Vella had signaled a taxi with her ride app, her first instinct on the way home had been to call Aunt Ellaine and report.

Her whole life, it had been Vella's job to debrief her aunt of her actions and decisions and wait for her judgment—and obey. That was the way things worked, and if she was honest with herself, she'd felt some comfort in it. Aunt Ellaine wasn't the perfect caregiver, but she'd been there after Sara and Vella had lost everything—their home, their parents, any sense of security.

That was not nothing.

Div Tower hadn't been easy, but ... they'd had a place to live. Sara had medicine for her illness.

Yet, when Vella had reached for her phone to call Aunt Ellaine, she'd noticed a message from her cousin Derrick. He'd wanted to know whether her security systems were working properly. They seemed a bit buggy on his end and he could drop in on Tuesday to give them a hardware upgrade.

Medea's obscure comment—was it just this morning? —about getting a phone call on that subject had flowed back through her mind. What the fuck did it mean?

Vella grabbed a pillow and screamed her anger into it. What the hell was she meant to do next?

Matthias fucking Medea was trying to control her like a puppet. He'd threatened Sara to make Vella comply, and it felt so familiar that it made her realize Aunt Ellaine did the same thing. If Vella disagreed or questioned her, suddenly Aunt Ellaine was murmuring about the Elixir potions and making passive aggressive comments about Sara's health and the extravagant price of keeping her medicated.

Also? Was she a Mors Dicen? No, it must be a trick. She was a Divinator through and through—both her parents had been Divs, hadn't they? She was related to Ellaine through her mother, so if she *were* Mors Dicen, it had to be from her father's family tree.

Frigging goddess, Vella and Sara might be part Div, part—

No. Nope. Not going there. Impossible.

But what *would* Aunt Ellaine do if she learned that she and Sara *could* have a connection to the Mors Dicen?

Vella went hot and then cold, thinking of how Medea had forced her to confess her deepest, darkest fear of what Ellaine *could* potentially do to her. To Sara.

Sara was fucking right. The best outcome would be if they were free of everyone. If they could just be regular witches, like Jacqui with her coffee shop, running their businesses, making their own money, not owing anyone anything. Even better, what if ... what if she could leave New York City altogether?

A distant childhood memory of life in Vermont whispered through her mind ... back then, she'd breathed deep and easy, surrounded by old-growth forests, mountains, rushing rivers.

Wouldn't it be something if Sara were healthy, they moved back to Vermont, lived together in an old 1850s farmhouse filled with antiques—Vella could run her business online and so could Sara with her studies, her art, her gaming, her ... well, honestly, illegal hacking.

And cats ... she'd have so many cats.

That would be true security—the freedom to make her own choices without having to defer to someone else.

But if she reported back to Ellaine anything at all about Medea, his club, his vamps, let alone Vella being Mors Dicen, or that knife ... Brianna, what were the odds Ellaine would yank their chains and force Vella and Sara back to Div Tower? Damn frigging high.

Too high.

No, better she didn't say anything.

But neither was she working with that dickhead, Medea—he could take his thirty thousand, his questions, his contract and shove them all up his ass. He had just as much to lose reporting her as a Mors Dicen as she did.

Vella was done; if she ever saw Medea again, it would be too soon. She hoped his nose healed crooked. Or better, got infected and fell off his face.

With that very pleasant image, Vella finally drifted off to sleep.

VELLA AWOKE to muffled sounds echoing from the floor below and fumbled for her cell ... two a.m.

Damn it, Sara's broken sleep was a constant problem now. At least they could have a chamomile tea together.

Vella pushed back the covers and came face-to-face with Sara. What the—

Shit. Not Sara downstairs.

"Someone's down there." Sara was holding their bat.

Vella snatched it. "Well, someone's about to get their head bashed in." She grinned, deserving some release after the night she'd had. She could pretend it was Medea. "Lock yourself in your room. Call the police. Don't come out until I tell you to."

"The fuck I am."

Vella growled. Save her from willful sisters.

"Fine. But you will stay back behind me—got it?" She crept, followed by Sara, to the top of the landing and listened, straining to hear where the intruder was. A large figure appeared at the bottom of the stairs.

"Where is she?" he demanded, slowly climbing.

Redoubling her grip on the bat, Vella bolted down the stairs, swinging. She slammed it into the man's chest, sending him crashing back down the steps. She followed, bat high and ready. The lights switched on and the man was now visible, gaping up at Vella, face pale, his wide eyes a startling blue.

Vella aimed for his forehead, and he rolled away, the maple slamming where his head had been seconds earlier. He lunged to his feet, and Vella swung it at his face again, catching him on the arm he'd raised to protect himself. He screamed in pain, his hand at a funny angle. Vella went after him again, and he dodged past and smashed through the window.

Glass shattered. Shards flew. And the figure disappeared into the night.

"I hope the Darklings get him," Vella muttered as Sara joined her. "Asshole coming into *our* house trying to steal *our* stuff."

Sara snorted. "Oh, the irony."

Vella swung the bat back up and strode through the shop, furious that all the drawers had been pulled out. Contents scattered. The front door was broken. Even her purse was on the ground—at least the fucker hadn't stolen her wallet.

Knock, knock.

Vella spun around. Shannah from Nocturnal leaned against the broken door frame, still wearing her security uniform. She had an earpiece on and said into the microphone, "Vella and Sara appear unharmed."

"What are you doing here?" Vella demanded, smacking the bat into her palm.

"Security." Shannah's eyes drifted past Vella's shoulder. Her mouth quirked into a half smile. "Hi, I'm Shannah."

"Sara."

Vella whirled around, and there was Sara, leaning against the counter, staring back at Shannah, gently twirling her long hair around a finger. What the actual frig.

"Please feel free to fuck right off." Vella tried to slam the door in Shannah's face, but it collapsed off its hinges and fell to the floor.

"Yeah." Shannah's half smile went full wattage and Vella realized she was younger than she'd first thought. Maybe mid-twenties? Not much older than Vella, anyway. "Your intruder broke your door. Also, your security system is disabled."

"Please, come in, Shannah. Tea?" Sara said.

"Stop being nice to the enemy!"

"Actually, do you have coffee? I've been working since midday and really need caffeine."

"Absolutely." Sara narrowed her eyes at Vella. "You

better tell me what happened at Nocturnal. What do you mean, *enemy*?"

"There was a thing, and fine, I'll tell you, but can we deal with that later? Right now, Shannah needs to fuck off, like I said, and *we* need to do something about this giant-ass hole in our window, not to mention the door."

Shannah tapped on her cell, and a moment later, she said, "Done. Matthias has someone coming to you right away."

"Thanks!" Sara said at the same time that Vella shouted, "What? No. I can take care of this."

"Too late." Shannah shrugged. "Shall we check your kitchen, Sara? We can inventory, and I'll take that coffee from you."

Entirely ignoring Vella's protests, the two girls vanished.

Vella grabbed her hair in her fists. "Argh!"

Then she looked over the damage to her shop floor. Not much seemed broken; everything was just jumbled and disorganized. The till was flipped over, paper, receipts, paper bills, coins strewn across the floor. She knelt, hands shaking, picking up the two halves of the selenium charging bowl and set them on the counter.

Sara and Shannah returned with steaming cups, and Sara reported that the kitchen and the offices were also a mess. "Thank the goddess my tech is fine, and everything looks like it's still here."

"Whoever they were, it appears they're looking for something specific," Shannah said. She stiffened, brought her hand up to her earpiece and nodded. "Vella, Matthias wants you upstate. Now. I'm under orders to bring you up."

"Well, sorry to disappoint—and to be clear, that was a

sarcastic apology—but no. Tell Medea that he can fuck right off too. I'm not working with him and I'm definitely not leaving my shop."

Shannah took a sip from her coffee mug. "We intercepted signals transmitting from here since we've been, ah, providing you with extra security, and we're fairly convinced your surveillance feeds are being monitored."

"No way."

"Yes, way. And if someone has bugged your cameras, chances are they're listening in to your cell and landline as well."

"I knew it!" Sara said. "But if we're bugged, why are you telling us this right now?"

"I'm carrying a signal jammer," Shannah replied. "In fact, our security teams have been jamming the signals off and on to see what would happen since the winter ball."

"Vella, remember how when we first moved in, Aunt Ellaine was so determined to put security cameras and audio *everywhere*—including our living space? And we argued and argued, and suddenly she just dropped the subject?"

"Has anyone been in touch about your surveillance?" Shannah asked.

"Fuck." Vella muttered.

"I'll take that as a yes. And that's part of why Matt wants you upstate—he wants you both secure after tonight and also free from your aunt's prying."

"Hell no." Vella slammed her fist onto the counter, making the broken selenium pieces jump. "We're not going anywhere."

"Vel, I want to go." Sara gripped Vella's arm, and real fear clouded her expression. "I don't feel safe here. Let me get my things." She dashed into the office to collect her tech.

Shannah bounced her eyebrows at Vella. "Guess we're going."

Swearing under her breath, Vella stomped back upstairs to grab their toothbrushes, Sara's meds, and some extra underwear.

10

It was noon on Sunday, and Matthias stood on the near-frozen shore of Lake Ontario, drawing in deep breaths of fresh air—trying to clear his mind and control his power. He dug his toes into the cold sand, determined to ground himself.

A few hours ago, Vella and Sara had arrived in the chopper with Shannah. Matt had come out to greet them, to be polite, generous even, smiling and offering them the hospitality of the Magicae coven.

As he was speaking, Vella swerved around him and kept walking toward the house.

Sara, looking fragile and gray, but retaining a mischievous twinkle in her eye had said, "I don't know what you did, dude, but she's pissed, and when Vella is mad, you better watch out."

Shannah shook her head at him. "Bro, whatever strategy you had in mind with this one, you fucked up. Like big time. Also, check the group chat; I've uploaded a video you'll find most illuminating."

Since then, Sara and Vella have been barricaded in their guest bedrooms, sleeping or something. Neither were speaking to him, and Shannah, the traitor, seemed to have taken their side. A pair of fucking Divs.

Only they weren't actually Divs, were they?

Matt, against his better judgment, once again pulled up the footage of Vella Knight wielding a motherfucking bat like a war hammer, beating the shit out of whoever that intruder was. She was effortless; she was relentless; she was straight up trying to kill the man. No hesitation. That's why the burglar had thrown himself out of a window. He'd instinctively known Vella didn't have a shred of pity within her—not when she was protecting her own.

She was a lioness.

A warrior.

And Matt was so turned on. Damn it to hell, why did his power react to her like she was a fucking flint to his kindling?

Breathe, calm, focus. He pressed his feet deeper into the sand, rubbing the soles of his feet raw; his toes were frozen. *Breathe, calm, focus. Breathe, calm, focus.*

Just *who* was Velvet Knight?

Gold flames burning in her eyes. That glorious grin, all teeth, she'd given him the split second before she'd bashed his nose in. *With her forehead.*

Want. Her.

The power clawed through his veins, snarled to be let free.

Hell. Grounding wasn't going to work this time. Matt strode into the frigid winter-gray liquid, clothes and all, and submerged himself just as his power pulsed out—latched onto the nearest element. He flooded the water with his energy. Boom after boom blasted in his ears, and who knew what the top of the lake looked like, but finally, *finally*, his power subsided.

And after an eternity, with his lungs burning for air, he pushed himself to the top and gasped in a breath.

Fuck. That had been close.

"Bit cold for a swim, isn't it?" Ronin's familiar, dry voice called from the shore. "What's going on here? Your power still surging around Rapunzel? Any clue what's causing it?"

Matt let his head hang, water dripping. "I don't know. But it's fine. I'm keeping it under control."

"Really?" Ronin drawled. "That's why you're in the lake fully clothed in the middle of winter?"

Matt just sighed. Ronin knew him too well. "Hang on a sec." Releasing all his glamours, Matt murmured his obscurity spell and settled it around himself and his Second. "What's the intel you've got for me?"

Ronin shrugged off his coat and put it around Matt's shoulders, and they sat together on a rock.

"Turns out Rapunzel's mom was Ellaine's youngest cousin. She acquired the girls after the mother, Olivia, and the father, Tony, died eighteen years ago at the height of the Mors Dicen raids and exterminations."

Matt shook his head in disgust. "E still refers to that time as *disbanding* with a straight face. How did the parents die?"

"No clue. Their records are vague. We found birth and death certs, but ... there's no real activity from when they were alive. Like schooling, jobs. Not many photos. Might be worth asking Rapunzel a bit about her background before the evil sorceress swooped in and stole them away."

"Maybe you could have a chat with Sara about that. Vella's not exactly speaking to me at the moment."

"Yeah." Ronin rubbed the back of his neck. "That ambush didn't go as expected. Did you notice how terrified Vella was of the knife? And she's so fearless with everything else. There's something odd going on there." Ronin chuckled. "By the way, how's the nose?"

Ronin reached out to boop it, and Matt dodged backward. "Asshole. It's *fine*. A little tender. Dave is very good at healing spells. What about the would-be assassin?"

"We hit a rather solid possibility. An image from a college yearbook."

"Name?"

"Lincoln Stewart."

"As in the Elixir coven Stewarts. As in—Charles' *relative*?"

"Yeah, a third or fourth cousin who was probably trying to get into high-level management before his abrupt and tragic ending."

"Hard to get good help these days." Matt grinned, feeling a surge of victory. "At least some of my politicking seems to be working. At our last Council meeting, I got real cozy with Councilor Priestly, offered to fund a remodel of the jails at all Div Towers, and Charles got totally bent out of shape. He was already annoyed about our hosting the winter ball. I think the assassination was his attempt to either kill me outright or warn me off. Ellaine should be furious; Charles is getting too independent for her tastes."

"As delighted as I am about any schism between the Divs and Elixirs," Ronin said, rolling his eyes, "don't forget Charles will most likely continue with his assassination attempts. Our surveillance teams are overworked as it is. Speaking of which, all the Magicae are here except Dorothy."

"What? Why—is she okay?"

"Just feeling a little under the weather and didn't want to make the trip up, so I hired a crew of Crystallos to guard our New York residence. Also paid them extra to stay quiet about our departure."

"Ah, shit." Matt tunneled his hands through his hair. He hated leaving any of their coven on their own. What if something happened back in the city and he was up here, unable to help? "I wish she'd come up anyway."

"The woman is ninety. We had to let her decide what was best for her."

"I know. You're right." Matt let out a deep sigh. "Well, we've warded and guarded the mansion to the very best of our ability. It'll have to be enough." He stared off into the distance, frowning. "I'm also freaking about having Vella and Sara stay here, witnessing our whole coven together."

"My greatest fear is what they report back to their aunt. But I do believe the risk *is* worth it. I mean, Velvet Knight is the key to locating the Mors Dicen runes, and finally, we have a hope of recovering our grimoires. This is huge! The one fucking missing piece in our entire plan—to our chance at a final victory against Ellaine—has just been delivered to us. And wouldn't such a success be all the sweeter by accomplishing it with her own niece? I did fuck up trying to force Rapunzel to comply, though. She's too bloody stubborn. I need a ... different strategy."

Ronin chewed on his lip, then said, "You know, another option could be to level with them? Be honest about our goal with the runes and why we're fighting? I think they could join our side. Vella and Sara aren't blindly loyal to Ellaine—there's no love lost there, in case you haven't noticed. Just fear."

"It hasn't escaped my notice."

"And Sara, in particular, seems ready to separate from the Divs. She and Shannah have been getting friendly, and Shannah told me how Sara insisted she and Vella leave Div Tower. Sara threatened to go to an out-of-state university if they weren't allowed to move out, illness or not."

"And Ellaine's been surveilling them within an inch of their lives. But none of that matters, Ronin. I don't trust either of them. Even if they *are* Mors Dicen, they grew up with Divs—Ellaine was their caretaker and indoctrinator. Do they believe in Div supremacy? Will they betray us if we don't manage them carefully? We just don't know their politics. Here's my new strategy: we'll leave Vella alone for now, let her relax, and get her guard down. I'm fairly certain she's withholding information from Sara, and that's something we can use against her."

Ronin stood, swiping dirt off his trouser legs. "Matthias Medea, let me say for the record, I think this is a terrible idea. If Vella is really a Mors Dicen witch, and you keep lying to and manipulating her, you could damage our chances of ever gaining her as an ally."

"And if I fuck this up, then everything we've worked for will be at risk. No. This is the right option." He stood and nodded at the house. "Come on, I don't want to leave the Divs alone too long. Let's head inside."

"About time." Ronin strode ahead and held open the kitchen door. "Clay just served lunch, so we can join—Ms. Knight."

Matt followed Ronin inside and stepped past him.

Vella stood at the counter, her customary glare in place. Was that just for him?

"Ronin ... Medea." Vella's eyes ran down his body. And damn, but getting turned on wearing tight, wet jeans was not fun. "Swimming full clothed ... interesting pastimes you have up here."

"Ms. Knight. Skulking around my house ... interesting pastime for a guest."

"Skulking? I'm looking for tea."

"Vella? Did you find—oh, hey, Matthias. Ronin." Sara's face was paler than usual as she entered the kitchen from the living room.

WHAT THE FRIG was Medea up to? Who went swimming fully clothed? Sadly, his nose looked like it had already healed ... maybe he'd spelled it or something?

But right now, none of that mattered. She turned to Sara. "You didn't need to come down; I would've brought it up."

"What do you need?" Ronin's voice was filled with genuine interest, but Medea's eyes were narrowed like Vella was trying to steal the silver candles or whatever the hell spellcasters kept in their kitchens.

"I'm looking for a herbal tea—something like chamomile—to help Sara sleep. I forgot to grab it since we were in such a rush to leave." Vella made sure Medea saw her glare.

"I just need to rest but find it hard to actually sleep." Sara's entire body weight sank against Vella's side.

Crap. Sara must be exhausted given how much she hated relying on others, let alone having outsiders see how sick she was.

"Do you need help?" Ronin stood up.

"Thanks, but we've got it." Vella wrapped an arm around Sara and moved them toward the door.

"And I won't sleep for long." Sara sighed. "Part of my illness, unfortunately."

"Ronin?" Matthias murmured. "Your sleep incantation?"

"You want to spell Sara?" Bile stung the back of Vella's throat.

"Just into a deeper state of sleep," Ronin muttered.

"You can do that?" Sara's eyes widened as she looked from Matthias to Ronin.

Wait, Sara was considering saying yes?

"If it's any help, Ronin has spelled me when I couldn't fall asleep." Matthias stood too and moved to Sara's other side like he was going to help Vella. But no way did she or Sara need a Magicae's help.

And why would a spellcaster have sleeping problems? Not that it mattered. "No, we—"

"Yes, please," Sara said at the same time.

"Sara. Can I talk to you alone for a minute? In the corridor?" Vella gritted her teeth into a semblance of a smile and helped her sister out of the room.

"What's wrong?" The bewilderment on Sara's face was genuine, and Vella had to grind her teeth to stop from yelling. "Everything."

Because frigging hell, maybe if Vella had told Sara about her nightmares—about what really happened with their parents—her sister would have at least an ounce of caution around the Magicae coven. What if the very witches who had killed their parents were still alive? Maybe ... even here.

"I don't think it's a good idea to be spelled into sleep," Vella finally said. "We don't know what might happen."

"I might get some decent sleep for once. Vella, I've had every other coven try to help me. Why not give the Magicae a go? I know you hate spellcraft, but I don't. Please? What if this really helps me?"

Vella held in a sigh. "How can I say no to you?"

"You can't." Her sister grinned, and it filled Vella's heart to see her sister smile.

"Fine. Let's get you in bed first."

It took most of her effort, but Vella helped Sara up to the shared bedroom they'd been given on the first floor.

"There you go, lay down. Want me to help with your shoes?"

"Yeah. And thanks," Sara whispered. "Feel like such an idiot getting sick."

"Hey, none of that. You're not well—it happens."

"Not after every meal."

"Well, you can have lots of little meals while we're here." Vella slipped Sara's shoes under the bed. "I'll talk to Clayton."

"He seemed nice."

"Yeah."

"They all seem nice."

All of them? Vella held in a snort. No one saw the good in people like her sister.

Shannah, she ... trusted. Ronin ... he seemed to do whatever Matthias ordered him to do. And Matthias? Pft, zero trust there. Except right now, Matthias needed Vella, so what was the likelihood he'd do anything to hurt Sara at this moment? Low. Very low.

And if Ronin could help Sara get a decent sleep, especially after the stress of the last twenty-four hours, then Vella would find a way past the bile coating her throat and let him spell her sister.

A light tapping on the doorframe had both Vella and Sara look up.

"Sar, I'll be back in one moment. Just need a word with Ronin."

"Don't scare him off." Sara raised one eyebrow.

"Not scaring him away. I promise." Vella nodded for

Ronin to stay where he was and then lowered her voice when she joined him outside the bedroom. "Be careful with her. Sara's unwell."

"I'm not a monster." Ronin's mouth twisted. "Heads up, I need physical contact. Her foot will do."

"I'll come with you." Vella entered the room first.

"That's fine. Just don't touch her unless you want to say goodnight, too."

"How long will it last?" Sara's eyelids were already closing.

"Whenever you want to wake up within the next twelve hours."

"You could help me sleep that long?" Sara yawned. "Next time, for sure. For now ... when does the party start?"

"Six."

"About then sounds great. I don't want to miss a thing."

"Six is perfect," Vella blurted. Sara hadn't slept that long for ages.

Ronin nodded, knelt at the end of the bed, reached under the blankets and closed his eyes. His mouth tightened, then he whispered, "Rest deep, rest true, let not the outside world intrude. Deepest slumber, take us there, where night and peace and comfort fare."

A small hum of energy rolled out like the softest winter throw rug to blanket the room. Sara sighed, and even her face, which had been pinched, relaxed.

For a moment, longing filled Ronin's expression, and then he scrambled to his feet.

"Ssh!" Vella glared at him.

"Not needed, she won't wake up." He backed out of the room fast. "I have to go."

What the hell? Well, the Magicae wasn't her concern right now, Sara was.

And, although her sister's expression remained easy and her breathing deep and even, Vella stayed a little longer to make sure the spell didn't do any damage. The goddess knew Sara needed genuine rest, but having the spellcaster spell her further couldn't happen.

The runes. Vella had to find those runes.

11

Vella lay on the guest bed, counting the minutes until Sara was meant to wake up—as if she'd leave the bedroom before then—and stewed.

She'd grown up surrounded by all the modern luxury Divinator money could buy, but Medea's massive split-level timber lake house was possibly the best home she'd seen in her life. Damn him.

Massive kitchen, living room stuffed with cozy over-stuffed chairs and sofas, bookshelves overflowing with books, crystals and houseplants; the massive log fireplace; the bay window overlooking Lake Ontario. It was like she'd walked into her fantasy from last night.

Worst of all, they had the sweetest little cat, Midnight, the color of satin obsidian. Aunt Ellaine had *never* allowed pets. Vella always *always* wanted a black cat.

To her intense irritation, physically, Vella felt energized away from the city, inhaling the clean, fresh air, the sense of earth directly beneath her feet. Even Sara seemed better—fast asleep beside her, experiencing deep slumber, which was unusual.

Once again, memories of her childhood home before she and Sara had gone to live with Aunt Ellaine swept through her. Goddess, she wished her parents were still living and she and Sara had never left Vermont.

Her phone buzzed, and Ellaine Priestly flashed across the screen. Vella's heart sank. She tiptoed to the ensuite bathroom and quietly shut the door before answering.

"Where are you?" Aunt Ellaine asked in her coldest, calmest voice.

Vella blew out a steadying breath. "Sara and I are at the Magicae residence in upstate New York. I've signed a contract with Medea to furnish several of his homes and clubs."

"The security systems at Arcane Antiques are completely offline, and *as you know*, the accuracy of our foreseers drops exponentially when you leave the city. How could you leave without informing me? And what about Sara? Have you no concern for her health?"

There it was, right on time. The constant prod of her aunt's control. Vella was sick to death of it. "Sara is here with me. We have her meds. And I think being out of the city is doing her some good. By the way, have you tested the sphalerite crystal ball yet?"

"Yes, yes," Aunt Ellaine replied. "No cure, I'm afraid. What you should be concerned with is the danger you are in now. We've been unable to keep up our surveillance. I had one of our senior foreseers follow Matt's movements for the next week, and on multiple occasions, he just disappears from their vision. *And* worst of all, most visions of you have dropped in accuracy to almost thirty percent starting tomorrow! You need to return home immediately."

"But *why* are you so desperate for me to be in New York? I'm twenty-three, and I run my own company and

Sara's turning nineteen soon. We're both adults. I'm here on business. Shouldn't we be free to do what we want and go where we want?"

"Because, *Vella*, you are a Divinator and as my niece, you have a role to play in the magical world—"

"To ensure the Divinator's success in their goals, I know—"

"And our coven's goal is to make sure that no harm is made to, or caused by, witches. And while Matt *may* be on the Council, he is unscrupulous. He collects arcana indiscriminately with his wealth and sells it on at a profit, whether legal or not. And did you not see his flagrant display of unapproved spellcasting? You should not associate with him at all. What kind of example is that as a Divinator?"

"You mean when he saved our lives at the winter ball?"

"Regardless, Vella, that spell was illegal." Aunt Ellaine went quiet. "Actually ... upon reflection, it might be good that you are up there now. There is the matter ... you recall the runes? The issue with Mors Dicen arcana remains. Our divination is *always* disrupted and unclear. I'd like you to search for the paper and the runes or whatever Mors Dicen object you may locate there."

"I'm curious, Aunt Ellaine, do you mean to use the runes yourself? I thought Mors Dicen magic is dark, evil and dangerous and should never be practiced."

"I would do *anything* to save Sara," Aunt Ellaine snapped. "Do as you're told. This is all about your sister's health."

Yeah, right. Vella, with a surge of joy at being difficult, answered, "I don't think I can manage it. Every room is occupied by Magicae at the moment. They're all up here for the party."

There was another pause, and Aunt Ellaine said, "Be home by tomorrow and don't disappoint me."

Vella switched off her phone, picked up a towel and screamed into it. She wished to the goddess she had access to a bat and Medea's face.

Every-*fucking*-body was giving her orders. She wanted to live her own life, make her own decisions. And now, more than ever, Aunt Ellaine's instructions were getting wilder and illogical. She was constantly contradicting herself and when Vella asked any questions, the answer was to evade and shove Sara's health in her face.

Could it be that the whole 'we're seeking a cure for Sara using arcana you steal' argument was complete bull-shit? She'd been stealing for years, and there had been zero success.

Was Aunt Ellaine after something else?

WELL INTO THE PARTY, Vella sat on the couch by herself, petting Midnight and sipping on her glass of delicious red wine.

"Top up?" Shannah came over with a full bottle of red wine.

"Thanks, but I'm good." Something told her to keep a clear head around these peeps. "I heard someone say you're from Madgewick. Is that like a town or—"

"Nah, it's Matt's home. But we all grew up there at some stage or another. It's near Glastonbury, in the south of the—"

"UK. Of course I know Glastonbury. It's got one of the richest histories for witchcraft in the world. It's absolutely on my bucket list to visit—imagine getting lost in streets filled with our history and lore."

"Who said Glastonbury?" Clay, a Black man maybe in

his early fifties, joined them, his eyes gleaming with interest. "That's my hometown. Growing up there was magical. All the vivid lights and festivals and beings from all over the world."

"It sounds wonderful." Longing sang through Vella. One day, she'd get there.

"Oh, it was." Clay wrapped an arm around Shannah. "Watching Shannah and Ronin, Matt and Amelia—Amelia still lives there—running around town used to make my heart happy."

"Hey, Green-tips, break time's over. You ready to get this game going again?" Sara gestured to the table they'd been playing at.

"Shannah?" Vella lowered her voice. "Thanks for playing with Sara. She looks happy."

As Shannah went back to the Dungeons & Dragons game, and Clay called out to Matthias to help him open a keg of Guinness—apparently Matthias's favorite stout ale—Vella took another slow sip of her wine.

As much as she despised Medea—she was fucking furious with his whole stunt at Nocturnal—Vella did not want to creep around this beautiful home, filled with lovely people, and skulk around searching for Mors Dicen arcana or that bit of paper with symbols Ellaine was so desperate for.

David and Clayton were so warm, friendly, open. Divinator parties were cold and sterile by comparison. There sat Queen Ellaine on the top, in beige, of course, in her ultra-modern monochrome-and-white living space, where *only* Divs were present, except for a few high-status Elixirs, and all jostling for power.

When Sara and Vella had attended, they'd been respected on the surface because of who their aunt was, yet whispering and laughing at their defects as Divs, saying she and Sickly Sara might as well be non-witches.

Meanwhile, here, at the lake house, were Magicae, Crystallos, shifters and vamps.

David and Clay were now taking turns playing the piano and singing popular pop songs. Their two daughters, Freya and Morag, the ages of nine and eleven, with massive gap-toothed smiles, were constantly running up to their dads and getting cuddles. Vella and Sara could have used an endless supply of hugs at that age.

Sara was deep in the throes of a Dungeons & Dragons game with Shannah as Dungeon Master, participating with Ronin and the two girls—when they weren't getting loving attention from their parents. Sara, geek that she was, adored role-playing games, and she'd been able to whip up a character in under five minutes and join in as a guest.

Vella had been invited to join in, but she was not in the mood. She'd much rather stew while petting this glorious little cat, who gently purred, thinking about how hard-ass Ronin, Councilor Medea's Second, was running a campaign for Shannah, Morag and Freya, which also meant he'd taken time to create adventures for a D&D game with his family.

In fact, Vella was coming to understand, they *were* a family. Not just a coven.

Medea walked around, friendly and charming, and no one showed fear as he approached—instead, they were relaxed and evidently already had a rapport with him. He was their clear leader, though, gravitating in his direction like sunflowers to the sun.

What the fuck did Aunt Ellaine mean by 'the good of witchkind' anyway because *this* looked like the answer to Vella—this kind of coven full of happy, content people.

And Sara with rosy cheeks, bright eyes, surrounded by friends ... playing footsie with Shannah under the table. Goddamn it.

Vella gently lifted the purring Midnight from her lap and went outside into the cold for some air. Shimmering stars filled the sky high above the lake, and muffled piano music and laughter echoed from inside.

Vella hugged her arms to her sides. She felt ... alone. If she were honest, that's how she'd felt most of her life.

The sliding glass door opened and shut behind her. Sandalwood and spice made her mouth water. Why did he have to smell so delicious, damn it?

"I owe you an apology, Rapunzel," Medea murmured. "I still want to work with you, but I shouldn't have been quite so forceful."

She turned and met his gaze.

His silver eyes dropped to her mouth, and that look alone was as powerful as a physical caress, making her body shift gears.

Good goddess, how did a male so ... consuming ... exist? It was like an internal electric tripwire connected Vella to the spellcaster and the moment she got close, *zap!*

"Do you mean that?" She took a step closer.

Watching Medea be this kind, attentive, respectful leader all evening had been hot. Not only that, but she'd also been realizing how shit her and Sara's life had been with Ellaine compared to the Magicae. What if instead of an enemy, Vella had an ally in Medea?

They stared, and deep in his silvery eyes, constellations of black stars swirled into existence. Vella opened her mouth to speak, trying to summon up the courage to say what was in her heart when the sliding glass door slammed open.

Sara came out, her face flushed with fury. "Why didn't

you tell me about the knife and being Mors Dicen?" she asked. "I'm so fucking fed up with you keeping things from me to protect me. Being sick doesn't make me stupid, Vella. You should trust me and let me make my own choices."

Sara stormed off, sliding the door shut so hard it bounced.

Medea looked downright smug. "Sylvie and her brothers are here with Brianna. They're waiting for us in the library."

"Motherfucker." Vella checked Medea hard with her shoulder as she went back inside.

How could she have been so stupid? Medea was just another version of Ellaine, manipulating her, controlling her with Sara.

12

Vella's fury dropped by maybe one percent when she entered the library. Wood-paneled walls, floor-to-ceiling books and rolling ladders. Midnight was now asleep, curled up in front of a massive and lit fireplace.

Was that a drinks cabinet—with Fireball Whisky!—in the corner?

Sara sat on a Chesterfield sofa across from Sylvie and the two male vamps, and Sylvie was reaching across and handing her sister something ... the knife.

"No!" Everything slowed down, and even as Vella bolted toward Sara, her legs felt like they were dragging through molasses. Her brain flashed images of living flesh calcifying to bone. Her heart became a black, empty void of loss—

And ...

Everyone was staring at her, surprised.

Then Sara scowled. "*Yes*, Vella, I have every right to know if I'm a Mors Dicen. But I'm not. Brianna isn't speaking to me. Damn."

"You're okay?" Vella asked, not believing it. "The bone wasn't poisoned?"

"Daughter, I hear you. What has happened these past centuries?" Brianna sounded distraught. "Please make contact, Daughter."

Vella stared at the knife, at Brianna, not sure what to do, what to think. Everything was happening so fast. "Please, Sara, return the knife to the box." Shit. Had Sara really not heard Brianna?

"Sara, are you telling the truth? You cannot hear Brianna?" Medea exchanged glances with Sylvie. Oh no, they better not be thinking of *that*.

"Don't you fucking touch her, Sylvie!" Vella snatched the knife, grabbed Sara and stepped in front of her. "No one is biting—"

A charcoal-hued veil snapped over Vella's eyes, turned everything close to black and white.

"Contact at last!" Brianna's voice was as clear as if she were right beside her. "And we are to fight? Excellent, Bone Wielder."

Vella knew she should be afraid, but *damn,* Brianna was a woman after her own heart.

"Fighting's good, but right now—what the fuck is happening? What is a Bone Wielder? Why are you calling me that?"

"*You* are a Bone Wielder. And I am now yours to wield. Who are we fighting?" Vella took a fighting stance, then spun around and surveyed the room. "The youngling behind you, this is your sister, correct? And the others are a mix of spellcasters and vampires, by their marks. Why do you wish to fight them?"

"We're stopping them from biting Sara. And how can you see what I see? And stop making me turn around."

Thank frig, Brianna listened, and Vella caught her breath as she faced Sylvie.

"That is what I do," Brianna close to shouted. "You touch me, I see through your eyes, and I aid you in your fight—how do you not know this?"

"I won't bite your sibling, Bone Wielder." Sylvie nodded at the other vamps. "None of us will."

"Hmm. Daughter, it seems there is no fight to be had here after all. How disappointing. Well, all is not lost. Come with me."

Vella tried to walk back but couldn't move her feet. Fear punched through her chest. "Brianna? Brianna! What's going on?"

"Calm, Daughter," Brianna murmured. "I am taking you with me."

And between furious pumps of her heart, instead of Sara and Matthias and the library, a lush emerald grassy field, mist pooling at the edges of a darker green forest, spread out before her.

What? Where the hell was she now?

Whispers of movement echoed behind her, and she spun around.

A stunning, fierce woman stood alone in the meadow. Windswept dark hair, braids at each temple, a line of thick black paint streaked across her face, in line with her eyes. She wore a mix of leather and animal furs, had a sword strapped to her back, and held a knife in her hand. And then she grinned.

"Calm, Daughter, you do not need to fear this place," the woman said.

"Don't tell me to be calm"—Vella didn't bother to hold back her scowl—"when I have zero clue where I am." The words clogged her throat. Was this real? Vella gave in to the urge and rubbed a hand against the pain in her chest.

Yep, this was real. She swallowed hard and found her voice. "You're the Brianna of the knife."

"Correct. I'm glad you're not so thick as to be unable to work out my identity."

"And I'm here because the knife spoke to me?"

"Not the knife. The—"

"Bone. Yeah, I meant the bone. So where are we? And what did you do to me?"

"You are in my memory. But how do you not know this? What is happening to the Mors Dicen training that our witches have such little knowledge?"

"I'm not Mors Dicen."

"Yes, you are."

"No, I'm not."

"Then how do you come to me here?"

"Good question. But a better one, how do I get out?"

"Look at your hand."

Shit. The bone-handled knife—she still held it.

"No, don't let go!" Brianna cried out. "Goddess be damned, Daughter. Don't you know anything? If you let go of the bone here in my memory, you will be trapped unless someone else comes to me. And those visits have been so few for so many years, who knows how long that might take? No, you cannot let go of the bone. But to leave my memory, you must focus your will and make it so. I used my will to bring you here; you use your will to leave."

"But you brought me here; you can send me back, right?"

"I can." Brianna crossed her arms. "But you need training, so I suggest you do it yourself. We must work together." She sighed. "You are no youngling—although your level of knowledge would suggest so. Tell me your name and your family."

"I'm not telling you anything." Shit, what did Brianna

mean, Vella was Mors Dicen? And fuck, she wasn't letting go of the knife if that was her only way out of here.

"Then you shall be here for a long time."

"I don't *have* a long time. Listen, the fact is it's a really, really long story, and I don't even know many of the answers you're asking for right now. Can you tell me ... who I am? Who my parents were?"

"I only know you are a Bone Wielder, my many, many times removed granddaughter."

"What *is* that?"

"Our people are warriors, and through our connection with bone, the strongest witches not only speak to the dead, but they also learn from the memories of past witches like me. I gave my bones to the coven to guide our Bone Wielders in their role as leader."

Vella's heart was racing. Everything Brianna was saying sounded so *right*.

But how? Her mother—no, she'd been Div through and through. Sweet goddess, then just who was her father?

Vel, you're part frigging Mors Dicen witch.

Which meant Sara was too, both witches descended from a disbanded coven. Except, why hadn't Sara heard Brianna talk? Vella's chest went tight, and she had to haul in a breath past the constriction that leaped up her throat.

She stared at the bone handle, aware of the humming in her palm where the bone pressed into her skin. So, this was the way home?

But where was home? Where she'd come from?

Sara's face flew into Vella's mind. Oh shit—had Sylvie or her vampires injured her? She needed to get back and find out what had happened.

The field and forest and Brianna disappeared, and instead of clear, fresh air, Vella dragged in a heavy breath filled with the scents of Matthias's library, and everyone who had been in the room only minutes earlier, was still there, although once again her vision was black and white. But thank fuck, she was back.

She dropped the knife.

Total darkness enveloped her. What the fuck?

"Hey," Vella called out. "Why are the lights out—"

"What? The lights are on," someone said.

No they damned well weren't. The hairs on the back of Vella's neck prickled, and her flight or fight response kicked in. She whirled around, stumbled into something—

"Watch out," someone else yelled.

"What? Who said that?" She threw her hands out and steadied herself. Were her eyes closed? Images seemed to move in the darkness, as if they were shut. She squeezed them tight and reopened them ...

Nothing but darkness.

Her heart took off, running faster than if she'd just finished a sprint, almost to the point of pain. "Why is it dark?" Was her voice squeaking? "I can't see—"

"Vella?" Sara said from somewhere nearby. "Are you okay?"

"You're a fast learner," Brianna's voice rang out; thank the goddess this time from afar.

"Shut up," Vella croaked. "I can't see anything. Why can't I see? Sara? Sara!"

"I'm here." Sara's little hand grabbed hers. "What happened? You went all silent, then suddenly yelled about the lights and the dark."

"Because it is. Isn't it? Wait. Can you see? I can't see anything!" Terror gripped her hard, and her head started to spin.

Shit. *Breathe, Vel. Do not pass out.* In ... and out. In ... and out.

The whirling sensation finally calmed, and she clenched Sara's hand for everything she was worth. Sara was there. Sara was okay. Vella was okay. She just couldn't see anything, that was all. A whimper escaped her.

"Daughter, you cannot see because you're paying the price for—"

"Vella? Here, I've got you." Matthias' voice rang out right beside her, and another hand grabbed her arm. "Vella, can you hear me?"

"I said I can't see anything—I can hear fine." She fumbled to feel the arm attached to the hand that held her. Wide wrist. Strong forearm. "Medea? That's you, right?"

"It's me. Are you saying you can't see anything?"

"Of course she can't." Someone nearby sighed. Sylvie?

"Why not?" Matthias hissed.

"Daughter, did you hear me? I said you are paying the price for exchanging your sight for mine. When you allow the bone to overtake your sight, you lose yours."

"What?" Vella froze, fear clogging her mind. "Will it come back?"

"Of course. Unless, when we are in a fight, you lose your eyes, although, given my skill, that is unlikely. Daughter, you must join with me more often so—"

"Fuck that. You think I'm just going to trust some stranger about my vision? I'm never touching you again. Matthias?" She fumbled for the hand holding her arm. "Find the knife, put in the box and close the lid. Now."

"Wait, Daughter, we are still talking—"

Thank frig. Silence from one voice.

"Vella. What just happened?" Sara's voice was as uncertain as Vella felt.

"I just—let me catch my breath." And think. Goddess but she had to think, what did this all mean? "You're okay, I'm okay. We'll be fine." She squeezed Sara's hand.

"Of course I'm okay." Thin arms wrapped around her middle. "The couch is right behind you—can you sit? Feel your way. There you go. Can you see anything yet?"

Vella squinted hard ... "Starting to. It's like the room's going from pitch black to dark—shapes are visible now." Thank fuck. At least Brianna hadn't lied about her visions returning.

"Thank the goddess." Sara's voice shook. "That's a relief."

"You're telling me."

"But, Vel? About the knife—why did you think the bone would kill me?"

"I—I've seen it happen before." Vella was shocked by how shaky her own voice sounded. "I witnessed ... someone ... calcified by a Mors Dicen skull after spell-casters cursed them to murder Divs—"

"What? Vel, no wonder you've always hated bones so much." Sara squeezed her, and Vella returned the hug.

"Correction," said Sylvie. "Elixirs and *Divinators* poisoned the Mors Dicen bones after Ellaine's coup as part of her extermination program. That is how the Mors Dicen covens in North America, Scotland and England were decimated."

"In our history lessons," Sara said slowly, "we were taught that Aunty E—in her official capacity as Divinator Councilor—and the Elixir Councilor Walter Montgomery prevented the Mors Dicen Councilor and her allies from starting a war after they rebelled against the Council, saving witchkind from strife and death, and thereby saving countless lives."

"We were there, youngling." Sylvie sighed. "Believe me

when I tell you, in London, twenty years ago, Ellaine and Monty orchestrated a coup, a power grab together. And they were wildly successful. Since then, your aunt has been keeping her boot firmly pressed on the necks of all non-Divinator covens and hedge witches—and tried her best with non-human magical creatures."

Ellaine's boot to her neck? Vella knew the sensation all too well.

"But why," Sara murmured. "Why has Aunt Ellaine gone after the Mors Dicen particularly? I mean, honestly, their magic does sound dark—they sacrifice witches and trap their souls in bone?"

"My dear child, the Divs have *always* targeted Mors Dicen in their desire for money, power and control. They reap financial gain by divination and setting themselves as the top coven. However, future paths can also be decided by past events, and through the bone, Mors Dicen can talk to the dead and understand that past—and therefore, the future. Divinators do not like competition and believe in their right to remain supreme. Luckily for them, humans are terrified of the ancient traditions of the Mors Dicen, so it has never taken much to paint them as evil."

Vella stared at the box holding Brianna, now on Medea's lap. How long had Brianna's soul been in that bone? How long had she been alone?

"Enough with the history lesson, Sylvie," Medea rumbled. "I have brought you two Mors Dicen witches— one even a Bone Wielder. Can you please *finally* give us the details on the runes?"

The fucking runes. Ellaine wanted them, and Matthias wanted them—both were lying to her, and both wanted to use her to locate them. Vella was sick to death of being jerked around for everyone else's plans.

She stood. "We're done here. Sylvie, thank you for ... I

don't know. Not being a massive dick. Sara, we only had enough potion for twenty-four hours, so we're going to need to get home early tomorrow."

"Yes, and we're taking Brianna, right?"

"Hell, yes."

Sylvie's eyes glowed even brighter—with what Vella could see was irritation. "I am glad you have reunited with Brianna, my dears. My brothers and I are pledged to the Mors Dicen. And I tell you this with total honesty, you should know about the runes, for they are *your* heritage, hidden by Mors Dicen *for* the Mors Dicen."

MATT TENSED as Vella glanced from Sylvie to Sara and back again. If Vella said no ...

"You know where these runes are?" Her eyes narrowed as she faced Sylvie.

Matt just stopped his breath from whooshing out. Fuck but that had been close.

"We know the vampire responsible for the paper that Matthias has." Sylvie met his gaze, and he could see the challenge she faced—she knew Matt's plan and what he needed to succeed, but she also had a blood vow to honor. "Years ago, she curated for an art gallery in England and, through her time there, came across information about the location of the runes. Shortly after, the Divinators waged their coup upon witchkind and—"

"What?" Vella shot to her feet. "The Divs saved witchkind."

"Bone Wielder, we were there. Believe me when I tell you, the Divinators did wage war. Just what do they teach you in your arcane history?"

"Not that." Vella's lips pursed, her suspicion evident.

Double fuck. This had to work. "So, this curator, will she take my call?"

"She will only talk to you in person," Sylvie said as they'd planned. "But be warned, she may want to taste your blood to confirm your honesty."

"Like you did me?" Vella's eyes narrowed.

"I can show you this time, if you like?" Alexander shifted closer to Vella, his expression more I-want-to-fuck-you than I-want-bite-you.

Matt tensed. No bloody way—

"No frigging way." Vella turned to Sylvie. "And where's the curator?"

"London." Sylvie looked from Vella to Matt. "I suggest you both go."

"Yeah, that's not happening." Vella stood, still holding Sara's hand. "Good to know where to find the runes, but we're calling it a night."

"In that case, we shall go." As Sylvie strode past Matthias, she whispered, "We will all be watching out for her. She has power, Matthias. And if your plan is to succeed ..." She tilted her head at Vella.

If his plan was to succeed ...

Matthias insisted on walking the vampires to the front door alone and, as soon as they'd gone, paused in the short hallway. Anticipation buzzed in his veins, and he rolled his shoulders to ease the tension because nothing could fuck this up.

They were so close. Even Sylvie thought so now.

The constant power running through his veins suddenly swelled, thrashed to be let out. Fuck. He'd let it out only hours earlier—why was it surging again so fast?

"Night, Matt." Sara's voice made him freeze.

Shit. *Control, Matt. Control.*

"And thanks for having us at the party," she continued,

thankfully oblivious to his struggle. "It was—well, it was eye-opening. Vel ..." Sara's voice lowered, but he heard her perfectly well. "Say goodnight. Don't be a total bitch."

"Pft. I'll be a bitch as much as I want. Fine, don't roll your eyes." She cleared her throat. "See you tomorrow, Medea."

Finally, the pulsing power in his veins receded just enough for him to turn around. "Tomorrow," he gritted out.

Vella gave him an odd look before disappearing up the stairs to their bedroom.

Damn, that had been close. This was one secret he could not let free. But why did his power want to crawl out of him now? Apart from when his parents had died, his power had always been under his control.

The muffled echo of Vella's voice as she spoke with Sara reached him again, and as if just that was enough, his magic gave a little hum inside him.

It was Vella. Somehow, his power connected to her, and more than that, wanted out around her. A shiver prickled up his spine.

Fuck.

ALONE IN THEIR BEDROOM, Sara and Vella stared at one another. Vella had shared everything with Sara, including Aunt Ellaine's increasing demands about Mors Dicen arcana and her desire for the bone runes. For the moment, Brianna was silent, maybe dormant.

They'd also discussed their situation: one, Ellaine hated Mors Dicen; two, *they* were Mors Dicen; and three, what did it mean *if* Ellaine knew? What did it mean if she didn't?

"I think you're right," Sara said. "We can't trust Medea either. He's up to something."

Medea ... Just what was going on with him? Just *who* was Matthias Medea?

"Vel, did you hear me?"

"Ah, yeah. Our best plan for now, I think, is to go home. I'm almost making enough money to pay for your meds outright, but we'll keep playing Ellaine's game until A: I'm making enough money—"

"*We're* making enough; I can get more commissions too."

"Okay, *we're* making enough money and B: we work out how to get an Elixir to make the meds without having to go through Ellaine and Charles. Then we leave town. Maybe without even telling anybody."

"We can pick a place out in the country with a decent witch community and access to hospitals."

The girls grinned at each other. Escaping Ellaine? Sweet goddess, *yes*.

The biggest truth that Vella had realized when she'd watched her sister reach for Brianna and expected her to die was that *Sara* was all that mattered. *She* was her home.

Fuck living in the city.

Fuck her debt to the Divs. They'd been paid back how many times over by all the arcana she'd stolen for them?

And fuck Medea.

13

———

Bone Wielder. *Bone Wielder. Bone Wielder.* Brianna and Sylvie's words had haunted Vella's dreams to the point she woke up at her usual predawn time.

She needed to focus—needed a run.

By the light of her phone, Vella dressed in her running gear, then pulled out the sheathe with Brianna.

Take it or leave it?

If she took the knife, maybe she could find out more about Brianna and the Mors Dicen. But she couldn't run with it—she was more likely to cut herself trying to run with a knife than anything else. And the odds of ever needing Brianna as a weapon were zero to none.

No, better she kept it here in the bedroom, in the box.

As she tiptoed down the darkened stairs, the window showed a deep steel-blue predawn sky, and on the ground floor, a dim light shone from the corridor. It was blessedly quiet. All Vella wanted was some time to think, to be alone.

In the living room, she found Shannah asleep on the

couch nearest the fire, covered by a thick blanket, head on a cushion, face half visible where she lay on her side.

"Early start?" Medea's silky voice rolled over her a moment before he appeared through the door from the kitchen.

Oh goddess, he wore dark track pants and a black fitted top that molded to that spectacular torso like a second skin. She swallowed the moisture that had pooled in her mouth—rolled her tongue back up—and grunted in acknowledgment of his greeting.

"And good morning to you, too, Rapunzel." One of those too-perfect brows rose. "Where are you going?"

She glanced down at her outfit while she finished tying her hair back into a ponytail. "You need to ask that? And keep your voice down. Shannah's sleeping."

"Who do you think put the blanket on her?" He folded his arms and frowned at her. "It's dark outside."

"It's almost dawn—perfect time for a run. And you don't have to worry about the Darklings. They never attack close to sunrise."

"I'll still feel better if you weren't alone. I'll go with you."

"What?" She glanced back at Matthias. "No, you don't need—"

"I was about to do a workout anyway; I'll run instead."

"I prefer to run alone." She gave him her best glare.

"And I prefer you to stay in one piece until after I'm done with you. So bad luck, I'm running with you. Plus, someone attacked you, remember?"

"Which was back in the city. But actually, yes, maybe you *should* come along. Your nose is looking far too undamaged, in my opinion."

"Ugh, you two, give it a rest." Shannah rolled over and glared at them through one bleary eye. "Just run. Or fuck.

Or get whatever the hell is going on between you out of your systems, but do it somewhere else. I'm trying to sleep off last night's red wine sesh with Clay. Man, he can drink."

Vella couldn't keep her lip from curling, just like she couldn't stop herself from glancing at Medea. But instead of the same antipathy, he had the audacity to look amused.

"Dick," Vella growled.

Shannah rolled over and pulled the blanket over her head. "For fuck's sake, *go*."

Okay, then. Vella shouldered past Medea, opened the sliding glass door onto the porch, and took in one lungful of crisp lakeside air. This was bliss. Wherever she and Sara ended up, she hoped it would be by the water.

She strode to the shoreline, the lake glinting under the fading moonlight.

Medea was far enough away, doing a set of warm-up stretches ... lunges that made the fabric of his running pants tighten around his butt. Arm stretches. Calves. Quads.

Her mouth went dry. Crap. Why did he have to be so frigging hot?

She purposefully spun away from the view and took off toward the east. Moments later, footsteps caught up to her.

"Vella, you really are a shit. I know this bay; this is our home. Why didn't you wait to follow me?"

"Because you're a manipulating asshole and I hate you. Please feel free to fuck off."

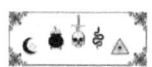

THIRTY MINUTES LATER, as the sun stained the sky over Lake Ontario a brilliant orange, Matt stopped on the rocky shore before the bridge to Hovey Island and inhaled the fresh, briny air. With his lake house far from sight around the bend to the west, and no one else around, the world seemed to condense to just him and Vella, and he gave in to the urge to let his gaze swing to where it wanted to go.

Fuck Vella? Shannah's words had played through his mind the entire run. And Vella's strong, muscled body had been impossible to ignore, to the point he'd had to turn away before his running pants gave away exactly how much he liked that impossible idea.

"Magnificent," she murmured.

The sunrise or her? *Focus, Matt.*

"It's fine," he lied. "So, any questions after last night?"

"Why? So you can come up with another way to manipulate me?"

Shit. Ronin had been so right. He really had messed up with his approach. He held up his hands. "How about we just chat—no blackmail? Just an honest conversation. You ask a question and I'll answer—if I can."

"Good caveat ... 'if you can.' But fine. What do you know about Mors Dicen magic?"

"Why don't you ask Brianna?"

"Because you just said you'd answer me." Her eye roll was perfection.

"Okay, okay. Don't run off. I'll tell you what I know." He checked out the water. "But first, looks like it's going to rain. Let's walk and talk. No way we can outrun it unless you want me to call a car?"

"Pft. I don't mind getting damp. So? Beyond it's outlawed, and what I've learned since I picked up the knife? There aren't any textbooks, and any internet references are so damn vague it's like an entire coven has been washed away."

"That's about right. Mors Dicen were one of the two warrior covens from ancient times. Through their connection with bone, the strongest witches not only spoke to the dead, but they also learned from the memories of past witches who gave their bones to the coven. Those powerful witches became their warriors and their leaders."

"And so, Mors Dicen ... anyone can do it?"

"Communicate to the dead through bones? Technically, yes. If they want to break the law." He stopped. "Although I've never seen a witch who practices it like you —conversing with a dead witch, wielding their weapons like you did the other night."

"Because that magic was outlawed years ago, during the rebellion—"

"You mean after the Div coup—"

"The what?"

"More of Ellaine's propaganda. Ellaine and the Elixirs orchestrated a coup, Vella. They took out the Mors Dicen and any other witches strong enough to stand up to them. They disbanded the one coven who might've been able to fight them, banned their magic, and anyone who has been caught making that magic since then is taken away and never heard of again. Even the history books have been rewritten ... Don't you wonder why the only teaching comes from Div books? No grimoires, no histories, no books are allowed to officially exist anymore that don't preach the Divs teachings."

What had Vella heard?

"What about your parents?" Pretending he didn't know they were dead was a dick move, but he pushed that aside. The need to know what—who—they were dealing with when it came to Vella outweighed sentiment. "Can you ask them?"

"They're dead," she whispered.

"I'm sorry." And he was. He knew that pain all too well. Purposefully reopening old wounds was fucked—especially when he'd known about her mother—but nothing mattered more than taking down the Council, not even Vella's feelings, which meant he needed to know how Vella came by her Mors Dicen magic, even if it made him an asshole. "What happened?"

"They died in the rebellion." She swallowed hard. "But I don't want to talk about that."

"Okay." Not okay. "What about their jobs? Did they work officially for the coven?"

"They were analysts at Div Tower; that's how they met."

"You and Sara were so young when your parents ... That's when you went to live with your aunt?"

"Technically, she's our mother's cousin, but yes, she raised us when we had no one else."

"Which is why you're so loyal to her?"

"You say that like it's a bad thing, but Aunt Ellaine did everything for Sara and me; she petitioned the Elixirs personally to help with Sara's meds; she paid for my degrees; she loaned me the money to start Arcane Antiquities. She leads our coven and the entire Council for the good of witchkind. Of course I was—am—loyal to her."

Was? Had that been a slip of the tongue, or was Vella starting to see the truth about Ellaine? Fucking gods, the number of times he'd heard *for the good of witchkind.* Bile burned in Matt's gut, but he didn't—couldn't—say anything.

"I just wish there was someone else—not just Brianna—I could talk to."

"I've got a hedge witch friend in the UK, Amelia; she knew several Mors Dicen fairly well, and it's from her I learned most of what I know. I'll see if she's got any more info I can pass on."

"Why?" The distrust was back in her gaze. "I mean, why are you helping me? It's not part of the blackmail deal."

A sigh escaped him before he could stop it. "Vella, not everything has to be about the blackmail."

"I think I prefer when it is." She turned, and her gaze searched his face.

"What are you looking for?" he whispered.

"*Your* truth. Just who is Matthias Medea?"

She stepped closer, and the gods help him, but he stepped closer too, until the inky sweep of her lashes made her lioness eyes even brighter and the freckles dancing on her cheeks seemed to glow.

Her gaze dipped to his lips. And when she licked hers, a groan sounded somewhere ... far away ... and he cradled her jaw; the warm, silky of her skin nirvana under his hands, and then she rose on her toes—

Running footsteps, more than one person, echoed from down the road.

Matt kept his hands on Vella's jaw even as he turned his head and slid his mouth to her ear. "Someone's coming," he whispered. "I'm going to spin around. You stay behind me. If it's bad, I'll fight, you run—"

"I can fight too," she whispered back.

"How? Did you bring the knife?"

"Of course not." She snorted into his neck. "But remember, I was kicking your ass until you used your magic on me in your bedroom." Her lips brushed his skin as she spoke, sending a shiver through him.

"I recall I was holding my own and didn't want to hurt

you, so then used my magic," he murmured back. "Are you sure you want to stay?"

"Don't worry, I'm not an idiot; I'll run if necessary. What about you? Do you have a weapon?"

Yes ... just not one he could show to Vella. "I'll use my magic. Whatever you do, stay behind me, and don't touch my hands. Last chance. I hear ... three people."

"I'm in. And you can hear that?"

"Shh. Coming from behind me. Can you see them over my shoulder?"

"No—wait. There. Coming fast. Thirty yards away."

"Then let's go." Matthias spun around.

Two men and a woman, all in their early twenties at most, approached at speed. The tallest male, with a sandy buzz-cut and built like a brick house, wore a cast on one hand; he led the other two, a dark-haired guy in a black puffer jacket and a blond woman in a lightweight blue fleece.

Black Puffer ran left, Blue Fleece right and Buzz Cut hung back, his hand jammed in his coat pocket. "Get her," Buzz Cut hissed.

"Vella? You got this?"

"Oh yeah." She cracked her neck and backed into him, guarding his back as he guarded hers.

Black Puffer lunged at Matt, Blue Fleece for Vella, but together, they ducked and parried and jabbed until Puffer and Fleece had to back off. The duo regathered, winded but not out of the fight.

Enough of this shit.

"Vella, don't move." Matt bent his head, turned his palms up. Gathered his power until his palm tingled. Then, right as Black Puffer and Blue Fleece reached them, he whispered his air spell, swooshed his right hand to the left and his left hand to the right.

Puffer and Fleece got swept up in a burst of air and thrown off their feet.

"What the fuck—" Buzz Cut's eyes went wide, then he reached into his coat pocket and pulled out a gun.

"Matt!" Vella grabbed his arm.

"I see it," Matt muttered. He shifted so his back fully covered Vella.

"Give her to us or I shoot." Buzz Cut stepped closer and his glittering blue eyes locked on Vella. Beside him, Puffer and Fleece were getting to their feet. "Fuck off, Spellcaster, we're here for the Div."

"Oh shit," Vella gasped. "You're him! The asshole who broke into our shop."

Motherfucker. Medea called his wind spell, and the gun went flying in a burst of air, then he dove at the man, calling, "Bind and call, come power now," and the magic visibly poured through his fist as he punched Buzz Cut in the gut. The fucker went flying three feet high.

"Holy shit!" Black Puffer shouted. He and Blue Fleece ran to Buzz Cut and picked him up just as a car screeched to a stop further up the beach. They stumbled to the vehicle together and scrambled in; the motor roared, and they all vanished into the mist.

Matt dropped the magic and spun to Vella, unable to take his eyes off her. "You okay?"

"Sweet goddess, yes. That felt so frigging good."

Gods but she was gorgeous. And the way she'd fought —holy shit! He'd already known she was fierce, but they'd worked so well as a team—she'd been like an extension of himself. If he had a thought, she was there already doing it.

"You smell really good, by the way, Matthias Medea." Her whisper made the hair on the back of his neck prick. Hells, it made everything prick.

She reached up on her tiptoes, and then the warm, delicious silk of her lips were on his.

He let her lead, but the moment her tongue touched his, energy buzzed through him.

Want. Her.

He cupped her jaw, held her still as he plundered. Kissed her beautiful mouth, over and over, licked into her, tasted her deeper. He nibbled his way to her ear. To her neck. A growl vibrated through him as he inhaled her delicious butterscotch scent. Licked and nipped at her warm skin. And her hiss when he bit down on her lobe— the way she pressed into him as if she liked that touch even more than he did—made the power in his veins surge harder. Faster.

And then he was back at her mouth, and he kissed her hard, giving in to the urge to taste her deeply. She hummed, a buzz raced across his skin, and then her tongue stroked his and chased him back until she was tasting him just as deeply, and—

Nothing. Just cold air. He opened his eyes.

She'd stepped back, breathing hard like him.

"Um, what was that?"

Vella shrugged. "I was feeling a little horny after that fight. Consider it your goodbye kiss 'cause we won't be seeing each other again, ever, after you drop me and Sara off."

Ronin may have been right. Perhaps he should've offered an alliance. Less manipulation, more truth? As long as he wasn't putting his people at risk?

Because, good gods, he just couldn't get over how he and Rapunzel had fought together. It had been like having a partner for decades. Like with Ronin at his side. Only Velvet Knight was so much hotter.

"Vella, perhaps we can start over? We don't have to be

enemies. What if I explain a bit more about the bone runes and why—"

"Medea, let me say this once and for all. Fuck you and fuck your runes." She turned and sprinted back toward the lake house.

Just as fucking well. His power was so close to surging out of his control that he had to kneel, shove his hands into the earth and release just enough energy to not cause an earthquake before he leaped to his feet and followed.

But gods, he wanted her. This warrior.

———

14

Vella, Sara, Ronin and Medea were seated in the chopper and heading back to New York.

The two men were working on tablets and using their headsets to keep their conversation private.

Sara had her laptop and was busy working on her latest artwork—or maybe something else, given the way she was keeping the screen to herself.

This left Vella to contemplate Brianna—maybe she had some answers about the bone runes? Because why were both Medea and her aunt after them? And why did they want *her* help, outside the fact she was Mors Dicen? *Seriously. WTF?*

Unfortunately, Brianna remained silent, recharging or something. Or maybe peeved that Vella refused to touch her again.

As the chopper descended into New York, the morning air cleared enough to make out the buildings in the distance—even Div Tower, sitting at the top of Central Park, gleaming gold, high above the city landscape. A nudge on her foot made her look up.

Medea gestured to his headset, and a moment later, his voice came through hers. "We're landing in ten minutes—it's a private helipad. But would you please reconsider our deal? I'll double the original fee we agreed on if you'll just come to England with me. There's a vamp there who could offer you more information about your past and the Mors Dicen."

And the fucking runes. "Sure," Vella said. "Why don't you give me her details and I'll visit her on my own?"

Medea was silent and Vella flipped him the middle finger. Ronin snorted and quickly covered his grin.

"Vel," Sara asked. "Exactly how much is Matt offering you?"

Vella glared at Medea as he replied, "Thirty thousand."

"Money *is* the answer to many of our problems. Maybe you should consider it. And a trip to England sounds amazing."

"I'm not going anywhere with him."

Sara sighed. "I wish *I* could go. Or even if we could've just stayed upstate longer. There's something about being in the country, the air—I've never felt so well in my life."

Vella's heart twisted again. Sara *did* look great, and they were both going back into the lion's den—their bugged and unsafe home. How long would it take to extricate themselves from Aunt Ellaine?

Ronin said, "Sara, Dave and Clay would be happy to host you again. The girls *loved* you."

"Well," Sara replied, "besides the weirdness going on between Vel and Matt—the thing is ... I need to take my meds daily. And a new batch has to be made fresh by the Elixirs every three days. So, I can't ever be away for longer than that."

"Elixirs make your medication?" Medea asked.

Ronin and Medea shared a long look.

"Why?" Vella asked.

Ronin's eyes grew bigger, but Medea only shrugged. "No reason."

HALF AN HOUR LATER, Medea was driving Vella and Sara back to the shop. He'd made a few more attempts at what he called "forming an alliance" but Vella wasn't having it. She stared out the passenger seat window. Sara sat in the back, plugged into her laptop once again.

Medea jolted in his seat, and his hands clenched the steering wheel. What the frig? Was he having some kind of—

"Shit!" Medea hit the clutch, the engine revved as he shoved the car into a lower gear, then he spun them into a U-turn.

"Hey!" Vella banged against the car door.

"What the—" Sara hissed. "Ouch."

Matt floored the gas, and they sped back in the direction they'd come from. "Come on ... come on ... Fuck. Fuck, fuck, fuck."

"Medea. What's going—"

"Not now." He pressed a button on the steering wheel, and a ringtone buzzed through the car's audio system.

"Matt?" Ronin's voice echoed into the car. "What's up—"

"The warning spell is triggered. I think it's been activated for a while now. We were out of range."

"Shit! Who?"

"Dorothy! I'm five minutes away. I need you to meet me there."

"I'll be there in ... thirty. Watch your ass."

"You too." The call ended, and Medea finally looked at

Vella. The frost in his gaze was colder than the air in the car. "I'm checking on someone, then I'll get you home."

"What happened? What do you mean your warning spell triggered?"

But Medea didn't answer, and inside the car, the air grew icier and icier. A shiver shot through Vella so hard her teeth rattled.

Frigging goddess. What was going on now?

MATT DROVE AS FAST as possible and skidded to a stop in front of the Magicae NYC residence. His coven were still making their way home from Clay and Dave's, and *damn it,* he should've insisted that Dorothy come up with them.

Come on, Dorothy, be okay ... be okay ...

He rang her again, and still no answer.

Matt clambered out and looked around. Several black armored Mercedes-Benz SUVs with tinted windows were parked in a row along the road. The vehicles favored by the SI. The ice that had flowed through him settled like a glacier in his gut.

"Stay here." Matt shut the door on Vella's upturned and questioning face. Behind her, Sara was pulling the earbuds out of her ears.

Bloody hell, he hoped they listened to him and didn't leave the car. But he couldn't hang around waiting to find out.

He took the stairs at a run, entered the code of the front door and shoved it open.

Bodies ... and parts of bodies, torn and ragged, covered the area. Matt recognized the Crystallo security guards' uniforms. Blood coated the marble floor.

His eyes followed crimson boot prints leading up the

sweeping staircase to the main living quarters—to Dorothy's rooms where the coven hid their last grimoire, the only one they'd kept from being stolen and locked away in the Central Library at Div Tower, including the body of historical works that Dorothy had created, accurate descriptions of the past that fucking Ellaine Priestly had been systematically destroying and replacing with her propaganda for the past two decades.

Dread slicked through Matt's gut. Bad. So fucking bad. Then adrenaline hit, and his heart jammed his chest.

Behind him—damn it to hell and back—Vella and Sara crept in, their eyes wide as they took in the scene.

"Good goddess," Vella gasped. "Go back to the car, Sara."

"Yeah. Sure." Sara stayed right where she was.

Matt *did not* have time for this bullshit. Ignoring them both, he made his way up the stairs and heard the women follow. Matt tried breathing through his mouth, but the thick metallic scent of blood was so strong he could also taste it on his tongue. As he approached, he could hear voices, followed by a hard smack and a cry.

"Dorothy!" Matthias froze in the doorway, unable to believe what he was seeing.

Their eldest, most venerated coven member was leaning sideways in her favorite rocking chair, her face bruised and covered in blood, particularly around her lips and nose. Her eyes were half-shut, she seemed barely conscious, her breathing loud and labored.

Ellaine Priestly stood in the overturned room, incongruous in her spotless white blouse, beige slacks and six-inch high heels. One SI with bloody knuckles loomed over Dorothy's diminished form.

Five more SI in their homogeneous black suits moved in and out of the space, continuing the search, breaking objects indiscriminately. Plants lay on their sides, the soil scattered everywhere, cracked photo frames and glass shattered, photos of smiling people crumpled and trodden on. In the bedroom, a pair were ripping through cushions and pillows with knives, sending feathers and bits of fluff floating through the air.

All the bookcases were empty, the books ripped and lying open and facedown on the floor. In Dorothy's wood-burning stove, the fire burned brightly, and Matt saw it was devouring their histories and their last private, ancient Magicae grimoire. Wrath scoured through him, hot and dark and dangerous, and the urge to scream, to let everything loose—the horror, the pain, the loss, the fucking rage at the universe—surged in a tidal wave through him.

By all the fucking gods. What good was being their leader when he couldn't even protect his most treasured members?

"Councilor Matthias," Ellaine said. "I gather you were completely unaware of the illegal activity Dorothy Churchill was engaging in?"

Fuck. He battened the emotions down. Way, way down, then felt for the buzz of magic over his skin.

"I did not." Matt agreed.

"This is ... all my doing. Matty did not know..." Dorothy said, her voice faint.

The SI smacked her hard upside the head. Dorothy slumped, boneless, unconscious now.

"No!" Vella shouted. She gaped around the rooms, horrified. Sara stood silently beside her, face blank.

Ellaine frowned slightly at her nieces; a look of annoyance ruffled her features for a moment.

"May I ask what brought you here to my residence?"

Matt asked, his voice as calm and even as he could manage.

"There was a Darkling attack, and we came to investigate. They ... damaged your security quite badly. When we inspected the rooms for more victims, we found Ms. Churchill and all her contraband. We'll be bringing her to Div Tower for further questioning. You realize we'll have to search the entire premises. When we finish, you may call in the police and clean up."

Matt closed his eyes in both despair and relief—he had removed all Mors Dicen arcana in his possession, but Vella had Brianna now. Would she betray them?

"Yes, Councilor Priestly," he said.

"There will be consequences, Matthias." Ellaine carefully stepped over the rubble of Dorothy's life toward the door. "Vella, Sara, come."

An oily slick rolled through Matt's gut, but he welcomed it. Because the fact he couldn't even show his grief and love for Dorothy was another disgrace at the feet of the fucking Divs and Elixirs.

But one day, one day soon, he'd grieve the loss of all those who'd died since Ellaine and Monty's coup. And do it in the fucking open, staring these assholes right in the eyes while their world crashed down.

15

"**H**i!" Derrick said as Vella, Sara and Aunt Ellaine entered Arcane Antiques. He joined them from the office, grinning, carrying his satchel. "I've been going over your equipment, Vel. Your network video recorder is fried, and I don't have everything to repair the unit now. I'll have to come back later. Oh, Sara, I've got your next batch of meds from Charles. He's trying something new, said this should help you to feel way better."

Sara automatically accepted the package Derrick passed over to her.

Both Sara and Vella had been entirely silent on the journey home while Aunt Ellaine sat up front with the driver behind soundproof glass, taking call after call. Vella noticed that her front door was fixed, the window repaired and the rooms clean, but she felt detached, like she was watching a film.

Had she truly seen all that blood?

"Come up to the kitchen," Aunt Ellaine said, her voice light and normal as if she'd never coolly, uncaringly watched one of her SI agents beat an elderly woman. "I'm sure we could all use some coffee. Derrick, would you be a dear and make it for us?"

"Actually, I'm not feeling awesome," Sara said. "Think I need to lie down." Vella jumped up, ready to assist her sister up the stairs. "No, Vel, stay. I'd like to be alone right now."

"Hmm. Sara appears distraught by this morning's events," Aunt Ellaine said as Derrick bustled around the kitchen and coffee maker. "Report, please. Present to me what you acquired—the runes, the paper with the symbols, the Mors Dicen arcana?"

Vella felt the sheathe pressed tightly against her back, where it was hidden beneath her shirt.

"I didn't find anything," Vella mumbled at her kitchen table.

She startled when Aunt Ellaine uncharacteristically slammed her fist down, causing all the coffee mugs and spoons to rattle and jump that Derrick had just set.

"Not acceptable, Velvet. The SI will thoroughly comb through every inch of Medea's mansion," she said, "but I fear they won't find anything. He has too many different locations. Or he may have sold it on ... the idiot. Velvet, it is imperative we locate the runes or find out where he sold them. The matter has become critical."

Aunt Ellaine glanced up as if seeing through the ceiling into Vella and Sara's bedroom.

"Okay," Vella said without much interest, wrapping her hands around the coffee mug, hoping to get some warmth inside of her.

She could still hear the thud of the SI fist on an older woman's skull; she could see her silvery flyaway hair, a halo around her bruised face. What were they doing to her now at Div Tower?

"For some days now," Aunt Ellaine was saying, "our foreseers have been reviewing events, including Sara's upcoming birthday celebrations. She's turning nineteen, and we were planning a party ... but ..." Aunt Ellaine's gaze drifted upward again.

The breath punched from Vella's chest. "What?" she asked, her attention properly focusing now.

"I'm—we're—sorry, Vella. But we saw a funeral, Sara in the coffin. On her birthday."

They had to be wrong. Sara was unwell, yes, but she'd been so vibrant the past few days. Vella forced words past the hot lump in her throat. "Prediction accuracy?"

"Ninety percent."

No. No, no, *no*. "But, the potion? Derrick said?"

"Charles is trying to make a difference, if he can. We have several Elixirs on task. No expense is being spared, Velvet. But remember—our visions show us events as they stand now—one tiny action can have a rippling effect that changes everything. Those runes I want are the singular, most powerful divination tool known to witchkind—they disappeared centuries ago. Those strange symbols you found in Matthias' room may be a clue."

Vella dropped her head against the table. Holy goddess, *Sara*. Was this really happening? Bile rose in her throat.

"Vella, sweetheart, please look at me." Vella battled back burning tears. Aunt Ellaine straightened, eyes bright, jaw steely. "We need someone to get close to the Magicae and find out how he is evading our foresight—this is also perhaps the best and fastest way to find the runes. He wants you to work for him, correct? Something about décor for his clubs?"

"Yes ... wait. You want me to spy on him?" Good goddess, was this really happening?

"Yes, I do." Aunt Ellaine squeezed Vella's hand. "This is the best course of action for your sister and witchkind. You can use the job as an excuse to stay with him, and if all else fails ..."

"Grandmother." Derrick gave a small cough. "If Matthias is interested in Vella and thinks she reciprocates his interest, he'll be expecting—"

"Velvet will do *whatever* needs to be done to get those runes for us." Aunt Ellaine turned back to Vella. "The job you've accepted from Matt decorating his clubs is the perfect cover." She smiled faintly. "Perhaps you do have a touch of divination magic within you after all."

As soon as they'd left, the tears Vella had held back spilled over. Sara's birthday was six days away.

But then she hauled in a breath. Tears wouldn't help. Finding those runes would. Which meant she had plans to make and plans to change.

16

The next morning, Vella paced outside around Grand Central Park, the world a winter land-scape. She dialed Medea's cell number on her recently purchased burner phone and waited.

"Who is this?" his deep voice snarled on the other end.

"I'm in," she said. "But it's sixty grand, and for that, I'll do up your clubs and help you get the runes. The vamps have info about them they'll only tell me, right?"

Medea didn't answer for a while. "Do you still have Brianna?"

"Yes, and Aunt Ellaine doesn't know I have her."

"Okay. Are you ready to form an alliance with me?"

"Just for the runes—and don't go getting any ideas, Medea. I am still pissed at you—nothing has changed there."

"Then we need to be up-front with each other. What's changed your mind? What are you hoping to accomplish?"

"Well, you should know some of that answer," Vella replied, feeling ill, thinking about Dorothy. "But, also, you know Sara's sick." Vella moistened her lips. "The Divs have predicted her funeral. On her fucking birthday."

"Does your sister know?"

"Fuck no—and my rule on this is absolute. You want this deal, then you cannot tell Sara about the prediction."

"Interesting ... but done. And I'm sure your Aunt Ellaine wants the runes to 'find her cure,' right? Have you considered she might be lying?"

"Yes, obviously. Gods damn it. Just shut up and listen for a moment. I can't take the risk she isn't telling the truth. She and her Divinators are skilled at their craft, as you well know. Sara and I need a safe way to leave Ellaine, and for that, we need money. And I'm starting to think that with Brianna, I might be able to figure out how to use the runes myself. Maybe Ellaine can't use them anyway. She's a Div"—Vella lowered her voice and whispered—"not a Mors Dicen. Maybe I can get Sara healed myself."

"I have lots of resources and money, but what if I need the runes for my own reasons?" Medea asked quietly.

"Well, duh, that's obvious too, Medea. But if we're in an alliance, then as long as I have the runes to find a cure for Sara, we can figure something out, can't we? After today, I can't work with Ellaine ever again, not one more second. Otherwise, I'm complicit. Sara and I always knew there was something, but ... Ellaine did her best to keep us from witnessing SI violence like that. Goddess, who knows what else she's doing?"

"We can talk about that later. Okay, the first port of call is just outside London. We need to get on a plane. Can you be ready in two hours?"

"Yes, but after the break-in at our place, I'm not comfortable with Sara staying home alone. I definitely don't want her at Div Tower ..."

"Would you be okay with Ronin or Shannah staying with her?"

"Deal. Meet you at mine."

EXACTLY TWO HOURS LATER, Vella took her packed suitcase down the stairs and joined Medea, Shannah, Ronin and Sara in the shop where her sister was pointing out the constellations on the ceiling.

They were all being very careful about what they said —which included any comments about what had occurred at the Magicae NYC residence—knowing the Divs were most likely spying, one way or another.

Earlier, Vella had explained her new plan to Sara on a notepad, and they'd burned the written pages afterward.

Vella tightened her grip on the luggage handle. What if something happened to Sara, and Vella was halfway around the world?

"Time to go, Rapunzel," Medea murmured. "Sara will be fine. Between Ronin, Shannah and Sylvie, nothing is going to happen to your sister."

"You can read me that easily?"

"Learning to."

Ronin grinned. "I have an *awesome* campaign for D&D planned. We're going to play along with Freya and Morag using videochat."

"Sounds good." Sara smiled, but it didn't reach her eyes.

Vella bit her lip. Was Sara looking worse? Or was that in her head? "Did you take your potion?"

"Yes, Mom."

Please goddess don't let this be the last time she'd see Sara alive.

Fighting back tears, Vella said goodbye, doing her best

to pretend this was just an everyday business trip to earn bug-out money instead of a race to save her sister's life.

But at least Sara was used to Vella's overprotectiveness and didn't complain about the second, third and fourth hugs.

And then she was sitting inside Matt's fancy black sports car as he navigated the city streets like a racer on a road circuit.

"You always drive this fast?" she asked.

"When we have a jet to make and a vampire to see, yes."

"Vampires." Vella sighed. "So, what can you tell me about them? I mean, I know they're nocturnal, so while they prefer to hunt and live in the night, they can survive fine in the day."

"Do you know that vamps—especially the older ones —like their worlds to be familiar? They can also be collectors, something about keeping their past with them, given they live so long."

"How long?"

"They physically age slower than humans, about one year to our ten. Sylvie tells me Lucretia is at least four hundred years old, but she'll look forties-ish, and she has absolutely lived every one of those years."

"Nope, definitely didn't know that."

So much she *didn't* know. From vampires to Mors Dicen ... Oh shit. *Brianna.*

"Matt, Brianna—the box, I mean—I don't want to put it in my luggage, but I can't carry it on the plane. And long term, I need something like a sheath to carry it unseen."

"We're traveling private. You don't need to worry."

"What? Private choppers. Private jets. Who the hell are you?"

"The nightclub business does well; what can I say?

Now, the sheath for the knife? I'll see what we can arrange when we land but keep it in the box until then. Not that I mind listening to you talk to the blade, but others ... We need to keep you low profile. And I want the fact you're going to London off the radar."

"I hate the whole keep-Brianna-in-a-box approach. There's got to be a better option to carry her. Maybe a sheath I can wear."

"Remember my friend Amelia? She might know of some ... options. I'll ask her. And here we are—this is the private airfield."

As he said the words, a retractable gate opened, and they drove into an airport. Private jets. Fancy cars and limousines. A shiver trickled down her spine.

Frig, Vel. What have you got yourself into?

Matt drove them right into a hangar, and in no time, she was sitting in a luxe jet with cream leather seats, crystal glassware and linen napkins, being offered a tour of the plane and a glass of champagne before take-off.

"Nothing for me, thanks," she murmured. "As long as this chair reclines, I'm good."

Matt declined a drink, too, and sat opposite her. "I know you're pissed at me." The midnight stars whirled in his silver eyes again. "And you have every right to be. I shouldn't have tried to manipulate you into working with me to find the runes."

"You think?" She settled back in the seat and closed her eyes. Gods she was tired. Between Aunt Ellaine's actions with Dorothy and the foreseer's vision of Sara's— shit, she couldn't even *think* the word—sleep had not been an option the night before.

"And that you don't trust me."

"No, I don't. Not outside of the fact you'll keep your word about my secret because I've got something you need. But how can I trust you on anything else? I don't know you, Matthias. Like, why do your eyes go all pin-pricky? How did you hear those people coming up at the lake house? How does your magic even work? So, who is the real Matthias Medea? And why all the secrets?" Something cold settled in her stomach, and she crossed her arms. "Trust? No, after all that, there's no way I can trust you."

Matt sighed and blinked. The stars in his eyes banked. "You ask a lot, Vella, without me knowing the same about you."

"I don't have anything left to hide!"

"The stealing and Mors Dicen magic are your only secrets?"

"The only ones that matter."

"To you, maybe. But you're right; you don't know me, and you have no idea what matters to me."

"Then change that."

"How? What do you want to know?"

I want to know you.

"Tell me something real about the great Matthias Medea, Magicae Councilor."

FUCK. Tell Vella the truth—even just one? The stakes were enormous. Make a mistake here and everyone he cared for was in danger. But if he couldn't convince Vella to work with him, then eventually, none of this would matter.

"How will you know I'm telling the truth?"

"You can do a truth spell, or you can just be honest and let me use my own judgment to decide if you're lying or not." Vella's chin rose, and she held his gaze like the warrior queen she was turning out to be. "This one's up to you."

"Fine. You want a truth? Here's one. I will do whatever is needed to keep my coven—my *family*—safe. And Dorothy?" The simmering rage that had shadowed him all day rose fast, and he clenched his fists. "That fucking cuts me to pieces. I've spent every second since that happened begging, coercing and bribing every contact I have to get her freed."

"You didn't call me."

"Why would I? We're not friends, remember? You're pissed at me, and you don't trust me. Why would I call you?"

Vella's cheeks paled. "Did it work?"

"Eventually." He controlled his exhale and shook out the tension in his hands.

"Is she ..."

"She's as well as can be expected," he bit out. Guilt made his stomach churn, but he clenched his jaw and didn't let it show on his expression. "Listen, I've got work to do, and you look tired. Why don't you try to get some sleep."

"I would, but I don't know if I can. It's like my adrenaline has been up and down so often in the past twenty-four hours I'm all discombobulated."

"That's to be expected. Adrenaline keeps you alert and gets you through stressful situations when you need to, but then your body crashes after. Balancing out again."

"I've crashed too many times, apparently. What about you? Where's your crash?"

"I've got more experience with balancing out after an adrenaline hit."

"Why?" Interest sparkled in her eyes. "Goddess, more questions. I am getting real sick, real fast, of all the unknowns piling up here. So, is this a question you can answer or another one of your no-gos?"

"No-go?"

"Yeah, when you basically tease me with information and then refuse to close the gap so I can understand what you've said, which you do a lot. Which just invites me to make up my own assumption, and bad luck to you if that's wrong."

"Well, in this case, it's not entirely a no-go. I'm a spell-caster; I'm used to balancing out energy to produce a cohesive spell. It's the same principle, and since I've been practicing spells since I can remember, it's as close to breathing as a trait can get for me."

"Wow, thank you. Another truth."

"Learning to read me now?"

"Looks like it. So, how do you 'balance out' the energy? And why is that important to your magic?"

"Balance is everything. It underpins the three pillars of spellcasting; therefore, it's the first lesson our coven teaches before we're even taught a single spell."

"What are the three pillars?"

"You really want to know?"

"Don't look so surprised. I like to know things, so sue me. Now come on, listening to you talk is helping to quiet my mind."

"Fine. It's not like this is a big secret, though. The pillars of spellcraft are balance in your emotions—that's how you connect with your internal energy source that allows the magic to happen. Then, balance in how you send your energy into the spell. And finally, balance in the spell's creation."

"And when the balance is disrupted?"

"Spells get fucked up. We get fucked up."

"Has that ever happened?" She shifted and got

comfortable in her seat. "It has, I can tell it—I *am* learning to read you now. So, when? And what happened?"

"Around you."

"Huh?"

"You put me off balance, Vella. I can't explain it."

"Is that a line? Did you say that to try and create some connection between us?"

"You really are distrustful. And in this case, no, it's the truth. So, any more spell questions?"

"Yes. I've told you how the Divs rate their magic, so now you tell me, how do you rate spells?"

"Short version? Unless you're looking to take the whole flight up?"

"Short is fine. As long as it's true."

Matthias rolled his eyes. "Unlike the Divs, we're open to sharing knowledge on spellcraft—after all, we're all witches; you could call a spell, likely just a simple one, if you wanted."

"Pft. Divs don't need spells."

"Then the short version will do. Just like the rule of three in making spells, the rule of three applies to the difficulty of a spell, and we measure that in breaths. So, one breath for a simple spell. Two for a complex and three for the hardest of spells."

"How many spells can you run at one time?"

"That depends on the individual power and control of each witch, but I can run multiple one-breath spells plus several two-breath spells concurrently. I can only run one three-breath spell at a time."

"Whoa," Vella breathed. "A three-breath spell is that hard?"

"Not just hard, they take all your energy—I can't funnel power to any other spells at the same time. And that's the basics of rating spellcraft. Now, weren't you going to sleep? We're heading to our contact as soon as we land."

"I'm trying. Just ... I'm still too wired to sleep yet."

"I could spell you to sleep—I'm not as good as Ronin, but I can handle a basic sleep spell."

"Let *you* spell *me*?"

"Don't look so horrified. It's just a small sleeping spell."

"Small or not, I'm never letting a spellcaster use magic against me."

17

S itting beside Matthias in yet another sleek black vehicle, with warmed seats to ward off the chill of the London late-night air, Vella eyed Medea for the hundredth time since he'd turned into iceman on the jet.

He'd retied his hair in another ponytail, revealing the intricate black and bronzed scales of the snake tattoo on this side of his neck. The tail dipped below his collar, but the head with its red eyes and fangs was clear, and the urge to trace the ink surged through her.

Shit. Down, Vel. The runes, focus on the runes, not an asshole, blackmailing spellcaster.

"Why are you glaring?" he said without turning.

"How would even you know? You've barely looked at me since we were on the plane. Was it something I said? Is refusing an offer of a magical sleep spell bad form and I've insulted you or something?"

"Refusing a spell on its own? No. Refusing a spell because you think the person is going to freaking take advantage of you? Yes, yes, that's insulting me at a core level."

"I wasn't refusing you." She ground her teeth. "I just can't ... go there for myself. To have magic done to me, on me, whatever you call it. It's me—I don't give up control. Ever."

"Why? Why do you have to have control?"

"Because I've never had it, okay?" Because of the internal cry, deep, deep down in her core, that craved it. Demanded Vella take control in whatever way she could. "And don't look at me like I'm some puzzle you're trying to figure out. I've answered your question, so if me refusing your spell is the reason you've had a stick up your butt, you can take it out and start talking to me." She snapped her mouth shut and held his gaze.

In his eyes, those flickers of obsidian flared, then he nodded, and the pinpricks disappeared.

"Stick removed. Sorry."

"Wow, did you just ... apologize?"

"Funny. Now the stick's gone, let's talk about Lucretia."

"Wait—Medea. What else do I need to know here?"

"Standard vamp rules apply. One you already know: don't lie and let her taste your blood. Although she's old enough, she might even scent a lie—so be careful with your words. Rule two: if her eyes turn black, run. Rule three: if you can't run, use your knife ... although keep that as your last option. I don't want anyone to know you've got the knife here."

"Why? How scared should I be right now?"

"Sylvie will tell Lucretia you're a Bone Wielder—you should be safe."

"What about you? I thought you get on with the vamps?"

"I get on with Sylvie and her family because we have a

personal relationship. Lucretia doesn't know me ... and I don't know her. So yeah, I'm tense."

"Then stay behind me; I'll talk to her first."

"You're protecting me?"

"Co-blackmailers need to stick together, right? Just don't go getting killed—yet anyway." Vella hopped out of the vehicle and froze.

A huge, crumbling stone building loomed into the night sky. This was a house?

"Close your mouth," Matthias murmured.

Crap. She flung him a scowl and then led the way up a short set of stairs to the double front doors, but before she could knock, the doors opened wide, and a stunning, tall, midnight-haired, green-eyed woman stared out at them from a dark corridor. She wore a richly embroidered kimono over leggings and a tank; her hair was styled in perfect waves like a movie star from a hundred years earlier, and she had enough jeweled rings and necklaces on her to fund a small nation if they were real.

"Lucretia?" Vella held one hand. "Hi, I'm—"

"Welcome to my home. Do come in." The woman swept her hand in a graceful arch toward the dark corridor behind her. "Please excuse the mess—the maid's day off and all that."

"It's a bit too ... dark to really see anything." Vella took a cautious step into the house ... castle ... whatever the goddess you called the building, acutely aware of Matthias at her back.

"Human eyesight." Lucretia sighed as if not being able to see in the dark was a crime, but a moment later, the hallway lit up with a bright pop of globes. Vella squinted —let her eyes adjust—and then she had zero chance of closing her mouth.

The double-height hallway led on forever with paintings and objects and tapestries and more objects hanging from, attached to or leaning against every inch of each wall. Matthias had said vamps were collectors. Hoarders more like it.

And thank the goddess for that hoard because Lucretia's packs and stacks were a slice of heaven. All these beautiful items that had been loved, regarded, used, worn, held, touched, caressed—

"Vella? Did you hear me?" Matthias leaned into her back. "Focus. We're here for a reason, remember?"

"What? Of course. Lucretia—your home is glorious. And is that triptych a *Kuniyoshi*? And look at that vase— sweet goddess, is it? It *is*. It's a Chinese blue and white Eight Immortals vase." She couldn't take another step. "I haven't seen one in real person—"

"Clean up the drool, Rapunzel," Matthias murmured at her back. "We're not here for pretty pieces."

"Pretty pieces? Oh no. These are globally significant—"

"You know your porcelain." Lucretia joined Vella at the vase, her eyes lighting up—thankfully not black. "I do love this one." Lucretia tapped a blush pink nail against her lower lip, painted the same color. "What was his name who gave that to me? Ah well, that eludes me. But the vase is a sweet reminder of our time together. He had the divinest eyes."

Matthias cleared his throat. "As lovely as this is—"

"If you enjoy the vase, you should see my collection in the front sitting room." Lucretia tucked Vella's arm into hers. "Come, we need to go this way."

Vella glanced back over her shoulder. Matthias was on their heels, his expression wary.

What the frig was she meant to do? Not that she had any choice. Lucretia might appear slight, but her strength was undeniable, even just with linked arms. The vamp led her down the corridor, past several closed doors and into what might have been a large room, with a fireplace on one wall and large curtained windows on the other—only it was impossible to make out the true dimensions because once again things covered every wall, crammed into each corner, encroached on the floor on all sides.

A sofa, small reading table and wingback chair were by the wall, but even more stacks of gorgeous antiques blocked the way to them.

Bliss. Absolute, total bliss.

The best way to handle this room was one section at a time. She'd start on the right and go clockwise. Wait. "No way," she breathed. "Is that a pair of emerald Japanese Meiji period silver wire cloisonné vases sitting on a table in the corner?" That's where she had to start. "Lucretia, this entire room ... your house ... you have the most amazing collection I have ever seen. I want to dive in and look at everything."

"Why, sweetling, you can look at everything to your heart's content. And you are right, that's another piece I came across many a year ago now. But do you know the designer—"

"Lucretia, can you excuse us for a moment? Vella, I need a word. Now."

"Hey, let me go—"

"What the hell are you doing?" Medea hissed as soon as they were back in the corridor. "What's with the bonding with the vamp thing?"

"Medea, have you seen Lucretia's house? I live my life for antiques—"

"Arcane antiques—"

"No, I *specialize* in arcane artifacts—my niche is ceramics—but I adore antiquities, period. And this place is a treasure trove. But fine. I get what you're saying. And I'm good. I'm focused."

"No more drooling over vases?" Matthias folded his arms.

"Drool is done. Trust me, I got this." She patted his jaw. "Come on, hot stuff. Let's get back to Lucretia."

"Excellent, you're back. I take it everything is fine? Now, as I said, apologies for the mess. I'm leaving town and have been busy packing all my babies—" Babies? Vella swung to Matthias, but then Lucretia cried out, "Stockholm! There you are. I've been looking for you everywhere, my poor baby." The woman—*vamp, Vel!*— moved in a blur of speed to the far end of the room and plucked something from the top of a cabinet.

When she turned around, she cradled a long-haired tabby cat in one arm.

Cat lady. The vamp was a cat lady. Did everyone have a cat except Vella? And wow, Lucretia might possibly be living Vella's dream life surrounded by the past and cats.

"Right." Vella moistened her lips and edged around a pile of books. "We're looking for information about a particular set of runes, and a—" Crap, what did she call Sylvie here? "—friend of yours thought you might know where we could find them."

"Why do you need these ... specific ... runes?" Lucretia's eyes sharpened, and she halted her cat stroking.

"To find a cure for my sister."

"Why these runes? There are runes everywhere; any good hedge witch, or if you must, a Divinator, would be an option for you."

"Unfortunately, even the strongest foreseers haven't been able to help. They—I—think these runes are my last hope."

Lucretia resumed her cat stroking, then asked, "Which runes?"

Vella glanced at Matthias. "Can you help out here?"

"They're an ancient set, believed to originally belong to the Mors Dicen, and they haven't been seen in a very long time. Your sister, Sylvie, directed us to you."

"Ah ..." Lucretia's gaze locked on Vella. "You seek the bone runes."

Bone? Shit. Of course they were bone. Vella couldn't restrain a shiver.

"Well, if Sylvie believes you need that information," Lucretia continued, seemingly oblivious to Vella's unease. "You are a Mors Dicen; this is your riddle. Only a Mors Dicen can access your coven's sacred bone runes. Surely you know that. No? Hmm, how very, very interesting." Her eyes sharpened. "Vella, you are a Mors Dicen aren't you?"

Double shit. "I am ... part, anyway. I don't know exactly, but I think my father must've been from that coven. Is that enough for you to give me the runes?"

"Oh, I can't *give* you them."

What? Panic welled in Vella's throat, broke off her words—

"However, I do hold the riddle that will lead you to them."

"Lucretia," Matthias interrupted. "We would be honored to see the riddle if you would show it to us?"

Lucretia ran her gaze up and down Matthias for one moment, then sighed. "Such a lovely specimen. Would you like to come with me to the countryside?"

Matthias stilled, then grabbed Vella. "That is a unique offer; however, I'm committed to helping this one."

"Oh well, another time, perhaps." Lucretia pursed her lips and turned her attention back to Vella. She took another dainty sniff of the air, then nodded and picked her way through the piles of things to a cupboard on the far wall. The vamp rummaged for something, then turned around, holding a small tin box. "Found you."

Lucretia removed the lid and drew out a pocket-size bound notebook. The cover had a raised image of a skull with a knife piercing through it.

Vella pushed Matthias to take it, but Lucretia shook her head and pointed at Vella. "If you want the riddle, you must take this book."

"*I* have to take it?" Shit. What now? Matthias didn't seem to know either when she shot him a glance.

An itch gathered at the back of her neck. She rubbed the spot—

"Who is there?" a male voice whispered.

"Who calls?" Another voice.

"We are here." Yet another voice.

Vella froze. Frigging hell, the skull and knife were made from bone. Multiple bones. She shoved the book at Lucretia. "Get that lid on now!"

The vampire's lips tilted in a secretive smile, but then she put the book back in the box. Closed the lid. The voices stopped.

Matthias touched her arm. "Vella, are you—"

But Vella shrugged him off and glared at Lucretia. "Don't ever open that thing near me again."

"Why ever not, Mors Dicen? This is your book."

Vella backed away. "No, it's not."

"It has the riddle you need to find the runes you seek; therefore, it is your book."

"The riddle is in there?" Matthias asked. "Vella, you need to take it."

"Then you read it." She crossed her arms. "I'm not touching that book. Ever."

"Lucretia, can I see the book?"

Lucretia shook her head. "It is not mine to give. It is hers."

"Seriously?" Vella blew out a hard breath. "Okay, how about this? Lucretia, since that book is mine—" A shiver raced up her spine. Why did everything have to be made of bones? "I am telling you to give it to Matthias. Matthias, find the poem, and here, take a photo with my cell phone. Just don't bring the book any closer."

Lucretia's brows rose, but then she nodded and opened the box back up.

The voices restarted their questions, but Vella held her breath and forced herself to ignore them until Matthias snapped several photos, and the book was back in its box.

He held her cell out, and Vella took it carefully—made sure there was zero chance of any bone residue or who the frig knew what else might be on it.

"Well, what does it say?" Matthias frowned at her.

Vella frowned right back. "Pushy, aren't you? Okay, here goes. It's written in four parts—"

"Stanzas," Lucretia interrupted. "They're called stanzas."

"Right." Vella held back an eye roll. "*Where ravens six crowd around, fire, serpents and bones abound. In the artist's wake, the enchanted lay, Find the truth, light the way.* Part— oops, stanza two. *Within the stone, they make their mark, From he who makes of rock his art. This northern well near Ramsay we lament, Those unjustly from this earth were rent.*" Vella paused and met Matt's gaze. "Any of this making sense?"

"No."

"Great. Me either. Okay, next stanza. *Where Poet's blood runs Rose red true, seek the cauldron with the brew. Neath sun and moon they make their meal, Within the lie the truth reveal.* That's a bit creepy. And the last stanza. *Now one more puzzle you must take, For the scroll, sense to make. But while this scribe knows not the key, From the Old World it must surely be."*

> WHERE RAVENS SIX CROWD AROUND,
> FIRE, SERPENTS AND BONES ABOUND.
> IN THE ARTIST'S WAKE THE ENCHANTED LAY,
> FIND THE TRUTH, LIGHT THE WAY.
>
> WITHIN THE STONE, THEY MAKE THEIR MARK,
> FROM HE WHO MAKES OF ROCK HIS ART.
> THIS NORTHERN WELL NEAR RAMSAY WE LAMENT,
> THOSE UNJUSTLY FROM THIS EARTH WERE RENT.
>
> WHERE POET'S BLOOD RUNS ROSE RED TRUE,
> SEEK THE CAULDRON WITH THE BREW.
> NEATH SUN AND MOON THEY MAKE THEIR MEAL,
> WITHIN THE LIE THE TRUTH REVEAL.
>
> NOW ONE MORE PUZZLE YOU MUST TAKE,
> FOR THE SCROLL, SENSE TO MAKE.
> BUT WHILE THIS SCRIBE KNOWS NOT THE KEY,
> FROM THE OLD WORLD IT MUST SURELY BE.

"Lucretia, how did you get this?" Matthias leaned over her shoulder and reread the text under his breath.

"It was entrusted to me by a Mors Dicen witch one hundred and thirty years ago. Sadly, she went on to die during the coup." Lucretia's face fell. "So many lost."

"Wait—she was how old?"

"I wouldn't know. Magic born of the dark energy ages differently—otherwise, how do vampires live so long? Now, you have your poem—"

"Where did you meet this Mors Dicen?"

"At the National Gallery, we both worked there for a time. I'm sure she mentioned one of the paintings ... but which one?" Lucretia shrugged. "Well, you have your riddle, and such a shame that I must leave town now."

"Why do you have to leave?"

"I have lived too long not to know when violence is rising. My babies need protecting, so we shall find a place in the countryside until the unpleasantness has passed."

"Do you mean the Darklings? You think they're going to attack?"

"Not the Darklings. Oh no, they are only responding to the void you left behind. No, I mean hostilities between the covens. Such terrible harm they caused last time, and now the tensions rise again. So, we shall leave. In fact, I must pack now I've found my final baby, and you must go."

"Void, *I* left?" Vella mentally grimaced. Did a vamp's mental state deteriorate as they got older?

"Yes! Absent magic causes unbalance, and the Darklings are simply seeking ways to restore that balance, which makes traveling at night rather tiresome. Luckily, I am every bit as dangerous as a Darkling. Now, Stockholm, let's go get you ready for travel, my baby."

Matthias tugged at her arm, but Vella had so many more questions.

"Time to go," he muttered in her ear.

"Wait, please, Lucretia. Last question—promise— about the Mors Dicen." She shrugged out of Matthias' grip. "And you, stop pulling me out of here. I need this."

"What do you want now?" Lucretia stroked the cat, but her gaze was sharper than ever.

Vella moistened her lips. "*Who* are the Mors Dicen?"

"The witches who saved our lives," Lucretia murmured.

Vella froze, and even Matthias stopped tugging at her arm. "What?"

"The War of the Witches here started in the late sixteen hundreds—"

"The seventeenth century? Are you talking about the Witch Trials, where humans persecuted witches—"

"'Twas that time; however, the War of the Witches happened when coven turned against coven."

"A War of the Witches in the sixteen hundreds? Lucretia, I've never heard of that, and sure as shit our history books don't show any covens at war in that time either. I'd know, I've read every book that ever existed in the Div library."

"Then I would say your books are incorrect—"

"Told you," Matt whispered.

"There are those whose knowledge of those times is ... intimate."

"But even if you're right"—Vella swallowed the urge to call Lucretia an outright liar ... that didn't seem good form given Lucretia had welcomed them as guests into her home—"why in the world would coven turn against each other when they already had humans to fight?"

"Fear. Fear started it all, of course. Fear that their coven would be next to be identified by the humans. The Divinators devised a plan to turn in their fellow witches while saving their own hides."

Vella recoiled. "That's disgusting."

"Those were disgusting times. But that's what happened. And the first to be given up were the Mors Dicen."

"But why?"

"Because they were already a threat to the Divinators," Matthias slowly said.

"Except, what I don't understand—and no one has been able to explain—is how?" Vella folded her arms. "In what way could someone who talks to the dead be a threat to the Divs?"

Lucretia cocked her head to one side. "Into every

coven, witches come in two ways—either with a natural gift, via blood lineage, that lets them participate in that magic without ritual or device—"

"You mean how in my coven, some witches can divine future events on their own, whereas others need a device to focus their power, like a tarot deck or a crystal ball?"

"And you mean in the Divinator coven; however, yes, you are correct in your analogy."

"Okay, that I get," she gritted out. "Still don't see any danger."

"For centuries, the Divinators reaped financial gain by setting themselves up as the coven to help others see their futures. They also used their insights into the future to make precise financial-based decisions, enabling them to amass wealth on a scale never seen before. However, future paths can also be decided by past events, and through the bone, Mors Dicen can talk to the dead and understand that past and, therefore, the future. Then there are the original Mors Dicen bone runes ... If rumors are true, those runes are the most powerful arcane device in existence."

"So it came down to money?"

"Money. Power. Control. Motivators for so many ills in our world—not just witchkind. But that is what led to the first Mors Dicen being handed over for trial by a fellow witch."

Really? Would Aunt Ellaine put money ahead of someone's life? No, surely not. A memory of Dorothy's pain-filled expression flew through Vella's mind and a cold shiver shook trickled up her spine.

If Aunt Ellaine really could ... would ... put money ahead of life, what would she do with Vella and Sara? No, Aunt Ellaine wouldn't hurt the girls. Absolutely not.

Vella bit her lip to stop from blurting, she still didn't

buy it. What witch would really turn another over? Not that a centuries-old story even mattered right now. *The runes, Vel, focus on the runes.*

"So why do *you* have a Mors Dicen riddle?"

"I see you also don't know the history of the vampires. That story started in the Witch Trials, too—the Vampire Queen was put on trial, believed to be a witch, but she was young, too young, and not able to withstand the human torture. A Mors Dicen witch named Hannah, herself a grandmother many times over, also in the same dungeons and being tortured, gave up her life to save that queen. And from that moment on, all vampires swore to protect the Mors Dicen, including protecting the riddle of their runes."

"Oh, shit." This was why Sylvie and her brothers had gone all weird with that kneeling shit back in New York. "But if the Mors Dicen had their bone runes, why hide them?"

"To keep them safe so they could be called upon when they needed them most."

"Except, there weren't any Mors Dicen left," Matt murmured.

"Correct. However, as sworn protectors of the coven, the vampires were asked to keep a clue in case it should ever be needed—one last way for a Mors Dicen witch to find the bone runes if that knowledge was ever lost."

"This riddle." Vella brought up the photo on her cell again. Could she really find the runes with this crazy poem?

"Have you ever given the poem to another Mors Dicen?" Matt asked.

"Every now and again, a Mors Dicen would pop up, but then almost as soon, they'd disappear. We could never work out how the Divinators knew their locations so well. And those rumors of Mors Dicen regathering ..."

"More Mors Dicen?" Matthias straightened.

"Alas, only rumors." Lucretia's gaze flicked to Vella for a moment. "No, these days, it is just the odd witch—coven or hedge—who has a remnant of that magic in their family tree. And, of course, they dare not practice that magic for fear of ending up jailed or worse." Lucretia's gaze locked on Vella this time.

"You don't get killed for practicing Mors Dicen." Vella frowned. "There are penalties, of course—"

"Oh, my poor child, you really don't know, do you?"

"What do you mean?"

"The Divinator coven will never let a Mors Dicen witch live. The risk to their continuing power, to their control of witchkind, is too great. And if you don't believe me, consult your bones. It appears to be past time you did so."

"But if the Divs are going around killing risks to their power, why don't they kill the vamps? You clearly have strength in numbers and hate the Divs, so why aren't they killing you off if that's their MO?"

Lucretia laughed. "Oh, they have tried. But we are harder to kill than witches. Their Elixir partners cannot potion us to death, and the Divs cannot see us to plot anything nasty enough to do us in."

"What? Why can't they see you?"

"We are part of the dark, like the Darklings, like the dark place where Mors Dicen magic comes from—and why they cannot see Mors Dicen when they are using their magic. Like ..." Her eyes drifted to Matthias for one moment. "Others. Now, I take it you wish to unravel the riddle? Feel free to use my home while I pack."

18

As soon as Lucretia left them alone, Matt opened his laptop and entered the poem into an internet search, but fuck, as much as he wanted —needed—to focus on the results, Vella's truth about needing the runes to save her sister's life made his gut churn.

Was Ellaine telling the truth about Sara's death? And even if she was ... he couldn't let the Divs get the bone runes.

Beside him, Vella dropped her head onto the table.

"Are you okay?" The words were out before he could stop them.

"Yes. Yes, of course."

"Your breathing doesn't sound like it. Do you want to talk about anything?" Like Mors Dicen magic. Her sister. The reason she craved control.

"What I want—no, need—is to find those runes." Vella sat up and stared at his laptop. "You're searching for information on the riddle? What have you found?"

"You really want to stay *here* to research the clue?"

Matt sat beside Vella at the black glass-topped dining table. "I get you and Lucretia have bonded over the whole antique thing, but she's a vamp. She can be deadly—"

"Lucretia is a being of taste and ethics."

"An ethical vampire?"

"Exactly. Look how she wouldn't give the book to anyone other than a Mors Dicen witch because she gave her word over a century ago. So if she says we're safe here, then we're safe here."

"You trust her that much after such a short time?"

"Yes. And plus, it's dark outside—we know the Darklings are still a risk—so at least here we can do what we need to."

"Which is find the bone runes. So, Lucretia said she met the witch who gave her the riddle at the National Gallery, right? But where to get started?" She took her laptop out of her oversized purse.

"I've entered the first part of the riddle—six ravens, a fire, snakes and bones—and the British National Gallery into an internet search. Look at this for the first result." He angled the laptop screen around.

"*The Brazen Serpent* by Paul Rubens. I mean, it's old. And famous. But where are the six ravens? Hold on." Vella stood back from the table. "Lucretia!"

"Yes, pet?" the words echoed back to them moments before Lucretia glided into the room.

"Does this painting look familiar?"

"Oh no." Lucretia gave a delicate shiver. "A Mors Dicen would never have chosen a Rubens. No ... it was something else ... a painting to do with magic. I'm almost done packing—don't be too long!"

"I'll try again." Matt deleted the last search. "Six ravens, serpents, bones, magic painting."

"Nothing ... nothing ... nothing. There are pages of

nothings. Shit. This is gonna take forever." Vella flopped into the seat beside him.

"You're not very patient, are you?"

"Never said I was. Try a broader search, just magic and painting." A new list popped up. "Matt! Sweet goddess, look at this painting. *The Magic Circle* by—"

"John Waterhouse. I've heard of it. And look, they're all here—six ravens, the bones, the serpent. Vella, you did it!"

"*We* did it. Who'd have thought we make such a good team?" Her smile warmed his chest, and when she made a fist, he'd given it a bump before he could stop himself.

Shit. Matthias Medea did not give fist bumps.

Head in the game, Matt.

"So, according to this website, the painting is at the Tate Gallery." She peered over his shoulder, and as her silky hair brushed his arm, heat hit him low in the gut. Shit. From her hair? "Maybe it used to be at the National Gallery. They do change hands. Let's check with Lucretia. Wait, why are you groaning?"

"No reason. You, uh, just look almost as excited by working through this clue as you do your antiques." And how else would she look when she was excited? Like ... flushed with desire? Would she ever look at him with that excitement?

And bloody hell, why did it even matter to him that she did?

He cleared his throat. "We need to get to the Tate Gallery."

"But which one?"

"How many are there?"

"Four locations. Let me in." She shoulder-bumped him, and he got her out of her way fast. "I need to do a quick search ... Where are you, *Magic Circle*? Where are you? Here we go; the painting is part of the gallery's permanent collection though out of rotation in their regular display. Crap, how are we meant to get a closer look?"

"I might have an idea there."

"What? How?"

"I have an old friend who's a significant patron of the arts. I'll see if she can help us."

"How will that get us a look at the painting?"

"Trust me, I've got this."

"Trust you—Matthias, I need to see that painting."

The frustration in her voice made him turn to her.

Mistake.

Because when she glanced up at him, she paused, and her gaze traveled from his pants to his shirt, to the tattoos winding up his forearms.

Her eyes widened, and the mouthwatering scent of her arousal hit the air—hit him hard.

His body tightened.

And then her gaze lifted to his, and those lioness eyes captured him, drew him in. The heat in his gut shot straight to his cock, and he swayed toward her—

"Vella?" Lucretia's voice cut the invisible cord reeling him closer. "How did you go?"

"We, uh, think we found it. *The Magic Circle* by John Waterhouse."

"John! That's the one. How I did enjoy our time together." Lucretia's eye took on a dreamy stare before she sighed and looked back at Vella. "Are you sure you wouldn't like to join me? I think you would find it most ... enjoyable."

"Where exactly in the country are you going?"

"Somewhere safe." Lucretia waved a languid hand

through the air. "I would take you and your sister both if you like."

"Thank you." Vella stared at Lucretia for such a long time that something twisted in Matt's chest.

Was she really thinking of not looking for the bone runes? Fuck. No, she couldn't leave him.

"That is tempting," Vella finally said. "Believe me, I have a feeling I would love to go with you. But I have to do this first ... Maybe in the future?"

"Dearest child, my houses are yours any time you wish to visit. Now, I am off. Do you wish to stay here or—"

"No, we have another job to do." Matthias checked the time on his cell.

"What?"

"Our public reason for being in London is for you to outfit my club here. Let's get that out of the way while we wait for my contact to get back to us."

It was close to midnight when he parked in front of the three-story steel and glass building that housed his London club and handed the keys to the valet. "Jimmy, great to see you tonight. Can you keep it out front in case I need to leave early?" He took out the first bill in his billfold and passed it over.

"Yes, Mr. Medea. And welcome to you and Ms. Knight."

Matt smiled and gestured for Vella to precede him through the entry doors.

"Wow, you just tipped him a hundred." Vella frowned like he'd done something wrong.

"What, Ellaine doesn't tip her valets?"

"Aunt Ellaine doesn't tip, period. Her belief is that the Divs deserve the service they receive. And yeah, it's shit.

I'm just ... adjusting, I guess, to seeing someone behave half decently."

"Only half?"

"You know what I mean." She swatted his arm, but he sensed she knew he was teasing. "And how did Jimmy know my name?"

"Most likely Shannah sent briefing notes to Gwen, my manager here. Shannah's particular when it comes to my overseas travel, especially when she's not with me."

"And why are we getting our bags out?"

"Because unlike you who changed on the plane, I've been in these clothes for close to twenty-four hours." He glanced at the queue of people stamping their feet in the cold night air, then stopped at the security guard. "Get a set of lights out to the queue. No shadows, anywhere."

"Worried about the Darklings?" Vella murmured.

"Of course." He strode through the doors, pulling Vella through with him.

Nocturnal London greeted him, music and lights, a packed dance floor, people talking and moving to the beat. But instead of the expected ease at the familiarity of the club, he couldn't lessen the tension tightening in his shoulders.

"Are you this busy every night?" Vella yelled. "Are they all witches?"

"Yes to busy. No to witches. There are a few witch-run breweries in town, and I don't have market share here like in New York. But we do attract enough humans to keep the place running in profit."

"Matthias, welcome back," a familiar voice called above the music.

He turned as his manager swept down the curved stairs. Her knee-length black dress, along with her icy blond hair piled back into a high pony, straddled the line between party and professional.

"It's been too long." Her gaze drifted to Vella and back to him before she grazed his cheek with a kiss. "You've really kept me waiting this time."

"Let me guess—another girlfriend?" Vella's words just reached him above the music.

He sidestepped Gwen's next kiss, no doubt aimed at his mouth, and slipped on his standard smile. "Gwen, it was remiss of me to wait so long between visits. Please let me introduce you to my newest business associate, Vella Knight. Vella, Gwendolyn Thomas."

"Please call me Gwen." Gwen held out one hand. "Business associate?"

"I'm an arcane antiquities specialist—helping Matt amp up the witchy vibe." Vella shook the offered hand, and the differences between the two women couldn't be more obvious. One perfectly put together, elegant. The other raw-edged but tough. Fiery. And with her chin raised and her gaze direct and unforgiving, every bit as strong and capable, and only one of them was making his blood pound right now.

Fuck.

"Matthias? I said I can hold a table upstairs for your ... associate. The next live show is starting soon." Gwen lifted her chin toward the second floor.

"What kind of show?" Vella squinted up at the windows.

"Volunteers enter the salon for public displays." Matt pointed to the windows. "Just like in New York. VIPs get to watch the PDS shows up close."

"PDS ... public displays of—wait, you do live sex shows here, too?"

"Yes, we do." Gwen ran a hand down his shirt, but her

gaze lingered on Vella before she switched her attention back to Matt. "Speaking of, since you're in town, will we get to see you in the salon tonight?" Gwen brought her cell phone out. "I can move participants and fit you in. Your associate is welcome, too, though if she prefers not to, I can join you."

Matt froze. Most women he brought here would jump at the opportunity.

Vella, in the salon, with him. Encouraging him to do whatever the hell he wanted. Be whoever he wanted. Temptation slithered through him. Except no, that *wasn't* why they were here, and right now, reading the tension in Vella's body, the tight line of her lips, she needed to get somewhere private. And quiet.

"Actually, Velvet's not in town for long, so we'll move straight to business and then I'll head to the VIP floor. I'll let you know if I have time for the show."

"Of course." Gwen's gaze flicked to Vella for a moment. Shit—he could see the speculation in her gaze already. He always participated in some way at the shows. "If you need anything, you know where to find me."

"I don't think she likes me," Vella said when Gwen had disappeared back into the crowd.

"Don't take it personally. This way." He slipped around behind the bar, gestured for Vella to follow, and then took the lift to the offices. Like New York, they were on the same floor as the salons.

Stark fluorescent lighting revealed practical, well-used desks—all currently empty. Printer. Tech area. Door to the server room. Nothing fancy at all.

"Another club office, huh?" Vella followed him inside, but her gaze was on him like she saw something she didn't quite ... understand.

"Starting to lose its glamour, isn't it? These are just

businesses, Vella. Front of house"—he waved a hand in the club's direction—"is all party, opulence and fancy lights, but the reality is, what you see here is a commercial enterprise with zero excitement, zero mystery."

NO EXCITEMENT or mystery in what she saw? Medea had never been more wrong because when Vella looked at him, those two words described exactly how she felt. But why did she feel like this around him? And exactly who was the real Matthias Medea?

She'd had a lifetime of believing the Magicae were responsible for her parents' deaths, were useless for society and were ruthless in pursuing their pleasures. And yet, every time Matt was away from Ellaine, he showed her a totally different side to himself.

Not that he wasn't ruthless ... because he was. And not that he wasn't a killer ... because he was that too. He'd taken out that assassin at his party without hesitation. But useless ... no, he was the total opposite there. And damn if she didn't find these sides so frigging desirable, the real drool problem was going to be over him and his snake tattoos.

Good goddess. *Seriously, get control of yourself, lady parts.* Yes, Medea was hot as all hell and a sublime kisser, but he was only working with her right now because he wanted the bone runes too.

"I need a moment," she said when she had her voice under control. "Can you ..." She waved at the door.

"You want me to leave *my* office?"

"Yes." She held his gaze.

"Fine. I need to shower and change, then I'll make some calls about the painting." He drained his coffee, the sleek column of his neck once again showing off the tattooed snakes winding up each side. He had more Magicae tattoos running up the muscles of his forearms, so if he wrapped his arms around her, she'd be surrounded by snakes. A shiver—hot and hungry—slithered low in her belly. "Vella? Did you hear me?"

Oops. "No, I was ... thinking. What did you say?"

"Come and find me when you're done—I'll be outside the second-floor salons. But heads up, if I'm out there, I need to be seen to do my thing, so don't go batshit on me."

"What does 'do your thing' mean?"

"I'm the owner of Nocturnal. I have a rep for being mysterious and lavish and hedonistic."

"Tell me something I didn't know." She didn't bother hiding her eye roll.

"How do you think I live up to that rep? I must be seen to be those things, dearest heart."

"Not your dearest anything. And what we need to do is find the runes."

"Which we will. But if I don't make it clear we're here for pleasure—"

"What?"

"You know, having fun. I get that concept is unfamiliar, but trust me on this. People will get suspicious of why we're here, which neither of us wants, correct? Now, do you need a reminder on how to have fun?"

"Seriously? I know how to have fun. What is it with you and Sara?"

"If your sister agrees, then it must be true. There's a show in one of the parlors now; once you've made your call, you can join me there unless PDSs make you uncomfortable?"

"I'm not a kid, Matthias. I can handle watching some

grownups play feelsies through a tinted window. Go, I'll meet you out there."

"As you order, Rapunzel."

Vella made sure he saw her eye roll, but as soon as the door closed behind Matthias, she took out her cell and called Sara.

She took her time, caught up on her health, the shop, her business, Ronin and Shannah. Apparently, even David and Clay had visited, plus Aunt Ellaine and the Elixirs with a new potion to try.

Sara hated the new meds—they made her physically ill, but Charles had assured her it would just take a couple of days for her body to adjust to the new formula.

And apart from the reaction to the meds, Sara sounded happy and hopeful.

The last sentiment Vella totally understood. Find the bone runes. Save Sara. Make a new life for them both.

Which only left the Mors Dicen as the outstanding issue.

Lucretia had said there were still a few witches with remnants of that magic in their bloodlines, but had anyone known about Vella's father? How far back did the magic line go? Surely Aunt Ellaine hadn't known—she would've told Vella and Sara years ago, if only to help them make sure they were extra cautious around bones.

But hell, how to find out for sure? Imagine that conversation with Aunt Ellaine. *By the way, there's something I need to ask about my dad, who must've been Mors Dicen.* Pft. That was one conversation she wasn't looking forward to. Although, at some stage, she would have to find out what Aunt Ellaine knew. Just not until she had the bone runes secure and a cure for Sara.

And sweet goddess. Vella Knight, part Div, part Mors Dicen. *Part Div, part Mors Dicen.* And what did having

Mors Dicen heritage even mean? Clearly, she had to be extra careful around bones.

Her cell beeped with an incoming call. Speak of the devil ...

Vella almost gave in to the temptation to send the call to voicemail, but that would only get her a temporary reprieve because Aunt Ellaine would ring and ring and ring until Vella answered.

Focus, Vel. She could do this—Aunt Ellaine didn't need to know everything, after all.

"You were meant to call in hours ago," Aunt Ellaine snapped as soon as Vella answered.

"I know." Vella clenched her jaw against the urge to hang up right there and then. "But we've found a starting place for the runes, a painting called *The Magic Circle* by—"

"John Waterhouse. I know of it. You believe there's something in the painting that will tell you where the runes are?"

"Maybe. The truth is, we've just started to investigate."

"And Matthias? Any sign as to how he's disappearing from our visions?"

"Nothing, yet. We're at his club now, and he's doing club stuff."

"Of course he is."

"I'll use this chance to make it look like I'm doing my job for him with the antiquities, which will leave tomorrow clear to search for the runes."

"And where are you staying tonight?"

"The Carrington Arms Hotel, not far from here."

"Matthias owns it—watch your back, Vella. And remember, the runes are the priority."

"Believe me, finding a cure for Sara is my only priority. Also, Sara mentioned the Elixir doctors have changed her meds. Can the foreseers retry their vision of Sara's ...?" Frig. She couldn't even say the word.

"One of our seniors still hasn't reported in for work, so we are under pressure with their workload redistributed; however, yes, I will try and fit that in."

"Then there's still hope."

"Of course there's hope. However, to be certain, find those—"

"Runes, I know. And I will."

"Good girl. You are to call me daily from this moment on. If I don't hear from you, I'll worry something has happened and will have to expend valuable coven resources on divining your location, which will reduce our ability to continue the search for a cure for Sara. And speaking of your sister, she had visitors today who aren't good company—talk to the Magicae Councilor and inform him that his shifter coven members are not welcome at Div properties."

Vella opened her mouth to automatically disagree— Sara and Vella could have whoever the hell they wanted in their home—but wait. Shifters? And not welcome? And the line went dead.

Not that her aunt's comments mattered right now. Sara had a potential cure, and Vella had a way to find the runes.

"Focus, Vel. Focus," she muttered to herself.

She brought up the painting again on her cell screen but couldn't make any more sense out of the poem riddle than they already had.

Time to see the painting in person. Which in turn meant getting this "seen at Nocturnal" business over and done with fast.

But crap, she was still in jeans and a sweater. Not exactly a standout outfit. Well, there was one way she could accomplish being seen fast. She grabbed her suit-case and pulled out the dress she'd worn at Matt's ball—so what if she'd worn it before?

THUMPING MUSIC GREETED Vella as she entered the packed, split-level top floor. On the lower level, lounges faced a wall of smoky red glass windows, and tall tables filled the upper level, presumably perfect for viewing the shows.

An act was taking place in the first salon, and whoever was in there must've been putting on some show, given that's where most people stared.

She scanned the crowd again ... Matthias ... Matthias ... Matthias ... Nope. No Magicae Councilor in sight. Crap. Where was he? She took out her cell.

"Looking for someone?" His rich voice rolled over her neck, and she couldn't contain a shiver as she spun around.

Why did he have to look so. Damned. Sexy?

"We need to work on the puzzle," she yelled over the music. And was it her imagination or did he pause to check out her dress?

"I have fond memories of this outfit, Rapunzel."

Nope. Not her imagination. "I bet you do." So did her lady parts. "Let's focus on—"

"I am. I put a call in to my contact. I'm waiting for their response now." He nodded at the middle lounge. "This one's mine."

As she sat down, one of the three women and two men behind the first red glass window caught her attention. "Is that ... Gwen? The mask makes it hard to tell, but the curve of her face ... She takes the club entertainment seriously, huh?"

"She takes her job seriously, yes." Matthias settled on a

seat beside her. And somehow, with all the music and voices and lights and even that view, hyperawareness of the too-delicious Magicae speared through Vella to the point she sensed his inhale ... exhale ... Her body warmed.

Shit. Time to focus on something—anything—other than him.

"Have you ever been in there?" she blurted. Damn it. So much for refocusing.

"On occasion."

"With her?" Why had her voice gone all tight?

"Are you jealous, dearest heart?"

"As if. I don't give a fuck what you do or who you do, as long as I get my runes—"

"Oh really? Not a single fuck?" He shifted closer, and goosebumps prickled across the back of her neck.

"Did you just ... sniff me?"

"Yes. You smell incredible, Rapunzel."

A warm and squishy sensation in her chest caught her off guard. She *liked* his compliments. *Get a grip, Vel.*

"Vella? This is where I do the nightclub owner thing. You don't have to stay, but if you do, things might get a little physical, although I'll keep it to the bare minimum, and you can tell me to stop any time. It's just for one act, your choice, though."

He *had* to do this. What did that mean?

"Will my staying help us get out of here faster?"

"Probably. Otherwise, someone else will come along, and I'll have to entertain them and start all over again."

"Fine. Let's just make it good so we can get to the real reason we're here."

"Um-hmm." He ran a hand lazily up her arm and then leaned down until his breath whispered over her ear. "The main show is about to start, so it won't be long."

"Sure." A shiver prickled up the backs of her arms.

"Can I get you a drink?"

"Sure," she repeated. *Ugh, Vella. You're here to put on a show. Get your head in the game.*

Then Matthias' lips tilted—was he amused at her reaction?—and the urge to wipe the smile off his face surged through her.

"Actually, a whiskey would be perfect. Fireball—if you have it—on ice." She waited until Matthias was coming back from the bar after ordering her drink, then reclined and patted the cushion beside her. "Sweetie, you should join me here. Let's enjoy the main event together."

Matthias' eyes widened for one moment before that customary bland expression—the one she was beginning to hate—returned.

As he eased beside her, the darkened window opposite their couch turned transparent, revealing a masked woman in a tiny dress, sitting in a wingback chair with two bare-chested men standing behind her, also wearing face masks.

One of the men had short dark hair, and the other had a heavily styled blond cut.

Style Cut shifted to stand in front of the chair—blocking the view of the woman—before he sank to his knees. Meanwhile, Dark Hair picked up the woman's hands and lifted them above her head.

Then Style Cut stroked his hands up the woman's legs and lifted one high. Kissed her calf, her knee, her thigh. Repeated with the other, but this time, he spread her thighs.

Vella's breath stalled. Holy shit, was he going to—

Behind the glass, the woman's head dropped back, her chest lifted, her hands strained in the clasp of Dark Hair behind her.

At Vella's side, Matthias shifted on the couch, and his

thigh pressed against hers; she took a deep breath, inhaled the delicious sandalwood and spice of his aftershave.

A memory from the first night she'd met Matthias resurfaced. How delicious he'd looked kneeling between her legs. How hot his hands had been on her thighs. How her pulse had spiked as his caress had swept over her panties.

In that moment, she'd wanted so badly to know how his lips would feel on her flesh. And she still did. If Medea dropped to his knees right here and now, and she lifted her skirt high, would he finish what they'd started that night?

Would he kiss his way to her clit? Would he nip or lick? Would he be rough and fast and feast? Or slow and languorous and take his time devouring her?

Her pussy clenched, and not even the server arriving with her drink, or a sip of her favorite drink, calmed the heat sizzling through her veins.

"Enjoying the show?" Matthias murmured.

"Mm-hmm." She took another sip of the Fireball and turned to him. "How much longer ..."

Matthias' gaze was laser-focused on her, and those midnight diamonds sparkled in the center of his eyes again. Goddess he was fine. Deliciously, dangerously, wickedly fine.

Then his gaze dipped to her lips, and she licked them before she could stop herself.

"Vella." He skimmed her jaw, smudged his thumb over her lower lip, and her breath caught—was he going to kiss her? Did she want to kiss him? His jaw tightened, and his deep growl reached her before he whispered, "Watch the show."

He turned her around, but he pulled her to him so she

was all but sitting on his lap, her skirt fanning over both their legs.

What the? She was on fire, and he wanted her to watch someone else get off?

She tried. Through the glass, the woman knelt facing the back of the chair. Dark Hair still stood, but now the woman had her mouth around his dick, and Styled Cut had dropped to his knees and was grinding his hips into the woman from behind.

But that scene had lost all interest. Instead, the hard length beneath Vella's backside consumed her focus. Her body drenched.

A low growl rumbled through Matthias' chest, vibrating against her back, and she dropped her head into the dip of his shoulder. Arched her back. Invited him in.

And then his lips were on the column of her neck in hot, messy kisses all the way to her ear. He found her lobe, sucked it into his mouth, tongued it. Nipped it.

The heat in her pussy turned to an outright ache, and she needed pressure on that spot. Now.

She squirmed to move his dick to where she wanted, but fuck, there were too many clothes between them.

She pulled his free hand around to her thigh, helped him pull the material of her skirt high—

"Are you sure, Rapunzel?" His whisper sent a hot shiver across her body, pebbling her nipples, deepening the ache between her legs. "Everyone here is watching us now, not them." He lifted her skirt higher, fingers digging into her thighs.

She pressed his hand to her thigh to stop him from moving and deliberately looked around. Gaze after gaze was locked on the tableau she and Matt made, and an entirely new thrill raced through her.

"That's the goal, right?" She tugged his hand higher,

and together, they rucked her skirt all the way to her panties. Matt flicked the ends so the material covered her pussy from sight, and then she placed his hand between her legs.

Finally, pressure where she wanted.

Those talented fingers dipped beneath the material, delved deep, and her moan was swallowed by the beat of the music. Then he drew her moisture up and over her clit. Swirled around and around. Tension built in her center.

Another swirl. Her hips rose.

A flick and press—

"Matthias, Vella, so glad you could join us." Gwen appeared in front of them, mask off, clothes on. "What did you think of the show? Oh, you're putting one on now—"

Show? What show? But before Vella could say a word, Matthias drew his hand from her, smoothing her skirt over her legs as he left her on the edge of orgasm.

Frigging hell, pussy-blocked by the woman who'd probably been dicked and licked every way possible.

Matt's cell beeped, and he held up a hand as he read something on the screen. His face tightened, and he rose in a long, smooth motion to his feet, pulling her with him.

"Gwen, good work tonight," he bit out. "We have to go."

Gwen's smile faltered. "Thank—"

"Vella, that matter we wanted to talk about. I have an update."

_____

19

The beat and throb of music shut off as soon as Matt closed the office door, but the hammer and pulse of blood in his cock kept pounding. Another freaking hard-on for the Div. He had to be setting a record for hard-ons here.

Shit, Matt. The role. Focus on the role. Control. Precision. *Revenge.*

But the Div behind him was proving harder to ignore than he'd expected.

"Matthias, what's the news?" She'd followed him over to the desk. Of course.

He dropped into the nearest chair. "My friend has arranged a private viewing of the painting. I've asked for that to happen as soon as they can fit us in."

"Seriously?" Vella's lioness eyes lit up. She sat on the desk in front of him, tipped her head back and, as her hair swung down her back, blew out a long breath. "Thank you, goddess."

When she raised her head back up, she was smiling—smiling—before her expression turned serious.

"Vella, why are you looking at me like that?"

She leaned forward, her cleavage rising high above the dress' neckline. "Because I'm curious."

Matt yanked his gaze back to her face.

"Out there, when you had your hand between my legs—"

Fuck. Hard-on number one million.

"I mean, you had to feel how wet I was." She tilted her head to one side. "And the fact is, I enjoyed the whole thing—the show, you. The thrill of everyone out there knowing what you were doing under my skirt, but no one seeing your fingers on me."

"You shouldn't say shit like that," he murmured.

"Why not? It's the truth. And I do believe you were the one who said sex should be based on at least one 'foundation of truth' back in New York. So, the question of the night—are you going to finish what you started?"

Matt couldn't hold back a groan. Who was this witch? How did she manage to make him so freaking hot he couldn't focus on his lifelong mission and, at the same time, bring out this bizarre sense of wanting to protect her —even from herself?

"Vella, that was all an act." He went to stand, except she'd see straight away that some things were indeed real. "I'm sorry I let it go that far."

"Bullshit." Her gaze went to his groin as if she'd read his mind. Hell. Maybe she could?

"Well, you're entitled to your opinion."

"Okay." Her raw silk rustled as she stood. And thank fuck, because he was walking a damned tight line with her already. "You can go to the hotel. I'm going to stay here for a while."

She took a lipstick tube from her purse and uncapped it with a sharp twist, revealing a deep, exotic color—like the point of change between the red and black beads on her dress. With one hand, she held her cell screen up like a mirror. With the other, her fingers moved with total precision as she layered her lush lips in that deep, bold red.

Finally, she pressed her lips together, then flicked the lipstick tube closed.

Hard-on one million and two.

"Vella. What are you doing?"

"Going back out there. We might be working together to find the runes, but you're not my keeper. And for the record? Sex doesn't have to be anything other than just that. I get the whole 'we're enemies thing,' outside this ... alliance to find the runes, but we can be enemies who have sex. Enemies with benefits. But it's no biggie; if you don't want sex, I can find someone else who does."

Matthias' breath punched from him. She meant every word.

"Fine." He said the word, but his blood was simmering, and the power that coursed through him at the best of times was so close to unleashing he had to clench his jaw. Somehow, he walked to the office door and held it open with one arm. Music thumped, matching the pound of his power and blood. "Enjoy your night."

She lifted her chin and walked to him, her tantalizing butterscotch scent making his mouth water. Her gleaming skin, those freckles begging to be traced. Her lush lips that someone else would lick—

He slammed the door shut. And when she turned to him, her chin rose again, the challenge in her lioness eyes impossible to ignore. "Rapunzel," he rasped. "From the moment you snuck into my bedroom back in New York, I've had this ... this ... craving for you." He stepped closer, forced her to look up to meet his gaze. "And every waking moment I'm either with you or even thinking about you, I've got a hard-on."

She rose on her toes, whispered over his lips, "Good. Because I like it hard."

A growl tore through him that he couldn't stop, and he pulled her to him, slammed his lips on hers, licked into her mouth.

She yanked his shirt out of his pants, and her fingers were on his abs, and he sucked in a breath at her touch.

He crowded her back to the desk, lifted her up. Laid her back over papers and who the fuck cared what else.

"So much fucking skirt." But then he had it all out of the way. "And enemies? Vella, when we have sex, no enemy shit, it's just you and me. And this."

She went to rise, but he pushed her back with one hand while he shoved her panties down her leg with his other until he yanked them off and threw them away.

And then she was his to view. Glistening. Lush. Mouthwatering. The need to make her come beneath his tongue shoved everything else away.

Not even the power tearing through him could stop this now.

"I'm hungry, Vella. So fucking hungry for you." He ran a thumb up her seam, then palmed the curve of those wickedly strong thighs and lifted her to his mouth. "I am going to fuck you with my tongue until you scream."

"Yes," she hissed. "Goddess, Matthias, I want all of that. All of you." A tremble vibrated through her, and she arched, lifting her pussy into his face.

And then her delicious taste filled his mouth, and he licked her again. Again. Her hips rose. She hissed. Moaned. He spread her thighs and tongued her deeply until her legs squeezed around him.

More power fed into veins, but fuck, he couldn't stop. Needed this. Needed her.

"Yes, yes, yes ... Matthias."

He shifted to her clit, sucked the nub of flesh into his mouth and lashed his tongue over and over and over. Vella hissed, arched higher still, and her legs gripped him tighter.

"So close," she panted. "More—"

But fuck, he needed to have some part of him inside of her when she came.

He replaced his mouth with his hand, then tongued her harder, faster, stabbing into her body—

"Fuck," she keened. And then her pussy clenched around his tongue, again and again and again.

Power shoved hard at the base of his spine, gathered in his cock, and even his palms tingled with the need to release.

He reared back, clenched the desk so hard the timber crumpled in his grip.

On the desk, Vella's breath sawed in and out, her chest rising with every gasp, her pussy still pulsing from her orgasm.

He could drop his pants, pull her down and spear into her right now—

Except, fuck, his power was too close to the edge. What if he blasted an elemental surge here? And it wanted to—his power freaking craved Vella.

Fuck. Fuck, fuck, *fuck.*

Control, breathe, focus. Control, breathe, focus.

Finally, he hauled in a breath and peeled his fingers from the desk.

"Matthias." Vella levered up on her elbow. Slumberous gold flames seemed to dance in rhythmic waves in her eyes, hypnotizing, seducing ...

"Knock, knock." Gwen's breathy purr announced her arrival a moment before she opened the door.

Seriously, what was it with people interrupting him and Vella in his offices? Except, this time, it was just as well.

He yanked Vella's skirt down and turned just as Gwen entered the office. "Gwen, how can I help?"

Behind him, Vella's dress rustled as she moved on the desk, and then she sauntered over to Gwen's chair, satisfaction blazing from her face in the tilt of her lips, flushed cheeks, mussed hair. Smeared lipstick.

"Matthias? Did you hear what I said? The team are excited to have you in the house tonight, and they've asked if you'll be staying for any more shows. Also, Henry, our security manager tonight, although I don't know if you've met him yet, asked if you'd like him to have a car take you to your hotel in case you wish to drink. He can also arrange for your vehicle to go into the parking garage overnight."

"Tell the team I appreciate both their enthusiasm and offers; however, I'll be leaving shortly. I'll stay for a longer visit next time."

"Oh, that is a shame, I was hoping to get some time in a salon with you." She stepped closer and ran a finger down his jacket. "We always put on the best shows, Matt. And as much as I enjoy my other partners, no one is quite as inventive as you."

Fuck, what was Gwen doing? He took a step back. "Gwen, I'm not going into the salon tonight."

"But you did the show in the lounge—oh." Her eyes widened, and she flicked a glance at Vella. "That wasn't a show. Apologies, Matthias. I didn't realize."

"Bullshit," Vella coughed.

Matt scowled at Vella over his shoulder, then turned

back to his entertainment manager. "Gwen, thank you again for your work tonight; however, we'll be leaving shortly." He ushered her back to the office door and shut it firmly behind her.

"Well, she was Captain Obvious," Vella drawled when he turned around. "Come on, she was trying to stake a claim, like almost every other female around you. How do you handle so many females throwing themselves at you? No, don't answer. I know—you just make the most of the meal."

"You seemed pretty happy to be eaten up."

"Yes, yes, I was. And I'm happy to finish what we started." Her gaze dipped to his cock.

And damn but he wanted that. Except he couldn't risk it, not with his power so close to the edge.

"Vella, we're in my office. Is this really where you want to fuck?"

"Who cares where we are? We just put on a show for your entire club, and I was okay with that, so why would I care about being in here?"

"Well, since you've had your fun, now can we go to the hotel?"

"Matthias Medea, I have zero idea why your panties are suddenly in such a twist, but fine. Hotel it is, and your loss."

"There's no loss. I simply think we both need to focus on what we're here for. The bone runes."

Vella grabbed her bags, lips pursed, back stiff. Undoubtedly angry at him.

Good. He needed her anger—welcomed it. Because he'd been so close to fucking her and for all the sex he'd had that had meant nothing more than release, instinct screamed that making love to Vella could never be just a physical act. Hells, what if he fell for her?

Sex with an enemy was one thing ... but sex with someone like Vella? Someone smart, funny, stunning. A warrior fighting for her sister's life. Someone bloody fucking wonderful.

That was the danger, because what if he fell for her? Fuck no, that could not happen.

He'd already fucked up so many lives—no way would he ever let that happen with Vella.

And the proof he was close to falling for her? Just look how his magic surged—when she'd come, he'd nearly blown his load right there, and with his power already heaving, he could have decimated the office, the club— and how many innocents would die then? If he'd lost control, then everything he, and so many others had fought for, worked for, lost for, would be at risk.

20

S unrise wasn't even a tint on the horizon when Vella hopped out of the car Matt had driven to the gallery, but the street and building lights cast a golden glow in the predawn air.

She tightened her coat and blew into her hands. At least her knee-high boots and jeans were warm enough. Matthias was in jeans and a gray cable-knit sweater that had made his silver eyes shine even brighter—damn it— and he shrugged into his coat as he joined her.

"Don't worry," Matt muttered. "It's too well lit for a Darkling attack. Plus, sunrise isn't far off."

"How do you know what I'm thinking?" She didn't bother hiding her scowl as they took the many, many steps to the front door. "Are you spell mind reading now?"

"No magic needed. They're on my mind, too."

Inside the glass door side entry, a sandy-haired woman in a bright blue pants suit and matching coat waved to them.

"That's Cressida," Matthias murmured. "My friend."

"Matthias." Cressida's smile seemed genuine, even

given the loco hour. "So glad you called. I'm always happy to help out."

"Thank you. You're the one always coming through for me—look at you out here before sunrise. And please, I'd like to introduce you to Vella Knight. Vella, this is Cressida, one of my first ever patrons from when I opened my original club. How's Tommy?"

"Well enough, although he hurt his back playing golf recently and is currently moaning that he can't be out and about."

"I can recommend a decent Crystallo doctor if he wants."

"Thank you, I'll let him know. And when are we going to see you again? It's been too long since you were over for a drink."

"Promise it will be soon."

"Excellent, now I can see you're in a hurry. But first, we need to get you through security. I called Michael Vo, the collection curator, and asked for a private viewing. He was more than happy to meet with us."

Cressida stopped at a fully kitted-out security checkpoint, with stairs and elevators beyond where she greeted the two guards by name. They handed Cressida, Vella and Matthias security passes on lanyards and led them straight through the security checkpoint.

"This place has more security than the vault in Div Tower," Vella murmured to Matt. "How did Cressida just get us in?"

"I made a donation while you were sleeping." Matt followed her through the security check.

"Must have been some gift," Vella muttered under her breath.

"Cress, thanks again for this. So where do we go?"

"Of course," Cressida said with an easy smile. "And here's Michael now. He'll take us to the painting."

A man in his thirties, with dark hair perfectly styled and a warm grin, approached from the stairs.

Cressida introduced them all, and Michael enthusiastically shook Medea's hand.

"Sorry to drag you out of bed so early," Matthias said.

"No—not at all. Thank you so much for your generous donation." Michael's smile was genuine. "And we're always happy to provide our patrons with personal tours before the facility opens. The painting has been out of rotation for a few months; however, I had the piece moved to an inspection room."

They'd moved the painting in the middle of the night? Vella cut Medea another look. His donation must have been huge.

Michael led them down a flight of stairs and through a series of stone-walled corridors to a glass-walled room. Inside, a large table filled most of the space, with desks and monitors on one wall, and at the far end, the painting in question sat on a black metal easel, illuminated by an adjustable spotlight.

"Wow," Vella breathed. "She—it's—beautiful."

"So, how close can we get?" Matt's hands were in his pockets, but the tension in his body screamed he wanted to go nearer.

"No physical contact, even to breathe on her. Stay a minimum of three feet back. Our staff will start to arrive around six, so you've got about an hour."

"Perfect. Michael, Cressida, I need to discuss the painting with my associate in private—is that permissible?"

"Absolutely. However, you will be on camera." Michael

gestured to obvious surveillance cameras at three spots in the room. "I'll be in my office—back out to the corridor, second door on the right. Cressida, would you like to join me?"

As soon as they were alone, Matthias walked behind the painting.

"What are you doing?" Vella glanced through the windows, but there was no sign of Michael or Cressida.

"The riddle says, 'in the artist's wake the enchanted lay.' A wake is the pattern in the water behind a ship, so we need to look behind the artist—as in behind their signature. The other side of their signature. Don't worry, I'm not touching the painting."

"You're breathing on it," she hissed.

"Just the back."

"Which Michael and Cressida will see on his monitors."

"Then we look fast. And what do we have here?"

"What?"

"Get over here and see for yourself ... Look, bottom left-hand corner." Vella joined him, and the warm scent of his cologne filled her lungs. Damn he smelled good.

Shit, focus, Vel.

"Is that a mark?" He pointed at the aged, simple timber frame.

"It looks like a T, but on its side." Vella held her breath, peered closer. "Could be just a mark made during the framing?"

"Or … an inscription. But what does it mean?" Medea's gaze dipped to her purse and then back to her face.

"Why are you looking at me like that?" Vella's stomach knotted. "What are … no. No way. You want me to get *Brianna* out here?"

"Unless you can think of another way to get the info we need? We're here, the painting is here. She needs to see it."

"But the only way for her to 'see' it is for me to connect with her, and you don't understand, she's … consuming. And I literally can't see afterward."

"She might also be a way of comprehending the riddle and finding the runes."

"What about the cameras?"

"Just keep your hand in your purse, don't take the box out, and as long as no one comes in and hears you talking, you'll be fine."

"Pft. Easy for you to say."

"I know." His voice lowered. "I wouldn't be saying it if I didn't think it's necessary for us to understand what the fuck is going on here."

"And how about the fact I won't be able to *see*?"

"It's what, five minutes? We just sit here until you get your sight back."

"Frigging hell, you have an answer for everything. No, don't speak. That was a statement, not a question. And fine, I'll do it. Just promise you'll keep an eye out. No one can see me do this."

"I'm not going to let anyone see you." He went still, and the lights began to dance in his eyes. "I promise."

She blew out a long breath. "Goddess knows why, but I do trust you." The truth of that statement sent a flutter of butterflies through her belly. "On this, anyway. Okay, here goes." She reached into her purse and thumbed the corner of the box free. "Can't believe I'm doing this."

"Can't believe you're doing what?" Brianna's voice cut through the room, and the prickling gathered fast and strong at the nape of Vella's neck. At least she was used to it now.

"Talking to you in a semi-public place," Vella whispered. "And to be clear—if someone comes, I'm going to close the lid or not answer your questions because I can't risk anyone hearing me talk to you."

"What absurdity—"

"Brianna. I need your help, and all along you've said that's why you're here—right now, I'm asking for it. Just, no questions, we don't have the time."

"I do not like this, Velvet."

"It's Vella. Or Vel."

"I think I prefer Velvet now."

Vella rolled her eyes. "Seriously? You want to quibble over my name?"

"Since I'm not allowed to ask you any other questions, yes, I shall call you what I like. Well, I'm here; what help do you need?"

"There's a mark I need help to decipher. Looks like a letter T."

"If you take me in your hand, I can see through your eyes."

"Touch you?" Fear made her knees weaken. "Is that necessary—"

"Why do you sound fearful?"

How about the fact she couldn't see anything afterward?

"Touching bone period worries me," she muttered under her breath.

"Which is utterly unreasonable," Brianna answered. Huh. Just how good was Brianna's hearing? "We are Mors Dicen; this is what we do. And may I add, you have already done it once before. I won't force you into my memories again, if that is what worries you."

Shit. Vella took a deep breath. "Fine. But I'm trusting you to honor your word about the whole memory thing, got it?"

"I understand."

"And I'll get my eyesight back—"

"Yes, yes. I told you the training of vision is a temporary state only."

Shit, shit, shit. So much for never touching Brianna's bone again.

"This better not go wrong." Vella felt inside the box for the cool bone, not smooth, but also ... not rough, and wrapped her fingers around the—

The charcoal-hued veil snapped over her eyes, just like what happened in Matt's lake house.

"What—why is everything so dark?"

"When you touch me, our senses combine. What you see, I see. What you hear, I hear. What you taste, I taste. This male with you in the room, he is Matthias, correct? I quite liked how you worked together. I also have him to thank for bringing us together, also correct?"

"Right on both counts. Do you know anything else about him?"

"Only what I have pieced together since I met you. You have also spoken his name many times since we last connected."

"So you can hear me talk?"

"When I am out of that infernal box, I can hear you—when you're close enough or not whispering."

"Can you hear anyone else?"

"Only Mors Dicen witches. What else do you wish to know about your coven?"

"Listen, we'll talk more about ... my coven ... I promise —but right now, I need your help."

"Oh no. What does this mark mean? And what are you seeking? I am aware you are hunting for something."

"A set of ancient Mors Dicen bone runes."

"Velvet. *Why*?"

"Why do you make that's so ominous?"

"Tell me everything."

"Well, that's the problem. I don't know anything— except that, apparently, there's a set of bone runes powerful enough to find a cure for my sister. They're so powerful even Aunt Ellaine wants them—"

"Aunt? So she is an elder of the Mors Dicen? Why does she not know of their location?"

"No ..."

"No, what? Velvet—what are you not telling me?"

"Listen, Aunt Ellaine is a Divinator ... and so am I. Part, anyway. Aunt Ellaine wants them for the same reason as I do—to find a cure for Sara. My sister ... she's dying. And these runes are the only way we can save her life."

"A Divinator is helping a Mors Dicen?"

"Our aunt is helping her niece—our coven has nothing to do with it. But the thing is, we don't know where the runes are."

"For a good reason. Vella, you do not know what power these runes contain."

Vella ignored the unease in Brianna's tone and focused on her goal. "So you do know of them!"

"Of course I know *of* them. For generations, Mors Dicen witches of uncommon and enormous power gave their bones until they created a set of runes to help not only link to the past but to see the future. They are the only bones we have that contain that power. But I do not think you comprehend how powerful—and therefore dangerous—they are. This goes beyond helping your sister—"

"I have to," Vella whispered. "There's no other way. Didn't you have someone you loved so much you'd do anything for them?"

Brianna's sigh echoed through Vella's mind. "Can saving one life erase posing a grave danger to many?"

"I have to try, Brianna. I will try. And nothing you can say will change my mind."

"Then I shall help you. However, you must agree to do one thing for me—and this is not negotiable, as you say."

"What?"

"You will train with me. I gave my bone to this knife so that my skill as a warrior would be passed to future generations—and that skill I can train into you. Well, do you agree?"

"Shit. I have to agree now?"

"Do you want me to look at this mark?"

"You are one stubborn witch. Did anyone ever tell you that?"

"Then you and I shall get on very well as you appear to be of the same ilk."

"Fine, I promise to spend more time with you, learning about Mors Dicen." Fact was, Vella did need to learn about the Mors Dicen. And Brianna was here ...

"Done." Brianna let out a delighted cackle, having gotten the better of Vella.

Not that it mattered now; she had a set of bone runes to find.

"Do you see the back of the painting I'm looking at?

It's called *The Magic Circle*, and it was painted last century. Are you familiar with it?"

"No. However, I have been in that box for over four hundred years."

"Shit. Of course. We're looking at a mark on the bottom; it looks like the letter T—"

"It is not the letter T. It is B. What languages do you learn in your times?"

Damn, maybe four centuries had driven Brianna mad? Who could blame her—

"The language this letter is from is called Ogham. Our ancient ancestors used it—"

"Of course." Vella mentally slapped her forehead. "That makes perfect sense."

"So you do know Ogham?"

"A little. And I can research to find out what else I need to know from here. Thank you. That's perfect. But wait—the bone runes, do you know their location?"

"No. I have not seen them for centuries prior to going into my box. However, my last recollection of their location was in the residence of our leader."

"Crap. Okay, thanks for the help with the mark."

21

Matthias checked his watch for the tenth time. "Vella," he murmured. "Michael and Cressida will be back in five minutes. Can you hear me? Are you ready to go? Have you got what you need?"

But instead of answering, Vella's eyes remained vacant, just like they'd been since she'd touched Brianna.

Shit. He had to make sure Vella didn't get caught practicing banned witchcraft. Cressida might be human, but all it took was one word in the wrong ears, and the Divs could find out about Vella's magic.

Except, how did he get through to her? He reached out for the knife—

"Stop," Vella ordered, her voice low and toneless.

"What? And thank fuck, you're speaking to me."

"We are still talking," she said again in that odd voice.

We? *By all the freaking stars.* He swallowed the lump that stuck in his throat. "Vella, is that you? Or am I talking with Brianna?"

"We are both." Vella took a harsh breath, her hand

appeared from her purse, and she stumbled into him. "Matthias."

"Vella." He eased her to the stool. "Are you back? Is it just you? Can you see this time?"

Her hand clenched at his shirt, and when her eyes opened, she looked everywhere except him.

"Matt, do not ever take the knife from me when I'm touching Brianna. Ever. Yes, it's just me, and no, no vision again." Her hands shot out, and she banged an empty easel. "Ouch. Where am I?"

"At the table in the center of the room. Here, let me show you—feel the edge?"

"Frig, this takes some getting used to." She gripped the table with both hands and took a deep breath, and he found himself taking one too. "Can you put a timer on? I need to know exactly how long this sight exchange lasts."

"Of course." He used his cell phone to set a timer. "We're still alone. Are you up to talking?"

Vella glared in his direction. "My vision's dark, I'm not catatonic. And Brianna recognized the mark—it's the letter B from the Ogham language."

"I knew I'd seen that mark before. It's a tree language, right? The letters stack on top of each other."

"Correct. I even studied it as part of my degree, can't believe I didn't pick it up."

"Don't beat yourself up; we're not all long-dead witches from the Middle Ages. Wait—is Brianna gone again? Did she hear me say that?"

"She's gone. And she can't hear you once I let go of the knife."

"Fuck, but I want you to tell me how that works. Later, anyway. What else did she say?"

"Brianna doesn't know where the clues lead, but she

does know about a powerful set of runes made by the Mors Dicen."

"Did Brianna say anything else?"

"Just that she'd been in that box for so long she's not aware of anything that's happened in the past four hundred plus years."

"Shit. There must be someone else who knows about the clues."

"We can try Lucretia again. She did invite me to her country house. And what about Sylvie?"

"Both are good options. But right now, what's happening with your eyesight?"

Vella squinted. "Everything's charcoal instead of black. How long has it been?"

"Three minutes. Is it enough for you to move if you had to?"

"Only if I wanted to fall over." Vella visibly swallowed, then crossed her arms, unfolded and refolded them.

"You okay, Vella? Not being able to see—"

"What? No, I'm fine." She let her arms fall to her side and lifted her chin. "How long now?"

"Four minutes."

Matt reined in his impatience because, as much as he itched to get out of the gallery, Vella's vulnerability punched him like a fist in the gut.

"I'm starting to see more. The charcoal areas have shape now, blurry, but enough I don't think I'll walk into anything."

"Okay, I've got our coats. Do you need to hold on to me?"

"Just your arm. Frigging goddess, this part I don't like."

"Relying on someone else?"

"Exactly that. If Cressida asks why we're moving slowly, we'll say I'm not feeling well."

Matt again resisted the urge to move fast, conscious of Vella in a way he'd never been before.

"It's probably a good idea not to do the whole exchange-sight thing with Brianna unless you're with someone you trust," he murmured.

"You think?" Vella's hand tightened on his arm, but then she let him go and paused. "Okay, I can see again. How long?"

He checked his cell. "Five minutes and fifty seconds."

"Felt longer than last time. I wonder if the length of impact on my vision corresponds to how long I use Brianna's sight. Shit, more questions. At least we're getting out of here."

"Michael's office is around the corner. I'll let Cressida and him know we're leaving, and then we can go."

But when they followed Michael's directions to his office, they found the door open and no one inside. In the distance, muffled footsteps echoed ... too many to be only Michael and Cressida. Shit.

"That must be them." Vella's shoulders dropped. "And I don't know why I'm whispering. But Michael said no one else would be here till six, right?"

"Right."

"I don't like the way you agreed with me then. Is it the security guards?"

"Maybe. But whoever they are, whatever the reason they're here, hanging around to find out seems ... unnecessary."

"Um ..." Vella swallowed like something was lodged in her throat. "You don't think Darklings would come inside here?"

"They don't normally."

"What about New York?"

"Aberration. For sure." Did he sound convincing? He strained his hearing.

"Great. What if this is another aberration?"

"Sh, let me concentrate. I can make out four voices, and none of them are the guard we saw on the way in ... or Michael or Cressida." Unease snaked through him.

"Are you using magic to hear that well? You did it back in New York, too."

"Something like that."

"At least they're not Darklings. That's good, right? No, not right. You're scowling."

"No, I'm not," Matt muttered. Damn but he didn't like this situation.

"And that's a grimace, not even close to a calm face. What's—"

"Listen, we need to find Cressida and get out of here. Silently. I've got a spell to hide our footsteps, but we need to be quiet." Matt gathered his energy, *fuck, let this be enough,* then took two fast breaths and murmured, "Come air to bind my call, craft yourself a solid wall, as silence reigns beyond our feet, as I will, so make it meet."

His palms itched with the power running through them, and as the air pressure around him deepened, he pushed out with his power until he'd encased Vella too. Only then did he let his breath out and take Vella's hand again to keep her close, then together they took off back up the corridor.

With the sound spell on, he couldn't use his other senses as effectively, so they ran until they reached the stairs; then, he stopped and mouthed to Vella, "Wait."

Holding his breath, Matt strained his hearing as hard as he could ... shit. Footsteps were still coming from somewhere behind them. But nothing from the floor above.

"Let's go." He gripped Vella's hand—

"Run. Run!" One of the security guards from the foyer pounded down the steps, eyes so wide the whites were visible, nostrils flared. "Get out—"

Two shiny orbs flew at the guard from behind and smashed into his back. A purple mist exploded around his head, and he crashed to the floor, his body thudding down every step.

Two unfamiliar women appeared at the top of the steps, hurled more orbs—

"Vella, behind me!" Matt dropped the spell muffling their footsteps, drew in two more rapid breaths and yelled his witchwind spell. A gale rushed up the corridor at their backs, whipped around Vella and Matt, and raced to the steps. Caught the orbs midflight and sent them back to their owners.

The women spun and ran, disappearing up the stairs before the orbs reached them.

"Matt! More coming behind us." Vella pivoted and pressed her back to his. "Can your wind go both directions?"

"How many?"

"Two guys. Two of those poison bubble things each."

Matt spun as both men launched an orb. He shifted his wind, caught the orbs and sent them hurtling them back. One man ducked, one didn't duck fast enough, and he fell to the ground in a burst of purple vapor.

"Matthias, don't move." Vella's tone had changed, and she whipped Brianna out of her purse and ran for the second attacker. The man grabbed something from a pocket, but before Matt could yell a warning, Vella flowed into a pivot and struck him with the knife.

The second attacker dropped to the ground, Brianna protruding from his chest.

Vella yanked Brianna free and wiped the gory blade on the man's shirt.

"Don't touch the—" He ran to her.

"Poison, I know." Vella dropped Brianna back into her purse. "Matt?" Her voice had returned to normal. "I can't see. I didn't use Brianna for long, but I—I need some help. Please?"

"I've got you." He took her arms.

"What about the two women? Do you think they might be dead?"

"There's no sign of them—dead or alive—which I don't like. We need to get out of here. Can you walk with me?"

"Just keep my hand and I'm good."

"Done." He tightened his grip. The way Vella charged toward danger ... "You're one hell of a fighter, Vella."

"Brianna is."

"I'd say you both are. How's the vision? We've reached the guard—" Shit. The purple bubbles had evaporated, leaving the guard lying on the ground, jaw locked, eyes wide, and no other sign of trauma. "Bloody hell. The poison evaporates or dissipates or something. Here, come this side; let's keep a wide berth. Are you good for the steps?"

"The darkness has faded enough to make out shapes, so I'm fine."

Still holding her hand, Matt took the steps as fast as possible, with Vella only stumbling a few times.

They reached the foyer and tripped over Cressida and Michael. They lay sprawled on their sides on the floor. Clenched jaw. Eyes wide.

"Fucking gods, no." Matt grabbed Vella and pulled her into his side just in time.

"Cressida!" Vella gasped.

Rage ... pure fucking fury ... suffused him. The air seemed to draw in around him like a vacuum had sucked all the oxygen out of the room—

"Is she ..." The shudder that racked Vella's body shook through him too.

"Don't touch her," he ground out. "Don't go anywhere near her."

"But why—who—"

"We'll figure that out later." An when he did identify them, the murdering fuckers were going to die. The rage resurfaced, a flame burning all his senses, but he tamped it down. Battened it away, deep, deep inside. "Right now, Cressida's gone, and you and I, we can't help her. And her killers could be anywhere." He led Vella around Cressida. "I'm going to muffle our steps again all the way to the car. But we can't talk—just run with me when I give you the nod. Got it?"

Vella's cheeks were pale, but she closed her mouth and nodded.

HER VISION HAD FULLY CLEARED by the time Vella leaped into the front passenger seat, heart pounding, hands shaking, and slammed her door shut. Matthias did the same in the driver's seat.

"Matthias, are you—"

"Not now." He shoved the car into gear. "We need to be gone before the police get here."

"Police? We haven't called them."

"Someone will have. But we need to be gone. And I need to change cars." He hit a button on the dash, and a moment later, a ringtone boomed through the car.

"Matt," Ronin's voice replaced the ringer. "What's going—"

"I'm in the car with Vella. You're on speaker. We need to change transport, something untraceable, now."

"Meet location?" Ronin replied with zero hesitation.

"Somewhere they won't be expecting us. Lucretia's house." Matt rattled off the address. "Message me when you confirm the delivery."

"Done."

"And, Ronin? Cress ... Cressida's ... fucking hell. She's gone. They killed her, and others." Matthias gripped the steering wheel so tightly his knuckles turned white.

Goddess, he was angry. And rightly so—why would anyone want to kill Cressida and Michael the guards? They hadn't been hurting anyone.

"Wha—fuck." Ronin's voice flattened. "Matt, what's going on? What do I need to know?"

"We were just attacked." Matt detailed a concise outline of what had happened. "As soon as you get the transport organized, I need you to hack into the surveillance network at the gallery and wipe all their footage."

"What?" Vella blurted. "Why?"

"And if I can't?" Ronin said. "It could be stored locally on a hard drive."

"We'll deal with that when and if we have to. Then you need to hack into the local police network. I want to know everything they do about the poisons and people killed today."

"The police, too?" Ronin's voice dropped.

"Ronin?" Vella cut in. "If you need help with the police network, Sara is my go-to for tech support."

"I'll keep that in mind. Matt, are you heading to Madgewick?"

"Not sure yet. Too early to tell if we'll need to head that far south."

"If you do, I can give Amelia a heads up."

"Yeah, I've already thought of that. I'll keep in touch regarding our movements."

As soon as the call ended, Vella twisted to Matt. "How safe are we right now?"

"As in this very moment? Not very. Which is why we need to get off the road and wait for a new car. Lucretia's out of town, so her place is perfect. We can't go back to the hotel, Nocturnal, or anywhere they might be expecting us."

"But who are *they*? And how did they find us?"

"Who they are? I have a good fucking idea. How they found us? No bloody clue."

"I can't believe they killed the curator and that guard. I mean, why—why in the goddess' name would they do that? Are they after the runes too? Wait. Remember at your lake house, Sylvie said there were other people—beings—asking about the runes."

"Whoever the hell they are, they're going down. But right now, we need to focus, Vella. We must find the bone runes."

"How can you be so calm? People are dying!"

"I'm calm because anything else is useless. We can do this, Vella. While I drive, look at the riddle again. We had a lead with the gallery from Lucretia, but I have no idea where to go next."

Shit, he was right. And Vella did have a goal—finding her sister's cure. Even so, her hands shook as she reviewed the picture of the riddle on her cell screen.

Within the stone they make their mark, From he who makes of rock his art. This northern well near Ramsay we lament, Those unjustly from this earth were rent.

Vella's heart stopped pounding, and she focused on finding the meaning that had to be hidden in the words.

AN HOUR and a half after leaving the gallery, they arrived at Lucretia's, but the tension that had ridden with Matt the entire drive refused to let go.

The call he'd made to Tommy on the way replayed through his mind. Fuck. Telling his friend that the love of his life had been killed just for helping Matt ... Guilt and anger twisted tighter in Matt's gut.

"We're here?" Vella looked up—she'd been absorbed by the poem for most of the drive, muttering to herself occasionally and punching various internet searches into her cell.

"I'll park around the back," he muttered.

"Um, Matt? I could see how much that hurt—calling Tommy, I mean—but what happened at the gallery with Cressida wasn't your fault—"

His cell beeped. "It's Ronin. The new car will be here in fifteen minutes."

Vella's lips firmed like she was going to pursue her line about Cressida, but he didn't ... couldn't ... talk about that guilt again now. He needed to focus, damn it, and letting his emotions out here and now wouldn't help anyone.

Something flared in her lioness eyes, and she glanced out the window for a moment before turning back to him. "I still can't believe you muffled our steps back at the gallery—you might've saved our lives, Matt."

"It's simple spellcraft." Thank fuck she'd changed the topic.

"I don't know nearly enough about magic—that's clear —but I am sure that sound thing isn't easy."

"Simple in its mechanics." The admiration in her voice sent a beat of warmth through his chest, but he brushed the odd feeling aside. Cress was dead. And others. Who the fuck cared how he did his magic? But Vella was staring at him like she wanted to know, and at least she was asking about his magic and not Cressida. "Sound is made by vibrations in the air. The spell just creates an air barrier around us so the vibrations can't travel far. Now, we need to work out where to go next and do it somewhere safe."

"Back to the hotel?"

"No, too risky."

"But our luggage is there—never mind, we can figure out a change of clothing later. So where the hell is safe while we figure out the next clue?"

"Good question. If I had my way, we'd be in a castle with fortifications and—"

"Castle! That's it." She punched something into her cell.

"What's it?"

"The next clue. I think we need to go to Edinburgh Castle."

"Scotland? Why?"

"In the late eighteen hundreds, a fountain sculpture was commissioned to remember all the women—and men—who were persecuted and killed during the Witch Trials. It's called the Witches' Well. That's north of us, carved in stone and has water. It must be it."

Matthias punched the address into a GPS map route on the car's dash display. "It's almost an eight-hour drive, although at least it's daylight now, so we don't have to worry about Darklings."

"Just whoever the frig else is after us?" She snorted and dropped her head back to the seat rest.

"One problem at a time." He eyed her pale cheeks. Damn but she was astounding. "And Vella? It wasn't just my magic that got us out of the gallery. You were amazing back there. That's the second time we've fought back-to-back, now."

"I had Brianna—"

"No, it's not that. You could've been a burden—and gods but that was what I expected, but you were the opposite. I get Brianna is good, too, but you were solid. You don't panic. You just plot a course, and whatever you say you're going to do, you stick to that plan. I can trust you with my back, and that's pretty amazing. I don't think ... I don't think I've felt like that with anyone other than Shannah and Ronin."

"Wow, not a burden. High praise, indeed."

"I'm serious. And I wanted you to know."

"Yeah, well, you're not too shabby yourself in the whole kick-ass department."

"Look at us now, huh? Two witches who started off enemies, actually getting on."

"I swear if you'd told me I'd be fighting alongside the Magicae Councilor not even one week ago, I would never have believed it."

"Ditto. And hey, I can see you're tired—why don't you sleep, and I'll drive for now. I'll wake you up if anything happens."

"No, I'm good. I'd rather think about the next clue and keep my eyes open ... just in case." She shivered and pulled her coat over her lap like a blanket. "Plus, I'll drive when you need to rest."

"Then here, I'll get the heater going. But if you do want to nap ... just for a few minutes even ... go ahead."

And as they drove north in a surprisingly comfortable silence, the anger and guilt in his gut hardened into resolve. When he found the motherfuckers who had killed Cress, they were going down, but right now, there were at least still two poison-wielding witches out there.

Focus, Matt. He checked his rearview mirror. No sign of danger ... yet.

22

"Vella." A hand on her arm shook Vella out of her sleep, and she shot upright. "Whoa, you okay there?"

She was in the car. Parked near a four-story brick and stone house, with the sun already casting long shadows over a green lawn and trees in the distance. In the driver's seat, Matthias stared at her with a wary expression.

"Sorry to wake you."

"I'm glad you did." She pushed her hair off her eyes and rolled her neck. "I wanted to stay awake for the entire drive in case we ran into trouble."

"Don't worry, you closed your eyes for an hour, max. Wish I could've let you sleep longer. I slept for a good two hours while you drove this morning, remember?"

"Look at us—actually sleeping in each other's presence." A yawn escaped her. "And yeah, I'm still tired."

"You're starting to trust me, aren't you?" A grin played about his lips, but his eyes stayed serious.

"Whatever." She refused to give in to the silly urge to

smile. This was too serious for jokes. "So where are we exactly?"

"Moor Manor, outside of Lamberton, just over the Scottish border."

"Why are we stopped here?"

"It's after four, and by the time we get to Edinburgh Castle, the grounds will be closed, and it'll be dark."

Running around in a darkened castle ... A shiver crept down her neck.

"I don't like the idea of being up there at night—not now. When do they reopen?"

"Half past nine tomorrow morning. I think we're better getting off the road tonight and driving up in the morning. But there's one problem."

"What?"

"Every hotel and motel we've driven past is already full—no doubt people are getting off the road well before dark with the increase in Darkling attacks. This is the first place with a room available—only one left, and just one bed. I booked it over the phone, just in case."

Vella rubbed her face, forced her brain to work. "It's Wednesday, right?"

"For a few more hours, yeah. Why?"

"I'm ... trying to figure out when I need to be back in the US."

"We can push on if you really need to, but it's risky. We just need twelve hours."

"So today is the seventeenth," she whispered, more to herself than Matthias. And he seemed to get it because he didn't speak. "Solstice is four days away. Okay, I've still got time. Let's get off the road for the night."

"Done." Matthias got out of the car, and she followed, shivering in the icy dusk air.

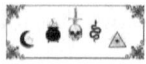

STANDING in the B and B's foyer while the reception staff checked them in, Matt couldn't stop staring at Vella. Stare? Bloody hell, more like he drank in the sight of her.

She'd insisted on paying half of the room cost, and after handing over her credit card, had wandered over to the grandfather clock taking pride of place on one wall, and now ran her hands over the timber, intense concentration etched across her face.

Even with her hair mussed, cheeks pale and shadows beneath her eyes screaming of her exhaustion, this incredible, strong, capable, resilient witch made his body hard and his chest warm ... and more, brought out a sense of admiration he never thought he'd associate with anyone outside his coven.

Just look at how she'd handled herself in that fight at the museum. The only other people he didn't have to worry about looking after in a similar situation would be Ronin and Shannah.

Fuck, that fight had been so many kinds of wrong.

And bloody hell, calling Tommy before ... his chest went tight all over again. He would never get over the awfulness, the uselessness, the sense of guilt at telling someone else he cared for that a life had been lost—and because of him.

"Mr. Medea, your room is ready." The receptionist handed over a heavy metal key. "We serve dinner in the dining room or can deliver it up to your room, and you're in room two-zero-three, second floor, second door on the right."

"Thanks." He joined Vella. "Are you finished communing with the clock?"

"Can you believe it's a longcase clock by Bryson of

Edinburgh? And I'm good now. Communing is finished. But this place is gorgeous. Hard to fathom being surrounded by such beauty."

"You really don't mind staying here?"

"Mind? Why by the goddess would staying in a four-hundred-year-old manor house, dripping in history, be a problem?"

"The one room thing?"

"Pft." She yawned as they reached the second floor. "I'm so tired I could sleep in an armchair. And even if they had more than one room, sharing makes sense."

He opened their room door and stood back so Vella could enter before him. "How about one bed?"

"At least it's big enough for us both." Her lips quirked.

Hard-on one million and three.

Thank fuck he had his coat as he shifted to carry it in front of him to hide his reaction. But then she stopped in the middle of the room.

"Vella?" He checked the place thoroughly. King bed. Two bedside tables. Coat stand. Chair beside a small table. TV opposite the bed. Door leading to ... He checked inside. Bathroom. And a window looking out over the town. "The place looks safe. But why are you just standing there?"

"I'm so tired I can't decide."

"Between?"

"Shower or bed. I might fall asleep *in* the shower at this rate."

Vella. Naked. Shower.

Fuck, if any more blood flowed to his cock, he was gonna pass out. "Right." He cleared his throat. "I can't help you decide, but I can sleep in the chair—"

"Matt, after everything we've been through, you and I can sleep in a bed together." She sniffed her arm. "But I stink." Her nose did that adorable wrinkle thing again that made his chest go warm. "Shower, that's decided. If you don't hear from me in ten minutes, knock hard. It'll wake me up. And then you should shower, too." She shrugged out of her coat and hung it on the stand.

"I stink as well?"

"Yes."

As the bathroom door closed behind Vella, Matt hooked his coat beside Vella's and took a sniff of his underarms. "Fuck." Well, there went the hard-on.

"Hey, Medea?" Vella called out from the other side.

"What's up?" He rested against the door. Naked Vella. The memory of that night in the club, with her body slick and pulsing with heat beneath his finger, seared his mind.

Fuck, but he had to get control of his desire. After what happened today, he needed to focus on protecting Vella, not fucking her.

"I'm hungry. Would you mind ordering something?"

"Sure. Do you want to eat up here or downstairs?"

"Up here's fine. And I'll eat anything. Literally."

Thank fuck. Being around other people right now was not high on his agenda. "Got it. Ordering food now."

"One last thing. Can you take these?" The door cracked open, and Vella thrust a bundle of her clothes into his chest. "I'm sure I saw a sign they do laundry here."

The bathroom door clicked shut; the shower turned on. A soft sigh echoed through the door. And his hard-on was back again.

Freaking hell.

Focus, Matt.

Fine, he'd get to work. Gods knew he had enough to keep him busy for the next year. He'd ordered their dinner, dealt with emails from Ronin and Shannah, updated them both on where he and Vella were and requested an update on Ronin's shadowing of the Div and Elixir Councilors when Vella emerged wrapped in one of the B and B's fluffy robes, her hair up in a messy knot, damp tendrils at her hairline wrapping around the base of her neck.

Water droplets gleamed on the freckles dusting her skin. He could lick them up—

"Thanks for dealing with the clothes."

He cleared his throat. "The receptionist said they'll be up shortly to get them, and dinner won't be too long. Do you want to grab a nap while you wait?"

"The shower woke me up enough to stay awake for food. There's a second robe in the bathroom, so you can give me your clothes when you've stripped, and I'll get everything to the staff when they come up." She tightened the robe.

Maybe the shower was exactly what he needed. Gods knew his mind was a maze of secrets and lies and guilt. Somehow, he had to reset and focus on what mattered. On what *must* be done.

In the bathroom, Matt passed his clothes back through to Vella and turned the hot tap as far as it would go, but even with his glamour spell dropped, and hot water pounding his shoulders and neck, the tension didn't leave his muscles.

What he needed was release.

He palmed his cock. The damn thing had been hard so fucking often that by the time he'd run his hand from the base to the tip, he was back to full mast.

He shifted his grip and pumped the shaft, again and again and again. Oh yeah ... and imagine if Vella had been in there with him. If she dropped to her knees, her beautiful amber eyes glowing up at him as she took him in her mouth.

His balls tightened. Pressure gathered at the base of his spine. Stars began to dance around the edge of his vision.

Fuck yes. Yes, yes, yes—

His cum erupted, and he emptied himself into the shower, over and over and over until, finally, the tension that had gripped his entire being for the last day released.

VELLA HANDED their clothes to the receptionist, who also confirmed their dinner would be up shortly—and went back to pacing the room. If she sat on the bed right now, she had zero doubt she'd fall asleep and then their food would go cold.

So she kept herself awake by running her hands over the stunning Maple & Co walnut mirrored-back sideboard on the far wall.

Heat slicked low in her belly. Her nipples tightened.

Shit, what the goddess—

The heat bloomed lower, and her pussy tingled like she had her vibrator right there. What the frig was going on? She gripped the sideboard—goddess but it was gorgeous—

Knock, knock, knock.

"Room service," a voice called through the door.

The heat swirled faster.

"Um, coming," she called out. Shit. She *was* on the verge of coming, but damn she wanted that food. She yanked the door open, tugging the vee of her robe tight. Thank the goddess for small mercies, the room service was on a trolley.

"Just leave it there. I'll grab it in a minute."

"Are you sure—"

The heat swirled faster. "Yep. Yep. All good. Thank you."

She shut the door hard, stumbled to the sideboard—

An orgasm crested through her, and she gripped the sideboard so hard it was a miracle she didn't leave claw marks in the walnut.

She swallowed hard, met her reflection in the sideboard mirrors. Her cheeks and mouth were flushed. Her hair had come out of its bun. Her robe parted. Her chest still rose fast beneath her harsh breaths.

What. The. Hell?

And crap—the food!

She'd just brought the trolley inside and dropped onto the bed when the bathroom door opened, and Medea joined her.

Well, sweet goddess.

With his silver eyes more brilliant than ever, his midnight hair loose around his shoulders, he'd belted his robe, but the thing was open to his belly button, revealing a deliciously hard, tanned chest, a smattering of hair trailing down—

"Thought I heard the door open. Perfect timing. Vella? Vella, is everything okay?"

"Sure." Was she? She'd just spontaneously orgasmed —almost in front of the poor frigging room service guy— and now she wanted to rip Matt's robe off him and have him for dinner instead of whatever was on the trolley.

No, she was not okay.

AFTER THAT SPECTACULAR ... bewildering orgasm, a full meal and a glass of cab sav, Vella leaned back into the oversize armchair and let a huge yawn overtake her. "Stick a fork in me, I'm done."

"Me too." His silver eyes darkened, and as she held his gaze, sexual tension gathered low in her belly all over again.

Whatever the reason behind her mysterious O, her body seemed to want more. *She* wanted more. Sleepy sex was a thing, right? Not that she'd ever slept—as in the true sense of the word—with a sexual partner before.

And she and Matt *were* sharing a bed, so the only question left was did he feel the same?

Enemies with benefits ... she'd been fine with that status quo before, but she didn't actually feel they were enemies anymore. They were working together, after all. And sure, for different reasons, but they'd also worked *well* together. Did she want to pursue sex right now? Would sex change the comfortable dynamic they'd finally found?

Matt stood up.

Time to decide: sex or no sex? Her lady parts cheered —definitely sex. All she had to do was proposition him—

"I'm going to set a boundary trigger spell around the building. Just in case." He took his coat from the stand and disappeared into the bathroom, emerging moments later in the coat and nothing else.

Wait. What?

"I'll keep the lights off when I come in. See you at sunup." The door closed with a solid click behind him.

Guess that was a no to sleepy sex.

Shut up, inner voice.

BUT AS TIRED as she was, everything else that had happened over the past six days filled her mind. Half an hour after Matt had left the room, the reception staff returned with their freshly laundered clothes—apparently, Matt had paid them extra to do a rush job—and she slipped her panties and shirt on, but sleeping in her jeans? No way.

She'd barely gotten back into bed before Matt returned.

"They returned our clothes." She rolled over to her side, better to see him, but in the dark, she could only just make him out. "Yours are hanging in the closet."

"Thanks." The bathroom light briefly illuminated him before he closed the door; it flashed on him again as he emerged, only for a moment before he flicked the switch, plunging them back into the dark.

"You're sleeping fully clothed?"

"In case we need to leave fast." The bed dipped beneath his weight, and she shifted well over to her side to give him room. "I thought you'd be asleep, for sure."

"I can't sleep," she whispered. "Everything's jumbled in my mind. Sara. The bone runes. The clues. Brianna. Darklings. The people trying to kill you—us—the people who have died." Her breath caught, and her shudder made the blankets shake. "Can I ask you a question?"

"Go for it."

He settled deeper under the thick blankets, and she rolled to her back and gathered her thoughts. *Focus, Vel.* So what if his big body took up so much space in the huge bed, or that his body heat felt so good.

"How do you stay so calm in the face of everything that's happened? Like dealing with the Darklings and being chased by assassins, and when Cressida—you know."

His sigh echoed into the room. "Vella, I'm not calm in those moments."

"Yes, you are—I see it. You handle the situations and then just move on to the next focus. That's what you said."

"You see a façade, Vella. One I work my ass off to maintain. What's really going on is the opposite—I am seething. But if I let that out ... then I'm not as effective as I need to be. Ready to sleep yet?"

Sleep? When she could be learning more about the spellcaster beside her?

"Maybe," she murmured. "But before that, thanks for not arguing with me about paying my share of my room when we checked in."

"Why would I? You're allowed to make your own decisions."

"Not normally. Whenever I'd go out with the Divs, they made all the decisions."

"Ah, hence your need for control."

"That might be some of the reason."

"Why did you let them?"

"It's ... complicated. Growing up, I was taught to show Aunt Ellaine, and the coven, the respect they're owed for everything they've done for us by never questioning, never arguing."

"Respect owed? They're family, aren't they? But fine, to each coven their own. What about others? Surely, you've spent time with non-Divs? Friends? Boyfriends? Girlfriends? Wherever your preference takes you."

"You want to know about me?" Vella couldn't contain her surprise at that, and she rolled back to face him. Damn but she wished she could see his face. He lay on his back, that much she could make out, but he shifted toward her enough that the gleam of his silver eyes became visible.

"Yeah, I do. Come on, Rapunzel. Open up a little. We're going to be together for another few days, by the look of it. Let's get to know each other—more than just as co-blackmailers."

"Okay. Let's see. You're right, of course. There have been non-Div friends."

"Romantic non-Div friends? Or is that also frowned on by the Divs?"

"Of course romantic. And mostly humans, but just because once a witch finds out who my aunt is, they get all weird. And don't roll your eyes. She's powerful, I get that. She scares witches off fast. What about you? Any specials among the multitude you've brought home?"

"You've heard all the rumors, then? And yeah, a couple. But like you said, life's complicated, and I haven't been in the right place to be more than a one-night stand to any person in a long time." He moved back to staring up at the ceiling, and she copied his move. Welcoming the dark to hide her thoughts.

"Do you want more than a one-night stand?"

"Sometimes ... I think it would be nice. But only when the time's right."

"Well, that's cryptic. Would you revisit any of the 'specials' when the time *is* right? I have a feeling at least one of them would wait for you if you asked."

"And there's the problem. What if the time is never right? I wouldn't want anyone to wait for that and miss out on their own 'special,' as you put it."

"Okay, so for you now, it's casual. Casual is okay, though—if it works for everyone."

"You think so?"

"Absolutely. A good friend, Jacqui—Crystallo witch and the best barista you'll find—has this saying: 'Don't jim someone else's jam,' which I love. So yeah, if one-night stands are the jam of the day, then as long as they're everyone's jam, go for it."

"And you? What's your jam?"

"Me?" The truth was that looking after Sara was her

priority. With every other moment filled with arcana retrieval jobs for the coven and running the shop, romance, like what happened in the books Sara made covers for, had just never happened to her. But she refused to worry about that. "Let's see, if I could have any jam at all, it would be blackberry. Sweet, sticky, but with bite." She smacked her lips, and his laugh filled their room like she'd intended.

"So, tell me about the fascination with antiques. I know you studied a dual degree, yet every time I see you with a piece—like the clock in the lobby here, or practically everything at Lucretia's—it's like you're seeing them for the first time."

"I am, for a lot of them. I was homeschooled, both high school and college, so most of my training was done via the internet and books. Which was fine—it got the job done—but before I opened Arcane Antiquities, most of what I'd seen had been retrieving artifacts for Aunt Ellaine."

"Why homeschool?"

"Aunt Ellaine thought it was best—plus, I got to stay close to Sara."

"And did you always do what Ellaine says?"

"Not always." She swallowed the lump that rose in her throat. "But I learned the hard way that you don't cross Aunt Ellaine. Once, when I was a teenager—gods, maybe fourteen or so—we'd had a fight because I wanted to go to a regular school with regular kids. I must've pushed the argument too far because Aunt Ellaine sent both Sara and me to our rooms without dinner, and we weren't allowed to leave for the entire night. I was fine, but Sara ... she didn't get to take her meds that night."

Matt's harsh indrawn breath echoed through the room,

but she was lost in echoes of the terror she'd felt that night—of not knowing if Sara would die. Of the pain that had racked Sara hour after hour. That night had been the longest, more terrifying of Vella's life, not knowing if Sara would live to see morning. The guilt and grief and horror played deep in her mind, but she pushed them away. She and Sara had a plan now. They'd make a life that didn't involve their aunt and find their happiness together, and that was all that mattered.

"Motherfucker," Matt spat. "She punished *Sara* to get you to obey?"

"Let's just say I learned not to disagree with my aunt. But what about you? Clay and Shannah mentioned you grew up in some place called Madgewick. Is that close?"

"Not really."

"What's it like?"

"It's … beautiful."

"You don't sound like you think it's beautiful. In fact, you sound …" Weary. Lost. Grief-stricken. "Tired," she murmured.

"I am, gods but I am that. But the truth is … Madgewick is me, as much as I'm Madgewick. And all the people who depend on me, on it, deserve to be safe and secure and every time something happens, I feel like it's my fault. Look at Cressida—if I hadn't asked her to help us with the painting, she'd still be alive. I hate it. So much death. So much pain." A chill accompanied his whisper to the point Vella pulled the blankets higher. "I fucking can't stand it."

"Matt, I'm sorry about your friend, but that wasn't your fault. Whoever these asshole assassins are, they killed Cressida, not you."

"Except, that's not the full story. I kicked over the hornet's nest with Charles, and if that's what these poison attacks are about, then yeah, it is all on me. Gods but I hope I don't end up killing anybody else."

So much guilt filled his voice that her own heart started to hurt, and she reached out a hand to him. And when he took it, she held it as tightly as she could.

"I think you're selling yourself short," she whispered.

"And I think you need to sleep. Vella, I know you don't trust magic and that you like to be in control, but how about I just help you relax? I'll add a spell to my voice so as I talk, you'll relax—become a little sleepy—and I'll stop when you fall asleep, which will then be a natural state, not forced."

"Like a calming spell?" Shit. Could she do it? Could she trust Matthias enough?

"Exactly. What do you think?"

She squeezed his hand. "Go for it."

23

M att had set his cell phone alarm for six a.m., but a buzzing around his wrist woke him up first. Vella lay on her side, facing him, one arm pillowed beneath her head, her soft breathing indicative of a sound sleep, and he eased the tangle of her red hair—she had curls, who'd have thought?—away from her face before he could stop himself.

Her lips were softly parted, and the freckles dancing high on her cheekbones glowed like some fae creature had sprinkled her with faery dust. Goddess but she was beautiful. His chest tightened. What he wouldn't give to be able to wake up like this every morning. He leaned closer—

The buzzing tingled again on his wrist.

Fuck. The trigger spell. Someone had crossed the boundary around the B and B, and given the sky outside was still dark, odds were against any guests being up and about. Maybe the B and B staff?

He wasn't waiting to find out.

He cut the trigger spell, called his glamour and shook Vella's shoulder.

"Vella."

She rolled over fast. "Wha—"

"Shh." He covered her mouth. "We need to go."

"Darklings?" she whispered into his hand.

"Doubt it—no screams." Frankly, he'd prefer it was Darklings—at least then they'd know they were safe inside in the light. "Get dressed. I'll check the corridor." As soon as she nodded, he withdrew his hand.

As she scrambled out of bed and yanked on her jeans, he eased the bedroom door open. Night lamps lit the empty hallway, so he held his breath and waited ... There. Front door. Footsteps—two people, hushed breathing, whispers he couldn't make out.

Poison attack in New York. Another in London. What were the odds of it happening again here?

Too fucking high. Just like the odds of them all being connected—although how was the mystery.

The hairs on the back of his neck prickled, and as soon as he felt Vella at his back, he grabbed her hand. "Staircase at the rear of the house," he whispered into her ear. "This way."

They'd reached the end of the hallway when footsteps echoed on their floor.

"Time to go. I'm doing the muffling sound spell again," he whispered. They ran down both flights of stairs, through the kitchen to a mudroom, and found the door marked exit.

And then they were outside.

Fuck knew who or what was out here in the predawn air, but with a fair idea of who *was* in the manor house, getting out fast was the only option.

"How do we get away from them?" Vella whispered

when they reached the parking area. "There are no other cars on the roads, and they'll see us from a mile away."

"Give me the box with the bone knife."

"What are you doing?" Vella shoved the box into his hands, and he threw the ignition key at her.

"Start the engine and keep it running. I'm busting their tires."

He grabbed the bone-handled knife and ran to the only vehicle not present when he and Vella had arrived last night. Stab and run, stab and run, stab and ru—

"They're here," Vella yelled. "Three's enough!"

Matt didn't waste time looking back; he just ran to Vella and leaped into the car.

"Buckle up, buttercup." She shoved the car into gear. "This is going to be fast."

He slammed his door, Vella spun the steering wheel and they took off.

He twisted around as two women ran after them, the building lights revealing their faces. They each threw orbs at the car—all of them falling short.

"At least now we know they didn't die at the gallery," Vella muttered as she glanced in the rearview mirror, then she scowled. "Why are you looking at me like that?"

"Rapunzel, watching you handle that gear shift might've been the hottest thing I've ever seen. I seriously have a semi right now."

"Well, good to know your jam, huh?" She smirked, and his semi stiffened all the way. Hard-on one million and four. "But gods, what a rush!"

Color shot into Vella's cheeks. She smiled over at him, and Matt's chest started to tingle. Damn but he liked seeing her happy. Bloody hell, when had her feelings become so important?

"VISITOR CAR PARK THAT WAY." Vella looked in the direction Matt pointed. "Then, according to the online map, the castle is a short walk up there."

"Perfect." Vella pulled into the parking lot and took the first available space. "Thank frig my heart has calmed down now. As exciting as that wake up was, I'm getting sick of people trying to kill us." She checked out the other visitors as they got out of the car. No overt threats.

"Me too," Matthias murmured. "In fact, let' s stay out of direct sight. We've got an hour before the gates open."

"What about that café over there? I'm hungry—we ran out of the hotel before brekky."

"Perfect."

Vella matched her stride to Matthias' as they skirted around one of the many tourist groups milling about. "Is it time to talk about the fact this might not be about the runes at all? You did have that poison attack back in New York."

"I'm thinking about it, all right. Which means you're in danger just by being with me. And that means finding out how they found us is my next priority. I have a feeling if we can work that out, I can end this."

"And them. I honestly thought they'd been killed by their own poison back at the gallery. Pfft, I wish they had been."

"Bloodthirsty. Nice." He opened the door for her.

"They killed totally innocent people and tried to kill us"—Vella lowered her voice—"so yeah, I wouldn't feel any remorse for them getting caught in their own evil. But what about the police? Surely, they're looking for us now."

"Ellaine and Charles are pressuring the lead investigators to look the other way as this is witch business. Plus,

Ronin was able to get in and scrub their surveillance records."

"Will it work?"

"Maybe. The Council has a history of making humans look the other way when they need." Matt's lips twisted.

"Hey, are you okay? What was that look for?"

"Nothing."

"I need a loo first, but get me a coffee."

"As you order, Rapunzel."

"Are you laughing at me? I don't order you around … much."

"Sure, tell yourself that. But all good. I've got the coffees." He laughed, and for a moment, genuine warmth glowed in his eyes. And something shifted inside her. And like a key in a lock, the certainty that this was the real Matthias firmed in her chest.

MATT HAD ORDERED coffees and something to eat and nabbed a table as far away from anyone else as possible when his cell rang.

"Ronin? Why the gods are you calling me at your four fucking a.m.?"

"Because Sara is getting sicker, and she's due to get her next medicine from the Elixirs today. It's killing me, us, because Shannah is the same, to see Sara so fucking sick and not tell her we think it's the medicine doing this to her."

"But we don't *know* it's the case. Are you at Arcane Antiquities now?"

"Yeah, Shannah and I are taking turns to stay overnight."

"Perfect. Get a sample of that medicine today and get it

analyzed. Find out what's in it, and then we can work out what to do next."

"How about fucking tell Sara? She needs to know. And you need to tell Vella—"

"No. That is absolutely not negotiable, Ronin. I need Vella to focus—*we* need her to focus—on finding the runes and then letting us take them so we can take this rebellion to the next level. And if Vella thinks Sara is getting worse, what do you think she's going to do? She's going to take the bone runes and run straight back to Ellaine—which is the absolute last thing we can ever allow to happen."

"You'd risk Sara's life for the runes?"

"Right now, what you're saying is an unknown since we don't even know if the Elixirs are harming her. And the fact is, I will do whatever is needed to make sure all witches—not just one—are saved. Ronin, we're finally close to having a way to stop Ellaine and you want to risk that? Get *your* head in the game."

"Matt, I think you're wrong—"

"And I think we can't risk it. Don't say a word, Ronin— nothing."

"Fine." The line went dead. Shit. Ronin was pissed.

As soon as she'd finished in the loo, Vella found a quiet corner in the café and made her check in call to Aunt Ellaine.

"Vella?" Aunt Ellaine answered on the first ring.

"Hi—"

"Where are you? Where have you been?" Vella bit back a sigh. How did she answer that? "And what are these rumors of you and Matthias conducting a physical display at his club?"

Vella straightened. What the frig?

"Vella, are you there? You simply cannot trust the Magicae—"

"Hold up, Matthias saved my life." She lowered her voice and explained what had happened at the gallery—minus her Mors Dicen magic use.

"Poison spheres?" Aunt Ellaine said after Vella had finished.

"That's what they looked like. Have you heard of anything similar? I have to ask—would Charles be behind this? Aunt Ellaine? Did you hear me—"

"Of course he's not behind those attacks."

"But are you certain? Who else could it be? The Second for the Elixirs lives in the UK, right?"

"Nevena Montgomery, yes."

"Maybe—"

"I said no. Neither Charles nor his Second would ever go behind my back, no matter how unhappy he is with the current state of affairs between our covens, so do *not* waste my time asking again." There was another pause, and then Aunt Ellaine's tone softened. "I will, of course, confer with Charles and see if he has any intel on the type of poison you've described. Now, I have to ask—how involved are you and Matthias?"

"As in romantically? No, of course not." Except for the whole enemies with benefits thing. And enemies who'd entered an alliance, who were getting to know each other and who saved each other's asses.

"Well, I did tell you to do whatever it takes. Vella, there are times when duty takes priority, and if that means sex with the spellcaster—even though I know you consider his coven the enemy after their involvement with your parents' deaths—so be it; he is just a Magicae."

Just a Magicae? What did that even mean? Wait—Aunt Ellaine really expected her to fuck Matthias to get the runes?

"Vella, did you hear me? I said Derrick and I are flying over—"

"Sure. Listen, I might have to restrict contact until we make sure we can stay hidden from whoever's following us. I'll call you when I can."

"But, Vella—"

"Bye." She ended the call and stared at the screen. *Just a Magicae.*

Vella glanced over at Matt—met his piercing gaze. He'd saved her life. He was decent to the people in his life. He was ... decent. Which was at odds with the man who'd blackmailed her and threatened her sister.

No. Whatever else he was, no way was Matthias Medea *just* a Magicae.

"That was Ellaine?" he murmured when she sat down opposite him.

"Yeah, it was either check in now or risk her calling out the National Guard, or whatever they call it here, to find us." She tucked her hair behind her ears. "Aunt Ellaine is going to ask Charles for any intel on the poison spheres and who could be behind the attacks. She's *said* she's sure it's not him."

"Why do you sound doubtful?"

"I don't know ... Aunt Ellaine mentioned something about Charles not being happy with our coven right now."

"Charles is unhappy with the Divs?" Matt's eyes narrowed.

"Yeah. Why?"

"Just good to know where my fellow Councilors stand with each other."

"I'm not here to help you figure out Council dynamics, Matt."

"I never thought you were. How's your coffee?"

"Good. And hardly a smooth subject change, there."

"Please. I thought it was a brilliant segue. Come on, the gates open in ten minutes. If we finish up, we can get there right on opening."

As soon as they reached the walkway leading up to the main castle tourist gate, Vella veered left. "There's the well. See by the wall?"

"It's smaller than I expected."

"But it's here. That's the main thing. And goddess, please let this be right. See the plaque? That was added later." She opened her cell phone. "So the clue says: *Within the stone they make their mark, From he who makes of rock his art. The northern well near Ramsay we lament, Those unjustly from this earth were rent.*"

"And look—we're right beside Ramsay Garden." Matt gestured to a signpost.

"This has to be it." As soon as they reached the fountain, Vella dropped to her knees—the icy flagstones sending a chill through her jeans. "If there's a mark, it'll be hard to see in the stone."

"I'll check this side." Matt knelt beside her.

"Okay, looking beneath ... frigging goddess." Vella's breath whooshed out. The weathered stone had a mark.

"It's here," she whispered. "Under the trough—it looks like a plus symbol, but this is the letter A in Ogham. I'm sure."

"So that means we have a B and an A. What does that mean?"

"Assuming the letters are creating a word, it starts with *Ba*. Ba what?" Vella took Matthias' hand and jumped to her feet. "Thanks. Sweet goddess, Matt—we got the next clue." The weight sitting on her chest lifted a little further.

"Did you just do a happy dance? I've never seen you this positive."

"Hell yeah. After everything that's been happening, it's about time we got some good news. It's a beautiful day. We're surrounded by all this wild gorgeousness. The sun's out, and we're so close now—just one more clue—to finding the bone runes. Matt! Of frigging course I'm feeling positive. The first time I've actually felt this way since I found out about Sara."

Last night's orgasm may also have helped ... but she wasn't mentioning that.

"I'm glad. And you're right—we need some brightness in this fucked-up situation. Here." He held out his hand, and she took it without pause. "We've got two Ogham letters and the next clue to decipher, so let's get back to the car. Can you send me the photos of the riddle? I want to take a look."

As soon as the car doors closed behind them, Matt took out his cell and read, *"Where Poet's blood runs Rose red true, seek the cauldron with the brew. Neath sun and moon they make their meal, Within the lie the truth reveal."*

"Where the poet's blood turned Rose red ..." What does that even mean?"

"And Rose is capitalized," Matt murmured. "A name? Is there a poet named Rose?"

"No idea. Let me check." Vella used her cell to do an internet search. "Okay, *loads* of poets with Rose as either first or last name. But the blood comment. Let me add that to a search. Huh. Apparently, poets like to write about blood, a lot."

"There must be something else." Matt's eyes narrowed. "Hold on—*where* ... That's the first word. As in a place or a location. 'Where the poet's blood turned Rose red.'"

"What's the next line?"

"Seek the cauldron with the brew."

"Like a witch's cauldron? Or ... it could also be an actual brewery—you know why breweries are called that, right?" Vella leaned forward. "There's a line of thought around women being the main brewers of beer back in the Middle Ages, and how they'd stand at their cauldrons in fairs and the like, selling their beer—their brew—and that's where the term comes from. So, it makes sense that a clue about a witch's puzzle would be in a brewhouse."

"How do you know that?"

"Arcane antiquities expert—remember?"

"So, we're looking for a brewery. But which one?"

"Surely that's in the clue. Maybe the poet or Rose references are the pub? It would have to be contemporary with the late 1800s." Vella started a new search. "Okay, not so many pubs, but still enough. And what if Rose is the street? A pub on Rose Street? But what's the poet connection?"

"Now, *that* I may know." Matthias punched something into his cell. "Here it is. The poet John Dryden was attacked outside the Lamb & Flag brewery on Rose Alley."

"A poet, an attack—there's the blood part—and the rose. Holy crap, that must be it. So where is this place?"

"Back in London. And I know it's a long drive, but we can't fly. It's time we stay completely under the radar.

Change our cell phones. Whoever these assholes are, they already know we're in Scotland, so we get cash out here, then no more bank or credit cards until we figure out who the fuck they are."

Vella let out a long whistle. "Right. Off-the-grid type of stuff. Then all we have to worry about is if they're using magic to track us."

Matt grimaced. "And we've also got an eight-hour drive ahead of us, so we're not getting back to London before nightfall."

"Then let's hope the roads are well lit." Her stomach twisted. "London, here we come. Again."

"Would Brianna know anything about the next clue? This pub was around when she was last out of the box, right?"

"It's worth asking." She blew out a steadying breath and, keeping her purse on her lap, lifted the lid on Brianna's box. "Brianna, before you say anything, I'm sorry for the long break, but it had to be done. And right now, I need to ask you another question about the bone runes. Brianna? Are you there?"

"I don't want your apologies, *Velvet*." Ouch, back to Velvet again. Brianna was pissed. "I want you to use your heritage correctly. And unless you have another bone teacher—"

"What's a bone teacher?" Vella glanced at Matt. His gaze was back on the road, but she sensed him listening to the side of the conversation he could hear.

"This is exactly my point. You don't know nearly enough to be wielding such power as you have at your fingertips."

"Then help me—"

"I need time with you, Velvet. Time. And not just in

conversation. You and I need to bond, and I need to see your world through your eyes."

"I'm in a car right now," Vella ground out. "This isn't exactly a good place—"

"What is a car?"

Shit. Shit, shit, shit. Brianna hadn't seen the world through another witch's eyes for four hundred plus years. How was she going to react to being in a frigging car? "Listen, we're going to stop somewhere. We're in Scotland, just out of Edinburgh—"

"Perfect. There are standing stones near that city that will enhance our connection. Take me there and then you may ask your questions, and I shall commence our training."

"You're blackmailing me?"

"I am helping you. Do not mistake me for a teacher without grit enough to ensure you succeed in your tasks."

Shit. "Matt, we need to make a detour."

"What?" He glanced at her purse. "Brianna's calling the shots?"

"Yep. She wants us to go to some standing stones somewhere close to here."

"There's one henge nearby I know of, and it's on private land, so that's a good thing."

24

H alf an hour later, Vella let out a long, low whistle as she ventured through the grass, around the craggy outcrops of rocks, and got her first magical look at the standing stones. Twelve roughly rectangular stones were gathered in a circle, perhaps twenty feet in diameter, and a thirteenth stone with a flattened top lay in the center.

Her breath caught, and she paused at the outer edge. "It's as if energy permeates the air like a live current is running somewhere close by. It feels ..."

"Magical," Matthias breathed as he stopped beside her. "What does Brianna say?"

"I haven't removed the lid yet. I wanted to get into the circle first. Can we—have you touched them?"

"The stones? Yeah. And the energy you feel? It's stronger within the circle."

"Do you know why?"

"I grew up hearing stories of how the stones contain the power of rituals performed within the circle, and over thousands of years, a lot of magic has been performed here. As an adult, I know these particular stones were erected on a ley line that directly connects Edinburgh and Tara in Ireland. You can touch them—they won't hurt you."

"I've always wanted to visit a circle of standing stones, thought my first would be Stonehenge, but here ... I don't even have words for how elemental they feel."

"Elemental?" Matthias cocked his head like he was regarding her with more than his usual interest.

"Yeah, hard to put into words, actually. Why?"

"Why don't you talk to Brianna? Maybe she can explain."

"Speaking of ... I get Brianna knowing of these stones, but how do you know of this place?"

"I have family up this way, and we used to visit when I was a child, and if we were visiting over a solstice, we'd always come here for a rite of gratitude. And you don't need to worry about anyone seeing us—the family who own the land aren't here at the moment."

"A rite of gratitude? I've never heard of that."

"Are you stalling, Rapunzel? I promise you can cross the threshold; it won't hurt."

Shit. She was stalling. But why?

Because Brianna was about to confront her with some truths that she had no idea if she was ready to hear or not.

Focus, Vel. Whatever the goddess had in store for her, so be it. This was just one more step toward finding the bone runes and saving Sara. Nothing else mattered.

She took a breath and removed the lid off Brianna's box.

"Okay, Brianna, we're here. You can tell me all about Bone Guides, and I'll ask you my question."

"Welcome to the circle, Vella."

"Wow, your voice sounds so clear—I can hear you better than ever before."

"The stan stones enhance our communication. Which will be of benefit as we commence your training. To begin, when a Mors Dicen witch comes of age—that's when their magic is stable enough to be trained—they are given a family bone, and the soul that bone came from becomes their Mors Dicen guide."

"So, I need someone to train me?"

"Vella, what disaster has struck your world that you know none of our sacred traditions? The Bone Guide is an essential rite of passage for the Mors Dicen. Otherwise, you know not what you deal with, what danger lurks, the opportunities and the wonder of the gift you have within you."

Yikes, this wasn't going to go down well. "Witches don't ... practice Mors Dicen anymore."

"Then we lost," Brianna whispered.

"Wait, you know about the rebellion that led to the Conflict of the Covens? I thought you'd been in your box for centuries."

"I know not this rebellion you refer to. However, my last witch, Hannah, told me the year was 1653, shortly before our last conversation. I had been with her since she was sixteen, and for six decades we worked together. Terrible persecutions had been happening to our kind, and she had me hidden in the floorboards beneath her bed so we could talk safely. We were speaking the night the Inquisitors came and tore her from her bed. They tied her hands to stop her taking me and letting me fight for her."

"Brianna." Bile rose in Vella's throat. "She was almost eighty years old, and they did that?" An image of Dorothy, back in New York, being smacked by the SI stole through

Vella's mind. Shit. Horrors were still being perpetuated against witches centuries later.

"Her screams have stayed with me all these years. I never heard from her again after that night."

"I am so sorry."

"Apologies have no meaning here. What matters now is ensuring your training. I had hoped her bones would be given to the sacred ritual, but as I have been in a box all these years, I never discovered if so."

"Wait, what sacred ritual?"

Brianna's sigh echoed through Vella like a brittle wind. "Another missing tradition. Our bones must be blessed at a sacred stan stone."

"A what?"

"The stan stones are sacred circles and henges where energy converges, where we gather and practice our rites, like the one allowing me to stay connected to this bone."

"I thought I could talk to any bone?"

"Any bone? Velvet, you need to start thinking!"

"I am," Vella ground out. "We're having this conversation, aren't we?"

"Don't be impertinent, Velvet—"

"Vella."

"Vella I like. It sounds capable and like you won't hesitate to use me when needed. Velvet sounds too soft for a Mors Dicen witch. But I will only use this name if you continue your training."

"Glad to know what you think of my name." Vella rolled her eyes—if only Brianna could see it. "So, back to the bones, who can I talk to?"

"Among other abilities, *your* witchcraft allows you to communicate with the soul a bone belonged to, if that soul has not reincarnated. Mors Dicen witches who give their bones to the sacred rite do so knowing they will never reincarnate and will be forever tied to that bone, to be there for the witches of our bloodline to come."

"That's some sacrifice," Vella whispered.

"It is not a sacrifice to be there for your family, Vella."

"On that, we agree. Which brings me to my question. My sister, can she practice Mors Dicen as well?"

"Any witch can undertake a Mors Dicen ritual, but witches of the Mors Dicen coven have this magic within them regardless. Now you must tell me something, Vella. What has happened in your world that the sacred rituals of our coven have been lost? That you, the strongest Mors Dicen witch I have encountered, know nothing of your craft? That I have not been called upon for so many years?"

Shit.

"Mors Dicen magic is banned." Vella winced even as she said the words. "And you go to jail if you get caught doing it."

"*What*?"

Vella grimaced. That screech had been so loud that surely Matt must have heard it. She glanced at him—but no, he remained by the edge of the stone circle, and then he mouthed, "Are you okay?"

She blew out a hard breath and nodded before returning her focus to Brianna.

"And who made this ban?" Briana continued.

"The Witches Council."

"A Mors Dicen agreed to something so preposterous?"

"Technically ... no. There were no Mors Dicen left on the Council when the decision was made. Twenty-four years ago, conflict broke out within witchkind. Witches versus witches. And your coven ..." Shit. How did she say this? "Your coven was disbanded."

"*Our* coven, to correct you." Vella's stomach clenched.

"Vella, you are a Mors Dicen witch. Make no mistake. And as strong as you are, surely you must be descended from one of the first three families, so discontinue the comments about my coven and commence saying 'our.'"

"But—"

"There are no 'buts' either. There is only training. We shall start with the simplest of moves. I trained for the majority of my living life as a warrior, and I have the skills to help you become a warrior, too. I fought with knives and short swords, with the bow and arrow, and by hand. What shall we start with?"

"I don't need to fight—"

"Vella. After what you just informed me, you absolutely must fight. You say that our coven has been disbanded, and it does not take the living to know you mean that disbanded equals death. And if you cannot fight for your life—who will? Are there other Mors Dicen now refugees from this rebellion?"

"No—at least I don't think so." Shit. This was all so confusing.

"Then, at the very least, you will be able to fight and protect your life. Come. I shall give you one lesson, and then I shall answer your question."

"I thought this whole conversation was a lesson."

"A lesson about your coven is different from a lesson on how to become a Bone Wielder. I never said what lesson I required in exchange for providing information."

"*Brianna*. You are—"

"Your Bone Guide, and in this, you will heed me, Vella, *daughter* of the Mors Dicen. Now, for this element of your training, I will take over your sight. We shall start with knife throwing. Do you see a target nearby? And no, not your Magicae."

"How did you know I was thinking of him?"

"Please. What male would you not wish to throw a knife at some stage? Now, this is the lesson. We are not in my memories, so you can let go of the knife; however, I shall guide your physical movement with the knife. To begin, we work on your stance. We place this foot forward, the other back—no. You are fighting me."

Give up control? Close to her worst nightmare. But Vella took a deep breath, forced her muscles to unlock, and let Brianna guide her movements until the Bone Guide pronounced Vella competent enough—for now.

"Well done, Daughter. Now, you may ask your question."

"The next clue has us going to a pub in London called The Lamb and Flag—it's one of the oldest breweries in the city. Do you remember it?"

"The Lamb and Flag … that is a familiar name. And I am not surprised to hear you travel there."

"Why?"

"Witches in those years often sold their brews from cauldrons and posits, and some of their brews were the most delicious ales. At least one family who worked in The Lamb and Flag in my last memory were Mors Dicen witches. And is the Magicae still traveling with you? Turn to him so that I can see him through your eyes again." Brianna let out a low hum. "Well, he may not be to my personal choice; however, you have mated with a fine specimen of a male."

"We're not mated."

"Do you wish to be?"

"It's … complicated."

"Bah. That is a word used to excuse yourself from going after what you desire. And if you do desire the Magicae, he certainly seems to reciprocate based on the looks he has been giving you. One piece of advice I can give for free—make the most of every moment, Vella. What I would give to see my beloved again. Now, I need to rest. Well done on your training—"

"Wait, you need to rest? How does that even work?"

"I have existed for over twelve centuries in one form or another. I need to sleep. And place my lid upon this box— when I hear your chatter, it keeps me awake."

VELLA PLACED Brianna back in her box—lid on—and instantly, the charcoal veil deepened to true darkness. And as if the removal of sight was a trigger, the rest of the world made itself known. The soft patter of rain-drops on her face and hands, the swoosh of the wind through and around the stones. The earthy scent of rain on the air.

"Vella, are you and Brianna still ..."

"No. We're done."

"And your vision?"

"Can't see yet. But it's okay; I just need to sit for a bit ... process what Brianna said. Do you mind giving me a few minutes?"

"Sure thing. Take the time you need." The rustle of clothing suggested he'd sat in the grass nearby.

"You can wait in the car out of the rain. No need to sit out here with me."

"I prefer to sit out here too, and it looks like the rain is clearing."

Sure enough, the droplets stopped. She pressed her hands on the stone beneath her. Something about the rock steadied her in the absence of sight, and she let herself take deep, even breaths as she processed Brianna's words.

Vella was a Mors Dicen ... a descendant of the coven

that had worked with the Magicae to kill her parents, along with so many others witches

Except, that wasn't the truth, was it? Everything she'd been taught growing up about the conflict of the covens ... a lie. The Divs had been the aggressors all along.

Shit. Shit, shit, *shit*.

The surge of magic thrumming through her veins crashed into a tumult of *what the fuck.*

And her vision had returned—although, as she looked over to Matthias, she blinked and looked again.

He stood between two stones with his shoulders hunched, hands in his pockets, staring downward. Beyond the circle, the rain came down harder, but on Matthias, it diffused as if he held an umbrella.

She spun around. Not just Matthias. The entire stone circle seemed to share his umbrella.

Was it this place? The goddess knew the magic that swirled through here felt more potent than anything she'd touched before. And then there was Matthias ... capable —frighteningly so. Focused. Captivating. And so frigging hot that the longer she stared, the more her body heated.

"Matthias," she called before she could think twice.

He looked up, his silver eyes reflecting the clouds above, and then he stalked toward her. And while the rest of her life seemed to be a tumult of WTF moments, one thing stood out in total clarity.

She wanted Matthias Medea.

Make the most of the moment.

25

"Vella?" Matt gave in to the urge and crossed to the center of the stone circle. Was she somehow ... glowing? Or was it a trick of the light? The moisture in the air kept tickling at his senses, but he held the rain at bay—although, thank fuck, Vella hadn't asked what spell he'd called. "Your sight's back?"

But instead of answering, she stayed still, her hands remaining on the rock, and her gaze locked onto his.

"Did Brianna say anything about the pub?"

"About the pub? No." She pushed off the rock. Stepped so close he could count her delectable freckles. "But she did give me one piece of advice. And I'm taking it."

"Vella? What are you doing?" Her gaze dipped to his lips before darting back to his eyes. His body tightened.

"You know how control is important to me; well, in this moment the only control I have is to decide what I want to do. And while I can't make you want me back, I'm owning the fact that I want you." She held out one hand. "To be clear. I want to have delicious, wonderful, messy sex with you. Here."

Sex with this magnificent creature?

Every ounce of blood flew to his cock, and he gripped Vella's hand like the lifeline she'd become in his storm of craving, clawing, demanding desire.

TINY PINPRICKS of warmth gathered in her palm, but Vella didn't move—just held on tight as the scents of fir and ancient oak melded with fresh rain.

And between one breath and the next, the heat in her palm grew, and tension pooled low in her belly. Hotter. Needier.

A shudder racked Matt's frame and he let her hand go, but before she could speak, he turned and cradled her jaw, and she had one fleeting look at his silver eyes before his lips crashed onto hers.

Heat and spice and desire exploded, and she greedily accepted his tongue. Tangled with it. Ferocious. Hungry. Demanding.

Pure. Frigging. Bliss.

A groan tore through him, and he hauled her into his body. She moaned at the contact, but it wasn't enough. She pressed harder, imprinted herself along every ridge of his magnificent body as he kissed his way to her ear, to her neck.

Heat replaced cold as if their bodies were pure energy, and not even the icy air could penetrate their cocoon of heat.

And then he bit the cord of her neck. Sensation arrowed to her pussy, and she hitched a leg around his hips. He groaned and cupped her butt, grinding himself exactly where she needed.

But that relief lasted all of one second before she ached for—

"More," she hissed. "I need more." Need *you*. But she shut the emotional shit down. This was about sex, specifically, the need to fuck this incredible male, so she pulled back and gripped his hand. "Matt, are we finally doing this?"

A blast of air hit the circle, and she held her breath, along with his gaze. Frig, please say yes.

"Vella." He cupped her jaw, smudged his thumb over her lip. "Yes, we fucking are. Because by all the gods, I need you too."

"Thank the goddess. Just hearing you say that ... all low and guttural and sexy ... it's like you sent a shaft of heat to my pussy."

His eyes narrowed. "But fuck. *Fuck*. We're in a henge. Outside. And you don't really know me—what I am, what I want—"

"Matthias, oh no you don't." She grabbed his wrist where he held her jaw and grabbed a fistful of his jumper with her other hand. Held *him* still. "If you don't want to have sex with me, come out and say it. Because I called you to me. And who cares if we're outside? This is private land—you said so. All that matters is, do you want me? As in hot, fast, wonderful sex *with me*? Because I am wet in more ways than one for you." She rose and nipped his lip. "Matthias Medea, you and I still have secrets. But right now, *you* are all I want. So? What about you?"

"Fuck, but you are spectacular," he whispered. He inhaled hard, and his silver eyes turned even more brilliant. "And I want you."

"Well, thank the—"

"Stop." He changed his grip and caught both her hands,

pushed her back to the stone. "You want to know what I really want? What I desire so much it's like a beast clawing inside me? I want to fuck you until you scream. I want to pour myself into you. I want to own your lips and your body and every inch of your glorious skin." His voice dropped. "Want you? Fucking hell, Vella, I want to destroy myself in you. You need to know I'm not talking soft and easy and gentle." His jaw clenched. "That is not in me, not now. Are you ready for that?"

Her body drenched.

His gaze roved over her face, the midnight stars in his eyes whirling faster, brighter.

"Yes," she breathed. "Sweet goddess, yes." Then, because it had already been too long between tastes, she nipped at his chest through his shirt.

"Vella," he growled. "I'm not in the mood to play."

"I'm not playing." She jerked her hands free and yanked her sweater over her head. "And I like to bite, just so you know."

"So do I." He shucked his coat and threw it over the rock, then sucked her earlobe into his mouth. "And *I'm* going to bite you where it counts."

A whimper escaped her; then they were kissing and nipping and licking as they tore at his clothes. Hers. Everything and anything that stood between flesh on flesh, and then, thank frigging finally, skin on skin.

But sexual tension already clawed through her veins. Savor later, sex now. She grasped his thick, hot dick.

Heat pooled in her core, and she hummed as precum beaded on the tip of his shaft. She swirled it around—

"Vella." His guttural tone was so low she could barely hear it over the blood pounding in her veins, and those beautiful stars in his eyes pulsed in sync with her heartbeat.

"Shit, Matt. Condom."

He inhaled hard. "Don't even move. I have this." He lunged for his pants, pulled a strip of foil packets from his wallet, tore one open and dropped the rest onto the ground.

He palmed the thick length of his erection and rolled the condom on, and her entire body clenched at the outstanding sight.

"Finally." She grabbed for him, but he stopped her with a look.

"First—I'm going to feast." His eyes darkened. "And yes, that includes biting." He dropped to the grass and grasped her thighs.

She sucked in a breath. Dark hair streaming down his back, cheekbones tight, glorious body kneeling at her feet, looking like a God of Old worshipping his goddess.

And as his gaze traveled down her body, she felt every inch of that deity.

She lifted her chin, held her shoulders back, let him look his full. And then she widened her legs. "Feast away."

Like she'd set fire to a fuse, Matt growled, and then his hands were parting her legs further, and he tongued her seam.

Sensation burst with his touch, and then he found her clit. Sucked. Flicked. Rubbed. Bit.

Vella cried out as energy shot through every nerve ending. "Close. I'm close," she chanted, and she grabbed his head, held him to her.

He shifted and tongued her entry, pressed deep right where she needed most and licked her, over and over—

Cold at her back. Fire in her core. Tension clawed. Crested.

Crashed.

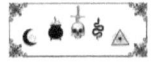

AS VELLA CAME APART under Matt's tongue, he drank her down, licked her until he'd consumed every part of her release. Power and desire thrashed in his veins to the point where one started and the other ended, ceased to exit. Hell, maybe the two were combined.

The urge to release it all into Vella surged through him. To show her the real him. Every single part.

Fuck. *Couldn't happen.*

And with the aftershocks of her release still quivering through her body, he rose to his feet, spun her around, and bent her forward.

"Hold on," he growled. And gripping her hips to steady her, he fitted himself at her entry, then surged into her body.

Wet. Hot. Silky. Fucking heaven.

She gasped, and her back arched, and fuck if those quivers didn't still rock through her pussy around him, squeezing. Enticing his release—

"Fuck, Vella." He gritted his teeth against the urge to lose himself right there. "Need you so much." His low voice was unrecognizable, but in full elemental contact with the air and water, with Vella around him and under him, part of him, everything else dropped away, and he responded to an instinct he'd never had before.

Rain drove down outside the circle. Wind whipped up across the grassy fields.

"Need you to know me," he growled. "Need you. Need you. Need you."

He pulled out of her clasp, thrust back in.

"Vella." His balls tightened. "Vella." Pleasure and power gathered at the base of his shaft. "Vella." He thrust again.

A whirlwind raced around the henge, faster and harder, roaring—

"Matt!" Vella tensed, her body clenched, then she shoved back, ground herself into him.

"Coming now. Fuck—" The pressure in his shaft exploded. His vision went black. Power surged. And he roared into the sky as he poured everything he was into her.

"Matt. What—" Her body tightened all over again. "Frig yes, frig yes, frig *yes*."

And then he held himself still because the power of his magic kept going, joining them, and he couldn't have moved if he wanted to.

26

That hadn't been sex. As Matt lifted his head, he sucked in the deepest lungful of air he could inhale, then marveled at where their bodies connected. At how Vella's head tipped back, her glorious hair tumbling around her shoulders. At her harsh inhales matching his.

Perfect in a way he'd never imagined possible. And definitely not sex. That had been a universe opening and devouring them whole.

"I don't want to leave you." The whisper was out before he could catch it. But he forced himself to ease out of her body.

"Frig," she hissed. Her body clenched like she really did want to keep him inside her. "Even that felt good."

"Tell me about it. One clench from your pussy and I'm already hard again."

"What can I say? My pussy's greedy." Vella snorted as she straightened. "When did it start raining so hard?"

When he'd been pounding her glorious body for all

he was worth. And shit, Vella deserved more than a fast fuck in the rain.

And *fuck*? That wasn't even right. What they'd just done ... Power hummed through him again in his veins, although how, he had no idea.

He held out her clothing. Damn but her legs were something else, and he unashamedly enjoyed the view as she tugged her jeans on, while getting dressed too.

"And now it's freezing—no idea how you did it, Medea, but you warmed me up so much I didn't feel the cold."

"Magic." Another lie. Everything he'd done with the elements had been totally unconscious. But he couldn't tell her that either.

"Now that's a handy spell. Got any more tricks you want to share?" Her lips quirked. "And you know what, as abso-friggin-awesome as that was, I am up for round two when we're not running—" Her eyes widened. "Matt. Your eyes."

"What?" He froze.

"They've gone black. Like not silver with the little stars dancing, but like, full-on, glittering black." Her eyes widened. "Matt. What is going on? Who are you?"

She shifted back from him, and a cold shiver crept up his spine.

Fuck. Fuck, fuck, fuck.

His gut tightened, but somehow, he kept his voice even. "Do you really want to know?"

"Yes."

Should he tell her the truth? *Could* he tell her the truth —this one, anyway? His throat thickened under the need to get this right—the weight of the risk if he got it wrong.

"Vella, I have already exposed so much by giving you

the trust that I have so far. One word from you to Ellaine could undo everything I've worked for."

"Just tell me," she whispered.

"You demand so much," he whispered back. "Are you asking to see the real me, Vella? Is that it?"

"Yes! You've been ordering me to trust you since we first met, but all this time, you've been the one keeping secrets. So yeah, about time you fucking trusted *me* and told me the truth. All of it." She folded her arms and backed up to the flat-top stone. "I'm ready and waiting, Medea."

Shit. He'd known this time would come—had to come —for his plan to succeed. But fuck, let him be right.

"If I tell you this, you'll be the one at risk, simply for possessing this knowledge—if your aunt finds out you know my secret and don't tell her, you'll be in danger, and if you do tell her, you'll put not just my life, but risking my entire covens' lives. Are you ready for that risk and responsibility?"

"Your secret is that bad?" He held her gaze without saying a word, and while her jaw tightened, she didn't back down.

He drew in a deep breath. Settled beside her on the rock. "This story starts with my parents. Our family property, Madgewick, borders an ancient forest. Mom and Dad used to tell me stories of how my mother came out of the forest one day, and my father was practicing his magic. He was in his late teens and couldn't master a particular spell. She gave him shite for it, then performed the spell perfectly.

"At first, he got mad, but then she offered to show him how, and the way they told it, by the end of the spell, they were in love. Bonded, forever. They didn't have a long time together—but they had a love that burned so brightly I still recall the warmth of just being around them."

"How did they ..." Crap. She bit her lip.

"It's okay," he whispered. "How did they die?"

"It was near the end of the war; the Magicae Councilor and his Second had died not long beforehand, and my parents were planning how to retaliate."

"Your parents were with the rebels?"

"They were. They died fighting for what they believed in," he murmured. "What was right. And will forever be remembered for fighting for our family. For all witch families. But fuck, they died so young." He drew in a harsh breath.

"Matt," she whispered. She reached out a hand to him.

And he grasped it. "But that's not all that happened that night."

He exhaled closely and cut the magic glamour on his eyes and face. Shit. What would she think—of all of it? His gut curdled, but she was right. He needed her, and hell, he trusted her, so it was time to reveal it all. "This is me."

He waited for the horror, the speculation ... but her eyes narrowed as her gaze touched the twisted flesh on the side of his jaw, his neck, his ear. The scar carving back through the side of his skull.

"Those aren't new," she finally whispered.

"No. They're old. Very old."

"Who did this?" she whispered.

"Before I tell—show you—more, I have to call another spell." He took the three breaths needed, then called his concealing spell.

Vella shivered as magic brushed past her, leaving goosebumps in its wake. "What did you do? I felt something."

"I hid this conversation from any magic sight. No fore-seer will ever be able to see this conversation in their visions."

"You have a *spell* for that?" Vella's eyes went wide. "And you took three breaths, so that's why you had to drop the glamour—you can't do the hiding spell at the same time."

He nodded. "I was sixteen when the Council's hit squad—today they're called the Special Investigators—came for my father and mother. Three witches: two Elixirs and a Div. And when I arrived in London to track down my parents, the same hit squad decided to make a lesson of me to the rest of the Magicae children, so they poured acid over me."

Vella recoiled, clamped a hand over her mouth, stifled the gasp he still heard.

"Yeah, it was fucking awful." Even that was an under-statement. But what else could he say? "Mind you, they only let me survive because my powers hadn't fully grown yet, and they didn't know what I was. And I can see your question—what am I? Go on, ask it again, Vella. What am I?"

"What are you?" Her whisper made the hairs on the back of his neck prick, but he welcomed her horror. She wanted the truth—now she was getting it.

He focused on his elemental power, and while it wasn't at surge level yet, he drew it forth enough to be visible in his veins.

"The stars." Vella froze. "They're everywhere now. Your hands, your face, not just your eyes. What are they? What are you?"

"I communicate with every natural element in our world. Air. Water. Earth. Fire. That power is in my blood, literally. It becomes visible when I draw it forward or if it has been unused for too long. Mostly, anyway."

Vella's eyes narrowed. "What magic is that?"

"It's not. I'm a Magicae, yes. But this is no spell." He held his breath. "I'm a Druid."

Vella stared at him for so long he wasn't sure she'd heard him. "Fuck. Off."

"It's the truth."

"Druids are extinct—"

"Not extinct. Living and breathing right in front of you. Although, I may well be the last."

"So, this is your big secret? Why?"

"You know why, Vella. Your aunt—the Council—would never let me continue to exist if they knew the truth. My power would be too much of a threat. So, I keep it hidden, along with my scars, far from their sight."

"But you're the Magicae Councilor—you're a spellcaster."

"I'm both. I told you my mother came from the woods the day she met my father. She came from the woods because she was a Druid. There's a dark energy opening in the woods, and she came through."

"They say the Druids are abominations," she whispered. "And that you—your people—created the vampires."

"That's what the Council teaches, but it's not the case."

"Then why hide it?"

"Because the Council decreed us the enemy." Shit. The stakes were too fucking vital for him to fuck this up. His throat thickened under the need to get this right—the weight of the risk if he got it wrong. "I have already exposed so much by giving you the trust that I have so far. One word from you to Ellaine could undo everything I've worked for."

"What ... what are you working for?"

"I have a plan to give witchkind their lives back."

SWEET FRIGGING GODDESS. She's just had sex with a Druid who was also a son of the rebel group who had killed Vella's parents. And Vella's own aunt had killed his family and assaulted him in the most horrific, vile way when he was still a kid.

"How could she do that?" The whispered words were out before she could catch them. Because what a stupid question—and irrelevant, right now, anyway. Aunt Ellaine had done this. Had killed an entire room full of witches, and then attacked a teenager for going to get his murdered parents' bodies.

The certainty of that truth echoed through her.

But Matthias seemed to understand because his hand tightened on hers.

"You know, the witchcraft books Aunt Ellaine gave us as kids always referred to the rebellion like 'witches were taught right from wrong.' But in fact, they were murdered. And injured. My aunt did that. Did this." Hot bile rushed up her throat, and she shoved it away, breathed deep till she had control again.

"Ellaine and Monty washed it all away. They ordered every coven to hand over their individual grimoires to erase their histories—and those who didn't comply were footed into capitulation. They banned any books that ever mentioned the coup, and they wrote their own accounts of what happened, to the point they almost succeeded in covering up their atrocities. Every single horrific act they perpetrated on my family, on anyone who allied with Mors Dicen and stood up to the Council."

"And now? You're telling me this ... showing me yourself—why?"

"Why you? Because I care for you. About you. Vella,

you are fucking spectacular. And I'm not talking about your eyes or your hair or the freckles that somehow dance across your cheekbones. All my life, I've been responsible for the safety and lives of others. And then there you were —fierce. Independent. Taking no shit. Sure as fuck taking no prisoners. And not really needing me at all."

"We were meant to hate each other." A half sob, half laugh, escaped her. "Goddess, Matt, after our coven's histories, we should hate each other, but—"

"I thought I did, and gods, I tried to. Then you went and fought like the lioness you are that night in my bedroom. You lied to me, tried to seduce me to cover up stealing from me."

"I did. And I would do it again." She lifted her chin.

"You called me a cold-blooded killer."

"You were. Are."

"You blackmailed me—" He rubbed his thumb over her palm.

"You blackmailed me first."

"You fought for your sister, for Brianna. For me."

"And I will again every time I have to."

"See, Vella? How could I possibly hate you? You are breathtaking. And I'm so fucking grateful to have had this time with you. Since the moment we met, I swear my eyes betrayed me every time I looked at you—those stars? That's the Druid power in me, drawn to you like some fucking ancient moth drawn to the light because there was no other way to live. And yes, I'm greedy and ruthless, and I will fucking annihilate anyone who ever thinks about hurting you. And if you want to take them apart yourself, which you are more than capable of, I'll deliver them to your threshold and help you bury the bodies."

"Matt." Her eyes gleamed, and she reached up and cupped his jaw.

He kissed her palm. "You don't have to say a single fucking thing. My words were my gift to you, not a burden you have to reply to or even acknowledge. And that's why I told you—showed you. You asked, and I've answered."

"And now? There's more, isn't there? More to why you're after the runes. Tell me everything. And you haven't misplaced your trust in me. After what Aunt Ellaine did to you? I will never let you or your coven be her victims ever again. And I get it now—it's not just your parents who were resisting, is it?"

He shook his head, eyes watchful. Body tense.

"Matt ... what do you want from me?"

"To help me ensure that every witch has the choice on how to live their life without the Council telling them how and what magic they can practice."

"But how do you do that?"

"It starts with Ellaine not getting any more arcane power sources—everything you stole for the covens in the past, that has weakened the remaining covens."

Oh shit. Vella ... Vella had been the bad guy. Everything she'd ever taken had been hurting witchkind. Not helping them.

The bile rushed up again, but she forced it down. "I want to fight." She leaped to her feet. "I'm going to use the bone runes to save Sara myself. And then I'm joining you."

"You'll stand up against Ellaine?"

"Sure as shit I won't be standing with her. After what she's done? She needs to be held accountable. Everyone needs to know—"

"Vella, I get your anger—gods but I get that—but you have to step carefully. If Ellaine gets any suspicion of what you're thinking, she will stop you."

"You want me to lie to her?"

"Yes. Hell yes. Why do you think I pretend to be meek

and mild and harmless around her and the rest of the Council? They must believe I'm not a threat; otherwise, they'll take me out and, possibly, the rest of my coven. So yes—you need to lie. And I have somewhere you and Sara can stay while you work out what you do next."

"The lake house? We might need to get further away—"

"No, here, in the UK. Madgewick, my family home, is south of Glastonbury. I think you'd like it, and you and Sara can stay there as long as you need."

Holy sweet goddess. Sara healthy, and both of them free to live their lives ... and finally helping other witches instead of hurting them.

"Done." She kissed him hard. Tasted hope and, maybe, the hint of a future she'd never dared imagine.

"You are amazing, Velvet Knight. Come on. Let's get going; we have a clue to find."

27

It was well into the night when Matt parked in a dimly lit multi-story parking lot in Covent Garden. He glanced around, made sure no poison-wielding assassins—or Darklings—lurked in the shadows as they reached the street level. "Let's stay in the light wherever possible."

"Fine by me," Vella murmured. "How far to this place?

"Ten-minute walk. We can't get any closer because this entire precinct is zoned pedestrian only." He eyed the dark smudges under her eyes. "I know it's late, but are you okay to do this? We could find somewhere to bunk down tonight and come back tomorrow if you need to rest."

"Define okay." She wiped her hair off her face where the breeze caught the dark strands. "We survived a poison attack. I'm tired and grimy, and haven't changed clothes in way too long. But ... we think we've figured out the third clue, and I have four days left to get the bone runes back to the US. No way are we stopping now."

They dodged another group of humans, and Matt

paused, pretending to check his cell while regarding them until after they'd passed by.

"What are you looking for?"

"Making sure we're not being followed."

"Shit." Vella tightened her coat. "Let's get this next clue and then get out of here."

"I like the way you think, Rapunzel." He strode beside her as they wove around yet more people toward their destination. "When you focus, you're all in. Plenty of people would've called it quits by now."

"Wow. Praise from the mighty Magicae himself."

"Not so mighty," he murmured. Mighty would've been stopping the attacks at the gallery. Saving Dorothy back in New York.

"Actually, mighty is a perfect word. You stopped that assassin at your party, you stopped the guys coming for Brianna at your lake house, and you got us out of the attack at the gallery. You've driven us partway across the country and gotten us back to London. Got *me* coffee and food—and I'm your enemy. So yeah, I'm going with mighty."

"Vella, stop." He grabbed her hand and turned to face her. The tip of her nose was pink, and her breath steamed into the air, but her golden eyes were clear and bright.

"What?"

I'm still lying to you, using you, and am nothing like what you think I am. Here you are doing everything in your power to save your sister's life—an act I can only commend you for, but if I'm right and your sister is poisoned, I can't let you save her.

"Nothing," he finally murmured. "Here, it's cold, and I could do with the body heat."

"Same."

She nestled into his side, and damn but she was the

perfect fit. Except shite, she couldn't be the perfect fit. Just look at what had happened to everyone else he cared for —let alone what he had to do with the bone runes.

No, Vella could never be the perfect fit for him.

"Matt, I said how much longer? Cold air stuffing up your hearing?"

"Yes," he lied. "Rose is the next street up. I can't get over how many people are out and about."

"They really aren't worried about Darklings."

"Right now, neither am I. Poison-throwing assassins are my concern."

"Good point," Vella muttered. They turned left onto a cobblestone road, buildings closing in around them. "And wow, this is an old part of the city."

"A lot of original buildings here. What did you say you found out about the pub?"

"Their website says the Lamb & Flag is one of London's oldest original breweries. The current pub has been there since the eighteen hundreds."

"Contemporary with the rest of the clues, then."

"Kind of. They underwent a renovation in the fifties, but the original brickwork is still there."

"Shit. Our clue was put in place before the works."

"Think they messed it up?" Her face fell.

"No bloody idea. But we're here, so let's find out."

The pub itself served customers from a hole in the wall facing Rose Street, but it also had a door with the pub's name stenciled onto the glass, and it led to a thankfully warm, cozy interior, currently packed to the brim with beings.

Paintings and photographs filled the room, with a bar taking up one wall. Behind the bar, a mirrored counter with glass shelves held different-sized bottles and vases. Another door led further into the building, and a bench seat ran along the back wall, with a mix of low and high tables crammed into the rest of the space.

A few people looked up and mostly, they all checked out Vella, of course—who wouldn't?—but all went back to their drinks and conversations.

"No one's throwing poisonous bubbles," Vella muttered. "Yay for small wins."

Matt held back a laugh. "Let's get a drink. Try to blend in."

Vella squeezed between customers at the bar, then turned back to him. "Guinness?"

He nodded, and a few minutes later, she handed him a pint of rich, thickly scented, stout beer.

"How did you know?" He took a sip.

"At your lake house, Clay mentioned your favorite stout."

"And you remembered?"

"Of course. Details matter." Vella took a sip of the apple cider she'd ordered for herself. "Now, where's the clue?"

"A table's free in the corner. Let's grab it and look around from there." He strode over, beating another couple by a fraction of a second.

Vella looked around as she sat. "This next part of the clue has me stuck. *Neath sun and moon they make their meal, within the lie the truth reveal.* So, we're looking for somewhere you can eat?"

"And a lie. A lie about where you eat?"

"What if the lie means to lie on something, like a couch or a bed? Are—or were—there rooms here?"

"Good point." Hell. "What about the *make their meal* part? This room is where people eat."

Vella scanned the walls. "There are a lot of artworks

here that appear old—look at those on the other wall, along with the early photographs."

"You're the art historian. Can you tell if they're real?"

"If I get up close, I can try." She left their table, squeezed between more customers, and stopped at a framed image. A moment later, she took out her burner cell, took a photo and darted back to their table.

"Look at this!" She put the cell on the table and enlarged an image on the screen.

"Shite," he breathed. "It's the pub."

Vella regarded him for a moment, then nodded. "And it must've been taken before the renovation since you can still see the brick walls." Vella whirled around to the bar, then back to the cell phone. "I see it!"

"What?"

"The clue isn't another painting—look behind the bar right now, and in the picture, you can just make it out. A vase, thirty inches tall, covered in gold gilt decorations at the top, and in the middle, facing us, is a scene of a couple eating a picnic, a shining sun overhead."

"You can make that out all from here?"

"Not really. But it doesn't matter because I've seen that vase before—it's a famous piece of ceramic from the seventeenth century."

"Then it's too early for our clue unless the mark from the riddle was added later?"

"No, the real vase is part of a private collection—which is how I recognized the design—the vase here must be a reproduction."

"The lie—that's the lie part."

"Exactly. I bet there's a scene on the other side of the vase with the couple in a lover-like embrace on the same picnic blanket but under a moon instead."

"Shite, Vella, you did it."

"*We* did it. Now, about the vase. The clue says inside—we need to look in it."

"Wait—where are you going?"

"To ask to see the vase, of course." She rolled her eyes. "Seriously, how else are we gonna see inside it?"

"I'll go with you—"

"No, you stay here. Mind our table in case we need to hang around." She darted through the customers and, in time, made her way to the bar. She spoke to the guy behind the bar, who shook his head, but then shouted a name. A woman came over, and she also shook her head.

Moments later, Vella dropped into the seat opposite him. "That was a no, in case you missed it."

"At least you tried. But don't worry, I'll get you that look."

"Magic?" She eased back in her seat.

"Time to put your distrust of spellcraft away, Vella. Unless you can think of another way to look at that vase?"

"Fine. Magic, it is. What are you going to do? You can't hurt them."

"A sleeping spell. As if I'd hurt anyone here."

"On them all?" She glanced around. "At the same time?"

Annoyance bit at her lack of trust. "You do recall I'm the Magicae Councilor, right? And you know how that works—passing a test of your magic strength before you can claim a seat?"

"I mean, yes, I know you have a lot of power. But there are twenty-plus people here."

"Let me worry about that—you see how to get behind the bar. And find an alternate way out of here, just in case."

"Sheesh, bossy much?" Vella whispered.

"When I'm spelling an entire room of people? Yes," he whispered back. "Go, I need to focus."

Now, how to conduct a mass sleeping spell without physical contact? Twenty-two adults, at thirty seconds for maximum effect per adult, he'd usually need over ten minutes. But he needed them all to sleep at the same time. So, he'd need to adjust the ritual ... Possible. But harder. A fuckload harder. And it would take every ounce of his two-breath spell control. He'd better be done with additional magic for the night after this.

"Done." Vella dropped back into her seat. "Through the internal door, the bar entry is to the left, emergency exit is on the right via a rear lane."

"In that case, let's do this now before this place gets any busier. To start the spell, I'll need to close my eyes, so you watch the room," he murmured. "And make sure no one falls off their seats."

"Falls off their—what do you mean?"

"You'll see. But, Rapunzel, and this is important; once the spell is set, you need to move quietly and fast; this spell won't hold for long and could easily break."

Matt inhaled and exhaled once, then took the deepest breath he could, and with his lungs full, sent a thread of energy from himself to the man beside him, then kept going from person to person until he was connected to everyone in the room and behind the bar.

Chest close to bursting, he ripped through the sleeping spell and sent it along the invisible threads of power.

His breath whooshed out. He opened his eyes, and one by one, the people in the room nodded off.

"Frigging goddess, you did it," Vella breathed.

"I'm connected ... to them all." Tension dug into him at every nerve ending. Shit. One stray breath and he'd lose the spell. "Like a ... spiderweb. Shit—she's falling. Don't ... touch her skin to skin."

"On it." Vella darted to a woman sliding off her stool and eased her to the ground.

"Go." Matt gritted his teeth. "Straining to hold the spell ... to so many people at once."

Vella took off, disappeared through the internal doorway, and a moment later emerged behind the bar.

He poured more energy into the spell as Vella climbed up onto the countertop, took the vase off the shelf and peered inside.

Little tugs pulled on the threads of his spiderweb.

"Vella?" he hissed. "People are waking up. Can't hold on for much longer."

Vella frowned. Fuck, that wasn't good. Then her eyes widened. "Inside," she whispered. "Shit." She ran her hands around the base of the vase. "If I make a loud noise, will they wake up?"

He eyed his spellees. "Yes."

"Then I'm coming out to you." She got down from the counter, then joined him moments later with the vase.

"Whatever you're going to do," he gritted out. "Do it."

"Crap. Watch out." She moved to the center of the room and threw the vase onto the floor.

Smash.

An instant tug on his spell dragged Matt sideways, and he stumbled to the table. He wrestled with the incantation, but the spiderweb of energy connecting him to everyone disintegrated.

Customers and staff raised their heads and blinked, almost like in a cartoon, as if they'd been asleep for too long on a hot day.

"I see something!" Vella grabbed a shard of the vase from the ground. "Got it."

"Then it's time to go." He grabbed their coats, wove around the pub patrons, still listing about and looking like they'd had too much to drink, and eased the door to Rose Street open.

Plenty of people were still around, so he and Vella should blend easily enough.

Three familiar figures rounded the corner of the street, the same three who'd attacked them at Matt's lake house. Their jackets were open. Buzz Cut pointed at the Lamb & Flag, and as he did, his jacket shifted, revealing a shoulder holster with a handgun.

Fuck. Who were these assholes?

Matt shoved Vella back into the pub, ushered her through the sleepy crowd toward the internal door. "Our friends from the lake house are outside. Rear exit—now!"

"Again?" She craned her neck to get a look—then froze, resisting his pushes on her back and staring at the floor.

"Vella? Vella! Go! They've got guns. It's too risky to take them on with so many people around."

Vella stopped pushing back against him and ran to an exit door at the back of the corridor.

They ran up the rear alleyway, reached a gap in the buildings and slipped through, emerging back out on Rose Street.

"Any sign of them?" Vella whispered.

"No."

"Then we need to wait and go back. As we were running out, I saw a chunk of the vase's base on the floor, and it had something else in it. I was so focused on getting the piece of vase with the Ogham mark that I didn't look at the rest of the vase."

"What was it?"

"Not sure, but it looked several inches long." Her lips tightened. "We need to see whatever that thing is."

"Shit." Go back, now?

"Come on, Matt. We've come so far."

"All right, I get it. Just let me look and figure out a way." He peered around the corner of the building and down the street past the pub. Maybe—

The trio who'd attacked them raced onto Rose Street from the pub's front door, one of them holding the remnants of the vase. Matt ducked back into the laneway.

"What? What did you see?"

"The fuckers chasing you and Brianna. They've got the rest of the vase."

"We have to go after them—"

"Whoa, slow down, Rapunzel." Matt grabbed Vella's arm before she could reach the street. "They have guns, remember?"

Screams echoed from the front of the pub.

What the fuck now?

Another scream. Another.

Matt eased around the corner again. People were streaming out of multiple establishments along Rose Street, all running toward the main road, many with bloody gashes all over their bodies.

"What is it?" Vella hissed.

"Good quest—"

From the shadows under the eaves of the pub and the buildings beside it, pitch-black humanlike forms emerged ... They grew larger, longer, split into two, then three, four ... more and more until they covered the walls and windows lining Rose Street.

And every time they touched a human, that person's skin split open in long, thin, bloody slices.

"*Darklings.*" Vella tugged at his arm. "What are you doing? We need to go the other way."

"I need to help the people in the pub. I put them to sleep, remember? They're still waking up and could be slashed to ribbons."

"What? You're going in *there*?"

"Listen!" He grabbed her hand. "Run to the streetlamp near the main road—the fuckers who are after you went the other way. I won't be long."

"Uh-uh, I should go with you."

Risk Vella? Now? "I can't. You don't understand. You're too important."

"Matthias, I honestly don't think I'm any safer standing there than if I'm with you. And what kind of magic do you have to take on Darklings anyway? Can you put them to sleep?"

"This isn't a sleeping spell. This magic is far more deadly." Fuck, he better be doing the right thing here. "Fine. But stay close—I want your hand on my back at all times."

By all the goddamned stars, he'd better be doing the right thing.

Another scream echoed from the pub. Vella grasped his jacket.

He took off.

28

H old on to Matthias? As Vella clutched at the material of his jacket in one hand, she couldn't imagine ever letting him go as they ran back toward the monsters.

The Darklings spread along the pub's wall, their humanesque shapes increasing in size even further, oozing into the pub through the street-facing bar.

More people stumbled outside. More gashes. More screams.

"Fuck. Vella, remember, at my back. Nowhere else."

"At your back. Got it." Frig, she wasn't going anywhere else.

With Matthias filling her view, Vella followed him inside The Lamb and Flag.

The first Vella saw of the Darklings was midnight shape after shape, so dark, there was no definition of body part, not even their eyes—if they even had eyes—and they seemed to be sniffing, or licking, the walls.

And as one, the shapes stopped whatever the goddess they were doing and swung to face Matthias.

"Matt," Vella hissed.

"Stay still." He drew in two fast breaths. "Light the path that I take, as I will so to make."

A tiny circle of light erupted from nothing in the air above Matt's hand.

"Witchlight," Vella breathed. Then she snapped her mouth shut because Matt was drawing in even more—this time huge—breaths.

"Enlarge the light to hide this night."

The orb floating above his hands pulsed once, twice, three times, and an acrid scent hit the air right before the orb exploded in a massive burst of radiance so bright Vella shielded her eyes.

The Darklings reared back; booming roars and shrieks echoed off the walls and retreated across the bar.

"Vella, let go," Matt ordered. "I need to go after them." He shrugged, and the moment she took her hand off his jacket, he leaped up onto the bar, his orb scorching bottles and glassware, but he kept forcing the Darklings back, following them through the door to the street-side bar and disappearing from her view.

Vella's heart punched hard in her chest. Shit.

She ran for the street.

Human screams and shouts echoed in the distance, but right there, hisses and shrieks filled her ears as the Darklings disappeared back through the eaves, hounded by Matt's glowing, pulsing orb.

Matt stood on the cobblestones, hands outstretched, tension stiffening every part of him.

"Vella?" Matt's voice had turned hoarse. "Can't hold this for long. Get ready to ... run."

"Fuck that. How can I help?"

"Can't," he ground out. "Almost—" He dropped to his

knees on the cobblestones. Head down. Body swaying. His witchlight blinked out.

"Matt!" But she couldn't run to him because the Darklings were still there—not many, but still deadly. Still bubbling and shrieking and hissing, reaching out at her with humanlike hands.

Sweet goddess, she had to stop them, but Vella didn't have a witchlight to blind them with. She shoved a hand into her purse and knocked the lid off Brianna's box. The lid fell out of her purse, but she didn't have time to worry about it.

"Darklings are here," she hissed. "Can you help?"

"So?" Brianna snorted like Vella was an idiot. "Why would—"

"No time. They're slicing everyone to pieces. Is there a Mors Dicen thing we can do to stop them?"

"Touch them."

"*What?*"

"You asked. I'm telling. Now touch them!"

Shit. Shit, shit, shit. Vella ran for the Darklings and reached out for the nearest Darkling's hand, squeezed her eyes shut—

Energy surged through her. All at once it seemed as if she were stuffed with too much energy, too much power. The charcoal veil dropped over her vision—just like when she connected with Brianna, but this time, she wasn't touching any bone.

She opened her mouth to cry out for Brianna, to scream at the pressure building inside her—but no sound could get past that roiling, heaving, surging electricity. The charcoal veil turned to black—

And cleared.

Her breath whooshed out, and she spun around—no sign of the Darklings—but damn she felt good. She felt so good—like she'd had a triple shot coffee and a bag of straight sugar all at the same time.

What the hell? And Matt—

He still knelt on the cobblestones. Head bowed. Shoulders slumped. "Matt!"

"Stay back," he whispered.

"Like fuck." She dropped to her knees, but he turned his face away from her. "Where are you hurt?"

"I couldn't save you," he whispered. "Are you hurt?"

"Me? No—"

Vella shifted to see Matt properly, and her stomach dropped. His scars were back.

She swallowed the knot stuck in her throat and focused back on his eyes. "Matt, are you hurt? Did they touch you? Why aren't you looking at me?"

He shook his head, then took a shuddering breath. "Not hurt. Used all my energy on the spells. You, though ... what did you do?" He swayed and she caught him just in time.

And what *had* she done? Zero frigging clue there. One minute, the Darklings had been reaching out for her, the next, they'd been inside her—but instead of splitting her open, they'd somehow dissipated and left her on some kind of high. Almost like she'd absorbed them.

Shit. Was Vella part Darkling now? Fuck. Fuck, fuck, *fuck*. So many questions—and no time to answer them.

"Here, let's get you to your feet. That's it. Lean on me. We need to get out of here before anything else happens." She tightened her grip on her purse. "Shit. I dropped Brianna's lid." She felt around for the shard. "And frig it, the piece of the vase with the clue must've dropped out too. Can you turn? We need to go back."

"Velvet Knight," a voice called from behind them.

The hairs on the back of her neck prickled. She knew that accent.

"Vella, get behind me." Matt wobbled to stand on his own as they shuffled to face the trio from earlier.

Buzz Cut held the piece of the vase Vella had dropped. The other two—surely only a couple of years younger than Vella—stood at Buzz Cut's back.

"If you hurt Velvet in any fucking way, I will take you apart until you're nothing but a speck of dust on the wind."

A thrill raced through Vella. Matt's magic might be exhausted—he might be physically shattered—but she believed every word he said. Was that the Druid in him?

"Mors Dicen." Brianna's voice rang out. "Don't hurt them! They are Mors Dicen."

"What?" Vella froze. "Them? No. No way."

"Vel? What's going on?" Matt's grip on her arm tightened. "Something I need to know here?" His gaze dipped to her purse.

"Wait. You speak to the knife?" Buzz Cut's eyes widened, and he glanced at the two behind him. "She's—"

"What do you want?" Vella stepped forward, but Matt held her tight. "Matt, I need to talk to them—"

"I couldn't protect you before. Like hell I'm not now."

Sirens wailing in the distance grew closer, and the two behind Buzz Cut grabbed his arm. "We need to go," the girl hissed. "We got what we need. Let's get out of here."

They span and ran into the night, and frigging goddess Vella wanted to go after them, but Matt staggered, slumped into her again. Thank fuck for whatever weird energy the Darklings had left her with because she held him up and managed to shuffle them both back down the cobblestones toward the carpark.

Emergency Services met them at the end of Rose Street, but since Matt had no actual injuries, Vella lied and claimed he was drunk, and they were let through without minimal issue—which made sense given how many people did need help.

Although, thank the goddess, there were no signs of anyone being killed.

With his weight bearing down on her, they staggered and stumbled all the way back to the car.

Vella got the keys, wrestled Matt into the passenger seat, then ran around to the driver's side.

"Matt? Where do we go now?"

"Madgewick," he whispered.

"Fine, but how—" Well, shit, he was out. Sleeping deeply, chest rising and falling.

Focus, Vel. Madgewick ... back in Scotland, he'd said his home was south of Glastonbury, so she brought up directions on her cell phone. She'd need more information on where to go once they got closer, but at least Matt could sleep till then.

Although, as she steered the car out of the parking lot, Vella darted another look at Matt.

Aunt Ellaine's comment from the ball at Matt's New York home played through her mind ... *Magicae use spells to make themselves look better.*

Sadness made her stomach knot. How awful to feel like he had to hide himself. But crap—he'd been hiding himself all along? How much magic did he have to live under a spell like that?

A LITTLE OVER three hours later, with her eyes stinging from the fight to keep them open and the air con cold enough to freeze, Vella fought off her gazillionth yawn and followed her cell phone map for the Glastonbury turnoff. Matt didn't even stir.

Mors Dicen witches. Darklings. Lost clues.

"Daughter? Did you hear me? I said the Darklings never hurt people in my day. I can only think there is some imbalance they are responding to."

"I heard you for the last two hours," she muttered under her breath.

But even Brianna hadn't been able to explain what had happened between Vella and the Darklings. And if Brianna didn't know ... What if Vella was the problem? What if Vella was somehow evil or had something terrible inside her that had drawn the Darklings to her?

And why hadn't Matt let her talk to the trio—damn it, she might've talked them around and gotten them to give back the last piece of the vase.

And more importantly, what the hell did they do now? She had to get that last clue piece.

"But have you listened?" Brianna continued, thankfully oblivious to Vella's thoughts. "Your words are slurred, and I can barely hear you. Clearly, you need to rest. Gods know I do. How is the Magicae?"

Vella glanced at Matt again. "Still out cold."

"Ah well, that is to be expected with spellcasters—their physical energy feeds their spellcraft so they will tire easily."

Easily? What Matt had done had saved countless lives.

"What feeds Mors Dicen?" The question was out before she could catch it.

"Our magic is of the earth, which is why grounding yourself in the grass or dirt or rocks is important. Do you have much of that in the place where you live?"

"I love to run in parks—but I don't have a garden in my actual house."

Brianna tsked again. "That needs to change. You cannot access your magic properly unless you feed it. You understand how magic works for each of the great covens, surely?"

"Maybe. Actually, no." The official Divinator training books hadn't covered the other covens.

"*What?*"

Vella winced. "You screeched that loud enough to wake Matthias."

"Pft. Nothing will wake a spellcaster who has depleted their magic until their physical energy is restored. Daughter? I heard you yawn. You are tired. This vehicle that you command ... if you fall asleep while steering, what will happen?"

"It's called driving. And if I crash right now? Things will get even more fucked up."

"Then you must rest. We shall continue your Mors Dicen education at a later time."

"But I still don't understand what happened with the Darklings—you just keep saying they're part of my magic, and I still have zero clue what that means."

"And *I* cannot explain it any other way. Now, I am almost asleep, and I do not wish to leave you alone until I know you are safe."

"I'm good."

"Pft. You just yawned again."

No shit. Between physical fatigue dragging at her eyelids, the storm of emotions colliding in her chest from all the night's revelations, and what she could describe as a crash coming down off that frigging Darkling-induced high, falling asleep at the wheel out of sheer exhaustion was a real risk.

"There's a gas station ahead. Well lit. I'll stop there—just for a few minutes."

"About time. I shall rest, too."

Finally, Vella pulled off the highway or motorway or whatever they called it here and pulled into one of the few empty parking spaces right on the edge of the lot near a small grassy parkland with just enough light to keep the Darklings at bay.

So many questions, but right now, she needed to close her eyes for a few minutes ...

LOUD VOICES WOKE VELLA, and she cricked her neck as she opened her eyes—oh shit. Still dark outside. Her jacket covered her like a blanket. And no sign of Matthias.

Her stomach dropped, and she fumbled for her cell: almost four a.m. So she'd slept for two hours. Sucked that it felt like two minutes. But more importantly, where was Matt?

She scrambled out of the car, yanking on her jacket and pulling it tight—and froze as a figure at the far end of the park, barely visible in the tiny amount of light permeating that far, turned around. Relief made her breath whoosh out.

"Matt?" She made her way over to him, scanning the area carefully. The lights were dim enough over here to make this risky.

"Vella." Matt turned, and his glittering silver gaze made her breath catch. And it took a full three seconds before the lack of scars on his face registered.

"You're better." A shiver shook her—from the cold, relief, or both, who knew?

"I am. Thank you for getting us out of there."

She crossed her arms. "Well, don't go doing it again.

Having you pass out from magic exhaustion—which I didn't even know was a thing—isn't high on my wish list."

"And you?" His gaze traveled with precision from her head all the way to her feet. "Vella, I saw what happened. You ... absorbed the Darklings. Without a single injury."

How? Why?

His unspoken questions hung between them, but she was too tired to try to answer—and what would she say anyway? She couldn't answer because she had zero frigging clue and what did it even matter when they had a huge problem right there and then.

"You're cold. Here." He stepped closer, and she gave in to the urge to sink against his chest. His sigh echoed through her. "You need to sleep, Rapunzel. You looked after me, now let me look after you. We can figure the rest out tomorrow—shit, today."

"There's no time for sleep, Matt. They took the last puzzle piece. We have to get it back. Without it ..." A lump caught in her throat.

Without that last piece, she couldn't complete the puzzle. Which meant not finding the runes. Not saving Sara. Tears stung Vella's eyes and left an icy trail down her cheeks.

"Hey, we've come this far. We're not giving up yet, Rapunzel. We just keep going—and believe me, I've got plenty of experience with persistence."

Hope latched onto his words. To the certainty in his tone and the strength in his arms crushing her to him.

"So what do we do?"

"We go to Madgewick as planned. But I just got a message from Amelia. She lives here in Glastonbury, asking me to go over now."

"Wait. At four a.m.?"

"Yeah. Which means it's serious. Now, want to tell me what Brianna said?"

"The trio who took the last puzzle piece? They're Mors Dicen. And why the Darklings flooded into me and disappeared? She had no idea."

"Fuck." Matt's arms tightened around her.

29

"So, tell me about Glastonbury?" Vella asked as Matt turned down a narrow lane, rundown buildings lining either side, and stopped beneath one of the few working lampposts. What lights were on revealed a town worn down. Darkened shopfronts. Uncared for. "I know it's nighttime, but I thought it would be ... more magical. Vibrant. At your party, Clay mentioned how this was a town for beings of all kinds and witches from all covens."

"It used to be." His mouth tightened.

"It's ... quieter than I thought it would be."

But Matt didn't say anything more, and by the time she'd joined him on the sidewalk, he'd shrugged his coat on, the dark material swirling around his legs like a mysterious, dangerous barrier, and while the grimace was gone, his usual casual expression wasn't in place.

Instead, his face was flat. Expression*less*.

"Matt, what's going on?" A chill raced down her back. "I don't like this."

"Just stay close. And don't tell anyone, *anyone*, you're from the Div coven."

Why would she? Right now, Vella was a daughter of two covens—how and why, she had no clue—but she couldn't hide from the truth anymore.

"This way." Matt headed down the laneway. Footsteps followed them.

"Matt, do you see those guys? They're watching us ... and not in a good way."

"Just locals checking us out. Nothing to worry about. The shop's right there, the green door across the laneway."

Warm, sage-scented air welcomed Vella at the shop's threshold, but then Matthias nudged her all the way in, and she caught herself on a long counter filled with a sparse selection of herbs and crystals.

A woman with dark curly hair, wearing black leggings and a fitted tunic embellished with a wild rose print, looking mysterious and stunning and vivid, stood with her hands on her hips, no amusement on her face, and a cat at her feet. Her gaze locked on Matt.

"Matty." The woman's shoulders dipped like she was relieved to see him. "Achelous Matthias Medea, what by Matronae are you doing?"

"Ak-u-lo—who?" Vella spun back to Matt.

"Amelia," he murmured. The woman launched across the shop, wrapped her arms around him and held on tight. And he hugged her back.

Ugh. What was it about this man and women throwing themselves at him?

Matt made a fast introduction between Vella and Amelia, but before Vella could say anything, the shop's front door opened, and the two guys who'd been watching them in the laneway stopped on the threshold.

"Amelia? You okay?" The oldest stepped forward. "Oh, Madgewick. Sorry. Didn't realize it was you. We thought some Divs were back causing shite."

"All good here, Jack and Travis. Thanks." Matt shook their hands. "Good to see you, lads. And no Divs here."

Vella's stomach turned to lead.

"And if I was a ... Div?" Vella couldn't help herself from asking after the shop door closed.

"This town would shut up shop fast, and you'd be moved out of here without a welcome. But Matty would never travel with a Div, so not an issue."

Never travel with a Div? Did half Div count? Vella traded glances with Matt—except he was looking around the bare-shelved shop, not at Amelia.

"Still as tough as ever?" Matt sighed.

"Out here, yes. I keep the façade for any Divs or Elixirs passing through that catch us unawares, but the good stuff is out back. They haven't stifled us completely, Matt. Don't worry. And we get the money you send us—"

"Amelia. You said we need to talk. What do you need?"

"Actually, *you* should come out back." Amelia's gaze flicked between Vella and Matt.

"Can you wait here while we have a word?" Matt squeezed Vella's arm.

As Matt and the stunning Amelia disappeared through a door—presumably into a back room—Vella stared at the witch's shop.

Bare shelves, indeed. But more importantly, why would Matt send this hedge witch money? Her stomach roiled again. Was this all because of the Council and Aunt Ellaine?

MATT FOLLOWED Amelia into the back room and took a deep breath of spice, herbs and potions. "You really do have the good stuff out here. Not even twenty years can fade the memories of the smell of this back room. Your mom always made the most amazing spice and fruit breads, and we'd be running around, but she never minded having us underfoot—"

"Matt, stop. There are some people here to see your friend." Amelia glanced at the ceiling. "But before I give them the all clear to come down, we need to talk. Just who *is* your friend?"

"They're here for Vella?" Matt's hackles rose. "Ams, who are they? What do they want—"

"Calm down. They're not dangerous—you know I wouldn't do that to you. But they want to see *her* ... your friend. They think they know her. And I just—I just need to know who you're traveling with, Matty."

"Fuck." He could go upstairs right now, but that would be breaching Amelia's trust, and she was too good a friend to do that without it being a life-or-death matter. "Okay. But if I think they're a threat—"

"To your friend? Or the cause?"

"It's ... complicated. Just tell me what you need to know before we can meet whoever's hiding upstairs."

"I need to know if you've brought a stinking Div into my house. I told them no way. Matty travel with a Div, let alone bring one into my shop? Never. Not the Matthias Achelous Medea I know. Matty? Matt." The color drained from her cheeks. "No. Tell me you didn't bring a—"

Guilt swirled in his gut.

Bloody hell, but what did he say? The fact was, they were in Amelia's shop, and right now, he'd just exposed Amelia to a deadly risk by bringing Vella here. This was a part of the leadership that he hated. How to know when the right time was to make a decision, when no matter which way he turned, there were risks and obstacles and the possibility of so many lives wiped out if he got it wrong.

"Vella's aunt is the Divinator Councilor. We're working together."

"Fuck off!" Amelia shoved him away.

"Ams. Amelia! Just hear me out. I told you this for a reason. We need you. I need you. And yes—this is for *business*. I wouldn't be doing this for any other reason, I swear to you."

"You want me to endanger my entire family for a Div?"

"Vella is more than just a Div. She's also ... a Mors Dicen."

Amelia's face went even more pale, and she stumbled back to the counter.

"And I'm trusting you ..." Matt took a deep breath. "Trusting you with that knowledge because she's in just as much danger if someone finds out before I—we—can finish this."

"The Div is part of ... the business?"

"I can't say, Amelia. I'm walking a tightwire of information here; too much bleed in any direction and everything we've fought for goes up in smoke. I just—can you do this?"

Amelia blew out a long breath. "Fuck. I mean, yes, I can. But I'm not leaving her alone in my shop any longer. She's already seen enough."

"What about whoever's upstairs?"

"We'll deal with them later. Right now, I need to talk to your ... friend."

VELLA WHIRLED around when the door to the backroom slammed open, and Amelia stormed into the shop, her hands fisted at her side, Matt following close on her heels, his eyes wary.

"You shouldn't be here," Amelia hissed. "For Matt, I'll take the job. But if you tell one other fucking Div about what I do—"

"Oh, for frig's sake, you called us here. Why would I say anything?"

"Because you're a stinking Div who looks down on everyone else."

"I am not looking down on you," Vella gritted out. She faced Matt. "If this is what we're here for, we can leave. I'm not putting up with this BS."

"Are you really a Mors Dicen?" Amelia snarled.

Vella's breath punched from her like she'd been bashed in the gut, and she shot Medea her best glare. "You told her?"

"It was necessary. Believe me, I wouldn't have said anything otherwise. And here's the thing—you need an alternative for carrying Brianna, and Amelia is the best person in town to help us find a lead-lined sheath."

"You want me to get a Mors Dicen sheath?" Amelia took a step backward, and her gaze shot to the ceiling. "We can't—I can't—if I get caught with lead-lined goods, I'll be taken, my shop and house seized at the very least."

"I know, Amelia, I know. I just need to know if it's possible."

"I can try—of course I can try for you. But ..." She glared back at Vella. "You really are a Mors Dicen?"

"Matt, are you sure *sure* about this?" Vella asked.

"We can trust Ams."

Pft. Matt might be in safe hands with Amelia, but judging by her glare at Vella, Vella was another question.

Although shit, she'd come this far. She reached into her purse and took out Brianna's box. "It appears I have some Mors Dicen somewhere in my family tree."

"Daughter, where are we now?"

"In Glastonbury. I'm talking with a hedge witch who Matt thinks can help us get a sheath so I can keep you on me instead of in my purse."

"Well, that is a smart idea. I am liking your Magicae more and more." Hers ... Damn if she didn't like the sound of that. "Vella!" Brianna's gasp made the hairs on the back of Vella's hair stand tall. "They're here. I can hear them."

Vella froze. "Who can you hear?"

"Vella?" Matt stilled, and those stars began to whirl in his eyes. "Has Brianna said something?"

"Them," Brianna trilled. "Your fellow Mors Dicen witches. Their voices are weak though—two so indistinct I can barely hear them, but one is clear enough for me to get a message through, nowhere near as powerful as you, though. I have told that one who is the strongest of them all who you are."

"*Brianna*. Who is—"

The backroom door opened, and the trio who'd attacked them at the lake house filed into Amelia's shop.

"We are here, Bone Wielder." Buzz Cut stepped forward. "Your coven."

"Shit. Not out here." Amelia ran to the wall and flicked the lights off. "Everyone into the back room. Now. I'll stay in the shop to keep a watch out."

30

In the sudden silence, Vella stared at Buzz Cut. "Who the frig are you?"

"Who are you?" he whispered.

"And I can answer you both," Brianna cut in. "You are Mors Dicen."

"I am," Vella said. And finally, her heartbeat returned to normal. "At least, partly."

"Vella is a Bone Wielder," Brianna cut in.

"A direct descendant?" Buzz Cut's eyes widened.

"Of that, I am sure. And I am Brianna. Who are you?"

"Brianna! Our elders told us about you. You've been missing for so long—"

"I know," Brianna snapped. "Centuries I stayed in that box. What is your name?"

"I'm Ryan. This is Liam and Ciara. We're not direct descendants of yours, but we're still Mors Dicen."

"But the coven was disbanded," Vella blurted.

"More like wiped out," Ryan spat. "And that's what we needed everyone to believe."

"Why?"

"So that those who lived could searched for our bones —the bones of our ancestors, like Brianna. If anyone knew we were alive, we'd be hunted down and killed by the SI. That's what led us to you, Velvet Knight. Rumors surfaced that the Magicae Councilor had a Mors Dicen relic in his possession, so we started to watch him. And then, last week we were at the Magicae's club when we all had this weird sensation—"

"An itch along your neck?"

"That's right."

"We didn't see anything, but we knew he—or you—had a sacred bone. We started following you then."

"You tracked me to London? And to here? But how?"

"That night I was in your house ... I put a tracker in the lining of your purse." Ryan grimaced and held out his hands. "We couldn't let another Mors Dicen bone fall into the hands of the Divs—and we thought you were a Div."

"I am," Vella whispered. "At least, half—"

"So why are you here now?" Matt stared hard at the trio, his distrust clear.

"When we were at The Lamb and Flag, I heard a Bone Guide—I didn't know it was Brianna, but I recognized the voice as one of our own. That's when I realized you're a Mors Dicen. And there are too few of us left to ignore that." Ryan took an audible breath. "I am twenty-four—and I'm the oldest of our coven. Unless you ..."

"Twenty-three," Vella whispered.

"But you're powerful. Even I can sense it, and knowing you're a Bone Wielder ..."

"Why are you looking at me like that?" Vella glanced between the trio. "Why are you all looking at me like that?"

"You're after the bone runes," Ciara said, her voice soft and lilting with an Irish accent.

"Why do you ask?" If they thought to stop her—

"We know you are. The fact that you're tracking the clues laid by our foremothers tells us everything. And as a Bone Wielder, you are the strongest of us, and if anyone can find a way for us to regather in safety, to rebuild our homes and our families, it is you." Her eyes filled with something like ... hope.

"What—oh no." Vella braced herself against the faith in Ciara's eyes. She had to focus on saving Sara, no one else.

"You'll need these." Ryan took a folded cloth out of his inner pocket and carefully opened it. "This is the piece of porcelain that you dropped back at The Lamb and Flag."

Vella took the shard of the vase and turned it over. Her breath whooshed out as she made out the mark indicating an Ogham letter. It had a single short horizontal line, with five shorter, evenly spaced vertical lines protruding downward. "The final clue."

"Not quite." Ryan took out another piece of cloth and unfolded it, revealing the yellowish, oblong-shaped object she'd glimpsed on the floor among the shattered remnants of the vase before she and Matt had run out of the pub. "It's a scroll, and we believe you need it, too."

"You're just giving them to me?" Relief made Vella's head go light. "Wait. You're Mors Dicen, yet even you don't know where the bone runes are?"

"No one alive does. And the bones of our Bone Guides who did know were all destroyed or lost in the coup twenty years ago." Ryan took a slow breath. "Vella, you are the only one left who can wield bone. Maybe some of our teenagers might grow into that power, but even then, they're years away from being able to. You are literally the only hope of the entire Mors Dicen coven."

"Teenagers. Wait, how many of you are there?"

Ryan glanced at Matt and resolve hardened his expression. "We can't say. We never say. But if the runes can help stop the Divs and Elixirs, and if what Amelia has told us is true, then you two are the right ones to use the bone runes. Just ... fight for us. Please."

Knock, knock. "Matt?" Amelia hissed. "Someone's coming. You all need to get out of here. Now."

"Here, take them." Ryan grabbed Vella's hand and placed both the vase piece and scroll in her palm.

"Wait. Matt, can they come to Madgewick? We need to talk—"

"Of course. But don't follow us directly. No one can know we've met you. There can be no suspicion from anyone. I mean, not a single fucking person outside of this group knows who you are."

"We don't go around yelling out our coven name." Ryan's tone was the most serious Vella had heard yet. And it made her pause.

Just what had these three been through?

"Come on. We'll work on the clue." Matt lowered his voice as they joined Amelia in the main shop. "Ryan, Amelia will give you my number to call when you arrive at Madgewick, but I mean it—you need to arrive later today. Zero connection between you and Vella."

"Car's gone, but you should two should go now." Amelia checked the window again. "The less people know you're visiting me at this time of day, the better and don't worry, I'll keep the trio here for most of the day—out of sight, though."

"Thanks, Ams. You are amazing." Matt caught the stunning witch up in a hug and kissed her cheek. "Call me if you can make the sheath work, and I'll drive in—"

"No way. I can bring it to you if—when—it's ready. Plus, I'd like to see Mr. and Mrs. B."

"Thank you. For the sheath—and for them." Vella nodded at the back room. "You don't understand how much this means to me."

"I didn't do it for you. I did it for us—for all witchkind." Amelia's gaze hardened.

Yep. Definitely no love lost for Vella. But right now, the other witch's feelings, one way or the other for Vella, meant zilch. All that mattered was being one step closer to finding the bone runes and saving Sara.

The moment they were back in Matt's car, Vella carefully pulled open the bag Ryan had given her.

"Can you see what's on the scroll?" Matt's voice was low. Tight. She glanced at him, but his face was in shadows, illuminated briefly under another working street lamp, then dim again a moment later.

"No. It's too dark, and I don't want to risk damaging it."

"And we can't turn the lights on. I need us to be just another car in the night. But we'll be at Madgewick soon."

"What was it like growing up here?"

"Magical. Amelia, Shannon, Ronin and I, plus a few others, ran around together and generally got into trouble."

Clearly, Matt and Amelia had a strong relationship ... one where they trusted and supported each other. Jealousy snuck through her, but she resisted the urge to pry.

Matt's words back at Stonehenge played back through her mind. He cared for Vella, and right now, that was all that mattered. Maybe ... maybe once this was over, they could tease this out further, see what a relationship would look like.

"So your house is called Madgewick?"

"It's the name of my ancestral home, where my family have been born—for more generations than I can count—and buried. And yes, we can hole up there."

"Phew. Not running for our lives would be nice for a chance. Wait—ancestral? As in, your parents are your ancestors or *ancestors'* ancestors? And when you say buried, please tell me you mean an actual graveyard and not under the floorboards or something?"

"Yes."

Vella swung back to the increasingly mysterious man beside her. "Yes to what—all of them?" *Frigging goddess.* "Are you like nobility or something?"

"No, but I am Baron Madgewick. And I can see the wheel turning—even in the dark. That title is really about me being responsible to the land and the people on the land."

"So it's an old property? Wait. Are you taking me to a haunted house or something?" Visions of a crumbling Gothic mansion spiraled through her mind. How amazing would that be? Historic buildings filled with antique treasures ... "And what's with Arkel ... whatever Amelia called you?"

"Achelous, pronounced Ak-uh-lo-us, is my first name."

"Achelous?" The name was familiar, and she— "The Greek god of water, no, rivers. Freshwater rivers." Vella let out a long whistle. "Your parents named you after a god. Cool."

"Only you would recognize that name."

"Art history major, and trust me, there are some breathtaking artworks with Achelous. Like the statue—"

"You can understand why I don't use it. Matthias is my second name. And before you ask, I have four names. Medea is my mother's family name. My father's name is Madgewick."

"Like the house? Sounds like there's an entire story I'm missing here, Matthias. Spill."

"There's no spilling. I'm just from a family who's been

in these parts for a very long time and whose house is named *for* that family. Now give it a rest."

Definitely touchy. But fine, she got that dealing with family—or the lack of it—was hard. But also, she'd learned something new about Matt. Inner-Vel cheered. Although why she had this insane urge to understand him was another mystery—and that was one mystery she shied away from understanding.

"So, Achelous Matthias Medea Madgewick, I'm going to talk to Brianna for a while." She sensed him glance at her as she stared at the box. "She needs time out of the box, and right now is perfect."

MATT DID his best to keep his gaze on the road while he focused on the one side of Vella and Brianna's conversation he could hear.

"I know, I can't believe it either. Three of them—and they hinted at more, Brianna."

And bloody hell. How had Matt never known about the remaining Mors Dicen? Did Sylvie know? If so, why had she not told him? She knew what he was trying to achieve.

"Yes, I'm yawning because I'm tired." Vella sighed. "I've slept for two hours in I don't know how long, and yes, everything *is* overwhelming right now. No, the Magicae is commanding the vehicle now. Yes, he's recovered his energy."

Matt sensed Vella's eye roll. But he understood Brianna's concern. How much more could Vella push herself before she burned out? And burning out was the last thing any of them needed right now—just look at what had happened to Matt.

Guilt roiled in his gut. He'd flamed out—zero spell-craft available. And while he could've called on his elemental control, everyone would've learned of his Druid secret.

Which would put Vella in way too much danger.

Once again, Matt was the risk to Vella.

Shit, she was already in so much danger—and he wasn't lessening that risk. He gave into the urge and glanced over at her profile. Fierce. Defiant. Compassionate.

Of course he was drawn to her. But that was the problem; it was as if the runes barely even mattered sometimes because she filled his thoughts. And that could not happen—he couldn't have emotional attachments, and yet here he was ... falling for someone.

Fuck. Did Vella even want that?

"I'd like to know more about how Mors Dien works," she said.

Focus, Matt. This was useful.

"Yes. Like"—Vella yawned long and hard—"how come Ryan and I heard you but not Liam and Ciara? Uh-huh. Really? Okay, so you're saying if you're an innate Mors Dicen witch you can talk to the dead while touching their bones. Powerful Mors Dicen can talk to the dead just by being around their bones—and really powerful witches can do the whole Bone Wielder thing. Believe me, I get that part. And then non-Mors Dicen witches, or those of the coven with really low power, can talk to the dead through their bones by undertaking some ancient ritual."

Now *that* made sense.

Vella yawned again, this time involving her entire body.

"Hey, Rapunzel? You're so tired you can barely hold a

conversation. Can your chat with Brianna wait? You need to sleep."

"You sound like Brianna."

"Brianna sounds eminently sensible, then."

"Yes, Brianna, the Magicae agrees with you. Pft. Then you and he should be the ones talking. No, I'm not sassing you." Definitely another eye roll. "Yes, I'll have a *decent* sleep. And that too." Vella pulled her purse securely into her lap and slumped back in the seat.

"Chat's over?" Matt took the turnoff to Madgewick. Thank fuck, they were almost home. "Brianna sounded ... miffed."

"You figured that out from my half of the conversation?"

"Not hard to."

Vella sighed. "Well, you got it right. Brianna is angry that I haven't had a decent slumber. She's also ordered me —when I wake up—to connect with some grass or dirt. Apparently, that's how Mors Dicen feed their magic."

"Interesting."

"Really? Why?"

"Grounding is something I do for my Druid powers, although any element will do, not just the earth."

He took the turnoff for Madgewick, and his gut tightened as familiar surrounds—barely changed since his last visit—sped past. Houses. Shops. Fields. Then the buildings grew sparser and sparser, and the forest loomed ahead.

"Wow, that forest ... even at dawn, all the mist, the gray skies ... spooky."

"It's haunted if you believe the stories they tell children to keep them out of the woods."

"And look at those gates—they're straight out of a

Gothic movie or something. This is your place, isn't it? But where is the house?"

"Back beyond the first line of trees." He turned the car onto the gravel driveway, and as he did, the gates opened with a groan audible even through the car windows. "We liked our privacy. Warning: as soon as we cross the threshold of the gates, you should notice a sensation. That's the magic of the property letting us through."

"Magic that can stop someone passing if you don't want them to? I'd like to know how to do that."

"So would I. That's magic long lost, I'm afraid. But it's tied in blood to my family."

Power buzzed through him as he hit the accelerator.

Vella hissed. "Ouch. You didn't say it would hurt."

"Impossible to avoid, unfortunately. Whoever laid that magic really wanted to ensure only Madgewicks—or those with us—step foot on our lands."

The driveway led up the slight incline, through the gap in the trees, and then there she was. Madgewick.

Vella's breath caught. And he would've turned to her, but he couldn't take his gaze from the house either.

Two dove-gray stone extensions spread out on either side of the main house, with a central tower rising to blend into the cloudy sky.

"Um, is this a castle?"

"Not quite." His gaze wanted to go to the trees beyond —to what lay beneath those trees—but he stopped himself and forced his focus back to Vella. "The original structure was fortified, that's the turrets and central tower on the main building, but then over the years, the other wings were added. There are a few outbuildings and stables as well."

"Stables? Outbuildings? A *castle*?" Vella whacked him

hard on the arm. "Who the hell are you, Matthias? Or Arche-whosit?"

"It's Matt. And I'm the Councilor of the Magicae coven, as well as the last child of a family who have lived on these lands for a very long time. Now, the Burrows—they look after the grounds and house—will no doubt be around here somewhere. I let them know we're coming."

"Stop stalling. I want to see your fancy house."

"Madgewick is old, not fancy. And you grew up in the Tower of Power—that's fancy."

"You're right, I did grow up in fancy, but it wasn't special to live in. No fingerprints left on glass or marble. Artworks so precious you could never touch them. No snacks in front of the TV. In fact, I hated it there. I prefer my house above the shop. As does Sara."

He steered the car to the left of the house and pulled into the garage. Vella was out before he could say anything—not that he had anything *to* say. But he took a deep breath before he followed her.

He hadn't even taken a lungful of the familiar, malty garage air when footsteps crunched in the gravel outside. And then Burrows, face grizzled, silver hair wispy, Fedora squarely on his round head, met him at the car.

"Matthias," Burrows' voice hitched. "Welcome home, my boy."

"Burrows." Matt swallowed the lump in his own throat.

"Well, get over here and give me a hug, and then out of this weather. I suspect the place knows you're back—about time, it's been three months since we last saw you—and this weather is its way of crying with joy."

And then he was embracing the man who'd helped raise him after his parents' death. A knot loosened in Matt's chest he hadn't known was there, but damn it, the bloody thing relodged in his throat, refusing to budge when he tried to clear it.

"Hi, Burrows, is it?" Vella stepped forward. "I'm Vella Knight. It's a pleasure to meet you."

Thank fuck she'd introduced herself because Matt could barely say a word.

"And lovely to meet you, too, Vella. So, are you a witch, too?"

"That I am."

"Well, Mrs. B and I are most pleased to see Matt's brought a friend home." Burrows glanced over Vella's shoulder and waggled his bushy brows at Matt.

Matt bit back a groan. "Ignore Burrows, Vella. Come on, let's get inside out of the rain. And I know you want to get stuck into the clue but you're so tired you're swaying. Burrows, is Mrs. B in the main house?"

"She is indeed. Setting up for breakfast right now."

"Lovely to meet you, Vella." Burrows doffed his hat.

"And you, too." Vella smiled, and Matt found himself taking her hand and leading her around to his home.

"Hey, are you doing that?" Vella nodded at the sky.

"What—oh, stopping the rain? Of course. Why would I let you get wet?"

"Do you just do that any time it's raining?"

"Only when it's safe."

What would she think of Madgewick? Clearly, Rapunzel loved antiques, but she'd also grown up in totally luxe surrounds, so would his home—

Fuck. What Vella thought of Madgewick had no bearing here.

"Wow. Oh wow. Wait. I couldn't see it properly when we drove in ... now I am ..."

"What?" His breath stalled.

"In awe," she whispered. "Look how the sun is just

hitting the top spires, turning them gold. What are they? Brass? And the stone must look gloriously pearlescent when the sun hits the rest of it."

"So you like it?" He held the door open.

Vella stopped on the threshold and tugged on his hand. "Matthias, your home is stunning."

"Just don't drool on anything inside—Mrs. B will be running after you with a cloth."

"Pft. As if I'd promise that. I have a feeling I'll be drooling everywhere, but don't worry. I'll clean up my own mess."

"In that case, welcome to Madgewick." He let the door close behind her.

"Welcome indeed." Mrs. B appeared to the right of the grand staircase. "Matty, you're home." And then he was enfolded in her crystal bracelet-adorned arms and hugging her back as tightly as she held him.

"Billy, this is Vella Knight. Vella, Mrs. Burrows—Mrs. B to most of the local kids—and Billy, short for Wilma, for me."

"Lovely to meet you, Vella."

"You, too, Mrs. B. And I love your crystals—they're stunning."

"You are a smart young woman. Now, would you like to eat or rest?" Her wise brown eyes sparkled. "Amelia tells me you've had quite the night."

"Actually, we have work to do—"

"Vella." Matt folded his arms. "You need sleep. We need sleep. How are we meant to figure out anything when we're both exhausted? I mean, I'm so tired that if I tried to call a witchfire spell, I'd probably end up making it rain, and I slept for three hours. You had what, two hours, max? And despite the gleam in your eyes—which I know is because you've spotted some antique you want to run over and touch—the fact is, you're exhausted. Hell, if fatigue was a Darkling, you'd be splitting me open right now. Uh-uh, I see you raising your chin at me and about to get all stubborn, but you know I'm right."

"Frig." Her shoulders dropped.

"Well, since that's settled, Vella, I prepared you a room on the second floor, right down the hallway from Matty; however, if you prefer to sleep in Matty's room, extra towels are out for you both. Matty's room has the loveliest ensuite—I'm sure you'll find it delightful." She bobbed her goodbye. "Well, I'll be off. When you wake, let me know and I'll make you a proper breakfast to get some color back into your cheeks." Mrs. B took off, her eyes twinkling.

"Did she just ask if we're sleeping together?" Vella let out a choked laugh.

"Pretty much. Billy's never been into subtlety. But the choice is yours, Rapunzel. Room of your own, or bunk in with me?" Hell. The words were out before he could catch them—but the truth was, he wanted her in his bed.

31

Vella awoke with her head on Matt's chest, his arms around her, their legs tangled, and without question, the biggest erection she'd ever felt pressed against her belly. His chest rose slowly and steadily with every breath, his eyes were closed, and in the filtered light, the scars were apparent on his face.

How would he feel about her seeing those marks again? Did he drop the spell that hid them every time he slept? She itched to know more, but he'd needed sleep just as much as her, and with his heart beating under her head and his arm almost protective in the way he held her, there was no way she'd wake him up.

By the goddess, Ellaine had a lot to answer for. Although right now, Vella had more pressing matters. A loo, then a clue, then saving Sara *herself*.

She eased from the bed, already missing the press of his body against hers, and padded silently into the bathroom.

Oh yeah ... this bathroom. Talk about heaven.

And she was finally awake enough to appreciate the

marble columns, huge central arch window looking out of a glorious tree-filled garden, ivy cascading out of planters, the rolled-edge claw-footed tub, and a shower big enough that Matt could host his coven beneath the multiple heads. Fine, maybe not the *entire* coven, but a good few of them. And perfect for Vella.

She threw off her shirt and underwear and padded into the marble enclosure, and after figuring out which handle matched which nozzle, she sighed as hot, hard water pummeled her shoulders.

"Knock, knock," Matthias' sleep-roughened voice echoed from the doorway. "Fancy some company?"

"Depends on the company." She turned, tilting her head back so water slicked down over her hair, and leaned against the cool tiles.

Matthias stood in the doorway. Sleep-rumpled but so damn hot everything in her cheered at the view.

"This bathroom is gorgeous, but what is it with you and oversized rooms?"

"I'm not exactly a small person."

"I noticed." She let her gaze wander down his body. "So ... the clue is waiting. But I need to wash my hair. Wanna help?"

His eyes darkened. "How long do we have?"

"Not long, but long enough." And then, thank the goddess, he was naked, standing before her like a Greek statue brought to life. Her own personal ancient artwork. Her mouth watered. But she danced out of his grasp when he reached out for her. "One thing."

"What? And why are you looking at me like that?"

"Because I have plans for your body ... when we have the time for me to savor you properly. But first, yesterday in the henge, when you came, I swear I orgasmed spontaneously. And it went on and on and on."

"Rapunzel, I thought you knew about sex with spell-casters?"

"I'd heard rumors of magic dicks."

"Hmm, that's not quite right. When a spellcaster comes, their power releases too, and their partner—or partners—experience the same release."

Vella's mouth dropped. "As in a guaranteed multiple? Sweet goddess, Matt, why haven't we been doing this sooner?"

His dark chuckle sent a hot shiver through her. "Let's see if we can make it happen again."

AFTER THE HOTTEST hair wash of her life, and Matt telling her to find him when she was ready to work on the clue, Vella called Sara.

"Vel? Where are you?"

"At Matt's home. It's called Madgewick. Still in the UK, but a few hours south of London."

"Matt?" Sara snorted. "You banged him, didn't you? Go, Vel. So how was it—did you see stars? Is fucking a spellcaster really that good? Tell me everything—"

"*Sar*! Seriously? How about we focus on how the hunt for the bone runes is going? Or, more importantly, tell me about you."

"Boo. You never tell me any of the good stuff."

"Fine." Vella made sure her sigh was long and loud. "It was good."

Sara's squeal made Vella smile. But the coughing that followed made her stomach drop. "Sara? You okay? What's going on?"

"Yeah, absolutely. Just have a cough. Nothing bad, Vel. Don't worry."

"Pft. You know who you're talking to, right?"

"Have to admit I did get distracted by the fact you finally got some with the spellcaster—and he is way fine. Mind you, they're all a rather delish bunch. Between Shannah, Ronin and the vamps, I'm surrounded by hotness."

"How are they going as housemates?"

"Pretty good, surprisingly. Although they are almost as meticulous as you when it comes to my meds and making sure I'm resting and eating right, blah blah blah." Sara's last blah ended with a yawn.

"Sara. They're looking out for you, which is a good thing, given you won't do it otherwise. What time is there?"

"Just after nine a.m."

"And you're tired already? Let me guess, staying up late playing D&D?"

"Yes, Mom. Now, if you're done checking in, I need to get back to work."

"Okay, okay, I'm done with the momming. But just ... please don't push too hard. And, Sar, you're going to love Madgewick; I think you should come here when you're well enough."

As soon as she hung up from Sara, Vella wound through the rabbit burrow of doorways and corridors and staircases to the ground floor and found Mrs. Burrows in a modern, fully outfitted kitchen large enough to feed the whole town of Glastonbury.

"Mrs. Burrows?" Vella knocked on the doorframe.

Mrs. Burrows looked up with a sweet smile. "Velvet, are you feeling rested?"

"Absolutely." And well and truly sexed as well. "And please, call me Vella—Velvet is what my aunt used to say when I'd get in trouble as a teenager."

"Vella, it is then. And Mrs. B is what the children call

me, not that they're children anymore. Now, lunch will be ready soon, but I can make you a cup of tea if you like?"

"Food would be amazing." Her stomach rumbled on cue. "Though, no thanks to the tea. I actually need Matt, but before I hunt him down, can I help you with anything here? I feel bad having you feed us—"

"Oh no. Feeding Matt and any guest of his makes my old heart happy." Mrs. B's gaze drifted to the window overlooking the grounds.

"Matt said he had to go outside. Would you know where to look?"

Mrs. B sighed, then went back to her stirring. "He always heads back there first thing when he comes home. Go out through the kitchen door and down through the garden all the way to the end. Turn left and head toward the wood and you'll see him soon enough—if you get to the folly, you've gone the wrong way. And the rain seems to have stopped, so perfect timing. Would you let him know I'm making lunch?"

"Of course." But as Vella stepped outside, the rain started again in a gentle drift. She could turn back or at least find an umbrella, but the sweet, fresh air was nice, and who cared about a little water?

She left the formal garden and spotted an odd little circular stone structure nestled near the rise of the land, looking back toward Glastonbury and off in the other direction ... the woods.

Vella kept walking, and soon enough, an itching along the back of her neck—not unlike when she was near Brianna—made her pause.

At the edge of the woods, a stacked stone fence ringed a small graveyard, headstones rising out of the ground here and there, and at the farthest end near the tree line, Matt stood with his head bent, staring at two graves.

And just like at the henge in Scotland, the misty rain diffused around him once again. Did he do it consciously?

Vella was through the gap in the stone fence before she could overthink the move.

He must've heard her, given his acute hearing, but he didn't shift as she carefully picked her way between the graves, although the itching along the back of her neck was hard to ignore.

Great, Vella. What were you thinking?

Clearly, not much.

She gave in to the urge to rub the back of her neck and made her way right to the end. One gravestone stood over two plots, each ringed with white stones.

Caelus Anthony Matthias Medea Madgewick
Niamh Ariadne Medea

MATT PAUSED at the door to his parents' study on the first floor. Vella hadn't said much at lunch, but then, when she'd asked him about his parents as he stood over their grave, he hadn't been able to say much either.

Their love had been bright and bold and beautiful.

And Vella ... Fuck. He could love her like that—bold and consuming and burning brighter than any sun he'd have imagined. But that couldn't happen. Loving her meant putting her first—and that was something he had no right to do. Had sworn not to do.

"Matt? Did you hear me? Are we going in?"

"Of course."

Shit. Head in the game, Matt.

The familiar, competing sense of loss and home twisted in his chest as he finally entered. Twin desks by the window. Packed bookshelves. Green leather couch by the fireplace.

He placed his laptop on the coffee table and ran a hand over the back of his mother's chair.

"How often do you come back?" Vella said from behind him.

"As often as I can—two or three times a year at least—but I want to get back more, stay longer, in the future." He didn't turn around. "After they died, it took a while to even make myself walk in here. As a kid, I'd play on the couch, under their desks, everywhere. As a teen, I did homework here while they worked. This was one of my favorite rooms in the house."

"Sounds special."

"It was. And one thing I remember is my mother's love of languages and puzzles—she was always reading new books on them right here, so hopefully, they're here near her desk, otherwise they'll be in the library."

"Can I help look?"

"No. And that came out harsher than I meant. Here in the study, some shelves and cabinets are spelled, and while I know—or can sense—which are, the last thing I want is you knocked out because of my parents' tendency to spell protect everything important."

"As in touch something and get spelled?"

"It's hard, but my dad was good with that kind of spell-craft, so yeah. Why?" When Vella didn't answer, he turned back to her. "Shit, you're shivering—here, I'll light the fire."

"Thanks, that'd be good. It's cold."

"Is that all, though? You're looking green too."

"Matt."

"What?" He whispered a fire spell, and as soon as the flames kindled, he turned to her.

She took a deep breath, and while she'd lost the look of someone about to vomit, a ghostly hue still tinged her skin. His stomach soured.

"Vella, what's going on?"

"You know how I don't like spells?" She moistened her lips. "Well, there's a reason for that—more than just my whole control issue. When I was a kid, I saw spellcraft used to kill."

"Who ..." Fucking hell. "Your parents?"

When Vella nodded, his blood turned to ice, and he eased down to the couch beside her.

"Gods, how old were you?"

"I was five. It killed my dad first—he picked up a spelled skull and, inch by inch, he calcified right in front of me. I must've screamed, and Mom came running. She went to him, tried to take the skull, and it happened to her, too."

"Vella." Knots twisted in his gut. "No wonder you hate spells."

"And bones," she muttered. "Spells I could handle, as long as they weren't being done to me, but bones ... Up until meeting Brianna in your room, I used to be so scared of them, I'd walk in a different direction if I saw one."

Hell. He rocked back on the seat. "I had no idea how hard this must have been for you."

"But you do what you have to, right? I mean, without Brianna, we might not have gotten so close to finding the bone runes for Sara." She shivered again and looked around the study. Was she looking for signs of spellcraft?

"Vella, even though I've never heard of a spell that does what you saw, I promise, the spells here are nothing like that. They'll stun you—maybe knock you out—but they won't kill you. We would never do that. Why don't you take a break? I'll investigate the puzzle—"

"No. No, I'm okay." She rubbed her arms. "Come on, let's figure out this clue."

She placed the piece of the vase with the last clue, along with the scroll Ryan had given her, on the reading table in front of them, and wiped her hands on her jeans.

"You look nervous. Can I help?"

"Just stay out of my light. I can't afford to tear the paper as I unroll the scroll—that might destroy a portion of whatever is written there."

Matt's gut tightened. "Please don't destroy the clue."

"As if. Okay, here we go." She visibly held her breath and, with her fingertips, unrolled the tightly wrapped scroll.

Matt held his breath, too, as roll by roll, a delicate parchment was revealed, with a fine line of writing in the center.

"What does it say?" he whispered.

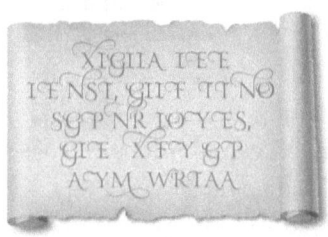

"Well, it's not Ogham. So that's a start. It's written in the same fancy script as the poem, but every letter is capitalized, and it has two commas. XIGIIA IEE IENST, GIIF TTNO SGPNR IOYES, GIE XFY GP AYM WRTAA."

"Shit." Matt couldn't stop himself from scowling at the scroll. "What language is that?"

"No clue. The final poem stanza says, 'Now one more

puzzle you must take, For the scroll, sense to make. But while this scribe knows not the key, From the old world it must surely be.' And that's it. There's no more to the riddle, so this scroll must be the next—please, goddess, final—part of the puzzle."

"You know the riddle that well?"

"After how many times I've read it?" She rolled her eyes. "I could recite that poem in my sleep. The problem is we have nothing else to go on—"

"Yes, we do." He nodded at the scroll. "Those words are there for a reason. We just need to understand why."

"You keep looking for your mom's books. Can I use your laptop? I'll search online the language on that scroll." She lifted her chin. "I'm serious, Matthias. I don't need comfort, I don't need to dwell on the past—I just need the runes."

"Okay, okay." He held up his hands when all he wanted was to wrap Vella up and hold her. Seeing your parents die like that? It had been hard enough for Matt as a teenager, and he'd only been there in the aftermath. But Vella didn't want to dwell—which he did get—so he grabbed this laptop from his satchel, logged in and opened an internet search browser. "Here you go."

"Right. Looking up languages."

"Can you read the last puzzle clue out loud again?" Matt asked over his shoulder as he started searching the shelves.

"'Now one more puzzle you must take, for the last of sense to make. But while this scribe knows not the key, From the Old World it must surely be.'"

One more puzzle. Matt mentally snapped his fingers. "The puzzle is the letters on the scroll. What if the letters aren't a different language, but a secret code? And judging by how the letters are grouped together, it might be a cipher."

"Okay, looking up ciphers instead of languages." She started an internet search. "Good news, there are plenty of online sites where you can encode and decode a cipher."

"What about types of ciphers?" He abandoned the shelf check and perched on the arm of the couch, over-looking Vella's internet search.

"First result is a Caesar cipher. You shift the letters from the ciphertext—I guess that means the letters on the scroll—up in the alphabet, historically by three. Okay, trying that. I'm entering the puzzle text into the online decoder ... Nope, still doesn't make sense."

"Any others?"

"Heaps of them, but I'm focusing on ciphers that existed when the clues were made. Next up is a *Vigenère* cipher, but you need a keyword to figure that one out."

"Vella, the riddle—the second last line literally says key."

"Shit, it does. Okay, this website says the keyword can be any length and any number of words."

"What about Mors Dicen?"

"Worth a try ... nope again. Nothing. Let's see. Magic. Witch. Bones. Of course!" Vella's eyes lit up.

"What is it, Rapunzel?"

"We already have the key. The Ogham letters form the clues. We just need to look up the last mark." She peered closer at the mark on the shard of vase.

"That's a letter?"

"Yep. Look here." Vella nodded at his laptop as she brought up a page filled with symbols made of intersecting lines. "This is the Ogham alphabet. All twenty characters."

"Okay." He compared the mark on the shard to the symbols on the website. "So the last clue is either the letter N or Q, depending on which way it's meant to be read."

"Oh, sweet goddess." Vella whirled and grabbed his hand. "Of course, it's N for sure."

"What?" Matt frowned as she practically dove back for his laptop. "What do you mean?"

"The three letters from each clue—B, A and N—spell the word ban, and ban is the Old English word for bone. Here, I'll type ban into an Old English translator. See?"

Fucking hell, she was right. Ban *was* bone. Which made perfect sense.

"We're so close, Matt!" Her smile was contagious and he found himself grinning back. "And the poem even says the key is from 'the Old World.' Entering ban into the decryption program ..."

Vella held her breath, and Matt did the same as the text on the screen transformed.

"Gods, Vella, you did it," he breathed.

"It reads, 'within her heart the stan stone holds the key to all wesan.' This is it. Sweet goddess, we did it."

Goddess was right ... Vella looked like one right now.

"We figured it out. Matt? Matt, you with me there? I said we figured the cipher out—now we just need to figure out what this text means."

"Of course. Here and present." *Fuck, Matt. Head in the game.*

"So, I know stan stone is a term for stone monuments,

like the stone circle we went to in Scotland, or Stone-henge. But I've got zero clue what wesan means."

"Wesan is an Old English term, too, I've heard it before." Matt paused, focused. *Wesan, wesan, we—* "Wesan means 'to be.'"

"Okay, so the scroll reads, 'within her heart, the stan stone holds the key to all to be.'"

"'Within her heart?'" He forced himself to focus on the revealed text on his laptop. "What does that mean?"

"Maybe under a stone? Surely not in one. And which stone circle is it referring to? I know there's lots of them across the country."

"But there is one more famous than any other—you just said it."

"Stonehenge. We can drive there, right?"

"Yeah, we can." Matt checked outside. "Listen, sunset is around four o'clock, which is less than an hour away, but it's an hour and a half to Stonehenge from here—and we don't even know if Stonehenge is the right stone circle."

"But what are the odds it wouldn't be?"

"It's a good lead, Vella." Matt rubbed her arms. "No, it's an amazing lead. But you and I need rest—not just sex—and I need to refuel so I've got plenty of magic in case we run into trouble. Let's take the night to research Stone-henge. Don't grimace—yes, the bone runes are our prior-ity, but we have what we need now, and running off into the night isn't smart."

"I get it. It's just, we already took time out today. I don't want to wait ..."

"I know. This is about your sister." Acid seesawed in his gut. "We've still got time, right?"

"Just. And you're right about not going out tonight, I

know. The main thing is, we found the bone runes." She leaped to her feet. "Thank you."

"We make a good team, Rapunzel."

Her eyes softened. "Yeah, we do."

"Better than you thought?"

"I can safely say that's an understatement. You know, I'd heard a couple of rumors about you before we met."

"Oh really?"

"Mm-hmm. That you were this ruthless, wealthy fuckboy witch who only cared about making money and living the high life. And that you had a magic dick."

Matt couldn't hold back his snort. But as Vella wound back around the couch to him, power gathered in his veins all over again. "And what do you think of those rumors now?"

"Now I know one of them is true. And let me tell you, my lady parts are very happy about that fact." That rare smile of hers lifted her lips, and he felt like he'd been given a gift right there and then. "And since we have all night to 'get ready,' how about you and I see how much fun a Mors Dicen-Div can give a Magicae?" She lifted onto her toes and, with that smile still hovering about her lips, kissed him.

A knock at the door made them both stop.

Mrs. B appeared with a tray of food, a steaming teapot, along with two cups.

"Mrs. B, what—" Vella took the tray. "Thank you, but you didn't have to do this. We could've come to you."

"Oh no, having guests in the house is too good a treasure to miss opportunities like preparing afternoon tea. Now, it's not much, just tea and toast. And, Vella, Matthias tells me you like blackberry jam—we have a grove of the thorny buggers right here on the property, and I make my own, so there's a pot of it along with your toast."

VELLA TOOK another bite of the perfectly balanced sweet-acidic-bursting-with-flavor blackberry jam on toast, reclined back into the couch, and turned to where Matt sat at the other end. "This might be the best thing I've ever eaten. You could bottle this and make a fortune."

"Already have one. And the blackberry grove is big enough for mass production."

"In that case, you can still bottle it, just give it all to me."

"That good, huh?" His lips tilted, and he finished his last bite of toast.

"Told you I was a jam girl." She considered the ridiculously, extravagantly, deliciously hot spellcaster over her last crust. "And you remembered."

"I have a feeling I'll remember every single thing about you, Vella Knight."

"And if that isn't the squishiest thing I've been told, I don't know what is."

"Squishy?"

"When someone says something that makes you go all warm and gooey ... here." She rubbed her chest.

"Ah, squishy. Yes, indeed."

"Look at you, sounding all fancy. You know, ever since we've been in England, your accent's gotten stronger? Like at the pub, you said shite instead of shit."

"Really? Now, that I didn't notice."

"Wow, looks like I'm noticing things about you, too." She put her cup down. Dusted the crumbs off her hands. "Like, even though you've come twice today, you're hard. Again."

He paused midway through sipping his tea, and those midnight stars whirled into his eyes again. And while she had no clue—yet—what those stars were, she recognized they were tied to Matt's intensity, which, right now, was focused all on her.

Heat pooled low in her belly.

"Rapunzel," he whispered.

"Spellcaster." She picked up the pot of blackberry jam, licked her lips. "You know, I love this jam."

"Really?" Matt's voice lowered.

"Uh-huh. But think I need to try it on something else." She stood, aware of his gaze fixed on her as she locked the study door and then stopped back in front of him. "And to be clear, because I don't like miscommunication, that something is you. Your magic dick, to be precise."

"Precision is always good."

"Well then." She smiled and dipped a finger into the pot. Licked it clean. His eyes narrowed. "Want to get naked again?"

A laugh escaped him, then he stood and yanked, ripped, shoved off everything he was wearing. And hard? *Good goddess.*

"Good boy," she said around the drool in her mouth. "Now sit still. I'm in charge this time. Got it?"

"Red, I am all yours." His lips curved in a wicked smile that made her lady parts tingle. "But fair warning. I love blackberry jam, too. And I haven't had dessert."

Puddle. Again.

But she got her shit back together and yanked a cushion to the floor. "You know, it really isn't fair for you to be this gorgeous." She dipped her finger back into the jam. "I think I should really cover you, right? This side, this side."

"Fuck." His hips rose.

She stopped. "Still, remember? Now, all the way from

here to the tip. Yep. Perfect." She rocked back on her knees. "What an artwork."

"Vella."

"What?"

"May I?" He caught her hand, brought her finger to his mouth, and licked around it, up it, sucked it. Her pussy clenched.

"I am so wet right now," she whispered. "I could jump you and—no. Not yet. I'm enjoying my handiwork."

She leaned in and licked up the mess she'd made. Swirled her tongue over the tip. Devoured every speck of jam until his hips were rising off the couch, his hands were fists at his side and the muscles at his neck were corded. Then she took him into her mouth, so deep he hit the back of her throat.

"Vella." His hands tangled in her hair. "You are pure fucking perfection." Then he was fucking into her mouth, groaning with each thrust. "Red, can't hold on—" He pulled back.

But no, she wanted this. Him. She dug her fingers into his thighs. "Then don't."

She took him deep again, urged him as far as he could go. He groaned, the echo rumbling around her, somehow through her.

"Vella!" His shaft pulse and his hot, salty cum flooded her throat.

Then the dampness between her legs ignited, and an orgasm exploded through her, forcing her eyes shut, squeezing a high-pitched keen from her throat and turning her world to fireworks.

When she finally got her breath back, she flopped onto the couch beside him. "Sweet frigging goddess, you really do have a magic dick."

She rolled to her side—came face-to-face with the eyes of the snake tattoos. Holy shit ... Were they *glowing*?

"Told you." He reached for her hand and squeezed it.

"What?" She yanked her gaze to his.

"The whole I-come-you-come thing."

"Yeah, I mean, I've already had it happen twice. But you were inside me both those times—I didn't know it would happen when I gave you a head job."

He traced her lip with his thumb. "Thank you. That was amazing. But did I hurt you? Was I too rough?"

"No, goddess no. I wanted that—every messy, tasty morsel of you."

"And do I get to reciprocate?"

"Oh yes."

32

L ong, delicious minutes later, Matt reached up and snatched the throw off the couch, rolled onto his back and pulled Vella into his side. She rested her thigh over his groin, and he grunted when her body fit perfectly against his.

"Was that a good grunt?" she whispered into his chest.

"Definitely. Apart from never looking at blackberry jam the same way again, I feel like you were meant to be right here with me. Or maybe I'm meant to be right here with you." His cock twitched at the brush of her knee.

"Hmm. Maybe both?" She picked up his hand and traced the lines on his palm. "Tell me about your magic. What does it feel like?"

"Like pins and needles, right in the center of my palms. As I call the spell, the sensation grows stronger until they pulse under my skin and that's when I know the magic is complete."

"Hot pulses?" Her laugh drifted over his chest, sending another wave of goosebumps over him. "Sounds ... sexy."

"It is a kind of release—not usually sexy, though."

"Well, by the look of your dick, you might be ready for another kind of release soon."

"I swear it's you—I've never had this many hard-ons, or for this long, around anyone else. Damn thing is trying to kill me."

"I have heard that's why men name their cocks—so they don't get killed by someone they don't know."

He laughed and hugged her closer. "I like this playful side to you."

"I can be playful."

"Really? Since when?"

"Since now." She tickled him under his arm. "But as fun as this has been—and I mean that—I'm ready to research Stonehenge."

"Online or physical references?"

"I would've said online ... but what physical references are you talking about?"

"The library downstairs—"

"Are those shelves spelled, too?"

"No to the shelves being spelled—that's only here in the study."

"Then why don't you look for any online references, and I'll check out your library. Which way?"

"Ground floor. Turn right at the bottom of the steps, take the first corridor on the left, then the third door on the right. Do not go into the second door on the left. In fact, I should come with you—"

"Good gods, no, seriously, you do your thing. I'll check the library. Think I can follow some door numbers. But what *is* behind door number two, or is that secret Magicae business?"

"Funnily enough, something like that. But fine, I'll keep going online. Plus, I need to talk to Ronin. I'll join you soon. If you get lost, check in with Billy. She has an uncanny tendency to be wherever you need her."

AFTER THREE RIGHTS, two lefts and the goddess knew how many circles, Vella ended up back at the bottom of the grand staircase.

"Mrs. B."

"Vella, dear. How can I help?"

"Matt said there's a library here and to ask you for directions if you've got a moment?"

"Ground floor, left wing, rear garden view. I'll show you since I'm heading over that way. What are you looking for? I can help with book locations if you need."

"Oh. Um, anything on hereditary magic." Which wasn't a lie—just not all she wanted to research. For some reason, telling anyone else she was researching Stonehenge didn't sit well.

"I'm sure there are works on that topic." They reached double timber doors, and Mrs. B pulled them open.

Double-height ceilings. Bookshelves floor to ceiling. Enormous windows looking out over the hills. And books ... so, so, so many books.

"This is magnificent," Vella blurted.

"It's been a passion in the family for generations. Now, which shelf?" Mrs. B fiddled with a yellow crystal on her necklace while she looked around—and within moments, the crystal began to glow.

"Mrs. B, are you a Crystallo? I've only ever seen crystals shine like that around members from that coven."

"I am indeed. You're a clever one, aren't you?"

"Not really." Clever would've been having the bone

runes by now. Or figuring out that Aunt Ellaine was a murderous bitch—although, the bitch part had never really been in question. But while she had Mrs. Burrows … "Can I ask a question? How do you and Mr. B. come and go with the whole only-a-Madgewick-may-enter-and-leave spell?"

"Mr. Burrows is a relative of Matthias."

"And Matt said you live here?"

"In the cottage at the other end of the estate, so I don't have to enter the property all that often, although I do like to drive into the town every now and again—and one good thing is I can leave the keys in the car since no one's able to steal it. Mr. Burrows just meets me at the gate and lets me back in if he's not with me."

"What about when you want to leave the property?"

"Oh no, the spell doesn't stop you there. You can go any time you like. Ah, here we are, magic lineage and hereditary gifts." Mrs. B took a blue-bound book from a shelf near the window. "There might be more—do you have a specific branch of magic you're interested in?"

"I'm not sure. It's more … my sister and I have different powers. But on top of that, Sara was born with a serious autoimmune illness. I'm trying to understand how blood sisters can end up with such different magic."

"Well, there are other influences on magic besides blood."

"What like?"

"Illness is the most common way. But a powerful spell-caster can also bind power—although that is perhaps one of the most complicated spells, or so I'm told. Some in my coven can use crystals to tune the frequency of a witch's power to heighten or diminish their powers. And the Elixirs were experimenting with something to that effect before their coup."

"Experiments?"

"Oh, it was a terrible thing. Not that there are many left who would remember. I saw firsthand children from our coven and others—from toddlers to young teens— who'd been given the Elixir's experimental potion. Within the Magicae coven, those poor children couldn't make a candle flame flicker with their power. And the others— the shifters were the saddest. They'd lost their ability to move from one state to another."

Vella's stomach twisted. "Who ..." Please, please don't let Aunt Ellaine be behind this too.

"Those experiments were run by the Elixir Councilor at the time—I'm sorry to say he was a Brit—Sean Montgomery. The Mors Dicen Councilor called for Montgomery to be jailed and his experiments banned, but sadly, their Councilor died the following day. Those were terrible, terrible times. Now, where is that book?—oh yes, here." Mrs. B pulled a book from the corner shelf and placed it on a reading table. "And now you're looking rather pale. I know it's distressing to think of, and I'm sorry to have upset you."

"It is awful. I can't imagine why anyone would do that to another witch, let alone a child."

"Control is the sad truth there, Vella. One witch controlling another."

"Did they stop?" Vella's chest tightened. "The experiments?"

"Oh yes. The coup erupted the day the Mors Dicen Councilor was murdered, and thankfully, Montgomery was killed a year later. Now, I need to get going, so I'll leave you to it."

Vella nodded, unable to even make words as disgust made her blood boil. How could anyone hurt children like that? But good goddess, so much harm had been done ... And if the Elixirs could do that to children, what else were they capable of doing? What if Sara—no. No, Charles was helping Sara. Sara herself had said she felt better.

She grabbed her cell and hit redial.

"Vel? What's up?"

"Why are you whispering?"

"I'm not. Just hoarse—told you I stayed up late last night with the guys."

"Sure you're not feeling sick?"

"Vel! Seriously—making me yell when I'm already hoarse is not right."

"You're sure you're feeling okay?"

"Oh my fucking goddess. Vella Knight, for the last time. I. Am. Feeling. Fine. Now, gotta go, got a date with a green orc's massive … club. Get it? Love you, Vel. Chat next time you're having a freak out over my non-existent health crisis."

And before Vella could end the call, the line went dead.

Shit. Was Sara lying?

Mrs. B's words about the Elixirs echoed back through her mind. One way to be certain.

"Vella, it's about time you called. Where are you now?"

"Actually, Aunt Ellaine, we need to talk about Sara. I just spoke to her, and she sounds … not great. You said Charles was making a new medicine—"

"Charles assures me the new medicine is working as intended."

"And the senior foreseers—have they seen anything new?"

"Nothing has changed." Aunt Ellaine paused, then her voice grew soft. The scary Aunt Ellaine—the version where nothing Vella said would change her mind. "Velvet, you have been away from your coven for too long, and I realize now this was too much to put onto you alone.

Therefore, Charles, Derrick and I are flying to London today. I expect you in London tomorrow to meet us."

Once more, the line went dead in Velvet's ear.

Frigging goddess. Ellaine was coming to the UK? Why? Had she worked out Vella wasn't going to give the bone runes back?

Vella grabbed Brianna, opened the library door—

"Oomph." Strong arms wrapped around her, and Matt's chuckle echoed in her ear. "Excited to see—"

"Thank fuck you're here. Aunt Ellaine is coming to the UK. She'll be in London tonight."

"Ah, there you are, Matty." Mrs. B called out from the end of the corridor. "You have visitors—three … well, you should come and see. They're with Amelia. And they have something for you, Velvet, dear."

VELLA TURNED the knife sheath and attached belt over and over in her hands as she sat opposite Ryan, Ciara and Liam on the library couches. Their serious expressions had her on edge, but she forced herself to focus on Amelia as the hedge witch explained the sheath.

"The handle section is lead lined, and if you flip the cap over, you'll have complete separation from Brianna, but there's also a small sliding window at the side, so if you have the sheath strapped on beneath your shirt, you just need to flick this tab and the top of the bone handle will rest against your skin.

"Thank you, Amelia. This is perfect. How did you get it so quickly?"

"Thankfully, the Council doesn't know where all banned magic artifacts are hidden."

"Vella, there's something else." Ryan shifted forward

on the couch and opened the locket that hung around his neck. A small piece of bone lay nestled inside, and an itch gathered at the base of Vella's neck. "There's someone I—we—want you to talk to."

"Ryan?" A masculine voice Vella had never heard before echoed through the library. "Ryan, I hear her—" The man gasped. "You were right. Another Mors Dicen."

Vella froze. "Who is that?"

"Grandfather. This is Vella."

"Hello, Vella." The voice was cautious. "It's lovely to meet you. My name is Steven."

"Uh, hi. Steven. Nice to ... meet you too. Ryan said you wanted to talk to me?"

"After everything they've done, I needed to be sure this wasn't a plot for the Divs to turn another of our sacred bones against us."

"The Elixirs poisoned them," Ryan whispered. "During their coup. Then the Divs used their foresight to see where we were gathering and laid the bones out as traps. That's how they killed so many of us—our parents, our grandparents, our brothers and sisters and cousins. But who are you? Which family do you come from?"

"I don't know for certain, but I'm guessing my father was Mors Dicen. Unfortunately, I can't ask him or my mom; they both died a long time ago. And as much as I get this is important, I'm here to find the bone runes for my sister—Sara—she's sick, and the runes are our last hope to divine a cure to save her life."

"Sisters?" Steven gasped.

"Velvet. Sara. Shit." Ryan's eyes widened and he stared at the locket. "Grandfather, do you think ..."

"Vella." Steven's voice lowered. "Our last Councilor, Honoria, had two daughters, Vespera and Sierra. They were taken near the end of the coup. Honoria's partner was Antony."

"You think both my parents are Mors Dicen?" Vella's stomach curdled, and pressure built in her chest until she had to force herself to take a breath. "No, my mom was a Div. The Divinator Councilor is my mom's cousin."

"There is one way to know for sure." Ryan took a locket from around his neck and opened it up. "Grandfather has a story you need to hear. He was there the day our Councilor and her family died. He also died that night, but he can tell you what he saw up until that point, and if you really are a Bone Wielder, he can show you—"

"From his memories. Yeah, I get that." But could she trust these three? "Brianna, any advice here?"

"Connect with this Steven," Brianna said softly. "See what his memory brings. Trust me, trust the bones."

Ryan dropped the fragment into her palm, and between one blink and the next, the library, Matt, Ryan, and the others, all disappeared.

In their place, a lounge room with a couch and a desk appeared.

"I know this house," Vella whispered.

A painting full of colors and multiple scenes filled the far wall. Her father's painting. Vella turned, and there stood an unfamiliar man, perhaps in his sixties, with dark hair and eyes.

"Hello, Vella, I'm Steven. We're in my memory now. This is the house of our Councilor, Honoria. I came here, this night, to tell her they were all in danger. Watch."

A dark-haired woman carrying an overnight bag ran into the lounge, straight through where Vella stood. A man—Steven—followed. "Antony," the woman yelled. "Get the girls. I'm getting our papers."

The woman spun.

Vella's heart stopped. Her mother. Honoria? No, her mother had been Olivia. Yet—there was no doubt who this was.

"Steven? How long do we have?" Honoria pulled an entire drawer out of the desk and dumped the contents into the bag she held.

"Minutes at best. What can I do?"

"Find our family grimoire. It's in the bookcase over there." She pointed to the shelves opposite them. "Antony? Did you hear me? Antony!"

Somewhere in the house, a child screamed.

"Ves!" The woman dropped the bag and ran out of the room.

"No, don't go!" Vella shot out a hand, tried to grab her mother. Tears burned at Vella's eyes, and her chest went tight, too tight to breathe.

But then the Steven in the memory followed, and Vella got swept along in time to see Honoria run into a room at the end of the corridor.

"Vel!" Honoria's scream echoed through the house. "Get back! Tony—I'm coming, babe, you're okay, we've got ..."

The child kept screaming, over and over and over.

Steven ran into the room, gasped.

Dread filling her belly, Vella had no choice but to follow.

Honoria and Antony, frozen. Dead. A skull in their hands.

Mom. Dad.

Burning tears ran and ran.

The child ran for them.

"No!" Steven grabbed the child. "Vel, come on, sweetie —we must go. Hey, Vel? Can you tell me where your sister is?"

Through her tears, the child pointed up to the second floor.

"Vel, you need to go upstairs, okay? Go up to your sister now. She needs you—can you do that? Your mom and dad would want you to look after her now. I'll be up soon."

Steven gave child-Vella a push, and she ran off.

Up to her baby sister.

I ran to look after her, just like I was told.

Crash.

Steven whirled around. The click of heels and the stomp of boots echoed up the corridor.

"Shit," Steven whispered. He ducked behind the window drapes just as the footsteps reached the end room. Burgundy fabric filled his view.

"Well. Monty, our plan finally worked," a feminine voice said. "They're gone."

"Excellent idea, poisoning their precious bones," a male replied.

"Yes, if only it hadn't taken our foreseers so long to locate the right opportunity. But well done on the poison —that is quite a sight."

"I really am impressed with my skill. And the children?"

"Our foreseers have predicted with ninety-nine percent accuracy that the eldest child of the Mors Dicen ruling family will hand the ancient bone runes to me. I know there are other Mors Dicen witches in hiding—and once I have their runes, I shall finally have the power to track down every last one of them."

"And the other child?"

"I think it's time to see if your experiment finally works."

"Excellent. I have been playing with some additional elements, so as well as removing her power, the potion will keep her sick, and if you stop giving it to her, she will die—probably within twenty-four to forty-eight hours."

"And is there an antidote?"

"None that we have found so far."

"Now *that* is perfect. I can use the youngest as leverage if we need the oldest to come to heel." She paused. "We'll remove everything useful, then burn this place down. No evidence."

Steven took a breath and eased from around the curtain.

Aunt Ellaine—younger, but undoubtedly her—and a silver-haired man stood in the doorway.

Aunt Ellaine? Vella's breath punched from her. Her tears stopped.

"Monty? We have a problem." Aunt Ellaine nodded to where Steven hid.

"Wait," Steven yelled.

But Monty took out a vial, threw it—the glass smashed at Steven's feet.

"Move back," Monty murmured, and his face was the last thing Steven—Vella—saw before the room went black.

33

"Vella? Vella? Can you hear me?" Matt glared at Ryan, whose gaze hadn't left Vella's since she'd started her communication with Steven. "Can you hear them?"

Ryan shook his head. "They went into Steven's memory. I can't hear a thing."

"I get that. So we just wait?" Shit. Matt dropped back to the couch as tears started to run down Vella's cheeks. Fucking hell. "She's shivering. Does Brianna have advice on what to do?"

"Let me check. Brianna? Vella's having a reaction to the memories—Yes, still breathing ... sitting upright." Ryan's gaze refocused on Matt. "Okay, Brianna says we are witnessing Vella's physical reaction to whatever is going on in Steven's memories, but as long as Vella hasn't passed out, she's fine. But Brianna ... Yes, of course. Okay, I'll tell him that, too." Ryan's gaze shifted back to Matt. "Whatever you do, do not take the bone out of Vella's—"

"Hand. I know. But how is this 'fine?'"

Ryan's eyes narrowed. "Because Vella is Mors Dicen. She was born to do this."

Good to see Ryan had a backbone. If he was the next strongest witch in their coven, he needed to have all the determination and grit that Vella had ... Shit. This was Vella's coven. And coven were family. Vella's family.

Something like ... jealousy twisted in Matt's gut, but he shoved that away.

He eyed the trio. "You should stay here. You know that no one can enter my property without a Madgewick, so you're safe—"

Vella let out a curdling scream. Over and over and over.

The hairs on the back of his neck spiked, and adrenaline surged, but fuck it, the enemy he needed to slay for Vella was one he couldn't reach. Fuck. Fuck, fuck, *fuck*. Once more, unable to help someone he lov—fuck. Cared for.

Finally, the screaming stopped, and Vella dropped the bone fragment. She fumbled for his hand and when he grabbed it, she squeezed like he was her lifeline.

"Matt?" Her whisper was barely audible, and he leaned closer.

"I'm here. Are you okay? What happened? Did someone hurt you? Was it this Steve—"

"Steven? No, no, he didn't do anything. And no, I'm not okay. Goddess, I am so not okay. Matt, it was awful." More tears ran down her cheeks, then she crumpled into him, massive shudders racking her frame.

"Vella? Fuck, your hands are icy. Here." He gently tucked her hand between his and began to chafe it. "Can you tell us what happened?"

"It was awful." Her eyes remained unfocused, but the slackness around her jaw told him everything. "I can't ..."

"Ryan, can you run out and ask Mrs. B for a bottle of Fireball Cinnamon Whisky? Vella needs something strong. I think we all do. Vella, you don't have to talk till you're ready." She burrowed into his side like a wounded animal—this lioness of a witch who, up till now, had stood up to threat after threat.

A chill flew up his spine. What the fuck had she seen?

IF SOMEONE CARVED out Vella's heart and shredded it, if Darklings flayed her open in tiny cuts until she was nothing but ribbons of flesh and blood, if she lived a thousand years and never slept, that still might not account for the way her body processed the grief coursing through her.

The library remained dark ... and while her vision had returned, right now, the absence of light was exactly what she wanted. Recounting the events from Steven's memories had been almost as awful as seeing it, although the whiskey and the warmth of Matt at her side had somehow gotten her through the retelling.

Goddess, how could they do that to Sara? To their mother, their father? To Steven? The tears came again, dripping down her cheek, off her chin, but they were hot and angry, fuelled by fury and horror and despair.

"Daughter? Are you there?"

"I'm here," she finally whispered.

"We need to talk."

"Don't know how much more I can talk right now."

"Where is the Magicae? He was there earlier."

"Looking after Ryan and Ciara and Liam." Matt had seemed to get how much Vella needed to be alone to process the awfulness of what she'd seen, and he'd gotten the Mors Dicen out of there fast.

"Daughter? Vella? Did you hear me? I asked if you are ready to talk? I have pieced together most of what occurred from your conversation with the Magicae, though I would like to hear from you what you believe I need to know."

"It's ... it's like you said, I am a Mors Dicen. Just not how I thought. They killed them, Brianna. That ... fucker who calls herself our aunt killed our parents, kidnapped us, and then all along, she's been poisoning Sara. And frigging goddess, I let it happen. I stood there every day when Sara took their—"

"No. No, you do not take that on board. You are angry. And right now, your anger is good. You need to use that to ensure you move forward with the information you have and do what needs to be done."

"Done? I need to get Sara away—except shit. We can't take her away. There's no antidote, Brianna. And if Sara stops taking that poison, she'll die." Vella doubled over, unable to hold back the keening cry that broke from her.

"Vella. Vella—you need to listen. You must find the bone runes more than ever before. They will help you find a path to the cure for whatever poison your sister has been given."

"What—how?"

"These bone runes are extremely potent. The witches who gave their bones were each powerful in their own right, and together, they provide enough magic to divine a vision of exactly the event you wish to see—the location, the people you seek out, their conversations, even the right path to take to find a specific outcome—like finding the cure to Sara's poison. You would not even need to be in close proximity, both in time and location, to the event, like a Divinator witch needs to be. If a cure exists in any form, in any place, the bone runes can find that for you."

"What do I do? " A tiny kernel of hope bloomed. "Do I touch them and then ask to see what will cure Sara? Brianna? Brianna—why aren't you talking to me?"

"I am thinking. By the goddesses' grace, Daughter, you have so much to learn. I presumed you knew how to divine future events; otherwise, why would you seek the bone runes?"

"You presumed wrong! But fine, I just need someone who knows how to divine." Vella rocked back in her seat.

"Not just anyone. Vella, if you do not know how to funnel the vision you seek—the act of divination—then you may get lost in the vision, just like you can become lost in my memories. And then you will never find the cure."

"Shit." Memories of her only—failed—attempt at divination as a teenager flew through her mind. She'd been close to losing herself that time ...

"Vella, all magic carries equally balanced dangerous and beneficial outcomes. You must remember that."

"Wait. Can a Div witch use the bone runes?"

"Yes, and the bone runes will increase the accuracy of their foresight, as I said; however, only a Mors Dicen witch can truly use the bone runes to the full extent of their power."

Did Ellaine know that? If so, why did she want them so badly?

"Fine, I'll figure out how to use the bone runes." Sara depended more than ever on Vella finding those bone runes. Determination surged and replaced everything else. "I just need to get them. We think they're beneath Stonehenge, an ancient—"

"Vella, every witch knows about the Stan Stones, or as

you say, Stonehenge. For as long as our stories tell, our clans met at the Stan Stones every winter solstice to celebrate the end of the shortest day and the beginning of the cycle of renewal. And each midsummer, we met to commemorate loved ones passed. We also visited when we had sacred rituals to conduct."

"Okay, so the riddle I'm trying to solve says the runes are beneath one of those stones. Do you know which stone it would be?"

"They wouldn't be beneath *a* stone. They'll be beneath them all."

"What?"

"You have so much to learn." Brianna's sigh made the hairs on the back of Vella's neck prickle. "Let's start at the beginning—"

"There's no time for a history lesson."

"Ah, but there you are wrong. If you seek something beneath the Stan Stones, then you must learn this lesson. There is no other way in. Patience, Vella. I know you are desperate to save your sister, but you must listen to me. I tell you this because to not know will lead to you failing in your goal, if not your death."

"Fine. Tell me."

"Actually, it is best if you take hold of me. We are about to conduct magic, Bone Wielder."

"I won't be able to see afterward, though."

"Your sight is the price you pay, remember?"

"Okay, okay." Vella swallowed hard. Rechecked the door.

"Mors Dicen is dark magic." Brianna's voice flowed with total clarity the moment Vella touched the knife.

"Is that a bad thing?"

"Oh no. This darkness is pure energy and the place where power originates—along with Druids, vampires,

Darklings and others. The reason you do not need a ritual to conduct Mors Dicen magic is that you are Dark Magic, Vella. It is in your blood."

"I get it, it's who I am. So, then, what?"

"Dark energy connects everything and everywhere, and you can tap into that energy. Follow it a little way or a long way to find what you seek. Use it to move things—earth, rocks, people. Use it to travel between locations. Use it to talk to others."

"Shit. So that's how I get under Stonehenge—I can move the rocks?"

"That's what you need to learn."

"Brianna, you sound awfully sly right now."

"Good. I am your teacher, and so far, you have not been an easy student. Now, find the deepest shadow, an absolute absence of light."

"In the fireplace," Vella whispered. "At the back, leading up to the chimney."

"Perfect. Lock your gaze on that darkness, feel the power gather at the back of your neck—"

"It itches," she whispered. "I need to rub it."

"No! That is the magic. Let it build."

"Really? Can't even scratch—"

"Vella! Do not scratch it—that rubs the magic away. Hold on to that sensation; let it grow, flow over your shoulders. Down your arms, all the way to your hands. Do you feel it there?"

"My palms are tingling like pins and needles. And … no way. I *see* the darkness—it's like a spiderweb connected to everything."

"I like that analogy."

"I stole it from another witch," she murmured. "Look how the strands shimmer, as if it's just rained on the web, except the drops here are like midnight stars ..." A shiver shook through her.

"Vella, focus, I feel you slipping—"

"I'm here." She took a deep breath. "Okay, so I follow the magic? Do I walk—"

"No. For now, follow it with your mind. Close your eyes and you will still see the spiderweb. Trust me, Vella. You can do this—just remember, don't let me go. I'll see you when you return from the dark."

"Wait—why aren't you coming with me?"

"Dark energy is a place for the living, Vella, and that I am not. However, I will be here when you return. Just remember—when you are connected, you can follow the strands of dark energy wherever they go. Focus and make it so."

Vella let her lungs empty. *Dear goddess, let this be the right thing to do.*

She focused on the dark energy, and then, like when Brianna took over her sight, a veil fell over her eyes, only this time, midnight stars filled her vision.

"I'm there! Brianna, I see it. Brianna—shit." Vella took a breath. She was on her own for now. But where to go?

Hmm ... well, there was one place she could return to.

"Leaving the library," she whispered to herself. "Out the door, around the corner, up the stairs, to the study door." Except, it was closed. Although, a trail of dark energy ran right up to it. Frig, this better work. She held her breath again and mentally followed the energy.

Matt stood behind his parents' desks, talking to someone—she followed the energy around. Ronin's face became visible on the laptop screen.

"The plan is in play," Matthias was saying. "We've worked for too long to risk messing everything up now."

It had worked; she was listening to their conversation! She *could* do this.

"Not that it matters after what Vella saw, but the lab results came back from Sara's meds." Ronin leaned forward. Vella froze. What about Sara? "As you suspected, a type of toxin. You were right about that. All this time they've been 'saving' Sara, they've actually been poisoning her."

"Shit," Matt breathed. "The fuckers."

Around Vella, the spiderwebs of power disintegrated, the room spun, and when she caught her equilibrium, she was in the library, with her human sight obscured.

"Motherfucker."

"Daughter, what happened? Vella?"

"Matt knew—all along, he knew about Sara being poisoned—and he never told me."

Fury rushed through her and Vella leaped to her feet. Ran into something shin-height. She gasped, toppled forward, and Brianna fell from her grip.

34

A n odd buzz along the back of his neck had Matthias recheck the spell he'd called to conceal his conversation with Ronin. Everything seemed in place, but he couldn't shake off the sensation.

"Matt? Did you hear me?" Ronin stood.

"No, just had to recheck the spell. What did you say?"

"Did Vella say if she was telling Sara?"

"I don't know. But shit. Ronin, Vella loves her sister, that's without question. And if Ellaine convinces Vella that only she can use the bone runes to save Sara, then Vella might take that option. And we *cannot* risk the bone runes falling into Ellaine's hands. Now more than ever, there is so much at risk—"

"Sara's *life* is at risk."

"*Everyone's* lives are at risk." Matthias rocked back on his heels, and his jaw clenched. "I hate this, too, Ronin. But I can't put one person's life ahead of everyone else. Nothing's changed. I can't let Vella take the bone runes back to New York."

"But what about Sara? She needs medical help. Urgent medical help."

"Then that's what we do. Get your lab sample to Ruby, the Crystallo Councilor. I'll call her next and set it up. Ruby knows the best docs that are not under the control of the Divs. I'll let Vella know we're working on an option for Sara."

"Matt, you've always been more my brother than cousin, so I need to call you on something—for your sake."

Matt paused. "If this is about Vella—"

"You're in love with her."

"This isn't the time for jokes. Wait—you're not joking." Matt dropped to the desk chair. "You are certifiable. And stop looking at me like that." He spun to the window. "Love? Vella? No, no freaking way."

Like her? Yes. Want her? Hell, yes. Respect her? Kind of, damn it.

"Matt, listen to yourself. When this started, she was the Div. The Div this, the Div that. But now she's Vella—your words, Matt. You are feeling something for her. And before you go denying it's even possible, look at how your mother and father bonded," Ronin said. "Why couldn't that happen to you too?"

"Because it *can't*."

"You say *can't*, but I see it happening right in fucking front of me! How you can't keep your eyes off her. How you orient yourself to where she is in a room. And you need to acknowledge your feelings, or you risk everything we've worked for going up in flames."

"That's it—I can't do that," he whispered.

"Can't? Why the fuck not?"

"Because I can't let myself think about a future like

that—a future with someone I love—until every witch is freed from the tyranny of the Council."

"Matt, you might not want it, but can you really stop caring for her? Like right now, how do you feel about her? And not the plan—just you and Vella."

How did he feel? Fuck, he felt too much. "I feel like she's the most precious thing I've ever seen or felt or touched. Like when she smiles, I've won some kind of prize. I feel ... fuck, I feel *right* when she's near me, and I just want to be near her. But then, on the flip side, every time I am near her, my elemental energy erupts. It wants out, to get to *her*, I swear. It's like claws raking under my skin, and it's growing stronger. But I can't disassociate how I feel with what we need. Because there is no fucking way I will ever put my wants ahead of our coven. Of the plan."

"The plan." Ronin hissed. "Are we really that close?"

"We are so fucking close—Charles is upset at Ellaine, Ellaine must be furious with Charles, and Vella is no longer stealing for the Divs. And once we have the bone runes, we'll find our grimoires, undo the spell Ellaine forced from me, and *then* we grind the Divs and Elixirs to dust. That's what I'm going to do. That's my promise."

35

M att's power was a raw, naked flame under his skin after he hung up from Ronin, and he gave in to the urge to find Vella straight away. With the shock of learning the truth about her family, about what Ellaine was doing to Sara, no wonder she'd been reeling.

Fuck. Fuck, fuck, fuck.

Mrs. B told him Vella was still in the library, but when he got there, the doors were closed and locked.

"Vella?" he called. "Vella? Are you there, honey? Can you hear me?"

One door opened with a whoosh.

"I'm not your honey." Vella spun and, with stiff, measured steps, stalked to a wingback chair by the window and sat, staring at the floor.

He walked around the last chair and paused. "Why is Brianna on the floor?"

"Because I dropped her there."

"Shit. You used her sight, and now you can't see, can you?" He put Brianna away and placed the knife and sheath safely on the shelf behind him. "Maybe you should only touch Brianna when someone's nearby."

"My sight is back. Kind of." Vella's chin lifted, but he could see now she wasn't looking at him, more in his direction.

"I get you're upset—"

"No, Matthias. You have no frigging idea how I am right now. I am furious that you lied to me." She leaped to her feet and shoved a finger in his direction. What the fuck? "That you fucking hid what you fucking knew about Sara being fucking poisoned."

"Shit. Where did you hear that?" He grabbed her arm. "Vella, you need to tell me now. Where. Did. You. Hear. That? Did you divine it? I thought you didn't have any foreseer skills?"

"Not the fucking point! And let me go right now or I'll pick up that knife right frigging now."

"I was holding your arm so you don't trip over the table right in front of you. And you can't get the knife because I put it back in the sheath—which you couldn't see because your eyesight has gone. But here. Letting go. Just watch your fucking feet."

"My sight's almost back, so don't go pretending to be the hero."

"I never said I was a hero, Vella. Not once."

"Oh I know that. A hero wouldn't think it's okay to leave a defenseless young woman being poisoned by the fucker who killed her parents."

"I don't think it's okay—I fucking hate what they've done!"

"Then why keep it a secret from me? And don't try to deny it."

His chest went tight but fuck if he was backing away from this now. "You're right. I wasn't."

"Motherfucker—"

"Bloody hells Vella." Matt shoved a hand through his hair. "How did you find out?"

"Who the fuck cares? Sara's being killed—"

"She's being poisoned, yes, but killed? No. And you told me that in Steven's memories, Ellaine said she'd use Sara as leverage against you. So what does Ellaine want from you, Vella? Because no way in hell will I hand the bone runes to Ellaine. And I can't let you do that either."

ICE FROZE Vella from the inside out, not because of Matt's scars or the midnight stars in his veins but at the utter determination blazing in his eyes.

A hysterical laugh escaped her. The Divinator coven thought this man weak. Useless. He'd played them all—including her.

Matt stepped forward. "Vella—"

"Don't come one single step closer, you motherfucking *asshole*." Vella backed away.

His lip curled. "What do you think I'm going to do? Hurt you?"

"What else am I meant to think? You were willing to let Sara get hurt for the cause. Why the fuck wouldn't you hurt me? You've been manipulating me from the start, but no more bullshit, Medea. Why didn't you tell me about Sara?"

"Because you put her before everyone else. And I get it —you love her. But I can't put one person before the rest of the world, Vella." Matt's nostrils flared, and the brutal intensity on his face almost took her breath away.

"It's all about the bone runes, isn't it? What were you going to do, Matthias? Take them yourself?"

"You knew all along I needed the bone runes—"

"But you've never told me exactly why. So? Time to come clean, Matthias. This has to do with your plot; I know it does. Well? Is it to kill Ellaine, somehow? Goddess knows I understand your rage at her—in fact, how you haven't killed her before now is hard to comprehend."

"It's not through lack of desire to remove her from this world, Vella. I *can't* kill her."

"What? Why?"

"After killing my parents and attacking me in London, Ellaine forced me to make a binding spell that rendered us—my entire coven—unable to kill her or directly order her death."

Vella's lips went numb. "You can make a spell that powerful?"

"I have the capability, yes." He nodded.

"But then why—shit. You can't undo the spell?"

"I'm powerful enough to craft the reversal spell, but that power is useless without knowing the ritual to make it happen—and the rite is recorded in one place only: somewhere in one of the grimoires Ellaine stole from us. And we don't even know where the fuck Ellaine is keeping them. Why do you think she keeps such a tight leash on all new magic? Ellaine knows how dangerous magic outside of her control is."

"Oh shit," Vella breathed. "So that's why you want the bone runes—to find your grimoire."

"That's one purpose, yes. But that's not the only reason. The bone runes are too powerful, Vella." Matthias' jaw clenched, and he shoved a hand through his hair. "More than anything else, the Divs can't be allowed to have them."

"I'm not going to give the frigging Divs the bone runes—"

"Vella. Can you use the bone runes to divine a cure? No. So you need a witch who can divine with them. And if Ellaine gets those bone runes she'll have more power than any Div witch ever has—look at how much carnage that woman has already caused without the most powerful divination tool witchkind has known. She cannot have them."

A river of fury erupted inside Vella and she let every ounce show through her gaze. "My entire life, Ellaine fed me this bullshit line about how stealing everyone's arcane artifacts was for the good of witchkind. And now here you are, telling me once again that for *the good of witchkind* I have to let my sister die. Well fuck you and fuck your good of everyone else, I will never give up on Sara."

Brianna. She needed her knife. But where—the book-shelf behind the spellcaster. Fifteen feet away.

Vella lunged past Matthias. Ten feet, five feet—

Matthias grabbed her around the arms and spun her to face him. "What are you doing?"

"Saving Sara's life." She yanked out of his grasp, but he didn't budge. "Let me go. Now."

"So you can hand the bone runes to Ellaine? Don't you get it? She will have enough power to kill everyone who ever tries to stand up against her."

"I don't care," Vella screamed as she fought his hold. "Those bone runes are my sister's life."

"But you don't *know* that. What if there is no cure? You said it yourself—in Steven's memory, Monty told Ellaine that very thing."

"I know it's a chance, and that's fucking enough for me. You're saving your family's life; well, I'm saving mine."

He stared at her hard. Breaths rasping in and out. Nostrils flared. Teeth clenched. Hair free from its tie and flowing everywhere.

And then he straightened, and his expression turned ice-cold. "You're right, Vella. We're both doing what we must do. And for that, I'm sorry." He whispered a spell and the air vise that had clamped around her arms back in his New York bedroom tightened around her again, this time from her feet to her shoulders.

"You fucker!"

"You can yell all you want. You can hate me, you can threaten to kill me—fuck, you might even do so one day, but I can't let you tell your aunt what happened here." He stalked to the doorway, though he didn't leave the library.

Moments later, Amelia ran into the room. "What's going on? We all heard the shouting—" Her eyes widened.

Vella jerked her head to clear the hair from her eyes since she couldn't move her arms and sneered at her. "What? Never seen a witch tied up with magic before?"

"Spellbound?" Amelia's mouth dropped open. "Matt, what's going—"

"Not now. I need you to get all of Vella's electronics from her room. Her laptop and cell are here but check her bags. Anything that could be used to call her aunt."

"But—"

"Just go. I need to figure this fucking mess out." He stopped by the shelf where Brianna lay.

Amelia's jaw clenched—a move so much like Matthias, Vella wanted to puke—and then she nodded and left.

"Medea, you can't do this." Vella struggled against the invisible bonds again, but they tightened even more. Shit, there had to be an out. "Wait, what are you doing with Brianna?"

"Making sure you don't do anything idiotic." He looped the sheath through the belt buckle at the front of his jeans.

"She's mine."

"Yeah, she is. And when you realize that makes you a Mors Dicen who can help end the misery of our people, you can have her back."

"You don't get to decide that—"

"Knock, knock, who needs a nice warm calming tea?" Mrs. B's voice echoed through the library a moment before she appeared with a silver tray filled with a teapot and cups.

She froze in the doorway, eyes rounding as she stared at Vella.

"Matty, what have you done?" Mrs. B's mouth pursed. "Matthias. Are you restraining Vella with magic?"

"You don't understand." Matthias' expression didn't change.

"I understand that you're doing what you think is best for us all." Mrs. B placed the tray on the table near Vella. "But is this the way to go about it?"

"No," Vella sneered. "It's not." She turned her wrists up but didn't try to wriggle again.

"Vella, you look like you need a cup of tea." Mrs. B poured a stream of tea into a delicate Aynsley Orchard Gold teacup.

"I need to get out of here," Vella gritted through clenched teeth.

"You're not going anywhere," Matthias said in his most mild tone yet.

"At least let her take some tea, Matthias." Mrs. B poured another cup. "In fact, you could do with one as well."

"I can't let her go, Mrs. B. She's too angry and not rational enough to be trusted—"

"I am more than fucking rational, you asshole! And I will—"

"See?" He sighed like Vella was the one in the wrong.

"Then change your spell. At the very least, let the girl drink her tea. Now, dinner will be ready in an hour, and I expect you to let Vella eat."

"Eat?" Vella's eyes were close to wild. "Mrs. B, I'm not *hungry*, I need to get out—"

"Well, I think you should. You've had a big day, and sustenance is important. I'll be back with the meal. In fact, why don't we all eat in here?"

"Not a good idea." Matthias stiffened. "Vella needs to see the reality of what's at stake here."

"No, Matthias. Vella needs a meal and some rest. You both do." Mrs. B settled her hands on her hips. "We'll be dining in here tonight. I expect you to have released your guest's arms by the time I'm back."

36

Two hours later, Vella still seethed as she sat at the far end of the couch, feet stuck to the ground as everyone finished their meals around her. The Burrowses sat on the sofa opposite. Matthias was beside Vella, at the far end—just as well he wasn't any closer or she'd have made sure he knew she was still furious at him. And Amelia had settled at the reading table by the window. The Mors Dicen trio were still nervous about being around others, and had elected to eat dinner in Ryan's bedroom.

"Vella, are you sure you're not hungry?" Mrs. B placed hers and Mr. Burrows' dinner plates on the trolley Mr. Burrows had wheeled up before sitting back down.

"No." Vella's stomach rumbled. "No, I'm fine."

"Well, I'll leave your plate with a lid just in case. So, Matthias, how is the program going to help the children in your new country?"

Matthias' gaze dipped to her stomach before he turned back to Mrs. B. "Ronin's taking the lead on the school programs, but we've got centers up and running in

Seattle, San Fran and Aurora, and we're actively looking for more locations."

"Oh, that's wonderful. Ronin has done a wonderful job. Is he finding many young witches?"

"Slowly, he is," Matt said between bites. "The main thing is that we're getting the word out to the kids of witches who died during, or just after, the war broke out. You can tell it's been tough for them."

"What do you mean, tough?" Vella's stomach rumbled again, but she ignored it. No way was she eating with these people. "And I don't know about any witchcraft schools."

"The Council stopped all formal witchcraft learning after their coup," Mrs. B said softly. "But when Matthias joined the Council five years ago—did you know he was the youngest ever to pass the test?—he discreetly reopened programs to allow any witch to learn their craft, regardless of which coven they belong to. He was already running them here, and he used the profits from the club to pay—"

"Billy, this isn't important," Matthias murmured.

"Oh yes, it is. Matty, you have always taken on so much responsibility." Mrs. B shook her head and traded a sad glance with Mr. Burrows. "But it's time you stopped feeling guilty for what happened with your parents and all the witches since then."

Guilt? What did Medea have to feel guilty about?

"You know, this is nice," Amelia said into the silence. "Shame we don't have Shannah here. That girl can party. Or Ronin, mind you, he was never up for the partying like Shannah."

"You people are loco! I'm tied up, and you're talking like this is a frigging picnic."

"No, Vella." Matthias sighed. "We're talking like a

family formed by love and affection and history. And, Ams, I wish Shannah and Ronin were with us, too."

"Well, I think we'll call it a night." Mrs. B elbowed her husband. "Matthias, Mr. Burrows and I are staying upstairs tonight. Out you all go now." Mrs. B shooed everyone but hung back. "Matthias, if you insist on this behavior with Vella, then I expect you to look out for her comfort—your mother would have had nothing less." Mrs. B smiled softly at Vella, then closed the library doors behind her.

Comfort. Right. Like that was ever going to happen.

Matthias stood and stoked the fire. Strode to the window. Stared outside into the dark. Strode back to the fire.

He'd retied his hair before dinner, and his glamour was back in place—did he do that automatically?—but as he stared into the flames, she saw the real man.

A ruthless asshole. Deadly. Manipulative. Everything he'd said of himself and what she'd called him. But he loved his family. That was obvious.

And goddess, she'd wanted to know him, hadn't she? Had been driven to reveal the mysteries of Matthias Medea.

She shivered. Well, now she knew.

"You and I are the same," she whispered before she could stop the words.

Matthias stilled, gaze remaining on the flames. "And how is that?"

"We will both do whatever it takes to save the ones we love, and I get that; I can't even fault you for it because I'm the same. For my sister, Matthias, I swear to you, I will go to the ends of our universe if needed."

"But what if you don't have to? Vella, just hear me out. There might be another way to find an antidote for Sara."

"And what if there isn't? What if the bone runes are the way to unfuck everything the Elixirs and Ellaine have done?"

"You're talking about an unknown—"

"And so are you! The only certainty we have is that the bone runes are the strongest divination tool that exists, and if a cure for the poison is out there, the runes will find it."

"Except that's not the only thing we know—it's also a guarantee that if Ellaine gets the bone runes, *she* will have that power. You've seen how much evil she's spread so far —who knows how many more lives will be extinguished?"

A chill swept through her.

"Are you cold?"

"Why do you even care?" Tears burned in her eyes. Frustrated, hurt, scared tears. She dropped her head back and blinked so hard those tears never had a chance to fall.

"I care." Matthias' words whispered over her, sending goosebumps prickling up her arms.

"For everyone else, maybe. But for Sara?" A sob filled Vella's throat, and she tried to curl up—but couldn't. So she wrapped her arms around herself and stared into the fire.

Frigging hell. Everything was so messed up.

Matthias wanted her to risk her sister's life.

"VELLA, VELLA. WAKE UP."

Vella jolted upright. Heart thrashing. Screams shrieking—

"It was a dream, Vella. You're okay. Take a breath." Matthias' low voice filled the void where awful cries had echoed only moments earlier.

She whirled around—but her feet wouldn't budge. Where was she? What had—

She lay in bed in a darkened, circular room. Matthias sat on a chair beside a fireplace filled with glowing embers. And even though she had a blanket, she was so, so *cold*.

Yesterday's events poured back through in a tumult of emotions that took her breath away.

"Shit, you're freezing. Hold on." Matthias stood and talked to the fire, put a hand in the flames—Vella sucked in a breath; how did he not hurt himself?—and the fire whooshed to life. Then he made a curling motion with his hand, and a burst of warm air surrounded her.

"Where are we?"

"The northeast tower. I carried you up—you were so tired you didn't even stir when I walked up all that mountain of steps. Speaking of, there's only one door in, and the stairwell leads back to my bedroom, so you can't get past me. I'll undo the final restraining spell on your feet when I leave. And I wouldn't bother with the window—we're six stories up."

"What time is it?"

"After four. Sunrise is still a few hours away."

Sara's birthday was one day away.

"Vel? Are you ready to listen? I've already got my team back in New York looking for an antidote for the poison. You don't have to use the bone runes to save Sara."

"How long will that take? You can't answer, can you? Because you don't know. But with the bone runes we can find out. I just need one Div who's a powerful enough witch to show me."

"And if you tell that one Div—and somehow, they agree to help you—they'll know that you've discovered

Sara's being poisoned. And how long then before Ellaine finds out?"

"And we're back to saving Sara versus saving the world."

"Vella, how can you ask me to risk everyone—everything—for an unknown after everything you've discovered?"

"And how can you ask me to not fight for Sara? Give it up, Matt. We're just never going to agree on this. So get me Brianna, and then get the gods out of my room."

"She's on the table behind you." Regret and something else ... something like despair filled his gaze, but Vella turned away. He had zero right to be upset because of how she felt about *his* actions. And thank frig, Brianna was there.

The door had barely clicked shut behind Matthias when the magic restraint on her ankles released and she dove for Brianna's box.

"Velvet? Thank the goddess, I was worried when I hadn't heard—"

"It's okay, Brianna. I'm here. We're together." She fumbled for the sheath. "And now I've got this sheath I am never letting you go again. The actual sheath is lead lined with a lid, so I can close it up when you need to rest but keep it open when we want to talk. There's also a panel I can slide open so I can have it rest against my skin, which will have us in contact, but keep my hands free."

"You have found a *cnamh truaill*?"

"A kuh-vaw tru-ill?"

"A bone scabbard. What you just described to me. Now tell me what has happened."

Vella ran through everything as fast and as accurately as she could.

"So now you are trapped in a tower, the Magicae has

the key, and he will not let you find the bone runes for fear of them falling into the hands of your true enemy?"

"Correct."

And frigging goddess, trapped in another tower—this one way more to her taste than the Div version—but in every other respect, it was exactly the same. Ellaine had kept Vella and Sara in that monolith of glass and marble for most of their lives—had only relented and let them leave when Sara had kicked up a fuss a year ago, demanding out of there or she'd stop taking the meds herself—and Vella had been so scared of losing her sister she'd persuaded Ellaine to let them set up their own home base.

And now it all made sense. All those years, Ellaine had used Sara to make Vella behave, destroying Sara's life one potion at a time to keep Vella under her control.

How the hell did they get out of this now?

"Daughter, does this tower have a window?"

"It does, but we're too high up for me to jump."

"Describe to me what you see. Every detail. Remember, I am your Bone Guide, and when we are touching, you can use my skills as your own—and I am an expert fighter, which includes superior balance. If there is a way out of this tower, I can get you there."

"Thank frig."

"Thank frig, indeed. However, as much as I can assist you in exiting the locked tower, I can't transport you to the Stan Stones."

"But that's all we need! I have an idea of what to do when we're out of here. Okay. So it's dark, but we're about two stories—um, about twenty-five feet—above the rest of the castle. There's a roof line below us, but it's only slim."

"Open the *cnamh truaill*, and we shall leave this tower. Trust me, Vella. We can do this, I promise you."

Shit. Shit, shit, shit—she opened the knife sheath.

The veil fell over her vision like normal and her grip on the window ledge shifted, her muscles bunched to hoist up.

Oh shit, she was jumping out the window? No. No, no, no.

"Don't fight me, Daughter. I have you. We are safe. Give me your control."

Good goddess ... She could do this. For Sara, she could do this. Vella let her breath out and then she was crouched, balancing on the windowsill, before she leaped to her right, sliding down the face of the moonlit stone tower until her fingertips grazed the ledge of a window below.

She gripped them tight, held herself there as she absorbed the shock of her momentum stalling. Using her feet to find purchase on the bricks, she pulled herself up fully into the darkened window ledge.

"We must break the glass, Daughter." Vella removed the knife from the sheath and used the bone end to shatter the pane nearest the handle before sliding back in its sheath. Moments later, she reached inside, unhooked the latch and eased the rest of the window open.

Dropping with silent grace to a marble floor, she stilled. No cries to stop. No shouting of her name.

"We appear to be in the bathing room. The only light is through the window, but I see a bathtub and other conveniences. What a marvelous space."

Thank fuck, not Matthias' bathroom. But still ... "Lock the door," Vella whispered. "Sweet goddess, Brianna. You did it! You rescued us from the tower."

"We did it. Together—had you not trusted me, ceded control of your body's movements, you would not have lived past the drop, and I may have hit the ground, smashed into a thousand pieces, none big enough to ever function as a Bone Guide again. Now let me go so you may recover your sight and proceed with your plan."

IT TOOK TIME, but eventually, she eased out of the bathroom and found her way to the library. Cell ... cell ... cell ... there! She grabbed it and ran out of the house. Her coat and purse were back in her bedroom; dawn was an hour away, and Darklings could be anywhere, but Vella didn't look back.

Sara was all that mattered.

37

A fter stealing the Burrows' ancient Range Rover, Vella tossed Brianna onto the passenger seat, texted her aunt to confirm Stonehenge was her next destination, and hit the gas.

And as she sped along the empty highways, as fast as if all the Darklings in the world were chasing her—which they could've been for all she knew—Matthias' face swam through Vella's mind. He was going to be pissed. Maybe even as angry as she was.

"Asshole." She banged the steering wheel. "Shit. Shit, shit, shit."

"That is a lot of shit," Brianna murmured. "Are you upset with yourself or another?"

"Oh, I'm mad at both me and him."

"You speak of Matthias?"

"Yes." A mix of fury and hurt and longing for a reality anything other than what it was jumbled and clawed through Vella's stomach.

"He is a rather remarkable specimen. Even I appreciated the view."

"You and a million other witches."

"What happened?"

As if the floodgates were opened, Vella poured everything out—every single thing.

"Vella, this Druid of yours—"

"Not mine."

"Well, that would be a shame given you sound like two strong-willed, powerful witches, and if everything he and you have said is true, your world needs witches like you to come together and create strong coven members to see in a new future for witchkind."

"*What*? After what I just told you, you want me to have kids with him? We just banged for cauldron's sake. And banged means fucked, to be clear."

"I gathered that. In fact, you appeared to have banged each other a lot yesterday. Children are still a result of banging in your day, aren't they?"

"We have ways of making sure children don't come from fucking these days. And we didn't just bang yesterday, we also banged at the standing stones—"

"Stop. You enjoyed carnal knowledge of each other *within* the circle of the standing stones?" Brianna's cackle made the hairs raise on the back of Vella's neck.

"I said we had sex. But same, same."

"Not entirely ... Was there an emotional bond of any sort? Vella? Hah. I knew it! There was. That, Daughter, is the key. Oh well, you shall just have to wait and see what has occurred."

"What do you mean? What the hell can occur from having sex with someone you like—*used* to like—in a henge?"

"We use the standing stones for rituals, Vella. And some of those are for bonding. And there are benefits to that, like having a strong mate at your side. My mate and I bonded the day we met, and though our lives took us to many different places, that connection has stayed true even to this day."

"You bonded? What does that mean?"

"It meant that Tara, my star, and I didn't just bond in our love. Our magic also bonded after we met between the stan stones and completed the ancient rite. I see this is another lesson. Vella, the power that lives inside every witch—no matter where that power springs from—can form a connection with another that can never be severed."

"Holy shit. So, Tara—can I ask, what happened to her?"

"At the time of my birth, the Mors Dicen were not one united coven, and Tara and I were warriors from different clans. Our love was forbidden, but when the bond happened, our families realized there was nothing to be done but let us be. However, we both agreed that supporting our bloodlines was the highest honor we could ask for; therefore, we each became Bone Guides, undergoing the sacred rite together. Tara was my moon and earth, and if you have found someone who is that to you, then you are blessed indeed."

"Brianna, I don't have that. After what he did, I hate him. And when he finds me gone, he'll sure as shit hate me."

"Hmm. It seems to me you are similar in ways that are important, believing that others' lives mean more than your own, that sacrifices must be made when times require them."

"You're still wrong. I'm not in love—or bonded—with a man I just met. Now hush, the visitor car park for Stonehenge isn't far away. I need to concentrate."

The car park was also empty, unsurprisingly so, given

predawn darkness still blanketed the ground. A shiver raced up Vella's spine, and she regripped the steering wheel as she followed the road past the official entry, using a mix of GPS maps and Brianna's advice to make sure no one saw her approach the sacred site.

"Almost there," Vella breathed. She could do this—no. She *was* doing this.

"What time is it?" Brianna murmured.

"Half past six."

"I would love to see the sunrise." The wistfulness in Brianna's tone caught Vella off guard. "If you were in physical contact with me, I would know this for myself."

"And I'd have zero chance of driving since you might be good in a knife fight and escaping towers, but you know jack-shit about driving a car. And I don't fancy being blind for even a few minutes here."

"I dislike it when your practical nature makes sense."

"Don't worry, it won't happen all the time. And look— there's the road we need. Okay, I'm parking here. The official visitors' center is about a mile away. It's brightly lit— guess they don't want to risk any Darkling attacks." She checked her cell screen, and her breath whooshed out. "And good news—Aunt Ellaine just got back to me. They're coming here."

"Are you sure that's wise? What of your Druid's words?"

"Not my Druid. And I'm not giving the bone runes to Ellaine forever—this is just until I find the cure for Sara and then I'm taking them back. No way will I leave them under that bitch's control."

"Then you're almost there. Wait, why are you not departing your vehicle?"

Vella took a deep breath.

"It is okay, Vella. I'm here," Brianna soothed.

"How do you know I'm scared?"

"You are breathing faster than normal."

"Since you've got mad hearing skills, can you hear anyone else nearby? Like Darklings? Or people with poison spheres or guns?"

"I hear none of that. But perhaps I will hear more when we are outside in the wind."

"Okay. Here goes." With her heart pounding and her mouth drier than dust, Vella made sure Brianna's sheath was firmly attached to her belt, secure in the dip of her lower back, but that the flap was open, then eased out of the car.

Her feet crunched in the frost-covered grass.

And rising in the charcoal sky, the monumental sarsen stones of Stonehenge. Goosebumps prickled up Vella's neck.

"Anything?" she whispered.

"The rustle of windswept grass. Bird calls and nocturnal animals readying for their rest. Nothing else."

"Thank frig." Vella tightened her coat.

"Your teeth are chattering now," Brianna murmured.

"Because it's so cold the air hurts. So where do I go?"

"Approach from the Heel Stone—it's to the northwest."

It took long minutes, but Vella passed the Heel Stone, and eventually, reached the circle of stones embedded into the earth. Up close, even against the predawn sky, the moss-covered ancient stone was incredible. "Amazing," she breathed.

"Vella!" Brianna hissed. "Someone comes—"

38

M att drove to Stonehenge faster than he'd ever pushed a vehicle. He'd woken up to the sound of a car engine in the distance, and bloody hell, he'd known instantly who had been driving, and while he'd tried to convince Ryan, Liam and Ciara to stay at Madgewick, they'd informed him if he left without them, they'd just follow on their own.

So fuck it, they were all together in his car. But maybe they could help convince Vella to go with his plan for the bone runes, and not hers.

Fuck. Fuck, fuck, *fuck*.

What if she still refused? She was going to hate him when he took the bone runes from her.

He pushed the car as hard as he could, but Vella must have driven just as wildly as he hadn't caught up with her by the time the Stonehenge visitor center lit up the dawn sky, its parking lot empty. But Vella would need to sneak up to the monument, so Matt followed the road around to the rear, and there—Mrs. B's car.

The tension he'd been carrying whooshed out as he pulled to a stop. Thank the gods he'd found her.

With the sarsen stones as his guide in the predawn air, Matt took off, running as fast as possible over the uneven ground, vaulted over a flat rock embedded in the earth, then ran into the center of Stonehenge.

Vella stood in the middle of the circle, and she spun around as he skidded to a stop, the rest of the Mors Dicen not far behind him.

"Matt. How did you get here—"

The hairs on the back of Matt's neck pricked one moment before a figure stepped out from between the sarsen stones.

"Matthias, so good to see you again," Councilor Charles said. "And what a pretty picture you make. You do seem to be cementing your relationship with the Divinators."

Ice settled in Matt's veins, and he deliberately shifted, this time shielding Vella.

"Charles," Matt bit out. "Early for an Elixir to be out and about." But was the Elixir Councilor alone? Holding his breath, Matt strained to hear around the site ... four sets of footsteps whispered through the air, two people coming from each side of Charles. Meaning the only way out was behind Matt.

"Councilor Charles?" Vella called out from behind him. "Are Ellaine—Aunt Ellaine—and Derrick with you?"

"Not at this moment." Charles smiled without a trace of warmth. "They're having a sleep in."

"How lucky for them." Matt forced a bland smile. "Vella, why don't you and your friends head back to the car and leave us Councilors to discuss Council business?" Matt caught Ryan's eye and gave a subtle nod toward the parking lot.

"Actually, Vella, stay right where you are." Charles reached into his jacket and withdrew a handgun. "Bonnie, Julianne, please join us here inside the circle."

The two assassins who'd chased Matt and Vella across the country stepped out from around the sarsen stones to Matt's right. They each held poison spheres and had tubes strapped to their waists with presumably more.

"And now, Henry and Gwen, you too, please." Charles stared at Matt with such delight that dread curdled in Matt's gut.

Gwen, the Nocturnal UK manager, and Henry from his security team stepped into the circle on his other side. Instead of poison spheres, they held handguns in capable two-handed grips.

Rage poured through Matt until his blood pounded in his ears.

But fucking hell, fury wouldn't help them here.

Control, Matt. Control.

"Matthias," Gwen purred in her trademark voice. "Shame it had to come to this."

"Shame is certainly the right word choice."

"There now, we're all here." Charles smiled. "Matthias, you look surprised. Ah yes, you didn't know the talented Gwen and Henry are part of my coven?"

"A hiring oversight I won't make again."

"That's for certain." Charles chuckled. An actual laugh. "Given you'll be dead."

"As lovely as hearing you have my death all planned out is, perhaps you could share why I have to die." Matthias tried to appear unthreatening. "I'm guessing you were behind the attempt on my life at the winter ball?"

"A last request?" Charles barked a mocking laugh. "Oh, I like this. And it is nice to share my brilliance." He pointed the handgun at Matt.

"Please, enlighten us." *Arrogant fucker.*

"Councilor Charles," Gwen called out. "Matthias is stalling you—"

"Oh, I know that. But we have them surrounded, and there's no help coming. The mighty Magicae reduced to worthless spells and stalling tactics; believe me, we have time for this story." Charles shifted his gaze to Matthias. "Now, Matthias, step to your right, please, away from Vella. And hands on your head, we don't want any of your freakish winds today, do we? Well, where should I start? The first attempt on your life, I suppose—that was a distraction. But it came with the added benefit of removing you from the Council."

"Which was important, why?"

"Matthias, you have been entirely too successful with your business. Wealth equals power, and I have no intention of allowing another Councilor to amass more of either commodity than I. And when you are gone, the lovely Gwen is going to help me take over your business."

Over his dead body. "How delightful of her," he murmured. *Control, Matt, Control.* "And the other attempts?"

"Those took planning—and I must say, these concoctions are rather impressive." Charles surveyed the poison sphere. "As soon as Ellaine decided to strengthen ties with your coven, it was time for you to go. Another coven will never be allowed to usurp the Elixirs."

Matt's breath caught in disbelief. His plan had worked —too well. And now Vella and the remaining Mors Dicen were all in danger.

"But how did you find us at the gallery?" Matt tried to infuse wonder into his tone. "And again, in Scotland?"

"He got one of Ellaine's foreseers to work for him," Vella whispered. "And you must have brought the Div to the UK so they'd be close enough to lock on a vision of us."

"Well done, Vella." Charles clapped his free hand on his wrist. "How did you work that out?"

"Only a skilled foreseer would have the accuracy needed to find us. And unless you have a hedge witch on your payroll—which I highly doubt—it has to be a Div. Ellaine mentioned one of her seniors was missing, but how did you get them to work for you?"

"A delicate persuasion potion delivered the night of Matthias's winter ball."

"That's why you needed the distraction of my poisoning." And now Matt needed a distraction …

"And it worked perfectly. In the attack's wake, no one noticed the foreseer come home with me, and from that night on, everyone has been so focused on finding who ordered your assassination they haven't worried about one missing foreseer."

"You fucker," Vella snarled.

"Vella." Matt tensed, ready to leap in front of her. "Stop."

"Yes, Velvet. Stop talking to me like that. And who are your friends?"

"Just locals who helped me get here." Vella backed toward Ryan, Ciara and Liam.

"Then it's a shame you brought them into a situation they cannot be allowed to leave. And Velvet? Please don't step any closer to them." Charles pointed at the trio behind her. "Bonnie, Julianne, if any of them move, take them out."

"Charles, you bastard," Vella snarled. "You can't just kill them—"

"*Councilor* Charles. And yes, I can."

"But surely Ellaine won't support this action. You'll be angering the head of the Council—"

"By the time anyone else gets here, it won't matter as I'll have the ancient bone runes, and the Elixirs will no longer be second best. Now, Vella, you are going to take me to the runes."

Matt glanced at Vella. Her lioness eyes were narrowed on Charles, and he could see her fury at the Elixir. And rightly so, given what the fucker had done to Sara all these years. But shit, if Vella went for her knife, and Charles shot her—

Losing Vella? For the world to lose Vella? Ice congealed in his veins. No. Fucking. Way. She mattered too much to those who loved her—including him, fuck it —and there would never be a world where he'd lie down and let Charles hurt her.

Fury rose in a firestorm, obliterating all other thoughts.

He dropped all his magic, including his glamour, and stepped in front of Vella. "You don't deserve to stand on the same ground as Vella. And I will fucking destroy you for threatening her."

"How touching. Shame you won't be alive to stop me. And before you die, I should say how nice it is to see your scars. I do like viewing the handiwork of my coven, even if I personally would've gone about your punishment in a more permanent way. An error I'll resolve now."

"Matt!" Vella yelled. She whipped Brianna's knife out from her shirt and threw the blade end over end, straight at Charles.

Crack. Crack. Crack. Gunshots split the predawn air.

Poison spheres flew. Voices cried out.

Matt wrenched on his elemental connection to the wind and sent a gale rushing around the tallest sarsen stones, encasing Vella and the Mors Dicen, holding back any more spheres.

Crack. Another shot. Another. More cries and shouts.

Vella. *Fuck, no. No, no, no.* Could his wind stop a bullet?

Matt roared his connection to the elements until he was part man, part air and earth, and then he was the whirlwind tearing around the henge, the earth opening beneath the stones.

He picked up Gwen and slammed her into one. *Crack.* Smashed Henry high into another. *Crunch.* He opened a chasm and dragged Bonnie under, sealing it over. Split the ground beneath Julianne and entombed her.

And scream after scream ricocheted around the ancient stones. Until they stopped.

39

W here one moment, roaring wind and screams and booming gunshots had filled the air, now, only Vella's harsh breathing echoed in her ears. And with her sight traded for Brianna's to throw the knife at Charles, Vella dropped to her knees, digging her fingers into the ground. A rush of energy made her head spin, and claw-like itches dug into her neck, but she steadied herself fast, strained to hear anything above her ragged inhales, exhales.

Focus, Vel, have to use your other senses now.

But shit! Matt? What had happened to him? He'd stepped in front of her. So many gunshots. So many screams and awful thuds and cracks and crunches as bodies were flung around the stones. Her heart stopped. No. No, no, no. He couldn't be dead. She had to tell him what an asshole he was but also how much she cared—

"Vella?"

"Matt? Matt!"

Strong arms picked her up and hauled her into a familiar, sold chest, and as she felt the pulse of Matt's heart beating beneath her cheek, relief spun with dizzying speed through her.

"Are you hurt? Vella?"

"Goddess, Matt, you're not dead—I thought you'd been killed."

Suddenly, his hands were cradling her jaw and his lips pressed to hers, but before she could gasp a breath, he'd pulled away. "I thought I'd lost you, too," he whispered.

"Matt, I can't see—I used Brianna's sight to throw her at Charles. Please, tell me that fucker's dead."

"Stay here. I need to check him and the others."

"Ryan, can you hear me?" Vella held her breath. "Brianna, are Ryan and Liam—"

"We're here," Ryan's thin voice came from behind her, followed by the soft hiccups of someone crying.

"Ryan and Ciara are hurt," Brianna said. "I cannot hear Liam. I think he has died."

"Oh goddess, no." Tears burned at Vella's eyes, and instead of walking, she dropped back to the ground. "Ryan, I'm coming to you. Talk to me so I can find you—"

"Vella, stop," Matt yelled.

She froze.

"Fuck, that was close," he said from right beside her. "Here, I'm picking you up and putting you on this flat stone. Do not move."

"No, I need to get to Ryan."

"There's poison everywhere. Just stay here until you can see again. I'll go to Ryan. And, Vella—Charles is dead. Along with the others."

"Thank the goddess." Her breath whooshed out. "Ryan," she called into the darkness of her missing sight. "Matt's coming. How badly are you hurt?"

"Gunshot, arm and hand—through the fucking plaster."

"I'm with him now," Matt called out.

"And Ciara? Ciara, where are you?"

"Ciara is alive, but her friend has died," Matt said in the same gentle tone he used with Sara. "And she can't touch him. Ciara, I need you to come away. If you touch the poison residue, you could die too. That's it, come on."

"Vella, Ryan," Brianna called out. "I hear motorized vehicles in the distance, faint, but they are coming."

"Shit." Vella relayed that to Matt. "It must be Ellaine and Derrick. What if they've foreseen this fight?"

"I called a concealing spell before you killed Charles, so they can't have seen from there on. Ryan, you and Ciara need to go now. Take my car. We cannot let anyone else find you."

"What about Vella?" Ryan whispered. "You should come with us."

"I can't. Ryan, I'm here for a reason that I *must* finish. But you go, and I promise I'll find you after this."

"Wait, you need Brianna." A moment later, Vella felt the weight of Brianna sliding into the sheath at her back. "I'll see you again soon, Vella of the Knife." Ryan pressed his hand to hers. "Blessings be."

"Blessings be," she whispered back. And then Ryan's and Ciara's footsteps faded as they left Stonehenge.

In the sudden silence, Vella took a deep breath. Frigging goddess, how did she and Matt work this out?

"Matt, Brianna has a theory that the bone runes are below us. I know we disagree on what to do with them, but we need—"

"To find the bone runes. I know. On that, we do agree."

"Find the true darkness," Brianna said. "Look to the tallest of standing stones, the one where the top flat stone frames the morning light on the solstice. Find the notch carved so the two stones fit together. There will be a place so dark no light can penetrate. Then you can connect to the dark energy and move the earth."

"But Brianna, I still can't *see* anything." Vella raked a hand over her face. "How can I connect to the darkness and get us under Stonehenge if I can't find it?"

"Vella." Matt's hand was suddenly holding hers. "I have no idea what Brianna just said, but you and I—we have been so used to working alone that we never ask for help. But if you need the earth moved, then I can do that. Druid, remember? Here, I'm going to carry you. Tell me where to go."

She whispered Brianna's instructions.

"There's a tunnel beneath us, and the earth will reveal itself," Matt repeated. "Okay, I'm putting you back on your feet now, but keep holding my hand. I'll reach down with my other and touch the earth."

Vella squinted, made out a huge blurry shape ahead.

"Bloody hell," Matt breathed. "The earth just opened at my feet, like a sinkhole, but with steps."

"Thank the goddess. We're almost there," she said to his outline. "But, Matt, I need to talk to you, have so much to tell you—"

"I know, gods, I know. But let's get under Stonehenge first. We've got twenty minutes, maybe a little more, based on how far away those cars are." He tugged her hand. "Do you want help down the steps?"

"Under Stonehenge," she repeated. "Can't believe you just said that. And yes. I need help. I can see better, but my feet are still a blur."

Then Matt's arms were around her again, and he held her tight as the cool, rich, musky earth enveloped them. Pitched them into obsidian darkness.

Matt whispered something, and a tiny ball of witch-light emerged into the darkness.

"Shit," Vella breathed as she took in what Matt's magic had revealed. "What is this place? And are there corridors? I can't quite make them out—"

"There's three tunnels," Matthias murmured. "All going in different directions."

"This is our sacred temple. What else did you think was here?" Brianna whispered.

"Nothing like this, that's for sure. I knew about the barrows—the tombs of our ancestors—but this ... And why are you whispering?"

"Because the creatures that lurk below Stan Stones can hear me as well as you. We must all be quiet. Do not awaken that which sleeps unless you want more blood to bathe this soil."

"Matt," Vella hissed. "We have to whisper; things might be down here."

"Things?"

"Brianna said creatures, so let's just go with things that might hurt us. She knows the way, though. Brianna? Where do we go?"

"Go to your right, follow this passage, wait—I sense something else here with us. Vella, you are not alone!"

A chill ran down her spine. "Matt, something—"

In the witchlight's glow, shadows moved along the wall. Humanlike figures stretching high over the tunnel walls. Matt spun, and the witchlight revealed more and more of the forms.

"Darklings," Vella breathed. "Everywhere."

"Fuck," Matt hissed. He yanked her tight to his back.

"Vella, I have told you before, the Darklings cannot hurt you." Even in a whisper, Brianna's tone carried her exasperation. "Nor can they hurt your Druid. You are both born of the dark energy that they travel through."

"Then why are they here?"

"That I do not know. But if you go into the shadow where they come from, you may find out."

"You want me to go *with them*?"

"What the fuck?" Matt hissed. "Vella, what is Brianna saying?"

"Shh, Matt, not so loud." Vella shared Brianna's advice.

"Good news about not hurting us," he whispered. "But *go into the shadows with them*?"

"Yeah, not happening. Listen, we must get the runes, and since we're unhurt, let's just move forward."

"Shh, Vella." Brianna's whisper was so quiet Vella had to strain to hear it. "You pass a place of great danger now. Do not look to the left, no matter what."

"Matt." Vella pitched her voice as low as Brianna's and recounted her words exactly. Then she picked up Matt's hand, clutched it to her, and with her heart once against thrashing in her ears, they inched through the tunnel. And was it her imagination, or were the Darklings crowding closer from every direction?

"Brianna says we're past the bad thing," she whispered into Matt's back. "And though we've got a way to go yet, we can talk again, just quietly."

Vella let her breath out, and as she did, the Darklings seemed to give Matt and her more space as well.

"Thank fuck. My hair stood that entire time."

"Can I ask a question? It's about your scars." He didn't say no, although technically, he didn't say yes either, so she pushed on. "You cast a spell nonstop to hide them?"

"Every moment of my public life, yes."

Vella's breath whooshed out. "That's ... a lot. Do you ever relax? Get to be just Matthias Medea?"

"In public, I am always what the Divs and Elixirs expect me to be: the playboy witch who runs nightclubs and appears useless and grovels to Ellaine and does what he's told like a good fucking lapdog."

Vella stared at Matt's back, battling back sorrow and horror at how he'd been living.

"Don't feel sorry for me," he murmured.

"Reading my mind again?" She squeezed the words through her scratchy throat.

"Reading your silence. But I don't want your pity. The truth is, I made my choice to be that man because, inside me, there's a river of hatred that feeds one goal: destroy the Council. And if that means pretending to be a pet for those I despise most, then that's what I will be. Nothing matters more than freeing witchkind."

Now, that was a sentiment she agreed with. Vella's chest went tight, and she thought Matt was finished when he slowed down and reached back for her hand. "But there are two things I do when I am alone—or just with family. I read and I connect with nature. Those are my jams."

Vella couldn't stop a small smile, not that he'd be able to see it. "Good to know you have something for yourself. And that explains all the books at your lake house."

"The tunnel is ahead," Brianna murmured.

A chill flew through Vella, but there was no going back now, so she shared Brianna's directions, then followed Matt and his witchlight into the next tunnel.

"I guess we're here." Matt stopped, and she stepped past him into a large, round, dirt-walled room with a stone altar in the middle covered in bones and boxes and urns.

"Brianna, any idea what these all are?"

"Sacred offerings, either hidden or protected throughout our history. You must be careful, Vella. Only touch the runes you are here for—to lay a hand on anything else may bring all the creatures under the stones to us."

"Well frig." Vella did another fast recount for Matt.

"Use the darkness," Brianna murmured. "Perhaps it can show you the way."

"Seriously? You want me to go into the dark energy down here?"

"And keep the Druid with you."

"Shit," she muttered under her breath. "Uh, Matt? Brianna thinks I should take you into the dark energy to find the runes, and yes, shit is going to get freaky."

"Freakier than it already is?"

"Good point."

"Vella, I trust you. Whatever you think we need to do, do it. I'm here with you."

"Matt, I have no idea why the goddess sent you my way, but right now, no matter what else happens, I am glad she did. Okay, here goes. Snuff that witchlight, spellcaster. I need the dark."

"As you order, Rapunzel."

Vella connected with the dark energy in an instant, the itch shooting into her neck, running down her arms to her palms, and then midnight diamonds highlighted everything she could see. Even Matt and Vella were covered.

"What is this?" Matt whispered.

"The place my magic and your Druid power spring from—according to Brianna. And look, the midnight diamonds are coating everything on the table. Keep holding my hand, but we need to get closer. I think I can follow the strands if I must, but I really don't want to down here."

"You can travel this dark energy?"

"That's how I discovered you knew about Sara's meds

—I traveled into the study when you were talking with Ronin."

"Really? You and I need to add eavesdropping to our chat when we get out of here."

"Busted. And fine. But wait, look at how the dark energy is everywhere except that skull in the center. I'm going to reach out and see if I can feel anything."

As soon as she did, an itch scrabbled at the skin along the back of her neck. "Thank fuck."

"That's it?"

"I think so. But if I'm wrong, get ready to run like all hell."

"Wouldn't expect anything else with you."

Vella took a deep breath and picked up the skull. Through the eyeholes, she counted eight roughly shaped oval runes.

"Is that them? Are your ancestors talking to you?"

"It's only eight runes—one aett."

"What? I thought runes were made up of twenty-four bones?"

"They are, but look around. I don't see any sign of the other two aetts. Maybe the bone runes were split up? And they're not talking to me, but Brianna said only the living enter the dark energy, which is why she's not here."

"Then we need to get out and confirm—"

"Wait, Matt, before we go, right now, you and I are hidden from the Div foreseers." With her free hand, she took one of his. "You don't need to call a concealing spell because their magic can't see us."

"Really? How do you know—Brianna?"

"Yes. And you should know they can't see you when you're using your Druid magic, and the same with the vamps. Any power or magic born from dark energy is invisible to the Divs."

"Fucking hell," Matt breathed. "Do you know what this means? I have a way to fight back."

"But why you? Why do you have to do all this? Where is the rest of the witching world standing up to Ellaine?"

"They don't ... because of me." He glanced down at his hands.

"What do you mean? Is this because of what Mrs. B said last night about you feeling guilty? Matt?"

He sighed, and a chill crawled into the cavern. "After the coup, our allies stopped fighting because of what happened to me—they'd seen the aftermath of the acid attack, and they didn't want to risk that for their children. And I wasn't there when my parents died so I'll never know if I could've stopped it. Those two facts are irrefutable. So yeah, I carry the weight of that responsibility—but how can I do anything else?"

"Except ... it's not just them, is it? Cressida—you said something when she was killed, about it being your fault. Is that how you feel, that everyone killed by the Elixirs and the Divs is somehow your responsibility?"

His jaw clenched, and still, he didn't meet her gaze. And her heart fractured—just a little. But enough that she couldn't stop her next words. "And me? Do you now see me as your responsibility?"

Finally, he shifted and faced her, the galaxy of stars once more whirring in his eyes. "You are," he whispered.

"No. No, I am not. I am my own person. I can fight, I can fuck, I can love or not love, and all of that is my decision. Not yours. But I see it now—you've been pulling away from me ever since we had sex at the henge—"

"What? We had sex again—"

"Yeah, but at the henge, you said it—you cared for me. And then, *bang*, I went from someone you could have fun with to someone you had feelings for. And like everyone else you care about, I became another weight around your shoulders."

"You're wrong, Vella—"

"No, I don't think I am. And you know what—I care for you right back, and I won't pretend otherwise. But, Matt. This guilt—this toxic guilt—is *your* issue, and you need to figure your shit out because I have my own battles. And first up is saving Sara."

40

Covered in glittering obsidian stars, with her lioness eyes glowing, Vella was every fierce midnight fantasy Matt had ever had—and never dreamed he might touch. And with her discovery about his Druid powers being invisible to Div foresight, she'd just given him an edge in this war he'd never imagined possible.

No wonder he ... felt so much for her. And she thought he was deliberately pushing her away because of his feelings? But damn it, he had to keep a level of separation—didn't he?

"Matt, I get why you don't want these runes in Ellaine's hands. I said before that I'd never work for her again, and that I wouldn't give the runes to the Divs, but ..."

He steeled himself because he already knew her next words. Sara. "And I understand why you think you need them. Except, your aunt—"

"No." Vella pulled him to her, and he tucked her against his chest, held onto her as tightly as she held him.

"She's not my aunt. You and I, when it's just us together, we are never going to call her that again. Ever."

"And your real name? Vespera?"

"I think ..." She eased back and stared up at him. "I think for now, let's just stick with Vella."

"Done. And gods, I wish we had more time to talk." Could talk to her more about his fears and his guilt and how it all mixed up to make him fucking terrified of losing her. "But I can hear the rumble of cars above ground. We need to go, *now*." He picked up her icy hand.

"Then we'll talk while we walk—because I have an idea. But it means you need to trust me. More than ever before."

"What do you mean?" He tightened his grip to transfer some warmth into her palm.

"I'll explain on the way. Just listen. Please."

Minutes later, with his stomach churning at Vella's whispered words, he followed her up the earthen steps and into the mist-shrouded inner circle, where bodies made macabre mounds through the drifting fog and blood splatter turned the sarsen stones rusty red in the rising sun.

"So, will you trust me?" Vella whispered.

"You're asking a fucking lot, Vella," he gritted out. "And hell, we don't have long—but there's something I must do before Elaine gets here." He knelt and dug his fingers into the ground, and with his Druid power exhumed the bodies he'd suffocated.

"Good call. This sacred ground doesn't deserve their contamination—" Vella's eyes widened, and she stared at the skull in her hands for a long moment.

"Vella? What is it?" Adrenaline surged and he leaped back to his feet.

"Nothing bad. It's the skull ... it belongs to a Mors

Dicen witch, too. I couldn't hear her when we were inside the dark energy. Yes, Tara? Hello, I'm Vella—Vespera, actually. But call me Vella, and it's nice to meet you too—"

Voices echoed beyond the stones.

"Shit." Matt grabbed her free hand. "Whoever's coming is close. I'm dropping the concealing spell." He reassembled his glamour. "The bone runes—"

"I know you fear Ellaine having them. But like I said, you just need to trust me."

"It's not you I don't trust. The immense power *she'll* have with them is what terrifies me." Along with the thought of what Vella wanted to do. "Vella, I can't risk—"

"The runes. I get it—"

"No, you don't fucking get anything. I can't risk—"

Ellaine and Derrick, along with Nevena Montgomery and two Special Investigators, strode into the circle.

The biggest threat had arrived, and everything inside Matt went on high alert.

Despite the horrific scene, Ellaine's gaze locked on Vella, and perhaps if Matt hadn't been watching her so carefully, he'd have missed the slight flare of the Div Councilor's nostrils, the triumphant gleam in her eyes before her expression returned to normal.

Murderer. Kidnapper. Abuser. And fucking perpetrator of how much more evilness? Power clawed through him, ready to—

Control, Matthias. Control.

"Vella, are you hurt?" Ellaine picked her way between the bodies and splatters.

"I'm not physically injured," Vella whispered. Fuck but she was doing an amazing job of holding herself together. "Charles and his coven members attacked us."

"Surely not?" Ellaine slowly spun around. Was she

comparing the scene to the vision that had led her to kill Vella's parents?

"It's true. I'm fortunate Matthias was here; otherwise, I'd be dead."

A shiver shook through Matt at just how true that statement was. Even if Charles had killed Matt, no question the Elixir Councilor would've killed Vella after—if—she'd delivered him the bone runes.

Gods but bring on the day he could destroy every last fucking one of them.

"Check all the other bodies and remove any personal identifiers," Derrick ordered the two investigators, then ducked down beside Charles' body.

"Watch out for the poison." Nevena Montgomery's voice rang out, cool and collected. She glanced at Matt, and something intense sharpened in her gaze before she turned back to the Special Investigators. "Standard safety protocols and call me if you have any questions regarding the toxins used."

"This is a knife wound," Derrick called out.

"I killed him." Matt buried his rage deep, deep down and forced a casual shrug. "He pulled a gun on Vella, and it was the only way I could save her."

"Did Charles say why?" Ellaine's gaze locked back on Vella.

"He wanted these." Vella held up the skull. "The bone runes."

"You did it!" Derrick leaped back to his feet.

"Vella, you wonderful, darling girl. Where were they?"

"Beneath us. Matthias has a new spell—" Vella's gaze cut to him, and he fucking knew what she was about to do.

Fuck. Fuck, fuck, *fuck*. All his plotting had come down

to this moment, but there was shit all he could do to stop Vella without risking her—and his entire coven. Not now. Not anymore. Fear and fury battled for supremacy, and fuck it, he couldn't give into either emotion.

"Councilor Matthias was reluctant to use the spell," she continued. "Because it's not approved yet, but I insisted you'd be okay if he used his magic to help us achieve our goal. And so he moved the earth right here beneath the centre stone—"

"And found them." Satisfaction bloated Ellaine's tone.

"Not entirely." Vella raised the skull. "There's only one aett here. Eight bone runes in total."

"Are you certain?" Ellaine froze.

Vella nodded. "Here, you should take it. I suggest we put it somewhere safe immediately."

Ellaine reached for the skull, only to pause. Her lips tightened, and a flash of fear crossed her face—the first time Matt had ever witnessed that emotion from Ellaine.

"Derrick," Ellaine called. "Have your team take this immediately. There's a box in the car it can be placed in for safety." As soon as the investigator took the skull, Ellaine let out a subtle breath. Interesting. "Matthias, you have my thanks for dispatching Charles."

"No thanks necessary." Matt forced back the urge to let every ounce of his power loose on Ellaine right there and then. If only he could—if only that magic wouldn't rebound and target the people he loved instead. "Vella's wellbeing is a priority for me."

"On that note, my niece needs to focus on her business; therefore, I suggest concluding the contract you have together."

"That would be a shame with so many of our mutual acquaintances aware of Vella's role and looking forward to seeing her work. However, Ellaine, whatever you suggest is best." He turned to Vella. "It's been a pleasure. I hope to see you back in New York—"

"Unlikely," Ellaine cut in. "Vella, you don't wish to see any more of Matthias, do you?"

"No." Vella turned her lioness gaze on him, this time emotionless. "Thank you for your help with the runes, Councilor Matthias, and your assistance here today. There is nothing else."

"Excellent, Vella. It is good to thank those who help us." Ellaine's polished smile returned. "Now, Matthias, considering Charles' untimely demise this morning, we will need to call a Council meeting to elect his replacement."

"Of course." What was the Div Councilor up to now?

"Given our next official Council gathering is the spring equinox, I suggest an interim Councilor—Nevena Montgomery, the current Elixir Second. Nevena has been especially useful to us here today and with other recent matters. I'll be in touch when you are back in New York to arrange the voting process. Vella, Derrick, Nevena, we are leaving. Matthias, I'll leave you here to clean this ... mess up."

Rage burned hotter than ever, but Matt battened the seething mess of emotion down. "As you say. The Magicae are here to support the Council in whatever way we can."

Ellaine nodded as if those words were exactly as expected and gestured for her coven to precede her.

But as they left the stone circle, Matt couldn't hold the power back anymore—and no doubt if they'd turned back, they'd have seen the burning need to raise the earth and stop Vella from leaving, to throw the wind at Ellaine and remove her from this world, whirling in his eyes.

Control, Matt. Control.

Finally, he turned back to the henge, but the power that ran through his veins tugged him to the north. What was—

Vella. While he'd lost sight of her beyond the standing stones, he sensed her walking past the Heel Stone like he had an internal Vella-compass.

A new layer of dread trickled through him. Fucking gods. Some how, some way, some*thing* had bonded between him and Vella. He turned around the circle. Was it the stones? Who knew what magics these ancient monuments wielded?

AFTER DEALING with the mess at Stonehenge, Matt crossed Madgewick's threshold in the early afternoon, and while Amelia met him at the gates, he held off any explanations until he'd checked on Ryan and Ciara. As expected, they were both being cared for and satisfied they didn't need his spellcraft to further help the healing process; he headed to his study and finally released his glamour.

"Where's Vella?" Amelia had followed him up. "What's going on?"

"Hold on, I'm calling Ronin. I'll tell you together."

"Matt?" Ronin's eyes narrowed as soon as he answered the video call. "What the hell's happening there?"

"We found the bone runes, and Vella has taken them back to New York." He dropped into the desk chair.

"What?" Ronin swore.

"Why?" Amelia said at the same time.

"She didn't see any other option." Matthias turned his palm over and let the flicker of his Druid magic show.

"Put that away," Ronin hissed. "You haven't called the concealing spell."

"There's no need. Vella discovered the Divs foreseers can't see my Druid magic in their visions."

"What?" Amelia dropped onto the couch. "You need to start at the beginning. Tell us everything."

"For that, I *do* need the concealing spell." Once their conversation was hidden, Matt explained what had happened.

"Wait." Ronin scowled. "Why the fuck has Vella gone back to the Divs?"

Equal parts pride and dread gathered in Matt's chest. "Because Vella is going to use the bone runes to find a cure for Sara."

"She went back in there after everything?" Disbelief shone in Ronin's eyes. "I can't believe she did that. And fuck, that you let her—"

"There was no 'letting.' Going back was Vella's idea. I thought at the end she'd realized how dangerous this is— for us all—but she took the bone runes anyway. And, gods, it fucking cut me more than I knew it would."

"Matt, what does that mean?" Ronin's face paled. "What have you done?"

"You were right, Ronin. I fell for Vella the night she broke into my room. But more than that, I think ... I think we've formed a bond."

"Holy fuck," Ronin breathed. "Is Vella aware? And does she know what a bond with a Druid means ... *Hell*. Matt, your face says it all. Why didn't you tell her?"

"Because I only figured it out after she'd left. And I'm hoping to have time to work through *that* before it becomes an issue. Once Vella's located a cure for Sara, she'll get the bone runes back to us, and we'll use them to find our grimoires. I'm not giving up, Ronin. I will never give up."

"You better be right. This could all go really fucking bad—"

"Real fucking fast. Yeah, I get it."

VELLA'S CAB arrived at Arcane Antiquities the day before Sara's birthday, in the late afternoon local time, but instead of the familiar noise and hustle of the village warming her chest, a cold void felt like it lived where her heart should've been.

The last conversation she'd had with Ellaine played over and over in her mind. They had been about to land in New York when Vella realized something she'd missed.

"Aunt Ellaine, Charles said he gave you and Derrick a sleeping potion, but you came less than an hour after him."

"He did. However, after your call alerting me to the poison spheres, I had our foreseers observe Charles, and in one of their visions, they saw him preparing a sleeping drug. So, when we arrived in London, I reached out to Nevena. Her family and ours have a long, loyal history, and she arranged an antidote that Derrick and I both took before Charles administered his drug. We then waited to see what he would do—never dreaming he would attack you, and none of our foreseers ever saw him attacking you either."

Wait. If Vella hadn't told Ellaine about the attacks, then Charles would've succeeded with his sleeping potion, and maybe Vella and Matt could've ended things differently?

Except, would they? She and Matt were just on opposing sides of the argument.

"Oh, and Vella, dear? One of our senior foreseers just

reported in—they confirmed they're no longer receiving visions of Sara's funeral; instead, they see her enjoying her birthday."

"That is ..." Vella's stomach revolted. Now she knew for sure—there had never been a vision of Sara dying. But that was okay; Vella still wouldn't have changed a thing because she did need the bone runes—to find the cure for Sara's poisoning.

So fucking thank you, Ellaine. Because now Vella had a way to cure her sister that she may never have had if Ellaine hadn't sent her after the bone runes in the first place.

"I can see you're overcome, understandable after the recent events." Ellaine had patted her knee and then gone back to her conversation with Derrick.

And now the bone runes were in New York. Yes, they were at Div Tower, but Vella knew the vault, knew how to get to them, and she knew one more thing ... Ellaine and her foreseers couldn't see Vella when she moved within dark energy so she would get those runes back, just as soon as she found a Div to help Sara.

Sara. Goddess, what was her sister going to do when she heard the truth about her poisoning, the bone runes ... their parents?

Vella closed her eyes and took a deep breath, but the scene of her parents' death replayed over and over in her mind. Like it had every other time she'd closed her eyes since leaving Stonehenge.

Goddess, it felt like her heart had been blasted into a million pieces.

But what right did she have to feel so bad? So many more deaths had been perpetrated at the hands of the Divs. And her—she'd been complicit in hurting her fellow witches.

She dragged in a shuddering breath, and icy shards seemed to claw into her chest.

Would she ever get truly warm again?

At least, thank the goddess, she was alone now. Ellaine and Derrick had stayed glued to her side the entire way from the UK to Div Tower, even following her into the vault to deposit the bone runes.

Their insistence on always being with her had set her teeth on edge, and more than once, the hairs on the back of her neck had stood straight up; only the reassuring weight of Brianna strapped to her back, along with the burning determination to destroy the Council and its control over witchkind, gave her the strength to continue.

And now here she was, home.

Sara and Shannah sat at the counter, both laughing at something on Sara's laptop, as Vella pushed the shop door open. She took a deep breath of sage- and lavender-infused air. Still nothing—no warmth, no welcome.

"Vella!" Sara leaped off her chair and hugged her sister.

Vella's throat constricted and tears welled. And a tiny portion of the void in her chest warmed.

"Vella, welcome home—hey, you okay?"

"Yeah, I'm okay," she squeezed out. Now for the hard part.

She risked a glance at the shop's surveillance cameras. On the flight back, Derrick had casually mentioned the cameras were working again, and Vella had no doubt now that the monitoring of her landline and cameras had been part of the Div's plot.

"Why don't we close here and go upstairs?" She forced a smile. "I've been away for a few days, and sisters need time together, right? And hey, Shannah. Thanks for stopping by while I was away."

"We had a great time. Turns out I'm a huge fan of Sara's art online—I just didn't know who she was."

"Well then, let's go make coffee and talk." Vella fought the urge to fidget as she followed Sara into the living room. "I want to share something with you, something I should've shared a long time ago."

EPILOGUE

It had begun with bones, and now it would end with bones. Vella entered the coven's solstice gathering at Div Tower, finally grateful for the icy void that had lived in her chest since she'd flown home the day before.

Because it was only that ice, along with the weight of Brianna strapped to her thigh, that contained her rage in a brittle, padlocked cage. And if that ice cracked, and her fury broke free, she'd deploy every weapon at her disposal to pulverize everything, everyone, into the ground.

And that could not happen. Yet.

So instead, she took careful note of every Div, from names to roles to power levels.

"Well, Vella. I am thrilled to see you taking part in official business." Ellaine patted her on the arm as they met by the Yule log.

"What happened in England showed me exactly how much the Council are needed. And after you all have done, I am more than willing to do my part as well."

Vella executed the line with the same coolness Ellaine displayed. Another reason to be grateful for the cold. In fact, the only times she hadn't been cold were when she was with Sara or the rare moment she let herself think of Matthias.

"Excellent. I'm only sorry Sara couldn't come."

"She had an unexpected client meeting out of town. But she'll be back soon."

"Are you sure she's well enough to travel?" Ellaine frowned in the perfect picture of familial concern.

"Absolutely." Keep it cool. Do. Not. Break. "The new Elixir potion has worked wonders. And I can always go to her if needed. And the bone runes? Any word on progress with a vision for a permanent cure?"

"I believe so. My foreseers told me only today they have found something very promising."

"Well, that is good news." More lies, but Vella told her own, too. "I can't wait."

"There is one thing. Locating the other second and third aetts is now this coven's priority."

"And therefore mine," Vella murmured. Truth this time. "Do you know anything about where they are?"

"No, unfortunately not. But then, we didn't know where the first aett was, and you found it."

"I had help. Would you recommend working with the Magicae again?" Vella forced a bland expression as she waited for a response.

"I suppose." Ellaine's lips pursed. "We still need to understand why he occasionally disappears from our visions. I have also considered your contract with Matthias, and as he said, it would reflect poorly on this coven if you were to sever the agreement."

"Whatever you decide"—she met her parents' murderer's gaze, unflinching—"Aunt Ellaine."

Aunt. That word threatened to crack the ice, so Vella

shored the barrier up, colder. Harder. But one day soon, she would never have to say that word again.

"You are a good girl."

"Thank you. Finding all the runes will be my highest priority." Along with taking down the Divinators, the Elixirs, and the Witches Council.

Vella forced her jaw not to clench, but inside, her heart picked up pace.

The Witch Wars were about to explode.

DEAREST WITCHY ROMANCE READER

Thank you for reading *Wrath* and stepping into the world of Witch Wars.

I hope you loved meeting Vella and Matthias, and I can't wait to invite you back to see what happens next in *Weapon*, Witch Wars Book Two.

While many of the locations and places that Matthias and Vella visit during the story exist in real life, I have absolutely taken liberties with people and operations.

And although research is one of my favourite parts of writing, please forgive any mistakes made in translating the Ogham, Irish and Latin—they are entirely my own!

GLOSSARY

Bone Guide: Mors Dicen witches who sacrifice the chance of future reincarnation to bind their souls to one piece of bone forever so they can share their knowledge and skills with future generations.

Bone Wielder: The most powerful of Mors Dicen witches who can channel Bone Guides to wield their skills for themselves.

Cnamh truaill: (*Kuh-vaw tru-ill*) specialized lead-lined, leather scabbard for a bone-handled Mors Dicen knife, with a sliding panel where the bone meets the wearer's skin, whilst leaving their hands free.

Crystallos: (*Christ-ello-z*) Coven of witches who draw their power from crystals and stones. Often use their magic for healing.

Divinators: (*Divin-ay-torz*) Coven of witches who draw

power from the energy of humans, often gathering in large cities to fortify their power.

Druids: Ancient (believed extinct) race of beings connected to the elements. Descended from the Old Gods and Dark Energy, they are rumored to have created the vampires.

Elixirs: (*E-licks-erz*) Coven of witches who draw their power from chemical reactions. Creators of magical potions ranging from food to medicine.

Hedge witches: Witches who prefer practicing their craft (in whatever form they find comfortable, except outlawed Mors Dicen magic) outside of an official coven.

Madgewick: Family estate and home of Matthias Medea, Baron Madgewick. The grounds are protected by an ancient spell only allowing blood relatives to cross the boundary.

Magicae: (*Magic-eye*) Coven of witches who draw power from within themselves and use spellcraft to create magic.

Mors Dicen: (*Mor-z Die-Chen*) Disbanded and outlawed coven of witches who draw power from the earth and who talk to the dead through their bones. Traditionally prefer to live in sparsely populated regions. Practicing Mors Dicen magic is banned.

Shifters: Ancient, patriarchal, secretive race of humans who can shift into animal form. Through millennia of evolution, family groups tended toward staying with one animal type, now known as clans.

Special Investigators: Witches who carry out the orders of the Witch's Council. Traditionally, they came from all covens; however, since the coup twenty years ago, they have only belonged to the Divinator and Elixir covens.

Vampires: Highly secretive, matriarchal, long-lived society of ancient beings who, legend has it, were created by the Druids. Able to taste lies from a human's blood.

ACKNOWLEDGMENTS

While *Wrath* is my book baby, it also exists from concept to draft to this final version due to the support, input and belief from some wonderful people who have my deepest thanks.

My dad, Chris, who sat through possibly the most convoluted white-board demonstrations of a story plot anyone has ever seen and who was a constant help with revenge plotting. My mum, Val, for plot chats and character names and read throughs. My sister, Julie, for the witchy inspiration and especially her help developing the calcification process (those chats were so good!). Henry, my wonderful hubby who, as always, never fusses when we're at the dinner table discussing death scenes and who comes up with the best left-field ideas and plot twists every. Single. Time. My kids (see also not minding the odd table conversations) but also for diving into impromptu brainstorming sessions and for putting up with a mother who while she's sitting right beside them is often in some dream world far, far away. And then the whole family who never mind when the Messenger group chat fills with options for names and places and titles and cover designs.

Fellow authors Jacqueline Hayley and Sarah L Richhelm, who were the first non-family readers and whose encouragement gave me hope my story didn't suck.

Wonderful humans, Jell and Dion, for the sensitivity reads. Thank you both so much. As someone without lived experience dealing with scarring and vision loss, your opinions gave me the hope and confidence that I've treated these topics genuinely, and with respect.

The three wonderful Beta readers who I might've adopted one night at a Readers Unleashed event ... Caitlin, Dallas and Naiomi. Thank you all for being fan-fucking-tastic humans! And to one last beta reader, Theodora ... thank you!!!

My writing family: Jacqueline Hayley, Tanya Nellestein, Samara Parish, Louisa Duval and Joanne Speirs #grateful for you all.

And then to *Wrath's* editors. Sarah Calfee, you are a STAR. For your approach to developing the plotline, for your time and dedication to help me get the best out of the story and the characters and myself, for the way you teach as you edit (I will now forever think in terms of authorial intent), *thank you.* From the beginning, your belief in *Wrath* absolutely pushed me to keep going and make Vella and Matthias' book the best damned story it could be. And I can't wait for your book! And one last thanks: Joanne Speirs. You are my second star. Pressing that final publish button is a scary motherfucker, and you honestly give me the confidence to hit it every damn time. Thank you.

ABOUT THE AUTHOR

Award-winning Brisbane author, HM Hodgson writes about wicked romance (steamy scenes a must!), intrigue and magic. Magic that moves worlds and takes her to another place.

In 2021, HM Hodgson won the Romance Writers of Australia First Kiss competition with the first kiss scene from her novel, Keeper Of My Heart, as judged by producer and director, Tosca Musk. Hodgson also won the Australian Romance Readers Association award for Favourite Continuing Romance Series 2022 with The Immortal Keepers.

When not writing or reading or daydreaming about her next literary hero, you can find her sipping coffee and eating chocolate (more often than not at the same time).

Keep in touch with HM Hodgson at:
www.hmhodgson.com

ALSO BY HM HODGSON

Relics and Legends

A Relic Of Magic And Gold

A Relic of Magic And Myrrh

A Relic Of Magic And Frankincense

A Wreath Of Thorns

A Spell of Longing and Death

A Sword of Stone and Magic

Cursed Nights

Book 1 Cursed Alliance

Book 2 Cursed Embrace

The Immortal Keepers

Book 1 The Last Keeper

Book 2 Keeper Of My Heart

Book 3 Keeper Of My Desire

Anthologies

The Love Hexperts

My True Love Gave To Me

Mermaid Kisses

Ghosts and Graves

www.ingramcontent.com/pod-product-compliance
Lightning Source LLC
Chambersburg PA
CBHW020247120726
47904CB00001B/118